Helen Mathers

Comin' thro' the Rye

Helen Mathers

Comin' thro' the Rye

ISBN/EAN: 9783337049539

Printed in Europe, USA, Canada, Australia, Japan

Cover: Foto ©Andreas Hilbeck / pixelio.de

More available books at **www.hansebooks.com**

INTERNATIONAL SCIENTIFIC SERIES.

The INTERNATIONAL SCIENTIFIC SERIES is entirely an American project, and was originated and organized by Professor E. L. Youmans, who spent the greater part of a year in Europe, arranging with authors and publishers.

The character and scope of this series will be best indicated by a reference to the names and subjects included in the list of volumes published; from which it will be seen that the coöperation of the most distinguished professors in England, Germany, France, and the United States, has been secured.

The works are issued simultaneously in New York, London, Paris, Leipsic, Milan, and St. Petersburg.

For sale by all booksellers; or any volume sent by mail, post-paid, on receipt of price.

D. APPLETON & CO., Publishers, 1, 3, & 5 Bond St., New York.

COMIN' THRO' THE RYE.

SEED-TIME.

CHAPTER I.

"It is the admirer of himself and not the admirer of virtue that thinks himself superior to others."

"'Poor Martha Snell, her's gone away;
Her would if her could, but her couldn't stay;
Her'd two sore legs and a baddish cough,
But her legs it was as carried her off!'

That's *mine*. Have you got anything to-day, Alice?"

"Nothing," says our lovely sister, lifting her head from "Paley's Evidences," "but Nell has."

"Bring it out, then!" says Jack, rapping the table smartly with his ruler.

Happy Jack! who is deterred from amusing himself by no such considerations concerning Scripture exercises and the like as lie heavy upon the rest of us; he is home for the holidays, and, as his soul is supposed to be well weeded and watered by his pastors and masters while he is away, it is left in peace while he is at home.

"It is a little vulgar," I admit, looking round, "but then you know you all like vulgar jokes. Not that this is a joke, —far from it, it is a veritable, properly-authenticated family—"

"Business is business," says Jack interrupting; "give us the epitaph first, and your remarks after."

"'Here lies the body of Betsy Binn,
Who was so very pure within,
She bust this outer shell of sin,
And hatched herself a cherubim!'"

"There! *burst*, not bust," says Jack, reprovingly; "don't expose your ignorance, Nell."

"It is not," I say stoutly; "burst is quite a leisurely way of doing things. *Bust* gives you the idea of cracking all over like a chrysalis and flying straight up through the air, as Betsy did."

"I don't think it's as good as Thomas Woodhen," says Alice, gravely. "His widow showed so much sense in adapting herself to circumstances."

"Or that other one," says Milly, looking up—

'Poor Martha Kitchen! her days were spent,
She kicked up her heels and away she went.'"

"I like the baby's best," says Jack; "that one on an infant three months old, you know—

'Since I am so quickly done for,
I wonder what I was begun for?'"

"Nurse told me of one yesterday," says Milly, resting her elbows on a Pinnock, "that she *saw* with her very own eyes—

'Here lies the unworthy son of a worthy father.'

The stone was erected by the father.'"

"That is nasty," says Alice; "the others only show extraordinary levity. I wonder what the people were like who made them up?"

"Shaky as to their grammar," says Jack, "and sadly in want of a dictionary!"

"Would you like a grammatical one," I ask, "and a *properly spelt* one? I don't say it's a particularly *good* one.

"Good Heavens!" says Jack, leaning forward. "Nell is—yes—no—yes, she is positively blushing!"

"I am not!" I say, looking at them all steadily. "No one ever accused me of such a thing before!"

"Then, to what," asks Alice, laughing, "may we ascribe this sudden access of color? Heat, modesty, shame, or pride, at having made a rhyme? for I do believe you have."

"Heat!" I say shortly; "how we shall broil in church!"

"Now, then," says Jack, "we must not permit the first literary effort of the family to die for want of air; let's have it."

"It is not much of it," I say, apologetically, "but our riddles and epitaphs were running so low that I thought it was high time some new ones were invented, and anything is better than nothing, you know! Here it is:

'Here lies the body of
Helen Adair,
Cruelly slain in the Flower of, her
Youth and Beauty, by
Amberley's Nags.
P. S.—Amberley's Nags were the only horses visible at, her funeral, for she died a Pauper.'"

"Ha! ha! ha!" goes Jack. "'Youth and beauty,' first rate that."

"And Amberley does nag at Nell shamefully," says Alice.

"And you all say," I put in, standing up for my bantling, "that my extravagant tastes will bring me to want some day, do you not? Only I don't see how I can ever be very lavish on nothing."

"The governor tells us every day that we shall come to the—union," says Milly. "I wonder if it is very bad?"

"They separate the sexes," I say, looking fondly at Jack, who is whittling away at a pencil in utter ignorance of my affectionate glance, "and I should never like *that*."

"What's the matter with Amberley?" he asks, looking up. "Has she got spasms?"

"Bilious," I say, nodding. "*She* calls it sick-headache, but I know better. She won't be able to get up till to-morrow, therefore can't harass our already too highly-cultivated brains with Paley and Pinnock. I wonder why Sunday is called a day of rest? It is not to *us*."

"I wish the holidays would come," says Milly, sighing. "Why should we have them in July instead of June? It can't make any difference."

"Amberley is not going away for her holidays," says Alice; "her brother, who is sixty, has got the measles. Did I tell you about her boots yesterday?"

"No; what was it?"

"You know we walked into Silverbridge? Well, she went into Summers's to buy a pair of boots, and she managed to squeeze her feet into a pair much too small for her, then said to the old man who was standing by with his mouth screwed up on one side, 'I think these will do, though they may hurt me a little at first.' 'Lor, miss,' said old Summers, '*that* don't siggerfy, that ain't of no account, but *I knows they'll bust!*'"

"And after that delicate warning did she take them?" asks Jack.

"She did!"

"Let us hope, then," says Milly, "that she will not wear them in one of our breathless scampers behind the governor, or she will come back without them!"

"I have done my exercise," says Dolly, speaking for the first time, "and so has Alan."

"Of course you have," says Jack; "did either of you ever do anything without the other? You eat, drink, weep, wipe up the blots from your copy-books with your noses, and, I believe, *snore* simultaneously!"

"I wonder how soon the bells will strike up?" I say, walking to the window and looking out into the broad, peaceful fairness of the Sabbath morning. There is no sound of work or voices abroad, the court is very still save for the voice of a thrush in the yew-tree yonder, who sings as gayly and loudly as though it were not Sunday at all, but common, homely week-day. The shrill bark of the grasshoppers sounds quite plainly from the lawn, the flowers are ruffled gently by the soft light wind; they have not changed their lovely garments or put on a different color because it is Sunday, happier in this than we mortals who make it a point of honor to smarten ourselves up for the Lord's day, and yet never emulate those dainty blossoms in their delicate, heaven-dyed tints. The cocks and hens pace gravely by, dirty and disreputable as on any other day, and I look at them with attention, wondering whether either of them has laid an egg, a practice in very great disfavor among the tribe, and am inclined to think, from the sidelong strut and complacency of a youthful matron of the Brahma species, that she has done her duty in that state of life to which it has pleased Providence to call her.

"I shall kill that pair of black Hamburgs to-morrow," says Jack, nodding toward two straggling wretches (why are *all* his fowls so lean?) who are scratching in blessed unconsciousness of the Nemesis of impecuniosity that walks behind them. "I want three shillings, and I don't know any other way of getting it."

"Mamma won't buy any more of you," I say with conviction, "the last were so stringy and thin that she said she dared not; the governor would call on the poultry-woman, and it would all come out."

"If he only knew," says Milly, "that after feeding their bodies in life he had to pay for their carcasses in death, how comforting it would be to his feelings! and every morning, *regularly*, he says their heads shall be cut off before night."

"And they deserve it," says Jack, with unusual viciousness, "for, of all the ill-behaved brutes I ever came across, they are the worst. They never lay eggs, or grow fat, or do any of the things all other well-regulated fowls are supposed to do."

"Mr. and Mrs. Skipworth are coming to dinner," says Alice, "to their quarterly festival, you know, and, thank goodness, we shall not be expected *to talk*. I wonder," she adds, with the gay laugh that never degenerates into a bellow like Jack's, or a cackle like mine, "whether she will wear her purple-satin gown?"

"I hope so," says Jack, unkindly; "for, sooner or later, I am certain that she will blow up in it, as Betsy Binn did, and sit calm and smiling in the midst of the purple ruins. Why should not the event take place to-day, indeed?"

Ding-dong! ding-dong! goes a squeaky little bell hard by; it is the voice of Silverbridge church, summoning its flock to worship. We are so near the churchyard that from our windows we can throw a pebble at the railings that close in the vault of our ancestors, by whose side we must all lie some day (if there is room), every one. There are so many of us though, that some will have to lie in state, and some simply, as poor folks do; those who go first will have the best place, those who go last the lower one. We do not pause to put away our books, but set off down the long passage and up the stairs and down more steps and up others, for the Manor-House is built with the especial purpose of breaking the necks, legs, and arms, of the inhabitants thereof, and though we from long acquaintance escape scot-free, so do not stranger servants, who usually pitch head foremost down one or other of the many pitfalls, and come heavily to grief. Our bedrooms are low and wide, opening one out of the other inconveniently enough, and they have latticed casements, through which the queen of flowers herself nods gayly in, reflecting herself in myriad shapes of crimson, yellow, white, and pink. Out of her beautiful breast drop those ugly parasites, the earwigs, and make themselves very much at home among our hair-brushes and the simple appointments of our dressing-tables. As yet these latter are primitive enough; they hold a glass of flowers, a pincushion, a few trinket-cases, a ribbon or two, and that is all. We have no powder, or cosmetics, or appliances for painting the lily, but look in our glasses and see our faces, pretty or ugly, just as God made them. Alice's mirror gives back a dainty picture enough as she stands before it, tying the brown strings of her quakerish brown bonnet that is just the color of the soft love-locks that lie rich and smooth beneath. I wish that you could see her as she is at this moment, with the freshness of a wild-rose in her exquisite cheeks, with the bloom of perfect health in her blue eyes, with the lovely severity of a sculptured Venus in the low white brow, and curved lips, and perfectly-modeled cleft chin, and slender neck. We are very proud of our sixteen-year-old sister, our eldest and our only beauty; we are not a bad-looking family, people say, but none of us come within a mile of Alice. Milly is handsome, after a sturdy, square, determined fashion, with a fine pair of dark-blue eyes, black-lashed, and a shock of lightish hair that sets straight out from her head in every direction. Now, if there is one thing for which we owe gratitude to the governor, it is for providing the family with such real, good, blue eyes. Reckoning his own and mother's, we number just twelve pairs among us; and by blue I do not mean that mixture of slate and gray, or green, so commonly misnamed blue, but a color as pure and vivid as the tint of a flower, from the clear, saucy blue of the forget-me-not to the deep purple that lurks in the heart of the violet. We are eleven, boys and

girls altogether, and I have said that we number twelve pairs of eyes of one color, so it is plain there must be one exception to the general rule, and that is me. My eyes were green from the day of my birth, and will be green to the hour of my death; mamma calls them gray, but where one's personal appearance is concerned it is always safer to believe one's enemies than one's friends.

"The governor is brushing his hat!" exclaims Jack, bursting in upon us spick and span in his correctly-fitting gloves and boxer, and we follow him precipitately. In the hall are assembled mamma, Dolly, Alan, and such of the young ones as are old enough to go to church, and the governor. He has finished brushing his hat and put it on his head, but as he is rummaging in a drawer for his gloves he does not notice our late arrival. And now he sets out, mamma by his side, the procession is formed, and we all tail two-and-two behind them. Across the lawn, through the wicket-gate, in at God's Acre, past our ancestors Geoffry and Joan, who lie in duplicate marble effigy aboveground, bleached bones below, flat on their backs, with their toes turned stiffly up, and their prim hands folded palm to palm. If the effigies are good likenesses, I should say that Geoffry must have been an obstinate, uncomfortable sort of old fellow, while Joan was pleasant to live with and very much under her lord's thumb. An impertinent rose-bush planted by Geoffry's side is holding its sweet red blossom to his marble nose, and from it he seems to be turning away disdainfully, just as, maybe, he did in life from all fair and pleasant things. Under the porch, along the cool dark aisle we go, and file into the long pew that seems expressly made for a man with many children. Mamma sits at the top, papa at the bottom; and the great object of our Sunday-morning existences is to get as far away from *him* and as near to her as we possibly can, hence various silent and rapid manœuvres behind his back that is.

as well for us that he does not suspect. To-day I am the hapless left-behind, and take my seat with a wrathful heart and a sickly smile that seeks to convey to my brethren the fact that I do not mind my situation at all, indeed rather like it than otherwise; there is, however, a covert grin on the row of triumphant faces to my right, that plainly informs me my little hypocrisies will not go down in *that* quarter. We all look upon the governor as a kind of bombshell, or volcano, or loaded gun, that may blow up at any moment and will infallibly destroy whatever is nearest to him, therefore our fears are usually lively when ill-luck plants us very close to him.

As usual we are early, so we sit and watch the old village people come in, prayer-book in hand, with the clean handkerchief folded on the top, and a rose or sprig of wallflower laid between, at which they will sniff between whiles, when they are not listening to an exposition of their sins, or looking to see if the quality has any new clothes on. The village hind comes in rosy-faced and well greased, he has taken his weekly wash, put on his weekly clean boiled rag, and, with the bit of roast-beef and pudding provided for his dinner lurking in his memory and tickling his nostrils, feels not unamiably disposed toward the wife of his bosom, and has no inclination to beat her as is his wont on week-days when he has a little spare time. In the gallery opposite sit the Sunday-school girls and ploughboys, an unruly tribe, impervious to the verbal remonstrances of Prodgers the schoolmaster, of which fact he is well aware, and possesses a more substantial claim to their regard in the shape of a stout cane, with which he discourses sweet music on their rustic backs, coming down with an inspiriting whack! in a pause of the sermon or interval of prayer.

Last Sunday he made a *faux pas*, for, being at the back of the gallery, and spying the unmannerly conduct of an obstreperous purple-cheeked lass in the first row, he leaned forward to take summary vengeance on the same, but alas! she was "so near, and yet so far," and in striving to reach her he overbalanced himself, and fell upon a cluster of maidens of tender years, who howled dismally, while the cane succeeded in doing no more than poking the crown of the offender's bonnet in! We did not smile, and papa could detect no unseemly mirth on our faces when he glanced sharply up and down our pew, for we have by long practice acquired the art of laughing inwardly, and can be in ecstasies of amusement without moving a muscle of our countenances.

At last Mr. Skipworth is in his place and the service begins. The governor makes his amens as fervently and loudly as the clerk, and we all follow, down to the very smallest child; in fact, such a wave of hearty sound runs along our ranks as might almost suffice to blow a thin man off his legs if placed directly before us. And now we have all settled our backs against the hard pew, we have planted our feet firmly on our respective stools, and we have opened our hearts and ears widely for such spiritual comfort as Mr. Skipworth may think fit to administer. Papa turns himself about and, resting his elbow on the edge of the pew, has us all safely under his eye. The sermon begins, and, though we fix our attention upon our pastor unwinkingly, we cannot follow his meaning, or indeed discover that he has any; his words beat upon our ears with a sense of wearying, empty babble. Is not a man supposed to select a text for the purpose of expounding it? But Mr. Skipworth does nothing of the sort. He walks up to it, it is true, and looks at us over the other side, he ambles round it, makes dashes at it, repeats it over and over again, but never really *grasps* its meaning and brings it home to us. In his ramblings he mentions Methuselah, and the name catching my wandering thoughts I fall to speculating about that old world-weary man, who must have been so tired of his life before God permitted him to lay it down. Surely his latter days were ghastly, gray, and lonely, with all his people and the friends of his youth lying in their graves and no new ones to fill their places! At what period of his life, I wonder, may he have been considered to be growing a trifle elderly, and did his father whip him after he was a hundred years old? What must his tailor's bills have come to, and how many Mrs. Methuselahs and little Methuselahs may there have been? Papa is not much past forty, and he has eleven children; if he lived until he were nine hundred and sixty-nine years old, how many might he be *reasonably* supposed to have? That is a sum, and more than my head, unaided by slate or pencil, is good for. I have not half exhausted the subject when Mr. Skipworth blesses and dismisses us, and we are out again, pacing along the narrow path that divides these soft swelling green mounds that we call *graves*.

How I pity you, poor, patient, forgotten, dead folk! I know that you are not here, that your spirits are transplanted to greater bliss or greater misery than the world ever gave you, but with my human heart I think of your bodies laid away in the earth's breast, not of your deathless, freed souls. They have buried you away so deep that not a glimmer of God's sunshine can pierce through to your dark, narrow beds. You are hidden away so close that the gurgling song of the thrush, or the shrill call of the blackbird, can never reach or thrill you; though your best-beloved were passing by, you could not stir one hair's breadth from your bondage; though you are cradled in the very heart of the earth, you cannot feel her throbbing pulses, smell her fresh flowers; her joy, her riches, and her sweetness, are not for you—not for you! I am sorrow for you, O dead! just as some day some one will, perchance, be sorry for me, and, looking down at the grass that grows over me, heave a sigh and say, "Poor soul!" and turn back as I am doing to the breath of God's air,

the caress of his south wind, and the thousand thousand treasures that he has so bountifully poured into the hands of the living.

We pass into the garden, cool with the shadow of the dark-leaved beeches, a rambling queer, old place, with many odd twists and corners infinitely dear to our hearts, for by their aid do we contrive to dodge the governor with surprising success. Away to the left is the kitchen-garden, ample, well-stocked, closely guarded, before which we are wont to sit down with watering mouths, and hearts as sighing as ever was that of Petrarch after Laura. This, our paradise, is inclosed by an envious and abhorred wall, too high to climb, too dangerous to jump, over which we have all in turn jeopardized our necks and legs and come to cruel grief, as many a bruised shin and dismal lump attest, while the potato-bed, which we always select to fall upon under a mistaken impression that it is softer than gooseberry-bushes, could tell many a tale of shame and disaster. At the present moment, however, we are indulging in no such monkey-tricks, we are walking two-and-two behind the governor, dutifully listening to his fulminations against Dorley, who has permitted two sticks and a stone to disgrace the velvet smoothness of the lawn. Dorley has been discharged without a character, departed from here to the union, from the union to jail, and from jail to the gallows, before we reach the house

"There will be some fun at dinner to-day," says Alice as we go up-stairs, "for Mrs. Skipworth had on her purple gown in church!"

CHAPTER II.

"There is no slander in an allowed fool though he do nothing but rail, nor no railing in a discreet man though he do nothing but reprove."

WE may not be a very uncommon family, I do not say we are; and we may be a very handsome family (with one or two exceptions), I do not say we are not; but I defy our worst enemy to accuse us of being a *sociable* family. We care for nobody, no, not we, and nobody cares for us! If we ever had any friends, which I strongly doubt, they have betaken themselves to foreign parts, or melted like snow, or died of a "waste" or—something; and as we have no relations—uncles, aunts, or cousins—we never see a soul. The truth is, papa quarrels with every man and woman he knows, on principle, and has come to the very end of his acquaintance, being (I think) heartily sorry that there is no one left that he can get a chance of being rude to.

Once a year, or so, some determinately peaceful neighbor, who is fond of mother, and wishes to know how she fares, drives through our hospitable gates, and in fear and trembling pulls the creaking body of our front-door bell, rusty with disuse as was ever that one belonging to poor, down-trodden, cowardly Mariana, who, in my opinion, was never worthy of the honor of being sung in verse. The sound of that bell, when it *does* ring, strikes as much consternation to our souls as the last trump might; from far and near we gather to see the fun, doors open, heads are popped round corners, the footman rushes hither and thither, seeking to ascertain the whereabouts of "master," lest unhappily he usher the daring intruder into that awful presence, and thereby secure his own instant dismissal. In the distance is seen papa furiously dashing his hat upon his head and rushing out of the house by some back-door, while the air is pleasingly filled with his shouts of welcome. (It is needless to say that he hates callers even worse than his friends, and with an intensity that you will find nowhere, save in the breast of a well-born, well-educated English gentleman, whose house and family are all that could be wished, and who has nothing in the world to be ashamed of.) Meanwhile the cause of the commotion cools her heels upon the doorstep, and is at last admitted, much as though she were something dangerous, or had come from a fever-hospital, or was suspected of having intentions on the spoons.

Once in every three months the Skipworths are invited to dinner, and there our entertainments end, for no other strangers eat of our salt from January to December. How it is papa has not succeeded in quarreling with the reverend gentleman, I cannot imagine, for goodness knows he has tried hard enough. Mr. Skipworth, however, is one of those dear, affectionate souls who find it absolutely impossible to quarrel with any one who has it in his power to bestow certain substantial gifts; and when the governor slaps him on the one cheek he is. Christian enough to offer to him the other, and, what is more, look as if he liked it. He is talking to mother now; a stout, sleek, pear-shaped man, whose legs always seem to me to have been swallowed up by his body, as the lesser rods were by Aaron's. He has a smile that would butter the whole neighborhood; a smile that Jack and I *hate*, and would wipe off his face with a duster if we could. Papa is talking to Mrs. Skipworth. How the broad June sun is flooding her purple gown and purpler face! How hot and kind and uneasy she looks, for her dress is stretched across her tight as a drum! Poor soul, she squints; not harmlessly, wonderingly, inoffensively, but *diabolically;* while one eye appears to be surveying the person she addresses, the other is firmly fixed on some one the other side of the room. Jack and I have worn ourselves out in speculations as to whether she can see with both eyes at once, or only one, whether she is literally able to keep her eye on two people at once, or whether she *makes up her mind* which eye she means to look out of, and drops that one and takes up the other at a moment's notice; in short, shifts the seeing power at will; whether—but our marvelings are not worth the writing down.

Plain as she is, there is yet something very unique and interesting about her—she has no children! And as she is probably the only parson's wife on record who has not half a dozen, she deserves to be chronicled as an amazing and historical fact. Greatness has its drawbacks, however, and she is not satisfied with her childless home; her husband does not like it either, and I have seen him glance at our overflowing numbers with a scarcely concealed bitter envy that sends a pang, I am sure, to the womanly heart beating so warmly under the gorgeous satin yonder, that would never be on her back if little feet were gathered about her, little voices clamoring for milk and bread-and-butter. And now we are walking in to dinner, and Jack, taking an unfair advantage of my proximity to him, trips me up in such wise that I take a header into my pastor's ample back, and am only saved from ignominious disgrace by the fact that the governor is too far ahead to notice the slight scuffle.

I wonder why people always feel so much more hungry on Sundays than any other day? Is it the sermon, or is it because we have kept our mouths shut so long that we have not taken in enough air? Anyway, we settle to our dinner in earnest, and there is a long, satisfied silence. I come to the surface first and glance around me, thinking how very like animals we all look, though we do use knives and forks and dinner-napkins.

Mrs. Skipworth looks uneasy; her dress certainly is *tighter* than it was in the drawing-room. Surely there will be an explosion soon. There is! She lays down her knife and fork, gives a mighty sneeze—a loud crack, as of hooks and eyes being violently divorced, is heard, then she settles herself in her chair and looks relieved. It is very strange, but there is no gaping fissure visible in front, therefore there must surely be one *behind*; yet James, who is at her back, has no speculation in his eye, and he does not offer to fetch a shawl to hide

her ruins, so it can't be *there*. It is certainly very mysterious. How delightful it is to sit still and to know that we shall not be called upon to provide conversation; for, of all the hard tasks the governor sets us, that is the hardest. When we were small children we were ordered to be silent, and bade never to open our lips in his presence. We never went to him in any of our childish joys or troubles, he took no interest in us; and we, who would have loved him if he had let us, came to have no feeling for him save that of fear. Now, that we are growing up, we are not afraid of him; but the old restraint lies heavy about us, and upon his bidding us to talk, lo! we find that the fountain is dry, and the harder we pump the less we bring up, and it is the daily puzzle of our lives to find " something to say," or to hit upon some safe subject concerning which we may furbish up a few remarks. We are not afraid of him; but, nevertheless, it is a degrading and mortifying fact that, whereas, behind his back, we are bold as lions, before his face we are meek as lambs, while our voices remain obstinately in our boots. If our lives depended on it we could not give one such whoop in his presence as we utter a hundred times a day when he is out of ear-shot.

The butler and footman hurry hither and thither, executing *impromptu* slides in their flights across-country, that move us to admiration; but woe betide them if, in their slavish haste, they clink one plate against another, or fail to appear at papa's elbow, vegetable or sauce laden, the very moment he is ready for a fresh supply!—while, as to the dishes, if, as soon as one disappears, another does not instantly take its place, his face becomes such a study of scorn and disgust as any living actor might seek in vain to imitate. We all sit round and watch him with a never-ending amazement not unmingled with admiration, and wonder how on earth he does it. His face seems to be made of India-rubber, and takes every inflection and shade of ill-temper and uncharitableness. I believe if we watched him till doomsday we should see some fresh contortion every day. He does not confine himself to *looks*, though— he acts. A dish-cover in his hand becomes a shuttlecock that the battledore of his wrath may send into the grate, or out of the window, or after James's rapidly-vanishing calves; it is impossible to tell where, we can only watch his eye and speculate as to the probable direction it will take.

To-day, however, there are no such compliments flying; and, if Mr. Skipworth does now and then intercept a diabolical look intended for Simpkins, what then? He is used to the governor's little ways. And now dessert is on the table, and papa is telling the reverend gentleman (who occasionally hunts on a cob as fat as himself) a pleasing little anecdote about a parson who came to grief last winter in ——shire. Taking an awkward jump, he rolled off his horse into a pond, from whence he piteously besought a passing squire to extricate him. "No, no!" cried the squire, dashing his rowels into his horse's sides, "lie where you are! You won't be wanted till next Sunday!"

Mr. Skipworth, who, in his travels across-country, has explored every pond, ditch, and brook for ten miles round, utters a feeble "Ha, ha, ha!" at which the governor, who is one of the pluckiest and hardest riders in the county, chuckles unkindly. Blessed hunting, that in winter takes him from the bosom of his family twice a week; and, oh! long-tarrying first of September, when will you come and set his feet among the stubble? We are eating strawberries, which, to my fancy, always smell and look so much more delicious than they taste. A jerk of papa's thumb presently dismisses us with our mouths half filled, and we walk decorously past his chair, but, once outside the shut door, scamper away like the wind to vent the spirits that have been so tightly bottled up for the last two hours. We all go our different ways—Alice and Milly to stroll about the garden, Dolly and Alan to some mysterious haunt known only to themselves, Jack and I to our birds and beasts. They are a rascally lot, consisting of the lame, the halt, and the blind, and in any eyes but ours would not be worth a pinch of snuff. We have a dog without a tail, a canary without an eye, a raven without a leg, a crippled rabbit, and various other poor wretches who have been compelled by the force of circumstances to part with one or another of their natural appendages.

Papa is safe for another two hours. He and Skippy will tell tales one against the other that would beat Munchausen into fits and make him green with envy; so we let out the rabbits, the parrot, and the raven, and they follow behind as we take our way through the garden and paddock into the orchard.

"Don't you feel rather patriarchal, Jack," I asked, looking over my shoulder to see that the rabbits are not nibbling at the raven, "like Noah?"

"No, I can't say I do," says Jack. "How he would grin if he could hear you comparing our measly little menagerie to his! Why, he had thousands of 'em!"

"So he had," I say, considering; "and how they all managed in the ark I can't imagine. They went in two-and-two, but of course they all had families; and, if there was only just room at first, they must have found it a tight fit after a bit."

"Very," says Jack, absently. "I say, Nell, will you get up early to-morrow morning?"

"I don't know," I answer, doubtfully. "You don't want me to go fishing, do you?" On such occasions I enjoy the proud distinction of fixing wriggling worms on the hooks, while *he* has all the honor and glory of the undertaking, and eats the fish afterward.

"No, you little silly, I'm not! It's something much better. Can you keep a secret?" (holding my arm tight).

"Of course I can!" I say, indignantly; and, extraordinary as such an assertion may appear from a female, I *can*.

"Well," says Jack, deliberately, "if you're not nervous, you know, or squeamish, like other girls, I'll take you with me; but you must not call out or scream, or any thing of that kind, or we shall be caught, and there will be a shine in the tents of Shem."

"I won't scream," I said, eagerly; "and you know I am not a bit like a real girl. You always say I am more than half a boy."

"I'm going," says Jack, eying me closely, "to see a pig killed."

"A pig?—O Jack!—you don't mean it! They squeak so dreadfully? I'm sure it must hurt them very much!"

"Nonsense!" says Jack, philosophically. "They are noisy brutes, and always make a fearful row over everything; besides, it's a very good thing they do squeak; for, if you happened to be frightened and called out, you know—for you are only a girl—the men would think it was the pig, not you."

"Oh!" I say, dubiously, for the idea that my voice cannot be mistaken from that of an expiring pig has not before occurred to me.

"The fact is, Nell," says Jack, glancing sharply at my face, "you're afraid, and I didn't think it of you—no, I didn't. However, I'll let you have till to-morrow to think it over; and, if, when I throw a handful of gravel up at your window at five o'clock, you are not dressed and ready, I shall know you are a coward."

"No you won't," I say, rebelling against this injustice; "if I don't go it won't be because I am afraid, but because I don't want to see the—the—mess."

"Make up your mind one way or the other," says Jack, carelessly; "if you don't come, I sha'n't say anything to you about it, but I shall know."

We fall into a silence, and sit down under a tree, and the parrot, who has been gravely walking behind with the rest of the riffraffs hops on to Jack's shoulder and swears fluently. His name is Paul Pry, and he is a sharp and ungodly bird, who has picked up many wicked sayings but never a good one. Jack brought him from school, and we are obliged to keep him dark for fear the governor should overhear his talk, and make his head pay the penalty of his manners. He gets very drunk when he has a chance, and reels about in his cage like a very disreputable, tipsy old man, muttering, "Polly very drunk," in a boosy voice. He is smart, but he never said anything half as clever as that parrot of which Jack told me, who attended a show of his brethren, held for the purpose of giving a prize to the owner of the cleverest bird present. He arrived last of all, looked round at the collection of feathered bipeds, cocked his eye at the company, and ejaculated, "What a d—d lot of parrots!" Alas! for morality, he won the prize, or so says Jack.

Under the trees it is very cool, very quiet. The sunbeams flicker faintly through the screen of green leaves and unripe fruit overhead; the gnats whirl giddily round and round, spending their one summer's day in ceaseless revolutions; the birds are singing their blithe, clear song, and, though they sing all at once, and each in a different key, there is not one note of discord in the whole concert. The sky is one stretch of deep, intense blue, flecked with clouds that show white as snow against its vivid color; a rustling, creeping little breeze, warm with the breath of new-mown hay and dog-roses, is stealing about us, frolicking softly with our hair and lips; and as I lie flat on the grass, that makes so yielding and luxurious a couch for our young bodies, I am lulled into an exquisite dreamy sensation of delight at the mere fact of existing on this bountiful, rich-hued, glorious June day. The parrot ceases to make naughty remarks, he puts his head on one side and appears to be thinking; perhaps he is remembering the days of his youth, perhaps he too enjoys the perfect day and hour, who can tell? The rabbits wander about, the raven stands motionless on the one slender leg that must ache so often; Jack is silent, but for some prosaic reason, I am certain, not because his soul is filled with pleasure.

"Nell," he says presently, while I am wondering why the clouds fall into grotesque likenesses of earthly things, not heavenly — human faces, castles, cities, hills—"I'm going to the top of Inky field, will you come?"

Never yet did I disobey Jack's behest, so I sit up, but very unwillingly. "The governor will see us," I say, suggestively; "Inky field is right before the dining-room windows, you know."

But Jack takes no heed to my caution, so we return to the garden by the way that we came, and inveigle all our animals into their abodes, save our crippled rabbit, who escapes to a verbena-bed, and there disports himself. A rabbit is an aggravating beast to catch; he has a way of remaining perfectly still till one's hand almost touches him, and then starting suddenly off in a jiggetty-jog fashion highly impertinent, while the pursuer measures his length upon the sward, angry and empty-handed. At last, however, he is caught, and Jack carries him away, while I sit down on an adjacent seat, and fan myself with the top of my double skirt, which I use as duster, fan, or for ornament, indiscriminately. Mother and Mrs. Skipworth have just gone in, but every one else is walking about in a leisurely way; Alice and Milly under the south wall, Dolly and Alan sitting close together in the sun like two plump little partridges, dogs straying about, and fry dimly visible in the distance, everything, in short, looks peaceful and comfortable, when from the veranda issue two black figures—can it be?—Yes, it is Skippy and the governor! Is the wine corked,

or have their stories run dry? I am too close to them to escape; not so, however, the rest, who vanish round corners, behind trees, over palings, anywhere, and the garden, that a moment ago was full, is now empty. Papa's approach may usually be known by the flight of everybody else in an opposite direction; and I think he has a vague suspicion of the fact, for he looks about him sharply as he approaches. Jack, lucky fellow, has hidden himself in the rabbit-hutch, and from a well-known loophole I see his eye fixed upon me with a mixture of pity and self-gratulation. I have pulled my hat straight, set my feet in the first position, and am doing my utmost to look modest, sabbatical, and cool. The last is the most difficult of all, and papa stops short and surveys me with the admiration that any new or particularly startling phase of my ugliness always evokes from him.

"What a mawk!" he says contemptuously; "can't you keep your mouth shut?"

I close it with a snap and a rebellious glance that he is about to call me to account for, when an unwary fry, venturing into the open, attracts his attention, and away he goes like a shot; horribly active is he, as any one can aver to whom he has given chase. I heave a deep sigh of relief, and turn away to make good my escape, when Mr. Skipworth lays a fat and detaining hand on my arm, and in an unctuous voice bids me sit down. He has got me into the seat, and wedged me in with his overflowing body before I get my breath back and recognize the fact that I am in for a sermon, and that he will presently come back and finish me off. I cast a despairing glance at Jack, who is close prisoner as well as I, but oh! the rabbits won't stand upon their hind-legs and preach him a sermon.

"My dear," says Mr. Skipworth, closing his eyes slightly, whether overcome by the sun or Madeira it would be hard to say (how I hate being "my deared!"), "did you hear the sermon to-day?"

"Yes, sir."

"And what did I say?"

"Something or other about Methuselah."

"No. I spoke of grace, the effects of grace. Without grace," he continues, folding his fat hands, and simmering gently in the hot sunshine like a seal, "we are lost, vile, miserable creatures, lower than the beasts of the field."

"You and I·may be," I say stoutly, "but mother isn't, she is much more like an angel."

"You are a wicked girl," he says, turning slowly and surveying me, "you are also *ignorant*. Do you not know that all mankind is born in sin, and that even a new-born babe is tainted with evil? It would appear that the infant is aware of that fact, for what is the first thing it does on coming into the world?"

"It howls," I say briefly.

"It weeps," says Mr. Skipworth rebukingly, "and why does it weep?"

"Because it's hungry," I say promptly.

"It does nothing of the sort," he says irately; "it weeps because it *knows it is born in sin*."

"Oh, poor little soul," I say, laughing immoderately, " I—I—beg your pardon, Mr. Skipworth, but—but it's such a ridiculous idea, as if it knew *anything*."

"Your levity is exceedingly unbecoming, miss," says my pastor, in a voice that reminds me of vinegar tasting through oil.

"I beg your pardon, I do really," I say again, stifling my mirth as well as I can, "but when you were a baby—I suppose you were a baby once, Mr. Skipworth?"

"I suppose so," he says stiffly.

"Did you never cry?"

"I have always been told," he says pompously, "that I was an unusually reasonable infant, and that my voice was seldom heard."

"Then you could not have been born in sin," I say triumphantly, "for you said just now babies cried *because* they were sinful, and of course if they don't cry they can't be sinful; don't you see, sir?"

But Mr. Skipworth does not see; my impudence has at last had the desired effect of making him turn his back upon me, and as he stiffly rises I make my escape, barely in time though, for I am scarcely hidden when the governor appears round the corner, looking red and heated, and as though the fry had led him a chase for which there will be a heavy reckoning to pay by-and-by.

CHAPTER III.

"... The morn in russet mantle clad
Walks o'er the dew of yon high eastern hill.'"

It is five o'clock in the morning. Through my open window come the pure notes of the lark's first song, the cloth-of-gold roses nod their creamy heads in at me, heavy with dewdrops, and whisper "Come out! come out!" Yes, but surely they do not mean to say, "*Come out and see a pig killed.*" My mind has somehow or other made itself up, and, though I every moment expect to hear Jack's footfall below, I am attired in a nightgown, no more. Who that has tasted the first spotless freshness of the early morning could go back to dull, senseless sleep in that white bed yonder? When Jack is gone I will dress and go out into the lanes and fields, and get a bunch of fresh wild-flowers. I will— There is Jack. I mount the window and present my white-robed form to his astonished and disgusted gaze.

"So you're not coming?" he asks, in an indignant whisper, heedful of Amberley, whose room is below mine, but reassured by the rhythmic regularity of her snores. "So you're a—"

"Don't be angry," I say, imploringly, "I'm not a coward, and I'll do anything else you like, but I can't do that."

"Oh! I dare say," he says, scornfully, "I dare say! Well, I'm going; but before I go I may as well tell you that I'm disappointed in you. I thought, mind you, Nell, I thought you were plucky enough to be a boy; but I was mistaken, you're only a girl."

"I know I am," I say, almost in tears, "that's just why I can't go and see it; boys feel differently about those things!"

"I should hope so," says Jack, significantly, "I should hope so," and turns on his heel and goes his way, pigstyward, leaving me to the miserable conviction that he is perfectly right, and I am a very small and cowardly person indeed.

By-and-by I pluck up sufficient spirit to put on the despised female garments that I hate so thoroughly. How cumbrous, and useless, and ridiculous they are! how my gowns, petticoats, crinolines, ribbons, ties, cloaks, hats, bonnets, gloves, tapes, hooks, eyes, buttons, and the hundred and one et ceteras that make up a girl's costume, chafe and irritate me! What would I not give to be able to leave them all in a heap, and step into Jack's cool, comfortable, easy, gray garments? When I am dressed I go through Alice and Milly's room on tiptoe. A sunbeam is lying on Alice's nut-brown head; a blackbird is singing on the window-sill, but she sleeps soundly on. Out in the garden the grass is all silvered over with dew, and the flowers are opening their beautiful eyes one by one; all night they have stood pale and still, but now, with the first quivering beams of the sun, they have awakened, and stirred, and trembled, turning eagerly toward their king, who is rising in such pomp of amber glory out of the great eastern plains of translucent sea-green sky. As yet there is that faint, chilly freshness in the morning air that is like some strange, intangible, wind-blown perfume, as though the breath of the moonlit night had tarried behind and were merging itself into the dawning warmth of the morning.

There are a nameless stir and throb of expectancy in the air, as though all Nature were awaiting the advent of her master; field and meadow, flower and garden, stretching out toward his golden splendor and swift vivifying beams.

When I have fed the animals—who are as wide-awake as though they had the work of the world to perform, instead of nothing to fill the long hours but sleeping and eating, while, strange contradiction! the human beings who have their lives to carve out, their names to make, and their souls to save, sleep soundly and long, awakened, not by the sun or the birds, or because they have had rest enough, but because (oh, prosaic reason!) they are *called*—I take my way across the dew-spangled meadows, where the cows are being milked, and John the milkman and Molly the dairy-maid are sitting on contiguous stools, and flirting at the top of their voices, loudly confiding to each other those gentle secrets that are usually supposed to be of a somewhat private character. There is nobody to listen though, save the brook, the birds, and me; and as I am behind them they are not put out of countenance by discovering that I have been an involuntary listener to their love-talk. After all, I dare say, flirtation at five o'clock in the morning is as agreeable and amusing as at any other time, and a great deal more sweet and wholesome than in the evening. I do not get much of a nosegay, for June, bountiful month as she is, gives not half the wild-flowers that follow Spring's footsteps and gem her mantle so preciously; I only find some dog-roses, travelers' joy, a few ragged-robins, a handful of moon daisies, some meadow-sweet, and honeysuckle.

Turning into the orchard, I run against Jack coming from the opposite direction; he withdraws himself with dignity, but does not look very angry, so I proceed to try and make my peace after a sneaking feminine fashion.

"Was it *very* nice?" I ask in a propitiatory tone.

"First rate; wouldn't have missed it for anything."

"Did it squeak much?"

"Awfully; didn't you hear him? There will be some prime bacon though, and I shall take a ham back to school."

Bacon! ham! Three hours ago it was a breathing, enjoying, reasonable pig; now—

"It is Pimpernel Fair to-morrow," I say, suggestively, hoping by a change of subject to divert Jack's thoughts from my delinquencies, upon which I am certain they are running.

"I know; but it's no good, the governor won't let us go."

"Mother is going to ask him; let us pray that the answer may be favorable."

Eight o'clock strikes as we turn in at the back-door, and at the sound we both start as if we had been shot. To drag off our hats, and make a rush for the breakfast-parlor, is the work of a moment; and by the skin of our teeth are we saved, for by great good luck the governor this morning enters the room at ten seconds past the hour, instead of on the stroke, as is his wont.

Now, there are laws and laws in our house, to break either of which is a very serious matter, but to be late for prayers is crime. To fall sick, tear our clothes, tell lies, steal fruit, and roll in the flower-beds, is bad, and will be punished accordingly, but to be late for prayers!—far better were it for that luckless wight that he or she had never been born. I wonder if, when I am quite old, I shall ever be able to forget that awful, sickening moment, when, having torn down the stairs at headlong speed, I found the door shut, and heard papa's voice booming away with angry fervor inside?

Our family devotions are conducted in a curious fashion, but one that is eminently satisfactory to our youthful and irreligious minds. The governor goes through chapter, prayer, and benediction as hard as he can pelt, without a moment's pause, from beginning to end, and when the chapter is ended, and we have rapidly reversed ourselves, we are scarcely settled on our knees when the book, closing with a smack on Amen! shoots us all up into the perpendicular again. Every now and then the morning scamper is agreeably diversified by the unseemly conduct of the canaries, who, when papa begins to read, begin to sing, and the louder he reads, the more shrilly they shriek, until he pauses to say, in a voice of thunder, "Take those wretched birds down!" then settles to his stride again with a furious countenance, while the culprits, from an abased position on the floor, twitter derisively.

Prayers being over, breakfast is brought, and partaken of much as the Jews partook of the Passover (save that we have seats), in hot haste and the shortest possible time.

I think papa's digestion has been murdered long ago, and ours are on the high-road to destruction, but, fast as we eat our meals, we heartily wish we could do it faster and get away.

This morning we are cudgeling our brains as usual to find a remark that shall be neither too fresh, nor too stale, nor too familiar, nor too dangerous, for ventilation, and every natural subject that suggests itself to our minds we reject in turn. The governor would not understand it, or he would wonder at our impudence, or—something. We are all nervously anxious to talk; it is from no obstinacy or contumaciousness that we sit tongue-tied, but somehow the stream that flows so over-bountifully among ourselves is in his presence reduced to a few scanty drops. Amberley is pouring out the coffee, limp, and meek, and drab, and fair, with putty-colored curls, concerning which we have never ceased to admire the self-restraint that has restrained the governor from pulling them in his frequent rages.

"Do you think it is going to rain, papa?" asks Alice, making her small votive offering in a voice that refuses to come boldly forth, but seems to be strangled half-way. The sky is one clear vault of blue, and it has not rained for a week.

"I don't know," says the governor, crossly. Apparently he has seen the pumping-up process, and is not grateful for the effort.

Alice looks over at Milly with a glance that plainly says, "Your turn now;" for it is a point of honor with us that, when one makes a remark, each shall follow in turn, and thus divide the labor of conversation.

"Dorley killed a lot more snails last night," says Milly, looking at papa; but the snails go the way of the weather, and no notice whatever is vouchsafed to this delicate *morceau.*

It is Jack's turn now, but he is stolidly eating his breakfast, with a mean and reprehensible indifference to his duty; therefore it devolves upon me.

"The pig was killed this morning," I say, starting with a tolerably loud voice, and dying gradually into a very little one. "It made such a noise!" But, alas! the pig goes the way of the snails and the weather.

There is an anxious silence, broken only by Amberley's meek voice offering the master of the house more coffee, but upon being told it is filthy stuff she collapses, as do we, and sit counting the moments to our departure. Jack sneezes violently, and we look at him gratefully; it makes an agreeable little diversion, but he must not do it twice, or he will he ordered out of the room. Papa has finished his bacon and coffee, and we are just thinking we may venture to rise and make our escape, when his angry voice makes us bound in our seats.

"Can't you talk, some of you?" he asks, eying us wrathfully. "There you sit, gobble, gobble, gobble, with never a word among the whole lot, and behind my back you can bawl the house down; a set of wretched dummies?" And so he dismisses us with a few more expressions of admiration and good-will.

"I am afraid Pimpernel Fair looks rather bad," said Alice, when we reach the schoolroom.

"After all it is not much of it!" says Milly.

No, it is not; and in our heart of hearts we despise it, with its one circus, its pen-

ny peep-show, and its fat woman; but it is better than nothing, and, when one has looked upon nothing but the face of one's own family for twelve months, anything is agreeable to the eye, and, now that it seems to be receding in the distance, Pimpernel Fair looks very attractive indeed!

Amberley comes in — Amberley to whom it is given to labor heavily at the tillage of our brains, and whom we look upon as a sedate and amiable old cow, who never kicks up her heels or does anything unexpected, but gives down knowledge in any quantity or quality whenever we choose to apply for it. She is a queer creature, Amberley. We used to play her tricks, and try to drive her out, as we did all our other governesses; but she opposed a passive resistance to all our endeavors, that in the end conquered us. We might as well have knocked our heads by the hour against a stone-wall. For oh! she is so meek! Give us a passionate person, an impulsive person, a person who loudly declares she will have her own way, but a meek, obstinate woman, *no one* can stand against her!

Lessons begin, and after our different fashions we attack the Tree of Knowledge. Alice goes at it gayly, and with a good heart; Milly weeps at its prickly rind; I skirmish round it; and Dolly and Alan sit down before it with moderate appetite. Happy Jack! who goes by with his dog at his heels; and, unlucky me! who possess the tastes and spirit of a boy and the useless body and petticoats of a girl!

CHAPTER IV.

"Jog on, jog on, the footpath way,
And merrily hent the stile-a;
A merry heart goes all the way,
Your sad one tires in a mile-a."

WE are waiting in the schoolroom for mother, who has gone with a serene front, but (we believe) trembling knees, to ask

2

her lord and master's gracious consent to our setting out for Pimpernel Fair. She has been absent a quarter of an hour, which we are inclined to think a hopeful sign, as his "Noes" are usually short and sharp, and for him to condescend to argue a matter promises well. Here she comes! We tumble one over the other to the door, and fling it wide. No need to ask her; she has "Yes!" written all over her in big capitals. As she sits down we swarm round her until she looks like something good encompassed by a hive of buzzing, noisy bees.

"You are coming with us, eh, mother?" I ask eagerly.

"No, dear, I think not; there is baby, you know."

"We are not going to have all the fry at our heels, I hope?" asks Jack, with some anxiety.

"The two nurses are going with four of them, and Miss Amberley will take you elder ones."

"Hurrah!" cries Jack; "if there's anything I hate it's going out in dozens. And what time are we to be back?"

"Six o'clock. And don't make yourselves ill with gingerbreads, dears."

"Ill!" we all echo in chorus; "who could get ill on nothing?"

"We have not a rap, mother," I put in on my own account. "There was a shilling somewhere among us last week, but it was so valuable, and we took so much care of it, that somehow it got lost. One of us hid it away, and forgot where we put it."

"I will give you a shilling each," says mother, "and you must make it do."

She takes out her purse that is so much too slender for the size of her family; and, though we all scorn the scanty shilling that is to fall to our share, we do not say so. Shall we give one additional pang to that tender, gentle heart? The governor must have his hunting, his shooting, his horses. We must be kept so long without a sight of the queen's countenance as almost to forget what she is

like; and I am certain that when we are grown up we shall be spendthrifts. When mother has given us our shillings and kissed us all round, she goes away, and we also depart to make our toilets, and beautify ourselves according to our scanty means and several lights. Alice puts on a white hat with a long white feather, sole tail of an ostrich that the family possesses, and considered by us Adairs to be the *ne plus ultra* of beauty and fashion. Whatever our other shortcomings may be in the matter of dress, when that feather is in our midst, and Alice's blooming face is under that feather, we feel respectable, and defy anybody to beat us. She also wears a white cloak and a black-silk dress, and, when it is all put on, where will you in the whole of England find a fairer, sweeter sixteen-year-old, than our Alice? Milly has put on her out-door gear as uncompromisingly as usual. Jack appears with a button-hole the size of a small cabbage, that gives him an uncommonly gay and festive air; and I, having tilted my Leghorn hat to the back of my head, for the better observation of men and matters, we descend and find Amberley awaiting us in a green bonnet and with a large smut on her nose. We admire the former, but are all much too delicate to point out the latter to her, so it goes to the fair with the rest.

Pimpernel is only a mile away; but a noonday mile in June is a long one, and by the time we reach the High Street we are very hot indeed, and very thirsty. It is the second day of the fair, and the fat farmers and their fatter beasts have waddled off the scene, while their smart wives and daughters have appeared upon it, and are walking about in raiment compared with which Joseph's coat was a mere joke, exchanging jests and cracking jokes with their friends and looking, thanks to the exceeding heat, very sticky and exceedingly moist. Behind and about prance their maid-servants and hinds; every Jill who has a Jack hangs fondly to his arm, and, while her large crinoline hangs affectionately against his legs, she casts scornful and triumphant glances at the unappropriated Jill who sidles by, deeply conscious of her forlorn and degraded state.

Hard by Punch is setting a bright example to the British householder as to the management of his wife and family, and we pause under the shadow of Lawyer Trask's door to see the instructive little drama played out, and the ends of justice defeated.

In the market-place is a queer edifice that looks like a gigantic house of cards, and upon the steps thereof, apparently too solid for the shabby structure, stands a man beating a gong that rends the air with its hideous tom-tom!—that is the circus. To our right a crowd of white-waistcoated, blue-coated, shiny-faced youths are shooting for nuts at a gallery which is presided over by a young person with black eyes and blacker ringlets, a brazen countenance and a nimble tongue. She seems to have as unlimited a supply of chaff as of nuts, and holds her own against all comers. Farther on is the peep-show, beyond that the merry-go-round, upon whose wooden horses the boys and girls are clinging with such giddy, delighted grasp, and round the corner the fat woman bursts upon our view, or rather her picture does, which has much the same effect. She wears a low-necked gown and short skirts, displaying a calf of which the circumference is about equal to our united waists. Her neck— We turn away shuddering.

"Now, what are we going to see first?" asks Jack.

What indeed! it is an *embarras de richesses.*

"The circus," says Alice.

"The fat woman," says Milly, who has been much struck.

"The peep-show," says Jack.

"Anywhere out of the sun," say I; so Jack, being the only male present, gets his own way, and we are speedily lifting the dirty red curtain, and standing on forms arranged in a circle, beholding im-proving illustrations of battle, murder, and sudden death.

The first scene represents a field, strewed with dead bodies, whose heads arms, and legs, are scattered around them in graceful confusion; a few horses seem to have gotten into the *mêlée* by mistake, and lie on their backs with all four legs turned up piteously to the gory sky, as who should say, "We kicked to the last!"

The beauties of this affecting picture are forcibly pointed out to us by the showman, who describes it as being the scene of a "most 'orrible massacr*ee*," as depicted by a "hi-witness."

We are next treated to an artistic study of murder in low life, the murderer being in hot pursuit of a young female in a nightgown, whose hair sets out straight as porcupine's quills from her head, and within an inch of the itching fingers of her pursuer, while behind him are laid out, in an ascending scale, the dead bodies of an old man, an old woman, and a child, the same being the victims he has just finished off.

In the midst of the showman's description of this *tableau vivant*, his voice suddenly ceases; turning to ascertain the cause of his silence, we find that he has temporarily retired behind a pot of beer, "Not before it was required," as he remarks when he returns to his duties. It strikes me that, before the day is over, his explanations will be somewhat hazy and obscure. And we see several more horrors which Amberley regards with extreme disfavor, as being possibly subversive of our morals.

When his stock of delicacies is exhausted, we adjourn to the pastry-cook's and eat sandwiches, buns, and tarts, with extreme relish, due heedfulness, and the nicest discrimination, for we are limited as to money, and must get its worth, if we can.

"I could eat 'em all!" murmured Jack, on our first arrival, gazing fondly at a pyramid of jam tarts before him, but experience soon teaches him that his eye is decidedly larger than his stomach, and after a decent tuck-in he is satisfied. Having drunk our lemonade, we betake ourselves across the square to where the circus-man is still sturdily beating his gong for the one o'clock performance, and mount the rickety steps, and go through the entrance to the red-baize-covered seats that circle round the arena strewed with sawdust. Although we know it all by heart, and just what is coming, what a thrill of excitement runs through us as we glance around us, at the eager faces of the poor folks and their children seated in the lowest place; at the dissipated pieces of orange-peel that are strewed hither and thither, suggestive remnants of the visits of those who could enjoy themselves without striving to be "genteel;" at the men with their brazen instruments, that will presently burst forth in a volume of sound more startling than dulcet; at our neighbors and their olive-branches, who, like us, possess the upper seats in the synagogue, but do not look at us, oh! dear no! The governor's sins are visited very fully upon our heads, and, though he never goes abroad to encounter either good looks or bad, his sins will be visited on his luckless children to the third and fourth generation.

And now the entertainment has begun; the pretty little girl in pink is taking her flying leaps through the hoops, and our hearts beat high with pride and delight as she clears them successfully, but a shiver runs through us as once she jumps short and falls. What a piteous quiver there is on the poor little painted face as the frowning, black-browed man, who cracks the whip, scolds her in a low, fierce voice; how we hate him and would like to make him suffer as he is making her! The clowns come in and make their jokes; old as the hills, no doubt, but to us exquisitely fresh, and we greet them with the hearty zest and admiration that no laughter, save that of childhood, ever knows. Presently something very dread-

ful happens; the hero of the piece (it is a grand piece, with robbers and horses and ladies and a splendid fight) who has been killed is being carried out, laid very straight and stiff on the shoulders of four men, with his eyes tightly shut, and the band is playing the "Dead March in Saul" very slowly and impressively, with a pause of several seconds between each note, when the music abruptly ceases, and, with a discordant crash, the musicians, instruments and all, vanish from our sight, and nothing is to be seen of them save a great dust that rises from their ruins. What has happened? The dead man is lowered to the ground, upon which he sits up and stares. We all gaze with fascinated and dilated eyes at the box from which the men have vanished. Are they killed? But sounds of wrath, of disgust, and vituperation, mingled with a rattling of bones and brass instruments, speedily reassure us on that point, and before long the missing gentlemen creep out one by one, very red in the face and dusty in the throat, and take up their station on the benches, which may possibly be trusted not to serve them the dirty trick the box has done. Once settled, they take up the burden of their "Dead March" where they laid it down, the dead man carefully stretches himself on his bearers' shoulders, and the piece is brought to a decent conclusion with "God save the Queen," to cover all deficiencies.

The sunshine makes our eyes blink as we emerge into it, and bend our steps toward the fat woman, to whom we must assuredly make our bow. The apartment in which that august lady receives us is out of all proportion to her charms, being in fact but a caravan upon wheels, across the hinder part of which is drawn a musty curtain, that we dimly imagine hides unsavory sights. As she lifts it and stands before us, I involuntarily draw back and get behind Jack, and Dolly gets behind me; her ponderous foot shakes the boarding as she approaches, and her huge body oscillates from side to side, like a badly-filled sack set upright in a cart. It is impossible to help feeling that, if she happened to tread on one of us, we should be crushed into pulp; for once report has not lied, and her picture has failed to do her charms justice, or represent her as she really is. "Look at 'er!" cries the showman, in a voice of rapture, hitching up her already short petticoats with his cane, and indicating first one colossal leg, then another: "*Look* at 'er, ladies and gentlemen! Did ever you see sich flesh, sich size, sich *proporshun!* And, mind yer, it's all real genu*ine* bony-fidy fat; no make-believes, shams, or sawdust in this exhibition! Look 'ere!" and he prods her with his stick in her overflowing sides, and he pinches her fat neck and arms as though she were a prize ox or sheep. "Turn round!" he says, and she turns slowly, as though on a pivot, and displays a back that is such a mountain of flesh as I have seen nowhere, save on the body of a prize pig. As she faces us again, a fat smile of pleased complacency dawns on her features at marking our amazement and admiration of her manifold beauties. At her knee, but overlooked in the neighborhood of her mountainous presence, stands a tiny dwarf, who nearly dislocates his neck in peeping up at her. It is plain that he admires her beyond all earthly things, and that she is to him, not only the lode-star of his existence, but the type of everything that is comely and pleasant to the eye in woman. Decidedly impressed, we take our departure, and repair to seek our fairings in the smartly laid-out stalls in the shadow of the old gray market-house. We buy mother a thimble, not that we are aware she is in want of one, but a silver thimble is a nice, useful, comfortable sort of a thing, that is sure to come in handy if you wait long enough, and we have no notion, we Adairs, of spending our infrequent money in kickshaws, or merely ornamental presents. We sometimes give her a purse by way of a change, and, when

she has had enough of them, we present her with a prayer-book; so there is a good deal of variety after all.

We pause for a minute or two to listen to the amazing lies of a cheap Jack, compared with whom Ananias was the most veracious man on record; and I, at least, look with some envy at the merry-go-round, remembering a day many years ago when I escaped from nurse, and surreptitiously took a ride on a side-saddled wooden pony that stood beside one ridden by Johnny Stubbs, the sweep's son, and was enjoying myself with all my heart, when a heavy hand made a clutch at my vanishing garments, and nurse's voice said in deepest wrath, "I'm *ashamed* of you, Miss Nell!"

The fun of the fair is just beginning as we turn our faces homeward toward Silverbridge. By-and-by it will become a frolic, later on grow into a carouse, last of all degenerate into a hurly-burly, where women will be seeking their husbands, and the same will be shaking hands with the town-pumps, and attempting to walk home in a circle. Most of the sober folks are leaving like us, and in the cool lanes, athwart which the sun is laying dark shadows, Lubin is kissing Phillis's ruddy and sticky cheek, blessedly unconscious of our near vicinity. With what honest delight do they gaze on each other's ugly red faces, and how enjoyingly does the smack!·smack! of their salutes come to our ears? The lady is not coy, and kisses him full as often as he does her, and almost as loudly. They are beautiful in each other's eyes, and long may their love last!

"I wonder," I say to myself, looking at Alice's flower-like face, "if any one will ever love *her* like that? or—or—*me?*"

Presently we overtake the fry, whom we have once or twice come across in the fair and avoided successfully; very gummy and warm and dirty and happy they look. If the governor could only see them! Fortune smiles on us to-day;

we do not meet him in the court, or in the hall, or on the stairs, so we are able to retire in peace to change our dusty clothes.

"Thank goodness, there won't be a walk to-night!" says Alice, sitting down restfully in her white petticoat on the broad window-sill. Thank goodness, indeed! Walks are the plagues of our lives and the terror of our existence. I do not mean those nondescript leisurely rambles that Jack and I are partial to taking, or the saunters that Alice and Milly affect; I mean a three or four-mile race over hill and dale at the governor's heels, which leaves us with aching, blown bodies, sore hearts, and angry souls. We resort to various cowardly and sneaking devices to get out of these excursions, but altogether in vain; severe stomach-ache even, and a prompt retirement to bed, avail us nothing. Papa is up to that trick, and we are promptly unearthed, dressed, and sent forth with the rest. We have even, on occasions, tried the desperate expedient of salts and senna, but even that cruel remedy failed us, for papa, believing our illness to be only another form of humbug, insisted on our accompanying him; therefore, from that day to this, we have left Messrs. S. & S. alone.

The Adair family out a-walking is a sight to be seen. The governor leads the way, steaming on in front all alone, like a ship in full sail, while behind him his family stretch out like pack of beagles, puffing, blowing, groaning, gasping, the elders well up to the fore, the youngsters, by reason of the shortness of their miserable little legs, straggling behind, while last of all comes Amberley, doing her duty like the Christian woman that she is, and praying that her second wind may come quickly. From time to time papa turns and surveys our scarlet and distressed countenances with a grim smile. After all, I believe he has some sense of humor, and only manages to support his own discomforts by witnessing the infi-

nitely greater ones of his children. Past cool sweet fields, where the cows are taking their meals at their leisure—happy cows, who have no father to harry them!—past easy stiles and broad flat stones to which our bodies seriously incline; up hill and down dale, across fields and down lanes, with never a pause for breath, or flower, or fern, and so home again "in linked sweetness long drawn out."

Next to those scampers we hate drives. Papa has several conveyances in which he jeopardizes the lives of his family, and makes our "too fretful hair" rise from our heads. First in danger is a very high gig, in which he drives a powerful rakish chestnut with a rolling eye, who invariably runs away twice or thrice whenever he goes out. In this, knowing her fears, he loves to take out mother, who has some respect for her own neck, seeing that it is the only one she is ever likely to possess, and by hook or by crook she usually manages to get out of going. Now and then, however, she is fairly caught, and drives from the door with a backward look at her assembled flock, that has in it the solemnity of a dying farewell. Next in danger to the gig is a mail-phaeton, drawn by a pair of fiery cobs, thoroughbreds, and matched to a hair, in which two of us girls are always made to sit, occupying ingloriously enough the seat intended for a man-servant. Many and many a time have we clung to each other with our breath gone, while the horses thundered on in their mad career, and the snapping of a rein or the smallest obstacle in the way would have probably sent us all to kingdom come. Providence, however, who apparently keeps special angels to watch over reckless people, has always brought us safely home, and will, I hope, continue to do so; for it is an ugly thought to be dashed into little bits on a heap of stones, with a horse's grinding hoofs hammering your face. Mother has a basket-carriage with two fat gray ponies, which are so far beneath papa's notice that they enjoy a meed of peace no other animals in the stable possess, and behind them we youngsters have many a pleasant amble and comfortable confab.

"Are you girls coming down to tea this evening or to-morrow morning?" asks Jack, putting his head in at the door. "The governor is just coming up the carriage-drive!"

CHAPTER V.

"Wooing, wedding, and repenting, is as a Scotch jig, a measure, and a cinque-pace: the first suit hot and hasty, like a Scotch jig, and full as fantastical; the wedding mannerly-modest as a measure, full of state and ancientry; and then comes repentance, and with his bad legs falls into the cinque-pace faster and faster, till he sink into his grave."

JACK and I went to see a wedding this morning that began yesterday, and was only finished to-day. It was not a mannerly-modest one though; far from it. We make a rule of attending all the weddings and funerals we can, but school-hours are a sad hinderance to me, and Jack often has to go by himself. We always watch the mourners with great attention, and have, after careful study of their countenances, made up our minds that it is almost always those who care least who are most demonstrative, and that dry-eyed grief is far more deep and deadly than a tempest of sobs and cries and wails. Not that poor people as a rule regret their dead very passionately; their hard, dull, working lives are so heavy to bear, that a trifle more or less misery matters but little. You will even see a mother with many children taking some comfort from the thought that the Lord has "provided" for the little ones taken away from her.

But I am forgetting all about yesterday's wedding. It was at a convenient hour, nine o'clock. So, having watched papa safely into the stables, we were soon across the lawn and churchyard, and in our usual hiding-place in the organ-loft. Mr. Skipworth was already waiting before the altar, book in hand, and looking decidedly cross, when the bride and bride-groom came in, followed by a few people. We couldn't see their faces, but there seemed something very wrong about the bridegroom's back, for he was lurching, tripping, and rolling from side to side, and, strange to say, the bride, a stout and buxom young woman, was supporting him! They reached the altar, and Mr. Skipworth began to read the service, but, when it became necessary for the young man to make his vows, nothing was heard but a series of hiccoughs; and, although the bride pinched and shook and whispered him energetically, no responses were forthcoming, and in another minute he had fallen an inert mass upon the chancel-floor.

"Oh, my!" exclaimed Jack in high glee, "he's *drunk*."

Mr. Skipworth shut the book in disgust and walked away; but the intrepid bride, with no trace of anger, raised her man, and with her friends' assistance conveyed him to the door.

We followed the couple to the village as far as we dared, and during the day contrived to get posted up as to the latest particulars. At noon he was fast asleep, with his head on the bride's lap; at three he was recovering, and calling loudly for beer; at five he was locked up by her friends for safety; at nine he was sitting with his head in a basin of cold water, forced thereto by the same hopes of enabling him to go to church on the morrow. And their indefatigable efforts have been rewarded, for this morning he came up to time, and was able to make his vows, if somewhat unsteadily, at least audibly. The bride's beaming face was a study as she bore her swinish and sulky mate away. Truly matrimony must have had charms for *her*.

It is a never-ending puzzle to Jack and me how people can like being married.

Dorley has a wife, a very fine woman, who beats him, and of whom he is intensely proud. Once she rather overdid it; and, as a worm will turn, so did Dorley; and, having represented to her that her little attentions were incompatible with the respectability of appearance Colonel Adair required from his gardener, it was agreed that they should separate, she possessing one-half of his wages and household goods, he the other. They had not been apart a week when Dorley came and gave papa warning. "He could not live without his missus," he said, "and he was going to her." And go he did; but matters were ultimately arranged, and Dorley came back to us with his spouse, who beats him more than ever, to his great satisfaction and content.

Dorley, however, if meek at home is not meek to us. He is a tyrant, and looks upon the fruits and flowers of the garden as *his*, while we are little thieves and pickpockets, who menace the same. And oh! he has to be sharp, has Dorley, or there would be never a gooseberry, peach, or apricot, to send in for dessert. I wonder where he is this afternoon? I wonder where everybody is? Though I have been prowling round the garden for half an hour, I have not met a soul.

It is very mean of Jack to go off and leave me in this way—on a Wednesday afternoon too. I did *not* think he would bear me so much malice about the pig; boys aren't forgiving like girls. I wonder what he is doing? Fishing? Bathing? Taking a scramble across-country with Pepper? It is too hot for that, for Jack loves his ease as well as anybody else. I wonder if any apples have fallen from the quarantine tree? I turn my steps toward it and look about; there is not one on the grass. I cast my eyes upward, and mark with approving eyes the rosy fruit hanging so stirlessly on the boughs. If only a breeze would spring up, and give those boughs a gentle shake, down would fall the apples at my feet, but the sky is one hard, fierce glare, and there is not the ghostliest shadow of a breeze abroad on the land.

Looking begets longing, longing in a depraved and energetic mind begets acting; and, seeing that the gentle gale my soul craves refuses to blow, I conceive the daring thought of myself acting the part of gentle zephyr. I look around; no one is to be seen. Dorley is invisible; the governor I saw fast asleep in the library a while ago; the coast is clear. In the twinkling of an eye I have swung myself up into the tree, and am shaking with a will. The fruit is falling in a bounteous red shower, when a voice directly below me makes me start so violently that I drop the bough and lose my footing. But, alas! instead of respectably smiting mother earth with my nose, I remain suspended, petticoats above, legs below. Even in this awful moment, the verse over the barber's shop comes into my mind:

"O Absalom! O Absalom! my poor, ill-fated son,
If thou hadst only worn a wig, thou hadst not been undone."

Only in this case, if I had been clad in Jack's clothes, not my own, I should not be undone. My face has disappeared into the crown of my sun bonnet in my abrupt descent, so I cannot see my discoverer. Can it be—*can* it be the governor? No, for if it had I should have received palpable evidence of his wrath before this.

"I wish your pa could see you," says Dorley's deliberate voice, sounding more sweetly in my ears than ever did song of nightingale; "'ow he would whack you!"

"I know he would," I murmur indistinctly from the depth of my bonnet. "Do, there's a good, kind Dorley, take me down!"

But Dorley has suffered many things at my hands, and, now his day has come, he means to enjoy it for a little while.

"You've been a bad young lady to me, Miss Ullen," he says slowly (and at the sound of his leisurely voice I aim a sudden kick at him with my dangling legs, for oh! at any moment *he* may appear on the scene, and then—). "You and your beasts has trampled my flower-beds and messed my lawn beyond believing, and you've stole my paches, broken my glass, and misbehaved yerself ginerally; and if it wasn't for yer pa, and his being so vilent, I'd leave you there for an hour, Miss Ullen, I would. Pr'aps, with the Lord's mercy, it might be a warning to yer. But I don't want to have nothing to do with murder, so I'll take yer down this time; only, if ever I finds yer a disgracing yerself in this misbecoming manner again, I'll leave yer there, Miss Ullen, sure as my name's Dorley. And kickin' won't do no good when you're in the wrong, miss; leastways, it won't wi' *me*."

He departs slowly in search of the steps, while I dangle at my ease in creeping, curdling terror, lest even now the governor may be turning the corner.

Dorley comes back at last, and disentangles me with some difficulty, and oh! with what joy do I once more plant my waggling feet on firm ground; never, never will I play the part of gentle zephyr again.

In the depths of my pocket, tenderly hoarded, fondly cherished, lurks a sixpence, which I disinter and hand to Dorley with my lips pursed up very tight.

"There, take it," I say; "it's for you."

"No, no, Miss Ullen," says Dorley, holding it out in his earth-stained hand, "I won't take it from 'ee! Happen you want it worse than I do!"

"Dorley," I say, drawing myself up with dignity, "I am amazed at you! Sixpences are *no* object with me, nor—nor—shillings, nor—half-crowns."

Having uttered this last astounding lie without winking, I walk away with a stately strut that I hope impresses him, and which is I suppose born of the occasion, for I never owned it before.

What a burning, breathless, sleepy afternoon it is! The earth seems lapped in a nerveless, luxurious, indolent slumber. The very flowers seem to have gone to sleep, and the birds to be taking a *siesta*. Passing the schoolroom window, I see Alan the solemn-faced, who is apparently not so overcome with heat as the rest of the world, indulging in the rather active recreation of spinning Dolly round and round on the top of the large schoolroom table. It is evidently a new treat to them, and I have not time to give the warning that painful experience has taught Jack and me, when whirr! whiff! the top of the table flies to the other end of the room, shooting Dolly into the fireplace, and Alan dances up and down, as though the perils his toes have just escaped make him anxious to assure himself of their integrity.

Piteous whimpers and groans from the fireplace announce extensive and painful damages to the poor little maid who was riding aloft so triumphantly a minute ago. Bruises and tears are, however, alike merged in the all-absorbing question of how the table is to be joined together again. In the middle of the room its legs stand stark and bare, like a thin little man, from whom his ample and overflowing spouse has departed.

All this while they have not been aware of my presence on the scene, but now as I remark, "A very pretty amusement, certainly!" with all the gravity and weight my thirteen years entitle me to display, they hail me joyfully, and with my assistance, and much puffing and straining, the divorced parts are put together, and Dolly has time to bewail her misfortunes, and Alan to rub his unharmed shins responsive.

Pursuing my prowl, I wander round the irregularly-built, three-sided court, and am shortly awakened from my abstraction by hearing a door bang violently.

Have you ever lived in a house, reader, where the merest chance sound, the bang of a door, the sound of a loud voice, or a distant noise, makes you start up, your nerves tingling, your heart beating, your body trembling, while an instantaneous photograph of falling chairs, flying crockery, broken bell-ropes, and dancing china, with a dervish dancing in the midst of the confusion, presents itself vividly to your eyes?

All this I see when that distant bang reaches my ears. To-day it means "Bills." It is an insult to papa's understanding for any one to dare ask for his money. We must be clothed, it is true, and fed, but shall the paying for these small trifles be taken as a legitimate, every-day duty? Perish the thought! It is disgraceful, it is unseemly, it is an upside-downness of everything, that these rascals should, week after week, be sending their paltry bits of blue paper in to him, and he resents the impertinence accordingly. Ah, poor mother! You are in the midst of that hurly-burly yonder; when I am older I will walk straight in and share it with you, now I should be ordered out. Experience tells me that the sooner I hide myself the better, for when papa is in one of these furies there is no safety for any one from garret to coal-cellar; in this mood he may even feel that a slaughter of the innocents is necessary for the rehabilitation of his peace of mind, so I hastily retire to the rabbit-hutch, which is in a central position, and thence watch the march of events. From my coign of vantage I presently see him come out, and throw his eyes hither and thither in search of prey, then he goes down through the garden and out of sight. I am just thinking that perhaps the house will be safer than my present quarters, when in the distance I see dogs, fowls, fry, nurses, Amberley, Jack, Alice, Milly, and Dolly, all flying toward the house, like autumn leaves before the wind. No need to ask what is behind them, only one person on earth could have that effect, so, remembering that there is safety in numbers, I join the flying squadron and reach the house with the rest. As we enter by the side-door, the rusty front-door bell is smartly pulled by a business-looking man in black, at whom we all peep privily from convenient lattices, and make up our mind that Providence sent him straight from heaven to be our deliverer. He has come to see papa, we ascertain later, and is even now closeted with him. I wonder how he will manage to so far smooth his ruffled plumes as to carry on any conversation that is not strictly vituperative?

We are all sitting together, save Jack, when we hear his steps coming down the passage, and he enters and closes the door with a cheerful bang, that does not make us all bound on our seats as the bangs of a certain other person do. There is a peculiar look on Jack's face, a kind of knowing twinkle in his eye, a modest elation in his glance, that owes its origin, I am certain, to some bit of news that he has possessed himself of, and which he is secretly enjoying in its full relish before imparting it to us.

"News!" we all cry, starting from our seats, "surely he cannot—cannot be —going away?"

Oh! those two delicious words, can any others in the whole dictionary contain such sweet music?

"I say," says Jack, vigorously repulsing the avalanche of female charms that threatens to overwhelm him, "I can't tell you anything, can I, if you stifle me?"

"Go on! go on!" we all cry, withdrawing hastily from the oracle.

"Well," says Jack, complacently surveying the row of open eyes, mouths, and ears, "he is *going away* (shouts of delight); he is going to-morrow (fresh rejoicings); and he is coming back next day (howls of dissatisfaction). Nevertheless, there is one assuaging circumstance, he is going early, so we shall have one clear day in which to accomplish our deeds of darkness."

"Hurrah! I know what *I* shall do."

"You'll take me with you," I say imploringly, "do."

"Can't," says Jack briefly, "I shall go out shooting."

We all gasp; Jack with a gun in his hands! Oh, if the governor could but— "What are you going to shoot?" asks Alice with interest.

"Blackbirds."

"Yourself, you mean," I say, nodding and feeling much hurt, and somewhat spiteful that I may not go with him to see the fun. "Only if you do, you must do it thoroughly; the governor hates sickness, you know; and, if you did have a bad accident, how you would catch it!"

"Funerals are expensive," says Alice. "On the whole I think papa would rather he only crippled himself."

"I shall take his new gun," says Jack, pursuing his own train of thought, and paying no heed to our cackle, "it's sure not to burst."

"I shall make treacle-tarts," I say, feeling my abasement very keenly, and wondering if Jack will relent. (I could make myself useful in picking the birds up.)

"What are you going to do, Alice?"

"I don't know," she says, turning a lovely, thoughtful face upon me, "there is so little mischief girls can get into. I think I shall make Amberley take me into Pimpernel, and I will have my photograph taken; it has never been done yet, you know."

"Whatever do you want a likeness for?" asks Jack, opening his eyes; "can't you look at your face in the glass fifty times a day if you like? And there's nobody to give it to, for we haven't a friend in the world, and you wouldn't give one to us surely?"

But Alice does not answer, she is wondering what the sun will make of her face of which—

"'T is beauty truly blent, whose red and white
Nature's own sweet and cunning hand laid on."

"I shall go with Alice," says Milly, promptly.

"And I," says Alan, the solemn-faced, "shall look over papa's new edition of the 'Ingoldsby Legends;' I've had one or two peeps at it already."

"What are you going to do, Dolly?"

"I shall take two Seidlitz powders with sugar, you know. They are so nice, and nurse says they make me thinner. I am never able to take them when papa is at home, because they make me look pale."

"Bravo, Dolly!" cries Jack, "happy the mind that a little contents. Well, girls, you shall have a fine dish of blackbirds for supper, and Nell's treacle-tarts, if they are eatable."

"Will you?" cries a terrible voice behind us, that galvanizes our recumbent forms into most intense and rigid uprightness, while every soft hair on our miserable young heads stands on end with freezing, curdling horror— "will you? I'll teach you, miss (with a fierce nod at Alice's pretty, trembling figure), to go gallivanting off to Pimpernel, to simper at a low photographer, you miserable, doll-faced, conceited puppet; (to Jack) I'll teach you, sir, to use my guns and bring me in a doctor's bill a yard long for mending your wretched bones; (to me) I'll teach you, you object, to waste my substance with your filthy treacle-tarts; and you, sir (to Alan), to maul over my books, while as to you (to Dolly), although I can't offer you Seidlitz powders, perhaps brimstone and treacle will do as well, oo—oo—oo—ooh. You deceitful, vagabond, shameless pack, get out of my sight; go!"

He need not tell us that twice, away we flee, every man for himself, and devil take the hindmost; along the passage, up the stairs, in at the nursery, to which we always flee on these occasions, for mother is nearly always there. At our heels comes the governor, and a lively time follows; we become a prose version of that deplorable story of ten little niggers, which we all know; as rapidly as they dropped off, so do we: this one for a cane, that for a Bible, another into space with boxed ears, until from beginning with a goodly number we end a forlorn remnant. Over and above our other punishments we are one and all sent to bed, and thither, when he has stormed himself away, we retire, only too thankful to have that refuge to sneak into. Anything is bearable while we are together, the only real misery he could inflict upon us would be to commit us all to solitary confinement. Jack comes in by-and-by, and sits down on the edge of Alice and Milly's bed, while I perch myself on a chair hard by.

"What fools we were," he says, with a dark look in his blue eyes, "not to have set a scout to watch, the sneakiness of him; why couldn't he have walked in like a man, instead of hanging about outside?" He gives his shoulders, which are still tingling with the sharp lash of the governor's cane, an impatient shake. "I can't think what fathers were invented for," I say dolefully. "I am sure we should have got on much better without ours. For my part, if I had been asked whether I would or would not come into the world, I should have said, 'Yes, and thank you kindly, sir, if you can arrange for me to have no papa?'"

"And yet he almost forgives our daring to exist, when he reflects on the number of times we have afforded him the exquisite satisfaction of beating us," says Jack. "Well, when I come back from school next Christmas, if he tries to beat the devil's tattoo on my back again, he shall find he won't get it all his own way."

"And we will hang upon his coat-tails," I say, comfortingly, "while the fry harass him fore and aft in countless swarms."

"Don't forget that he is going away," puts in Milly; "I was turning that sweet thought over in my mind the whole time he was making that row."

"He will lock us all up," I say with conviction. "He will never go away and leave us free to do all the things he heard us arranging to-night."

"You little silly!" says Jack, crushingly; "don't you know that he thinks us all dummies, and no more believes us capable of daring to do anything that he has forbidden than that the moon is made of green cheese? I sha'n't shoot to-morrow; I mean to do something worse."

CHAPTER VI.

"Happy in this, she is not yet too old
But she may learn; and happier than this,
She is not bred so dull but she can learn."

BREAKFAST is over, and the monotonous burden of our sins sung into our ears, from the saying of amen at prayers to the last drop of the governor's coffee-cup, is over. It has been very bad, but in listening to his fulminations we have been let off the active misery of conversation; and on the whole, for we are very hardened sinners, we almost prefer the breakfast to our usual ones. He is standing in the hall now, brushing his hat, and the sound sends a thrill of delight through our bodies; we know the full import of it so well, though we hear it so much, much too rarely. Up the carriage-drive comes the sharp trot of a horse's hoofs; it is the dog-cart that is going to take him to the station. Simpkins carries out his traveling-bag (the old varlet is as pleased in his heart as we are, he too will get a little holiday), and we all go into the hall and make a frosty peck, one by one, at the governor's face, occasionally hitting his nose or eyebrow by mistake. He eyes us keenly to see if he can detect any indecent joy upon our faces, but they are perfectly blank and stolid, to such abhorred hypocrisy have we already brought our innocent, indeterminate, pink-and-white features. He kisses mother (how droll it seems to see him making a peck at anybody!); and now he is in the dog-cart, he is starting, he is giving a sharp look at our assembled countenances, he is off, and has turned the corner of the drive. Still there is unbroken silence; then, as the last sound of the wheels dies away in the distance, the delight that has been running riot within us, breaks forth in exclamation, laughter, leaps, dances, whoops, and (on my part at least) rolls of bliss. When they have subsided a little—"Children," says mamma, "I have something to tell you."

"Won't it keep, mamma dear," asks Alice, "till some day when we are not quite so happy? We don't get many treats; had we not better have them one at a time?"

"It will keep," says mamma, smiling; "but I shall tell you now. We are going away."

Going away! We know the sound of those words well enough as applied to the governor, but as applied to ourselves they have a strange, unusual flavor—a romantic freshness that breathes of distant lands, gorgeous cities, and unknown, mysterious pleasures. None of us have ever been away from home in all our lives, save Jack.

"When, mamma?" we ask, after a pause; it takes a little while to get used to the idea that we are going away without requiring any further knowledge on the subject.

"To the sea!" The answer strikes us dumb again. Have we not longed ourselves sick for a sight of it? Have we not splashed ourselves from head to foot over a dirty pond in trying to make real waves with stout sticks?

"When, mamma, *when?*"

"Early next week. Your papa has heard of a house that will suit us."

So soon! it takes our breath away. "And is he coming too?" I ask anxiously.

"Not for a fortnight." We draw a deep sigh of satisfaction.

"What strolls we will have!" says Alice. "And donkey-rides!" "and shrimps!" "and peace!" "and cuttle-fish tooth-powder!" "No walks!" "or pun-

ishments!" "No one to call us dummies!" "or make us talk!" "or send us to bed!"

"Come along, Dolly," says Alan the solemn-faced. "I'm going to begin packing up."

Jack and I go out in the garden and discuss our plans—what beasts are to go with us, what to be left behind. Paul Pry must come, of course, and the raven and the canaries, and Pepper, the tailless. Dorley must take care of the rabbits; and as to the fowls, they have lately misbehaved themselves so perseveringly that it would cause us no great sorrow if, on our return, we found papa had made a holocaust of the whole lot. Possibly the amazing news puts out of our heads our several intentions of evildoing; at any rate we get into no mischief to-day, and merely walk about, laugh, talk, and stretch, not only in the schoolroom, but about the house, just as if we were used to doing it every day of our lives.

The governor comes back a trifle sweeter than he went. For once business does not seem to have rubbed him the wrong way; and somehow the few days slip away, and the golden morning of our departure arrives.

The coach stands at the door. It is going to take us all the way, and we are packed within it close as herrings, happy as lords; every nook and corner inside and out brimmingly full; where a body is not squeezed in, a hamper or a parcel is, and how we shall ever be got out again is something of a mystery. We have smuggled all our little private belongings in safely. Under my petticoats lurk the birds and Paul Pry, who, with the sense of a Christian, utters not a sound, raps out not a single oath; a large basket of quarantine hides its modest head under mother's legs; the young ones firmly grasp spades and buckets as though they expected to find the sea upon the road; Amberley embraces five distinct bundles, bandboxes, and bags;

the babies, set bolt up on end, utter fat little chirps of satisfaction. On the door-step stands the governor, to whom we have just said good-by with a freedom and affability that I think astonish him as much as they do ourselves; for once in his presence our voices come honestly forth; for once we kiss him, and I at least feel that I *love* him. And now the last forgotten parasol is handed in, the last servant has climbed with many a creak to her place on the roof; the coach-man cracks his whip. "Chirrup, chir-rup," go the canaries. "Hip, hip, hur-r-r-ah!" goes Paul Pry. "Bow-wow!" goes Pepper, wriggling her head out be-tween Jack's legs.

"Oh!" says Dolly, with a deep sigh.

"Balmy!" I ejaculate, pushing my hat to the back of my head; and away we go, nodding and smiling, and saying good-by! good-by! to the little gentleman on the door-steps, who somehow looks quite in-significant and a little forlorn now that he is not the centre of a dozen duteous white slaves.

"We are off!" says Alice.

"We are dreadfully hungry!" sigh Dolly and Alan, pointing their prophetic noses at a bulging hamper that obtrudes its portly body in an uncomfortable way between nurse and Balaam's Ass, the un-der nursemaid. It is only eight o'clock, and we had breakfast at seven, and it is rather early to be setting out; but when everybody is so anxious to start, so ready to go, why should there be any unneces-sary tarrying? Yoicks! away we go, along the dewy, bloomy lanes, between the fresh, green hedgerows, with the early breath of the morning blowing coolly in on our happy, eager faces; past the staring, silent cows, and the dull laborers who, poor souls! are going about their work just as on any other day, who are not tast-ing our first delicious, strange draught of "going away!" We feel like pilgrims set-ting out for an unknown land; we do not know what is before us, whether of sweet or sour, but that it will be something very

different from anything we have ever known before we are perfectly certain, and that is enough for us. Jack pooh-poohs our transports and pretends to have seen everything that we observe before, which is not right of him, for I know he goes to school in quite an opposite direc-tion, and by train; whereas traveling by coach is a very different and far more knowledgable thing.

We keep our eyes very widely open all the way, and observe with interest how the country changes as we near the coast, and how blue the cottage children's eyes are, as though a bit of the sea had got into them and staid there. Happy folks are always hungry, and by ten o'clock we are clamoring to attack the hamper; at two we are dying of want and finish it up; at four we pounce upon the quarantines (which were to last us a week, Dorley said), and eat them all up, every one. We get rather fagged the latter part of the way; our bodies are stiff and tired, and we cannot stretch them. By degrees one voice ceases, then another; one of the babies cries; Paul Pry makes remarks that he should not before the children. We look very different from the noisy, bus-tling, smiling people who started a few hours ago.

By-and-by we are startled out of our apathy by a shout without of "The sea! the sea!" and we leap up to the sight of a broad, boundless expanse of deepest, darkest blue, that thrills us through and through, and holds us spellbound with a breathless delight and strong awe. How our souls seem drawn toward it, though our bodies remain in the coach! Present-ly (I do not know how it happens), we are standing before it, gazing almost de-liriously at the glittering, belted-in treas-ure. When the first shock is over, how we stretch out our arms to it, as though we would clasp its beauty in our embrace! How we stoop and dabble our fingers in the strange, salt liquid! How we stand watching the waves lapping softly over each other with no fuss or hurry, or effort, rather as though they were in play, not earnest, but, as we quickly find, impelled by an on-coming strength that makes the babyish ripples resistless as fate, inexorable as death! We gather trails of brown sea-weed, and, when our hands are full, cast them away for others. We are distracted by the abundant riches of the feast set out before us; something new, unimagined, and wonderful meets our eyes at every step. Into my heart comes a dim ache that is not keen pleasure or satiety, but a passionate regret that my soul is not bigger, grander, capable of holding more of the great tide of rapture that sweeps through me in such a mighty flood. When Amberley comes for us I turn away as one in a dream; from a long way off I seem to hear her exclamation at our condition; though indeed I am well aware that we are as forlorn, dirty, dripping little wretches as any to be found in the kingdom, all save Alice, over whom untidiness and dirt hold no power.

As we go inland my senses seem to come back to me, and I hail with delight the jolly, red-brick face of our new abode, which appears to smile jovially upon us and bid us kindly welcome. Inside it is in a most immoral, delicious state of topsy-turvydom—luggage, servants, children, and animals, all mixed up in the most admired disorder; babies crying, small fry falling down-stairs, servants rifling half-filled boxes, canaries shrieking for water and groundsel, Paul Pry cursing his fate with peculiar bitterness and intensity from his perch on Minerva's head, to which he has evidently betaken himself for safety. It is a fine burly-burly, and, if papa could only walk in and see it all, his appearance would put the finishing stroke to the scene and make it Bedlam.

We sit down to a nondescript meal, but can scarcely eat for talking. A thousand tongues would not express the half that we feel; and oh, how bald the words are that language provides for expressing a great delight! Deeply im-

pressed as Jack is, he can find no words whereby to convey his admiration of the ocean than by those of "jolly" and "stunning."

It is too late to go out again this evening, so we go to bed that we may be able to rise with the first streak of daylight on the morrow. Sleep binds me so safely though, that, on Jack's calling me, I am scandalized to find it as late as six. What a lot of time we have wasted already!

In half an hour we are out on the beach and among the rocks, making queer discoveries; for instance, that shrimps and crabs do not grow scarlet but drab; also that the saying, "stick like a limpet," has a sound, healthy truth of its own that many proverbs have not; also that the seaweed-covered rocks have a remarkable knack of slipping away from our feet, compelling us to turn somersaults more rapid than elegant. We hunt for and find delicate shells, curious rose-hued freaks of Neptune, and we muse over them, marveling in what sea-palace the carver lurks who casts up to us such dainty and mysterious shapes. We hold the bigger ones to our ears, and listen intently to the faint murmur that must, we think, so exactly represent the shoaling noise the sea makes at a great distance. We have listened to the same murmur before at Silverbridge, and nurse always told us it was the sea that we heard.

After breakfast we accompany Amberley and our sisters in a sober trot through the one long street that forms the town of Periwinkle, and sit down on the shingle where, apparently, the beauty and fashion (!) of the place do congregate, for no other purpose than to watch the rows of fat and lean kine who are taking their daily dip in the sea hard by, bobbing up and down in the sun like seals, with snaky locks of hair clinging round their cheeks, and tight, sticky bathing-gowns that most lavishly display their charms, or the lack of them.

Jack and I have a hot dispute as to whether a very lean woman or a very fat one looks worst in the water. *I* say the former, *he* says the latter, and implores me on no account to submit my person to the public gaze without at least six thick bathing-gowns put on, like an old-clothesman's hats, one above the other.

They are a gruesome spectacle, these fat matrons and lean old maids; even the young girls, who might be good-looking if their faces were dry, have an unsavory appearance, for salt-water seems to have an ugly knack of washing out shams, stripping off borrowed charms, and leaving the original visage clear and visible. Aphrodite herself must have found it rather a hard matter to look as handsome under the circumstances as she did. It must be on the principle that there is always something pleasing to us in the misfortunes of our friends that makes these people flock to see their acquaintances *au naturel*, sans crinoline, sans bustle, sans pads, sans everything, save their own unembellished bodies and countenances. I wish the performers would go through their paces with a little more vigor and spirit, take a good sousing header into space, and look as if they liked it, instead of taking a dip as though they were going to be hanged; coming up, not smiling, but with shut eyes and screwed-up nose and mouth, sputtering, coughing, gasping, groaning, and holding on to the rope as though they were being shipwrecked. Others do not go so far as the heroism of dipping; they hug the shore and sit basely down on the sand, letting the water ripple over them by degrees. For decency's sake one could wish the process were less gradual. Others again shiver on the steps of the machine, and are afraid to venture in at all.

Now and then a daring young woman creates enormous excitement by lowering herself carefully into the water, and bringing her pink toes to the surface in the first position, stares up unwinkingly at Father Sol. Gallant creature! the pint or so of salt-water that she swallows is but a slight set-off against the glory she achieves, and the admiration her prowess evokes from the lookers-on.

Jack and I soon weary of looking at this raree-show; and having promised Amberley not to drown ourselves, not to get into a boat without a boatman and with a large hole in the bottom, not to sit upon a rock until the tide surrounds and flows over us, not to climb to the highest pinnacle of the cliff with the express intention of toppling over it to the rocks below, we take our departure, and speed the morning hours well enough.

Oh! the sea is a rare playfellow, for, unlike many a human one, he never wearies you! Each day he wears some new aspect, compels from us fresh wonder, admiration, and fear. He is terrible in his angry splendor of wind-tossed, thundering breakers, when his surface is all deep-green valleys and towering, snowy-crested mountain-tops. He is soft, tender, caressing as a summer breeze, with his shoaling, rippling murmur and lazy, creeping wavelets. Sometimes he is sulky, not angry, that is when the sun has hidden his face; then he catches the reflection of the sky and is sad-colored and dull. Another day he will lie calm as a lake, like a great monster soundly asleep, and we do not love his monotonous peace; dearer far is he to us when he stirs and flushes and quivers in the sun, his kingly breast sown with millions upon millions of sparkling diamonds. He gives no sign of the dark secrets he hides away so deep, so deep; of the water-slain bodies that lie below with the swish! swish! of his green waters, swirling over their pale, drowned faces, of the souls that trusted themselves to his smiling mien and silvery whispers, and whom he has drawn down, down! to the sea-chambers, of whose treasures we can but dimly guess from the rainbow-tinted shells and bloomy seaweed that are now and again washed up to us from their depths.

Has not the sea its cities and towns and gardens and dwelling-houses? Do not flowers as lovely, as glowing, as fragrant, grow in those silent gardens as any the dry land affords? They must have rare jewels down there; pearls such as no mortal empress ever wore; precious stones, common as pebbles on the shore; rare and costly gewgaws, plentiful as the sand, with goodly store of gold and silver, rifled from the gallant ships laden with splendid store of merchandise brought from foreign lands. Oh! it must be a rich land, and might be a fair land, if that great and countless army of the dead did not claim it so urgently for its own.

We have not been in Periwinkle a week; we have not learned one-half his moods, one-half his secrets, when something happens—something that sends me shuddering away from him inland, and makes me hate the sound of his voice and the dazzle of his brow.

Jack and I are standing on the beach one morning, watching a haul of mackerel in. The men have been pulling for hours. "It is strangely heavy," they mutter; "the net will break;" but by-and-by it comes safely in, and we all gather round to where it lies on the edge of the sand, with the waves rippling gently up to it. At first I see nothing but a glittering, brilliant, opal-tinted mass of glistening fish, which sparkle and scintillate in the sun, as they leap to and fro in their restless, unknown agony; then I make out a strange, dark, shapeless mass beneath them, that is—what? A dead man, with horribly discolored face and wide, staring eyes, looking out with dull and awful meaning from among the quivering, leaping fish for which the net was cast, and which has brought in *this*. A woman thrusts her way through the crowd and falls on her knees beside the net. "*My lad!*" she says, "*my lad!*" .... He went out alone in his boat a week ago, and did not return; but she said she knew he would come back, and she has been watching for him night and day.

"Come away," I say to Jack, dizzily; and we go away, away inland, and it is

3

many a long day before I love the treacherous sea again and can forget.

We do not see much of Alice and Milly, who prefer the town and the shingle to the rocks and the caves; and it sometimes strikes Jack and me as odd that, when we *do* come across our sisters, all the black, gray, and blue coats belonging to the youth abiding in and sojourning at Periwinkle should be in their immediate neighborhood. But then Alice is so lovely; who can help liking to look at her? The very girls turn and stare at her. with that grudging, unwilling, breathless interest that I am already learning to know is the highest compliment one woman can pay another; and which I shall never, *never* wring from any of my own sex. I may even fall to the degradation of being called "nice-looking" by them.

Alice looks demure as a nun; and how can the pretty soul help it if rude men *will* stare at and follow her about? All I know is I love to look at what is pleasant to the eye; and if I had been born comely should have carried about a pocket-mirror with me, and refreshed my eyes with a sight of my charms every five minutes, while nobody would ever have admired me half as heartily and appreciatingly as I should have admired myself.

CHAPTER VII.

"Some there be that shadows kiss,
Such have but a shadow's bliss;
There be fools alive, I wis."

It is nine o'clock, and I am making my toilet for the night, and smiling to myself at a ridiculous story Jack told me just now about on old sailor down here. He would like to be devout, but has not time to save his soul, so has copied out the longest and finest prayer he knows of and pinned it over his bedstead, and every night and morning, when he turns in and turns out, he looks toward it and says, "'*Thim's* my sintiments, O Lord!'" I have time, plenty, so there is no fear of my following his example. As I take a last look out of the window preparatory to jumping into bed, my attention is arrested by the extraordinary appearance presented by the hedge that lies on the other side of the road, which appears to be animated with what might be a row of uneven trees swaying to and fro, if, on this stirless night, there were wind enough to stir anything.

It is growing dark, and in the uncertain light it is difficult to pronounce distinctly on the phenomena; but I, nevertheless, come to the conclusion that the bobbing objects are hats, hats which may be reasonably supposed to have human beings inside them. "Burglars!" I say to myself promptly, and descend to Jack's room, which overlooks the back garden, not the front. He is not in bed, so returns with me, and surveying the enemy with some interest, squashes my theory by saying: "Burglars! Why, you little sawney, burglars hide, they don't hop up and down like Jacks-in-the-box; besides, there are too many of 'em!"

All at once a light breaks in upon me. I have surreptitiously read two or three words which have given me some small insight into the imbecile practices of courtships, and now I am able to put two and two together, while Jack, poor lad, is completely at sea.

"I know!" I say, nodding my head violently, "I know! it's *lovers!*"

"Lovers!" repeats Jack, quite unimpressed, and in a most scornfully contemptuous voice; "how exactly like a girl with her silly notions! Whom do you suppose they'd come after, miss; *you?*"

"No; but there is Tabitha, you know, and Balaam's Ass" (Balaam's Ass is our under nursemaid, whose obstinacy is so incurable that years ago we gave her the above name, which has stuck to her).

"Very likely either of them would get a lover, is it not?" asks Jack, peering about. "Perhaps you would not mind *cook's* having a chance?"

"It may be cook," I say, brightening up; "I heard James call her 'an old flirt' the other day, and she was so pleased."

"I should say it *was* cook," says Jack, grinning, "for one man would not be of much use in that quarter; perhaps if they all stood in a circle they might be able to clasp her charms. No, it's not cook, it's somebody or other in the schoolroom under, for I just saw one beast deliberately kiss his hand toward it. I'm going down to see who is there."

"Wait a minute for me," I say, furling an Elijah-like mantle around me, and, so equipped, go down the stairs with him. We go into the schoolroom, but there is nothing there; nothing, that is to say, but Alice and Milly, who are sitting by the window in their white gowns. We retire and walk slowly up-stairs; halfway Jack stops short and looks at me. "It's not cook," he says, deliberately, "and it's not Tabitha, nor Balaam's Ass; it's *Alice.*"

Alice! I stand staring at him. "Are you mad?" I ask at last.

"No," he says, walking on, "but I'm disgusted. To think that those impudent—" The remainder of his speech is lost in a mutter. He is very young, but he has in him the germ of that dislike (so tenacious in the breasts of all Englishmen), that every brother, husband, or father has, to having his womankind looked upon too familiarly or too nearly by any stranger.

"What a row there will be when papa comes!" I say, drawing a deep breath.

"Serve her right too," says Jack, as he vanishes into his bedroom, and I retire to bed with a troubled mind and a resolve to give my sister a friendly warning to-morrow. Finding an opportunity, I put my arm round her neck, and, looking into her fresh face, that is not, I hope—

"A violet in the youth of primy Nature;
  Forward, not permanent; sweet, not lasting;
  The perfume and suppliance of a minute,
  No more—"

say, "If I were you I would not have quite so—so many, dear; there will be such a row when papa comes!" Alice laughs, blushes, and is about to answer, when mother comes in, and no more is said.

We go out donkey-riding this afternoon, everybody except Jack, who is too proud. A small drove of asses has been chartered for the occasion, and at the appointed hour they stand at the door meek and stubborn, each provided with a small boy, whose duty it is to "whip up" the aforesaid beast and make it "go." Amberley's charger staggers ominously as she mounts him; and, when seated, her long legs touch the ground, but she would rather die than be left behind, or prove unequal to the emergency, so she hitches them up and leads the van with some dignity, and, I think, much discomfort. Alice has the best beast; it has a broad back with a fat body, and she sits on it at her ease, shaded by her cool straw hat, under which her face takes no yellow reflections as does mine, looking as the Queen of Sheba may have looked in her young and palmy days. Mother has insisted on our taking two or three of the fry, strong-backed, stout-limbed boys, of whom there is an endless succession after Dolly, so we make a goodly cavalcade as we jog away with our attendant *gamins*.

Now there are few things pleasanter than to idle along the Devonshire lanes in summer-time on a well-grown, broad-backed, peaceable donkey; one is not at the trouble of walking, nor yet at the trouble of riding; one can just amble along at leisure, enjoying the air, the sky, and the light that quivers on the path through boughs that meet coolly overhead. There is a dreamy sensation of utter rest as one wanders in and out of the tangle of lanes that seem to have no beginning and no ending, but to indulge this feeling, the boy with the stick, whose whacks, regular as the flail on a thrashing-floor, fall upon your animal's hide, must be left behind; there is little romance in these darkly-shaded, flower-starred lanes to the tune of such music. We have a few mishaps by the way. Amberly is painfully thin, so is her beast, and their bones do not agree, so every now and then she slips noiselessly over his head and glides into the ditch or dusty road. We get used to it after a bit; so does she, and takes it as a matter of course. Dolly's steed walks into a turnstile and is with some difficulty disentangled. The fry have, to our great relief, long ago succeeded in goading their asses into a trot, and have vanished amid clouds of dust, closely followed by their attendant sprites, yelling with delight at the spirit their several *protégés* evince. At Alice's request our party of beaters have fallen behind, so we pace silently along the dim green lanes, meeting neither man nor horse; it is all as hushed, as still, and as solitary, as an uninhabited island.

Loathfully we turn homeward at last, and are met at the house-door by mother with the intelligence that the governor is coming to-morrow. Our jocund laughter ceases, we all dismount anyhow, and go in-doors to sit down under the shock of the intelligence which (though we know it must arrive some time or other) comes upon us like an ice-cold shower-bath. We all seem to have forgotten our days of bondage during this past fortnight. Farewell, *dolce-far-niente* days. We did not make half enough of you while you lasted; and now you are gone, and we shall never get any at all like you again. Farewell, social breakfasts, leisurely dinners, pleasant strolls, and general ease of body and soul! Farewell, donkeys, crabs, shrimps, rocks, seaweed, early walks, and natural conversation.

Now that those happy days are gone, I become aware that Jack and I did not *half* fill them. We might have got into so much more mischief, done so many

more things, enjoyed ourselves twice as
keenly. How shall we ever pull ourselves
together by to-morrow? Morally speaking we have fallen to pieces during the
last fourteen days, but all that must be
seen to at once. We must put on our
stays, gird up our loins, and look sharply
to our manners, morals, and clothes; the
very expression of our faces must be altered, and our voices be brought down a
great many notes. We must get out of
that loose and ridiculous habit of laughing at everything and nothing; we must
smooth the gay smiles out of our faces,
and he or she who has any dimples must
put them away for the present. The
schoolroom must be set in order and some
schoolbooks laid about to look as though
they had been used, the dining-room must
be polished till it winks again; James
must be awakened from the sloth into
which he has fallen, and the cook stirred
up to punctuality; the fry must be
promptly broken of the habit they have
lately fallen into of tumbling down and
cutting open their heads, noses, or legs;
in short, the whole house and all that
dwell therein must be thoroughly revised,
weeded, and drilled against the ordeal of
that awful to-morrow that is rushing upon
us as fast as it can pelt. It does not seem
half an hour ago that mother told us the
news, and, lo! the night has passed away,
the morning has come and gone, one
o'clock has struck, and in the distance
we hear the smart trot of horses' feet,
and we know that behind that cheerful
trot sits our uncheerful governor.

We are drawn up in well-brushed,
well-scrubbed, solemn-faced ranks in the
schoolroom. There is not one vagabond
smile among the whole lot. And now he
is in the hall, he is kissing mother, and in
another minute stands before us. Why
can I not infuse into my salute that
warmth and alacrity that I did on wishing him good-by on the Manor-House
door-step? Why, indeed! As we pass
in review before him, he looks at each
from head to foot; but we all pass muster

safely until he comes to the last of all,
Alice. We know what is coming when
his eye lights on a certain portion of that
young woman's dress—nothing more or
less, in short, than a crinoline row. The
fact is, Alice loves a big crinoline; papa,
accustomed to the straight up-and-down
charms of *his* mother and grandmother,
hates it; and as sure as ever her petticoats
swell beyond a certain limit there is a fearful to do, and the whole house is turned
upside down and out of windows. Now,
Alice knows the length of tether permitted to her perfectly well, but she is under
a mistaken impression that the more bal-
loon-like her skirts, the more charming
her pretty form appears; and when she
wants to look particularly ravishing, puts
on a little more crinoline, just as a South-
Sea islander put on a little more paint;
and in the excitement and novelty of the
Periwinkle life, she has forgotten her parent's little prejudices, and stands before
him confessed in all her amplitude of five
yards and a half.

It is odd that she should be caught,
though, for her crinoline is like some mag-
ical flower that opens and shuts, expands
and contracts, according to the state of
the weather, i. e., papa's temper. If he is
in an amiable or engrossed mood, she
usually lets out an extra reef or two; if
he is in a bad one, she collapses at a moment's notice and looks like a folded but-
terfly; but Alice's admirers have evidently turned her ideas topsy-turvy.

"You disgusting spectacle!" says papa,
deliberately looking at her from top to toe,
"you object! Go to your room and take
that vile barrel off, and if you ever dare
appear before me in it again, I'll pull it off
and burn it!"

Off goes Alice, whisking a pile of books
from the table in her passage to the door;
she does not mean to do it, poor pretty
Alice, it is only an evil trick played her by
that fatal combination of whalebone and
calico, but the governor thinks she does,
and flies after her. Thank God, she is too
old to have her ears boxed, and he soon

returns, but, oh! we heartily wish we had no ears at all, as we sit for half an hour listening to his tirade against Alice, mother, Amberley, and his own evil fate in marrying to become the father of such a daughter. (It was the best thing he ever did in his life.)

CHAPTER VIII.

"If she be made of red and white,
Her faults will ne'er be known,
For blushing cheeks by faults are bred,
And fears by pale white shown."

THE clock is striking eight, and we are all hunting *ventre-à-terre* for the family book of prayers. Not once since we came to Periwinkle have we looked upon its goodly face, and now it is revenging itself by refusing to come forth and save us from utter disgrace. If papa discovers that we have eaten our morning meal without the seasoning salt of chapter, prayer, and benediction, then woe, woe, woe betide us! We distractedly turn the book over and over, but *nowhere* does that much-coveted old brown cover meet our eager gaze. Overhead we hear his war-like tread as he walks to the toilet-table; he is putting on his coat, now he has opened the door, and is telling mamma she is the laziest woman in Christendom, and a disgrace to her sex; his foot is on the stair, oh!—o—o—oh! We tumble madly over each other in a dancing agony, and a pale tear trickles down Amberley's nose, when, hallelujah! I have found it, wedged in with its back to the wall, between the "Arabian Nights" and the "Pilgrim's Progress." We are saved by the skin of our teeth, and fly to our seats with thankful hearts while Alice finds the place, and sets the old marker, "Jesus wept," with its back broken in three places on the open page. He is in the room before she has done, and having received our morning salutes, and glanced sharply at Alice's collapsed charms (she looks like Samson shorn of his strength), rings the bell for prayers. He is half through the chapter before the servants can get in at the door; but that is of little consequence, they would not hear a word if they were present. Breakfast passes over better than might be expected. There are so many safe remarks we can make about Periwinkle; every man and woman we see is not an enemy, the mention of whose name must be shunned as the plague.; and I am even able to provoke a smile by remarking that it is difficult to hear the sermon on Sunday evenings because the sailors snore so loudly.

I think that if we were to travel much we should find plenty to talk to him about; become quite colloquial, in fact. Ah! travel's a wonderful thing for enlarging the mind. No wonder splendid Will said, "Home-keeping youths have ever homely wits" (of course he meant that for girls as well).

After breakfast our troubles begin. We go for a walk, and make the depressing discovery that in every deep there is a lower depth, and that, bad as the Silverbridge walks were, the Periwinkle ones are infinitely, immeasurably worse.

The governor is apparently as impervious to shingle as to ploughed fields, for he leads the van without a falter, while we flounder, slip, and stumble after him like a badly-drilled squad of infantry. The sun is fiercely smiting our backs, blistering our cheeks and noses, making us feel that our bodies have suddenly grown gross and heavy and suffocating; our clothes might be of woolen, so irritatingly do they chafe us. It is one of those broiling mornings when existence under a green tree is bad enough, but existence taking a race over a glaring shingle is diabolical.

We are bound for the rocks now uncovered by the receding tide, and over them we are going to Cod's Bay, a fishing-village of evil reputation and bad smells, that hides its dirty head round the corner of the cliff. It seems near enough, but, judged by the endless succession of slippery bowlders that intervene, we find it a very long way indeed, and groan in our spirits as we slide and scramble after our leader, who bounds on in front, agile as a chamois, and twice as sure-footed as his progeny. Not one cropper does he come; but Amberley makes up for him; she slides majestically down the rocks as though born to the accomplishment, and even *sits* in the pools among the scurrying little crabs, whence she has to be fished out by our united efforts. She makes no complaint though, far from it: her bruised shins, damaged elbows, and wet petticoats, all come in the day's work.

We reach Ood's Bay at last, looking as though we had fallen among thieves, and take our way through its one unsavory street, and climb a hill that would be trying in mid-winter, but in these dog-days is simply brutal. In two hours' time we get home, blowsy, footsore, and worn out, knowing that our evil days have indeed begun. Somehow the hours go by, and blessed nightfall comes.

At the present moment I am standing with my hands behind my back, affectionately regarding a crab, garnished with frequent prawns and abundant bread-and-butter, which Jack and I have provided for supper, as a set-off against the disagreeables of the day. He has gone to fetch a jug of cider; when he comes back we shall fall to. I walk to the open window and look out. The dim gray of night is creeping over the land; the cold salt smell of the sea blows faintly but most freshly up across the town; the lights yonder look like coarse reflections of the bright restless lamps that quiver and burn in the pale vault overhead. I lean my elbows on the window-sill, and look across at the rose-garden, that, like many another in Devonshire, is on the other side of the road; and whence a fragrant whiff comes now and again, and makes a disastrous discovery. Those moving shadows yonder, what are they? Followers! Not one 'or two or three, but *dozens!* O Alice, Alice! do I not

know well enough what will happen? In five minutes the governor will come in from the garden at the back of the house, and sit down to supper (his seat faces the road and the hedge to the left of the rose-garden), he will see them—he will rush out—and here conjecture fails me.

Jack enters, bearing the cider. "Jack!" I cry, rushing at him, "they have come, they are *here*, dozens of them!"

"Beetles?" asks Jack, abstractedly, his thoughts plainly running on the crab who is waiting to have his body dissected.

"Lovers!" I say, shaking him by the arm; "oh! what *shall* we do?"

Jack goes to the window. Below we here the scraping of chairs, the rattle of plates; the lamplight streams across the road; evidently Alice is in full view of the enamored host, for there is a sudden movement in their ranks, and they increase their capers tenfold, much as you may see Chucky, the pig, curl his tail and grunt excitedly when he sees a delectable wash approaching.

"If they would only keep quiet," I say in despair, "perhaps he would not see them. Do you think they *know* what a dreadful man he is?" Jack vanishes. A thought strikes me; seizing my night-cap, I lean out of the window and wave it energetically, pointing first at the room below, then at the town yonder. Surely, surely, my nightcap says, as plain as it can speak, "Go away!" Alas! to them such is evidently not its meaning, for at sight of my modest signal, at the dim vision of my white-robed form, the besieging army seems inspired with fresh vigor, and even begins to clamber over the hedge. My flag of danger is construed as an amatory signal pointing to indefinite favors, perhaps a love-letter. In another moment I hear a chair pushed sharply back below; the next I see the governor tearing across the road. He is up the hedge and over it before you could say Jack Robinson; but, quick as he is, Miss Alice's admirers are quicker, and he shortly returns furious and empty-handed. I am so petrified at the catastrophe my well-meaning efforts have brought about that I am utterly incapable of moving away; so, when the governor returns, and casts his eye over the house in search of the waiting-maid to whom he attributes the ovation, he beholds *me*—nightgown, night-cap, open mouth, and all. He shakes his fist wildly at me, and the gesture breaks the spell. I turn to hide myself in bed, but before I can reach it the governor is before me. I receive a box on the ear, that makes me see two enraged parents, two crabs, two jugs of cider, two night-caps; then, with a thunderstorm of abuse and wrath bellowing about me, I am hustled out of the room, down into Jack's—a narrow slip of a place overlooking the back garden, and which is only—oh, horror!—partitioned off the governor's chamber. There I am left crabless, supperless, tearless, to reflect on the extreme folly of ever meddling in other people's affairs; no matter what one's intentions may be, since the better they are the worse the results seem to be. Alice comes by-and-by, bringing me supper and comfort, as well she may, since her sins have brought down upon me the sentence of a three days' imprisonment to the house. Finally, for I shall have plenty of time for reflecting on my woes, I fall asleep. I scarcely seem to have reached the land of Nod, when I wake suddenly and open my eyes widely on—what? At first I am divided between a doubt whether it is papa come to finish me off, or that I am at last face to face with a ghost; it is so difficult to make out anything in this half-light (for the green window-blinds are very thick and dark), and it cannot yet be more than very early morning. Do ghosts seize you by the arm and shake you till your teeth rattle in your head, and the breath is nearly out of your body? Do ghosts—

"It's four o'clock," says a voice in a harsh whisper; "wake up, Master Jack, wake up."

"Master Jack!" *James!* I disappear under the bedclothes like a shot; but if I think I am going to be left there in peace, I am much mistaken. To leave Master Jack snoring in bed when (I now remember) James has received particular injunctions overnight to eject the same, however unwilling, is no part of his duty; so he punches and prods my prostrate body with a most laudable vigor, making violent efforts to dispossess me of the clothes. To these, however, I cling like grim death, wrapping them about me as tightly as a hedgehog in his skin, and for a space there is a desperate tussle, intensely ludicrous by reason of its silence, for neither of us dares to make a sound for fear of the governor's hearing; finally, altogether worsted and confounded, he goes, and I am left to sit up in bed like Marius among the ruins of Carthage. Presently Jack's head is popped gingerly in at the door, and he stares a good deal at the sight of the tossed bed, my tangled locks, and flushed, indignant countenance.

"Has the governor been taking a turn at you?" he asks, in a whisper.

"No," I answer, solemnly, "*Jeames.* I am black and blue. He thought it was you, you know."

"Oh, he did, did he?" asks Jack, sitting down on a chair, and going off into a noiseless explosion. "I quite forgot to tell him—" He rocks himself to and fro in an agony of mirth. "*I* know what *his* awakings are."

"And so do I," I put in with conviction. "I'm sure they are nothing to laugh at."

"I must go," says Jack, indistinctly, "or I shall burst;" and he goes away on some unlawful excursion or another that I should have loved, leaving me to moisten my sheets with unavailing tears. How slowly the hours creep by! how shall I ever get through three whole days? For once in my life I enjoy the honor of lying in my bed while the others are all scurrying down to prayers. I eat my breakfast in a slatternly way with a book before me.

I dawdle through the morning reading
Shakespeare, for oh, blessed oversight!
papa forgot to set me any tasks. I pass
my afternoon in imaginary conversation
with two blackbirds and a linnet, enjoying with a certain complacency the knowledge that all the others, Jack included,
are expiating *their* sins in the burning
sun at the governor's heels, over shingle,
rock, and sand. But by the time night
falls I am heartily *sick* of my own society.
I am longing to be in the midst of the
chaff and noise and bustle of my brothers
and sisters. If papa wants a recipe for
making me ripe for Bedlam, he has only to
shut me up alone for a fortnight. Somehow the days drag away, and I am released, free to go down the stairs or up as
my spirit wills. Below I find things very
crooked indeed ; *he* is in a state of chronic
ill-temper. Alice looks alarmed ; she is
red one moment, pale the next ; and the
very day of my readmittance to the family bosom, disaster marks us for her own.
We are waiting the announcement of dinner, and the governor is looking out of
the window, prepared to quarrel with
anything, from the thrush singing yonder
to the baker's boy with the bread, when
a smart dog-cart drives slowly past, in
which are seated two graceless, handsome,
wide-awake Oxonians, who stare deliberately in at every window in search of
Alice's blooming face. Papa turns round,
and I think he is *black* : he can put two
and two together as well as any other
man, and he *knows*.

"Go to your room, miss!" he says to
Alice.—"So *this* is the care you take of
my daughters?" he asks Amberley.

Poor Alice! poorer Amberley! poorest
mother! We have one of our extra,
double-distilled, most virulent rows. It
is not worth writing down ; no one would
believe it if I did. Let it suffice that, out
of all the windy talk and abuse, one abiding resolve remains : Miss Alice will go to
school immediately, and a stronger, firmer hand than Amberley's shall be paid to
crush the naughtiness out of her. The

governor, as I have more than once remarked, is a man of action, and in an
incredibly short space of time he has
found a school and schoolmistress after
his own heart and pattern. All prelimi-
naries are arranged, the day for her departure is fixed, and to us all there is
nothing left to do but to lament. All too
soon the day and hour come round, and we
crowd about her with our kisses and farewells ; weeping in every degree,. deeply
and bitterly, loudly and effusively, silently and painfully, according to our several
natures ; every one down to the babies
furnishing his or her quota to the stream.
"Good-by, lovely sister, good-by." For
how many weary, long months shall we
see your sweet face no more?

———◆———

CHAPTER IX.

"Love is a familiar, love is a devil ; there
is no evil angel but love. Yet Samson was so
tempted, and he had an excellent strength ;
yet was Solomon so seduced, and he had a very
good wit."

IT was a year ago that I waved my
nightcap out of the window at Alice's
lovers ; she has left school altogether now,
and is home for good. She has been the
terror of her schoolmistress, the admiration of her schoolmates, the delight of her
pastors, masters, and every pair of male
eyes that have lit upon her, in the straight
and narrow precincts of her sheltered,
quiet life ; and now she has come back
to us lovelier, waywarder, more bewitching than ever. Strictly speaking, we are
not at home ; we are at St. Swithins,
whither papa, having no very pleasant
memory of Periwinkle, has brought us
for the holidays, and for the setting up
of mother's health, which of late has been
indifferent.

St. Swithins is a long, long way from
Silverbridge, and, the governor's doughty
reputation not having spread so far, the
residents of the place actually *call* upon

us (oh! it makes me smile to think of it) quite comfortably, and, as a matter of course, without the slightest notion of the danger they are running; and *he*, in the most baffling and unaccountable manner, not only forbears to shout "Not at home!" in their faces, or hold the door wide open for them to walk out, but permits mother to return these visits; and though he never goes out himself, does not forbid her partaking of the very mild and temperate amusements offered—croquet, five-o'clock tea, and the like. With mother goes Alice, who has, I think, high jinks. Whether papa is tired of living like Diogenes in his tub, or whether he finds it a new sensation to be treated just like any other man, I know not; at any rate a change has come "o'er the spirit of *his* dream," and it is positively refreshing to see him sinking the misanthrope in the moderately ill-tempered, retiring English gentleman. If he goes on at this rate he will be quite convivial by the time he is sixty, and excellent company at seventy; while at eighty years he will be so jovial that he will be quite sorry to have to go away; he will be beginning to enjoy life so much. (Happy thought! why did not he begin *earlier?*) It was only yesterday I saw him shake hands and walk down the street with old Mr. Tempest, who has, it appears, a place near Silverbridge; but as the latter has never lived there within the memory of man, papa has had no chance of falling out with him. As it is, he is probably saving up the old gentleman as a *bonne bouche* to demolish at some future day. Mr. Tempest is an invalid who spends his life in wandering about the world in search of health, thus he has chanced on St. Swithins, which is by the faculty considered salubrious. He has a son, tall, straight, yellow-haired, with brave blue eyes that might belong to us Adairs. He looks nice, but neither Jack nor I have ever spoken to him yet.

St. Swithins is a dull little place, but none the less does that pretty young woman, Miss Alice, in all the pomp of her seventeen-year-old, pink-and-white beauty quickly gather about her as fine an army as she did at Periwinkle. She was only a bit of a girl then; she is grown up now, so there are no more unseemly scrimmages of admirers behind hedges, or flying columns on the beach; things are conducted respectably, and it is no longer a question of a kiss of the hand or a love-letter, but of love and marriage. Yes, love and marriage; and if we don't look very sharp after our Alice she will be carried off by somebody or other, to a dead certainty. Over and above half a dozen indiscriminate lovers, she has a shadow, a tall, bronzed, dark-faced, handsome shadow, that every young woman in St. Swithins has vainly tried to make her own. Captain Lovelace, however, has his own ideas about female beauty, and until his eyes lit on our sister's fresh, saucy, charming face he has never felt inclined to lose his own identity; but now —one, two, three, and away!—head over heels into love he falls, and Alice follows at a respectful distance. There have been some half-dozen public meetings, one stolen one, a rose given and exchanged, eager words spoken, a proposal made and answered, a kiss or two (who knows?), and Alice, with a promptitude that does her credit, has made up her mind that she loves him; that she will marry him; and that, if papa does not see things in the same light as she does, he must be brought to reason.

Young people are very intolerant, very daring; they defy circumstance, and would rule the world in their own way, and in return receive many a hard knock before learning the inevitable lesson of giving in. So, one fine morning, when the governor is unsuspiciously swearing over the weekly bills in the library, Captain Lovelace is announced, and, with a pluck that does him infinite credit, requests the honor of Miss Alice Adair's hand in marriage. (We are all listening at the door, Alice in the post of honor at

the keyhole, the rest of us spread out behind her, anxiously looking forward to
the excitement of seeing the bold wooer
shoot out through the open door with
considerable assistance from behind.) We
can almost *hear* papa's gasp of amazement
as he sits in the midst of his disordered
papers (he usually dances on bills) and
stares at the young man; then he pulls
himself together, and refuses the proposed honor with a clearness and brevity
that admit of no mistake. He has, however, met his match for once.

Captain Lovelace hears him out, then
quietly remarks that, having obtained
Miss Adair's promise, he is content to
wait to time for the fulfillment of his
wishes, and is sure that, although Colonel
Adair may refuse to give his consent now,
he will do so at no very distant date.
Papa gasps again; but I think an unpleasant recollection of his daughter's willfulness crosses his mind, and in his next
speech, although he still repudiates the
wooer's pretensions, there is more bluster,
and less determination than in the first,
and oh!—miracle of miracles!—he has
not yet tried to kick him! After that,
the deluge; and it would not astonish us
if the governor suddenly fell on the young
man's neck and kissed him, and, sending
for Alice, wept holy tears over them both,
saying, "Bless you, my children!"

Captain Lovelace is speaking. He is
asking what reasons Colonel Adair has
to give for this summary refusal. Can
any exception be taken to his character,
means, or position? Has Colonel Adair
other views for his daughter? No; he
has none, and he knows nothing to the
detriment of Captain Lovelace's character, pocket, or place in life, and he is
forced to say so; for this is no woman to
be stormed at, or child to be whipped,
but a man who will have his answer. It
is not easy to say no, no, no, over and
over again, because it *is* no to a question
that requires a more reasonable answer;
thus papa, pressed for his reasons, can
find none, save that Alice is a mere child,

far too young to think of marrying for
many years, etc.

"I am told," says Captain Lovelace,
"that Mrs. Adair was no older when you
married her; you did not then consider
her youth a drawback?"

"What Mrs. Adair did is no affair of
yours, sir!" says papa, fiercely.

"None whatever," says Captain Lovelace, "save that it forms a precedent."

There is a pause, and Alice makes a
significant face to convey to us that the
governor's countenance is the reverse of
angelic. The fact is, he is in a dilemma. He has had some experience of his
daughter's admirers already, and he knows
perfectly well that, if Tom is not in love
with and wanting to marry her, it will be
Dick or Harry, and that if this young man
is sent to the right-about, there will be
fifty others popping up before him, asking the same troublesome question. He
also knows that Miss Alice has a spice of
his own willful, perverse temper in her (as,
indeed, it would be odd if she had not;
I often wonder we are not all demons),
and that she is not very likely to prove a
meek little fool, who will see all her lovers rapped on the head and sent about
their business without knowing the reason
why; and altogether, for once in his life,
he is compelled to think instead of to
act.

There is some more conversation and
pretty sharp practice between the two
men too; and more than once it seems
probable that our expectations will be fulfilled, and the parting guest sped over our
listening ranks, but in the end—oh, wonder!—the lover prevails, and wrings a
most reluctant permission from the governor to pay his addresses to our sister
for six months, and, if at the end of that
time no specks are discovered upon his
character, or vice in his ways or words,
he shall be considered engaged to Alice
for an indefinite period, matrimony appearing dimly in the far horizon. (Papa
is a sly old fox, he means to make fools
of them both; as soon as ever they press

for anything tangible he will send Captain Lovelace adrift, he only wants to gain time.)

Our faces express even more amazement than delight. We had so confidently reckoned on a violent scene, an unseemly exodus, and, behold! . . . We all tumble backward over each other as the door opens and her victorious sweetheart comes out, and catches her up in his arms like a baby, and what happens next I don't know, for we all scamper away like mad.

For many a day papa's face is black as ink, and he surveys Alice with a wonderfully equal mixture of scorn, impatience, and wrath, as though he found her a most indelicate and unpleasant spectacle. It is very strange that fathers who fell in love so naturally and comfortably when they were young, should so bitterly resent and feel so utterly disgusted at their children's doing the same. If he had his way he would keep all his daughters withering forever on their virgin stalks, and when they were miserable peaky old maids turn round upon them and twit them with their incapacity to get a man to marry either of them.

For the first time in my life I am in a position to critically study the ways, looks, and words, of a real handsome young pair of lovers. (I think all lovers should be young and good-looking; I can't fancy faded or elderly people peering into each other's dull faces.) I should not have so much opportunity, but that, after patient and dispassionate trial of all her elder brothers and sisters as gooseberries, she has fixed her choice upon me, as being the sharpest, most unseeing and most unhearing of the lot, and fully one-half my time is spent in boudoir, garden, or summer-house, craning my neck round corners in anxious watch against the governor.

Charles Lovelace is supposed to pay two or three decorous visits a week, and sit in the drawing-room opposite Alice, with mother for dragon, talking of the weather. In reality he is here every day, and twice a day; but he is not proud or above being towed in and out, and on occasion hidden in the shrubbery or a cupboard. Once or twice it has been a very close shave, and nothing but a special Providence and good luck has saved him from ignominious discovery. Their two faces look rarely well together, dark and fair; the bold, manly beauty of the one against the round, feminine, dainty perfection of the other. I think no woman's face ever shows its beauty to such advantage as when seen beside that of a man. How unweariedly they make love! How untiredly they utter their love-talk, of which now and then a word or two comes to my ears (I always turn my back upon them)—pretty, fanciful, tender stuff, that makes me smile and vaguely stirs my heart! If ever I have a sweetheart (and why should I not, since it is a well-known fact that all the plainest women marry before the good-looking ones, and to be married one must of course be courted?) I hope Dolly will make as excellent a gooseberry as I do.

When Charles is paying lawful visits, he brings with him a little book, called "The Bundle of Sticks;" where he picked it up it would be hard to say; and this he reads diligently if papa ever comes into the room where they are sitting. The sarcastic twitch of the governor's nose and lips as he looks from the one lover to the other is something to be wondered at. Now and then, when his back is safely turned, they go out together for a stirring spin in Charles's dog-cart, in which he drives two fiery gray ponies tandem, and a very charming turn-out it looks, with the two handsome young people smiling over the white rug; and every one thinks so, save the disappointed old and young maids of St. Swithins.

CHAPTER X.

" Those that Fortune makes fair she scarce makes honest; and those she makes honest she makes very ill-favoredly."

WE are at a children's party, Dolly and I. Jack was asked, but is too proud to come. It is five o'clock, and the sun, who has been standing over us all the afternoon, frizzling our brains, and making himself obnoxious, as he only knows how to do in the middle of July, is kindly sinking somewhat in the west. We have, with the usual insanity and waste of very young people, been playing at all manner of energetic games, and are now engaged in the comparatively mild recreation of " Kiss-in-the-ring." Kissing is not reprehensible until one is grown up, I suppose; at any rate these little girls take their boisterous forfeits quite placidly, occasionally return them even with an artless generosity that is not half appreciated by the stolid recipients of the same.

I am not a little girl, but a big one, and there is no boy present old enough or tall enough to kiss me unless I choose. Besides, no one has caught me yet, I can beat them all. I always was good at running; that and jumping being the two doubtful accomplishments Jack has taught me to perfection.

I am laughing heartily at the dismal fate my last pursuer has just met, his white-duck trousers being in fact one green smudge from an involuntary acquaintance he made with Mother Earth, when Mrs. Floyd, our hostess, comes across the garden, and by her side is that yellow-haired laddie, young Tempest. Hardly a laddie though, for he must be twenty if he is a day, and has the square, broad-shouldered figure of a man.

A not particularly clean piece of cambric dropped at my heels, and a vision of a nimble youth of tender years scurrying away in the distance, sets me off in fleet pursuit. He has a good start, so I do not catch him, but walk slowly round until I come to Teddy Minto, who is the spryest on his legs of the assembled company next to me. He is after me like a shot; but though I take him twice round the ring, his fingers do not once touch my gown, and I dive in between Dolly and Lily Floyd victorious. All at once young Tempest joins the ring; and presently, on receiving a dropped token from Lily, rushes after, catches, and kisses her to her huge delight, for is he not the biggest person present? I wish Jack was here! He would not care about it though, he would think it beneath him, while I—it only shows what an insignificant creature I am—love it. I am enjoying myself down to the ground.

" Look, Nell! " cries Dolly, unloosing my hand; and turning my head, I see behind me the symbol that invites me to pursuit. Off I set with a will, but I do not come up with the hare, who is young Tempest; on the contrary, his long legs bear him away with a fleetness that moves me to grudging envy.

" I wonder," I say to myself, as I walk round swinging the pocket-handkerchief, " whether *he* could catch me? We will see." Lightly I drop it behind him, swiftly I fly along; but I am not a dozen yards away when he is up with me, and I am caught, without his ever giving me a chance.

" Now for the forfeit," he says, as he lifts me from the ground and stoops his head to mine. I meet his saucy, bent face with a vigorous slap that turns it scarlet, but he never moves or blushes, only looks at me with frank, amused blue eyes, before which my sudden anger melts like snow before the sun.

" Put me down," I say, and he puts me down. " I hope I—I didn't hurt much? " (looking up at him rather anxiously). " I did not mean to do it quite so hard, only you should not be rude, you know."

" Lily did not mind," he says, looking down on me with a queer smile.

"But Lily is not grown up," I say with dignity. "Lily is only ten."

"And you?"

"I am a great age," I say, nodding, "but I shall not tell you how much."

"Are you not tired?" he asks. "Would you not like to sit down?" I look round; the ring is broken up; the boys and girls are strolling about; Mrs. Floyd has vanished.

"I don't mind," I say; "but we are going in to tea soon." We sit down under the beech-tree and look at each other. "I know who you are," I say, smiling. "You are young Mr. Tempest."

"And you are little Miss Adair," he says.

"How did you know that?"

"My father knows your father; besides, I sit opposite you in church."

"Do you?" I ask with some dismay. Can he have marked any of Jack's and my ungodly tricks during sermon-time? For at St. Swithins's we sit behind papa, not beside him.

"Is that your eldest brother who sits beside you?"

"Yes," I say, proudly, "that is Jack. There is nobody like him."

"Is he here?" asks the young man, looking round.

"No, he would not come. You see he is fifteen, and he likes boys. He used to be satisfied with me, but now—" A tear trickles down my nose, and I turn my head away. It is a very, very sore subject with me. "It is all such a mistake," I say, rubbing my nose and eyes hard, "that I was not a boy, you know. He and I would have been together always, whereas now—it is very hard!"

"Very," says the young man, and indeed he seems to understand. "Who is that pretty little girl yonder? She looks like a crumpled pink-rose."

"Does she not?" I ask eagerly; "that is Dolly, my sister."

"You are not a bit alike!"

"I know we are not," I say, looking at her with pride; "my sisters are all pretty, every one; I am the only unpre-

sentable one out of the whole lot. Now if you were to see Alice—"

"I have seen her," he says; "she is quite lovely. But you are every bit as good as Dolly, or—nicer."

"Oh, no!" I say, laughing; "you need not bother about saying anything like that to me, please; I am quite used to being plain. Nurse comforts me by saying that the ugliest children sometimes grow into the best-looking folk, but I know better."

"George," says Mrs. Floyd, bearing down upon us with all sails spread, "you promised to help me give the children their tea; are you coming?"

So we go in and eat cake and drink coffee, and by-and-by, having washed our hot faces and hands, and smoothed our tumbled locks, we assemble in a large room, forty souls odd, for the purpose of dancing. The Floyds' governess sits down to the piano; but alas! whether it is the painful consciousness of their extreme neatness, or whether they are really unequal to the duties of "footing" a polka, all the little boys present hang together in groups, and look askance at the row of shiny-cheeked, smooth-headed damsels, who are waiting to be fetched out.

This uncomfortable state of things having lasted for some time, the female wit (as is usual when things are at a dead lock) comes to the rescue, and Madge Weston, a black-browed miss of twelve, rises from her feet and walks across the room to the halting army. "I shall dance with you, Olem," she says decidedly; and, taking the biggest boy by the arm, she leads him away. The spell once broken, each little girl walks boldly up to the boy that is goodliest in her eyes, and bears him off triumphantly, though some of them utter feeble protests, and show a tendency to hang back. And now they are off, giggling, ambling, floundering, and young George Tempest, entering hurriedly, looks about the room, and then comes up to me.

"I can't dance," I say confidentially,

as he sits down beside me; "it is like a donkey gamboling in a drawing-room. Can you?"

"Pretty well; but I should have thought you knew how; you are quite the nimblest runner I ever saw."

"One does not want to be nimble in dancing," I say gravely, "or it must be reduced to a method to answer. Jack says my head always hits the ceiling when I try to waltz."

"Miss Dolly seems to be laboring under difficulties," says my companion, glancing toward my little sister, who is ambitiously trying to reach the shoulder of the very tall, lanky boy she has selected as partner; "he has lost her altogether two or three times. Supposing you and I see what we can do?"

"It would be worse than Dolly," I say, laughing. "No, no! let us sit still and look on. I want to ask you something, if you don't mind. Is Mr. Tempest your real father?"

"Yes. Why?"

"You are not a bit like him," I say, considering his comely features and the fresh bright look that, let folks say what they will about the expression that comes with years, etc., is goodly and pleasant in a young man's or a maiden's face. "He looks so dried up; so, so brown. Do you know, it is very rude, but Jack and I always call him the *Mummy!*"

Young George Tempest laughs, and reassures me as to a doubt that has just crossed my mind, as to whether that was a suitable remark to make to a young man about his father.

"Don't you think that on the whole papas are a great mistake, and that we should get on much better without them?"

"I don't know," says the young man, smiling, "but you surely would never say that of mothers."

"Never!" I answer, energetically; "but tell me, what does your father do? Does he expect you to talk? Does he insist on your going out walking with him, all the lot of you, except your mother?"

"I have no mother," he says soberly, "and no brothers or sisters. No, he does not make me walk unless I please; but I am his walking-stick, his pourer-out of medicine, his lackey" (rather bitterly), "who wanders all over the world with him, learning no good."

"Learning no good!" I repeat. (I was always rather like a monkey, and fond of echoing other folks' words.) "Have you not a profession? Do you not do anything? You are old enough!"

"Ay!" he says, and a sudden shadow falls upon his blond, bright face. "I was to have gone into the army, and even had my commission in the guards, but at the last moment my father refused to let me join. He said I was his only son, that he could not live many years, and so" (with a short, impatient sigh) "I am knocking about with nothing on earth to do. If only Providence had sent me one or two of your brothers!"

"I have six," I say proudly; "there are five running after Dolly, but I could not spare one of them to you."

"I suppose not," he says, with a smile. "Do you ever smack their heads as you did my cheek this afternoon?"

"Sometimes! only, to tell you the truth, they are getting rather beyond me. Were you angry when I slapped you this afternoon?"

"Very! I hope you will never do it again."

"But then *you* must never do it again."

"But I did not."

"If you were I," I say seriously, "you would be sick of the very name of kissing; we have such oceans of it at home!"

"Ah! I suppose so. Your father must be very fond of you all?"

"Very!" I say, with a wry face, "but it is not *he* who is lavish in that respect" (I giggle inwardly at the notion of his going about the house kissing us promiscuously), "it is my sister; she is engaged, you know."

"To Lovelace? So I have heard."

"I am gooseberry, you see," I continue, "and I do get so tired of it all. Do you think our fathers and mothers ever required gooseberries?"

"I don't know," he says, laughing; "but I suppose they did pretty much the same as their children do."

The polka is over, and very hard work the dancers have apparently found it, for they are all, boys and girls alike, *crimson.*

By-and-by we dance a quadrille, young Mr. Tempest and I, and he guides me through the mazes of that mysterious dance with much discretion. I wonder why the sight of two people *chasséing* to each other always reminds me of two amiable ponies, who curvet about face to face with each other, preparatory to turning round and letting out their heels in good honest kicks? We do not kick up our heels though; and when the dance is over go to supper, where we eat chicken and tipsy-cake with the hearty and unjaded appetite of youth, and then, for it is past ten o'clock, we all say, "Goodnight, and thank you," and go away to put on our cloaks and hats.

Balaam's Ass is waiting for Dolly and me, and George Tempest takes my little red cloak from her hands, and ties the ribbons under my chin.

"Good-by, little Red Riding Hood," he says, "and shall I ever see you again?"

"I shall be sure to run up against yon sooner or later," I say, nodding; "St. Swithins is so very little; besides, do you not live at Silverbridge, and are you not going back to live there some day?"

CHAPTER XI.

" . . . . We are such stuff
  As dreams are made of, and our little life
  Is rounded with a sleep."

WE are in August now, and there is no coolness anywhere, not in the house, nor in the garden, nor in the sea; twice to-day have I dipped in its salt waters, and each time I have come out of it ten degrees hotter than when I stepped in. Through the dining-room windows yonder we can hear the manly bass of the governor, and the shrill little pipe of the Mummy, following each other in friendly monotony, and out here, under the big linden tree, are sitting Jack, young Mr. Tempest, and I.

The weather has surely softened papa's brain, for, not content with shaking hands with Mr. Tempest, he invited both him and his son to dinner, and has just peaceably partaken of the same with them; mother, Charles Lovelace, and Alice, being also of the company. George and I are old friends now, and he gets on very well with Jack, so he has forsaken claret for our company; and very sociable and merry we are as we sit and fan ourselves with cabbage-leaves, for oh! though the sun is sinking, he has heated the earth so thoroughly that it is red-hot through and through; it is impossible to think of even the hours of the night being cool.

Yonder, in the winding ways of the formal garden, Alice and Charles are walking with their heads touching; she is holding up her white-silk train with one hand, and her pretty little feet are peeping in and out, while the white roses in her breast and hair are no fairer than her round arms and neck.

"I wish we were at Silverbridge!" I say, swaying my cabbage-leaf gently; "it goes to my heart to be sitting here, gooseberryless, currantless, raspberryless, while all the little Dorleys are, I am certain, taking their nasty little fills! Mother wanted to have the fruit sent to us once a week, but papa said it was to be preserved."

"I hate preserves," says Jack, "nasty apologies for fresh fruit; blackberry, jam's good, though."

"Did you ever make jam of sloes," I ask George Tempest, "that cleaves to the roof of your mouth and won't be swallowed?"

"Never! Did you?"

"Once, but we only made one pot, and it lasted years; whenever we were very hungry, and quite at our wit's end, we used to take it out and look at it, but never got any further, and at last it withered up. I wish I knew where to get some blackberries now, large, juicy, soft ones, like raspberries; but it's full early, I don't think we'll get any worth having before September."

"I saw a lot this morning," says George, "as I was riding across the lower"—("Jack!" calls mother, in the distance, "I want you") "landslip," finishes George, as Jack goes. "Would you like to go and get some?"

"So much!" I say quickly. "Are there many?"

"I think so; why cannot you and Dolly come with me to-morrow morning?"

"We are forbidden to go out alone," I say, thoughtfully; "you won't mind Amberley coming?"

"Indeed, I do," he says, laughing. "What do you want with that stupid old woman? We could have such a jolly morning."

"So we could," I say, considering; "I think I could dodge her all right; but how about the governor?"

"He goes for a ride sometimes."

"Yes, but not always. Supposing he were to inquire for us and we were missing?"

"What then?"

"What then? Oh, nothing!" A vision rises before me of the condition of the household under the circumstances, and his simple question makes me smile.

"Don't take any notice of him," says George, indifferently (it is all very fine for *him* to talk); "I shall be waiting on the Parade for you to-morrow morning at eleven o'clock punctually."

"I am afraid you will have to wait," I say, disconsolately; "but never mind, if we don't come, you will know it is not our fault!"

"The governor!" signals Jack, beckoning in the distance; so without waiting for farewells I hastily decamp. By-and-by the sound of music rising from the drawing-room gives us a new sensation. Never within the memory of man, certainly not within ours, has the piano's modest voice been uplifted in papa's presence; but, lo! at the magic touch of company its long-frozen melodies stream forth, and there is a convivial, rakish, bacchanalian sound about the festivities below that lifts the hair from off our youthful heads in amazement; we should not be surprised even, if on peeping in we discovered papa affably turning over the pages of Alice's music; he may, for all we know, be drinking tea. This mildness of temper if agreeable is alarming; can he be going to have fever or a fit? or has the sun actually melted some of the obstinacy out of his brain? Middle-aged gentlemen don't act in direct opposition to all the traditions of their past lives for nothing. If his wits would only go on softening until he is just like anybody else! I fall asleep with the cheerful tune of "Kiss me quick and go, my honey," in my ears. Somehow it seems indecent as sung before the governor.

We have all slept, risen, dressed ourselves (of all the machines that are yearly invented for reducing labor to a minimum, why is there not one for turning us out ready dressed? Who is there that does not now and then kick against the wearisome, ever-recurring duties of the toilet?), listened to prayers, eaten our breakfasts, and scattered hither and thither to our several pursuits and occupations. It is holiday-time with us, so I am not expected in the schoolroom, and my present object in life is to ascertain what the governor is doing, where he is going, and whether there is any dire chance of his catching Dolly and me just as we are trotting off to "pastures new." I carefully track him to the library, and am presently surprised and relieved by the appearance of his man of business, who is shown to that sanctum by Simpkins, and left for four good hours, I hope. And now to find Dolly. I have not mentioned to that young person that I meditated taking her out, or her eyes would have become so round that everybody would have suspected she was up to mischief, and on searching inquiry she would certainly have let it all out. I discover her in the nursery with Alan, learning Scripture history—the fag-end of a punishment given by papa weeks ago. I give nurse a hug—dear old soul! is she not like a second mother to us?—but wish she would turn her back; for if she is loving she is shrewd, and is too well acquainted with my knack of getting into scrapes to trust any one of her charges to my tender mercies. She is hemming dusters and rating Balaam's Ass, who with her usual obstinacy has been doing that which she ought not to have done, and leaving undone such things as she ought to have done. Apparently she has been taking the air on the leads, for nurse is remarking with a violent sniff, that "rent will soon be dear in these parts if so much beauty is seen disporting itself on the tiles." (B. A. is the most ill-favored young woman I ever saw.)

"Like Bathsheba," says Alan.

"Nurse," says Dolly looking up from her book, "who was Bathsheba?"

"Nobody in particular, Miss Dolly; nobody you have any call to ask about. A woman."

"She was an improper person," says Alan, unexpectedly.

"Sakes alive!" ejaculates nurse, holding up her hands; "whatever is the boy talking about?—Hold your tongue, Master Alan, and mind your book."

"I sha'n't," says Alan, resting his chin on his hand and regarding nurse with meditative eyes. "You know it as well as I do. I heard Jack humming something the other day about—

'That naughty little dragon,
And she without a rag on;'
4

And I asked him who *she* was, and he said *Bathsheba*. And I looked it out, and I sha'n't ever think much of David again, psalms and all."

Nurse looks at him helplessly as he returns to his book. Why do our elders always look so completely put out of countenance when we show any signs of shooting up in unexpected directions? They did the same when *they* were children.

Taking advantage of her departure to quell a riot among the boys in the next room, I catch Dolly's hand and pull her away with me.

"May not Alan come?" she asks, looking back.

"No," I say in a whisper; "I only want *you*." I trot her into my bedroom, and, having informed her of the trip I propose taking, ask her if she can get at her hat and jacket without nurse's knowing.

Yes, she can, and, all delight and round eyes, she departs on tiptoe, obtains the coveted articles, and in five minutes, after patient and careful dodging of mother, Amberley, Simpkins, and Alice, we stand on the high-road, and are scampering away as fast as we can pelt toward the Parade.

Oh! the bonny, bonny sea! Though I see and stand by it every day, it always gives me a new delight every time my eyes light thereon. It is only half-past ten; there is plenty of time to spare, so we betake ourselves to Tippet's, the confectioner; and, as—oh, wonder!—I actually possess a sixpence, we indulge in one bun each, one sponge-cake each, and a pennyworth apiece of bull's-eyes. Delicious! We are thirsty, but lemonade is beyond us, so we drink water unthankfully (why does every one take kindly to adulterated and manufactured drinks, and turn away disdainfully from the only pure liquid the world contains?) and then take a comfortable little trot round the town, gluing our noses to shop-windows; pausing to look at the omnibus starting for the railway-station; helping to pick up

an unfortunate pair of twins who have
been rolled out of their perambulator by
an elder sister, aged seven years; standing still to watch a man walking round
and round his horse in the vain effort to
mount it; diving into a chemist's shop
to get out of the way of old Mr. Tempest; feeling, in short, very dissipated,
very happy, and intensely, grandly independent. Eleven o'clock is striking as
we reach the Parade, and at the far end
is George. Seeing us, he steps out briskly, and in another two minutes we are
shaking hands and laughing over the success of our undertaking.

"We must be very quick though," I
say, "for some unlucky spirit may put it
into his head to ask for us, and then—"

"How do you do, Miss Adair?" asks a
voice behind me. Turning, I see Bobbie
Silver and two or three other young fellows, friends of Jack.

"How do you do?" I say, rather chap-
fallen: they will see Jack presently, and
tell him they saw me down here alone.
Oh, the ways of disobedience are very
crooked!

"And where is the duenna?" asks
Bobbie.

I am opening my mouth to answer him,
when in the distance I espy Balaam's Ass
bearing down upon us with a portentous
mien that betokens some deadly tidings.
The words I am about to speak die in my
lips; my open mouth remains open; my
widening eyes enlarge to their fullest
extent and remain fixed. The young men,
marveling, turn to ascertain the cause of
my petrifaction.

"If you please, Miss Helen and Miss
Dolly," says Balaam's Ass, appearing in
our midst, "*your pa says you're to go home
and go to bed directly!*"

She might have whispered. . . . I do
not look at Bobbie or George. I look nowhere; I see nothing. Why does not the
earth open and swallow us up? Somehow, I do not know how, to this day, we
get ourselves away.

"How dare he do it?" I say, as I

climb the steep hill that leads to our abode,
with bitter tears raining down my burnt
cheeks, hot anger and outraged pride
scorching my heart, "just as we were so
happy, Dolly! How shall I ever look one
of them in the face again?" And I am
fourteen years old! Truly "pride goes
before a fall!"

CHAPTER XII.

"This is the excellent foppery of the world,
that when we are sick in fortune (often the
surfeit of our own behavior), we make guilty
of our disasters, the sun, the moon, and the
stars; as if we were villains by necessity, fools
by heavenly compulsion."

My last little escapade has cost me dear.
Not only have I been condemned to a
week's imprisonment in the house and
grounds, but the edict has gone forth that
I shall be sent to school without loss of
time. I have long ago wept my eyes dry.
I do not think that I shall ever be able to
cry any more, not even when I find myself set down in the midst of a crowd of
nasty, spiteful, odious, chattering girls; if
there were a few boys I would not mind,
but to have nothing but petticoat company for five months will, I am certain,
drive me mad. If Dolly were coming
even, it would not be so bad, we could at
least hold together and talk about home;
I should not be so miserably lonely then;
but no such luck, Amberley is still good
enough for another two years' cultivation
of that little person's mind. How I shall
hate the needlework, and the bread-and-
butter, and the making my own bed every
morning! and, oh! how I shall have to
mend my manners and revise my vocabulary! Remarks that are merely spicy
among ourselves might be regarded by a
schoolmistress in a different light, and our
freedom and ease of invective and retort
be considered immoral.

Everybody is out this evening, papa
and all, and I have not a soul to speak to
but Paul Pry, who does not understand

If I do talk to him. I cannot even make myself of use by playing gooseberry. How Alice will miss me when I am gone! The ghost of a tear comes into my eye at this touching thought (which is after all nothing but that *pitié de soi-même* that is at once so pitiful and so natural). They cannot choose but miss me, though, I befear me, the cause of my being so regretted will be but selfish. Love on, poor lovers! By Christmas your billings and cooings will be over, and you, Mr. Charles, will be sent to the right-about. How the governor's patience has lasted as long as it has done, I can't imagine. It is dull work marching about here all alone, with no fruit-trees to rob, or sociable soul to exchange remarks with. I have not seen George since that fatal day, although he has been here two or three times. Somehow I cannot forgive him for having been a witness to my disgrace, and I owe him a grudge for having a nasty little father who did see Dolly and me when we bolted into the chemist's shop, and, meeting papa on the hill, told him, but with no malicious intent, that he had just seen us; hence the catastrophe. There never was anybody as unlucky as I am; everything has gone wrong with me ever since I was born, and everything will continue to do until my death, which is certain to take place in some unseemly, unexpected manner, at some unsuitable time and spot. I suppose my own bad conduct is at the bottom of most of my misfortunes, though. Now, that last *fiasco* was caused by love of blackberries, *ergo* greediness, which is distinctly a failing of my own, and nothing to do with an unlucky star! I wish I could commit my sins with my eyes shut. I know so perfectly well always when I am doing anything wrong, I see the good and the evil so clearly, the one on the right hand the other on the left, and yet, oh, shame! I nearly always choose the ill. Perhaps it is because I know my own wicked heart so well, that I, who am the merriest, noisiest, happiest of us all, have such

deep, bitter fits of depression and misery now and then. In comparison with the keenness of enjoyment is the power of enduring pain, they say. If ever God see fit to send me a great joy, I shall taste its sweetness to the uttermost; but if a great trouble come upon me, I shall bear every jot of its weight and hardness, and never seek to shift it to other shoulders, or contrive to bear it lightly. Clearly I am in a lachrymose and dismal frame of mind this evening; generally speaking, after a good howl, my spirits fly up to the skies, but this time I do not feel any the better, and if tears were forthcoming I would begin it all over again.

As I stroll along the coppice that divides our grounds from the high-road, I hear a gay young voice whistling, "My Love she's but a Lassie yet;" it sounds quite cheerful, and almost puts me in spirits. I hope he will not go away directly, for, oh! I do hate to be all alone without a human voice within ear-shot. I have not looked upon the countenance of man, woman, or child for a whole hour; to see anybody would be company, so I mount the hedge preparatory to taking a small peep over it. Even a commercial traveler, or a rustic Lubin waiting for his sweetheart, would be nicer to look at than these still, straight trees and the stupid, silent grass. Popping my head somewhat suddenly over the hedge, I find myself face to face with George Tempest. For a moment I stare speechlessly at him, then I drop the boughs, vanish from his sight, and run fleetly down the coppice. I hear his voice calling "Nell! Nell!" after me, and in another minute he has overtaken me, and stands in my path.

"Won't you speak to me, Nell?" he asks, rather blown and out of breath with his exertions.

"Can't stop now," I say indistinctly, turning a scarlet countenance over my shoulder; "somebody is calling me."

"Nobody is calling you," he says quickly, "are you angry with me, Nell?"

"Angry!" I repeat, turning round

my face, which is, I think, assuming its normal tint, "why should I be angry?"

"Come back into the coppice for a little while, then," he says; "you can't be going in yet, it is only seven o'clock."

For a moment I hesitate. I am ashamed to look him in the face, but will it not be intolerably dull all alone in the empty house yonder? I turn and walk beside him. "Do you know," he says, "that I have been looking out for you every day, and all day for the last fortnight, but I have never caught a single glimpse of you?"

"For the best of all reasons," I answer; "did you not know I was in punishment?"

"No!" he replies indignantly. "What a shame! and pray whose doing was that?"

"There is only one person in the world who has the power to make us miserable," I say, "and you know who *that* is."

"But you have not been locked up," he says, looking puzzled, "for one day I was here with Jack, and I am certain I saw you in the distance, and went in hot pursuit, but you had vanished. When I got back I asked Jack why you ran away, and how it was I never saw you now, and he said he didn't know."

"Good boy!" I say, laughing, "he would not betray me. It is not nice, is it, when one is beginning to be grown up, to be kept prisoner for a fortnight?"

"He is a wretch," says George, vigorously; "how he can have the heart—"

"I want to ask you a question," I say, looking up at his face, reassured by the unsmiling look it wears—"did you—did you—laugh much?"

"About what, dear?"

"That—that morning, when we went out blackberrying."

"No," he says, gently, "I was far too angry for that."

"And Bobbie Silver?" I ask, with my head turned away, "did *he* laugh?"

"I don't think so," says George, with some slight confusion in his voice, that plainly tells me whatever he did *not* do, the others did.

"I shall never forget it," I say, turning my red face full upon him—"*never!* You see I am just beginning to be grown up. . . ."

"Never mind!" he says gently, "it is *he* who ought to be ashamed of himself, not you!"

"And you will promise," I say, anxiously, "never to laugh, never even to think of it, or I could never feel comfortable with you!"

"I promise," he says, gravely; "and now tell me, is it true you are going to school?"

"Quite true!" I answer, "horribly true! To-day is Friday, and I am going next Wednesday." I thought I had no such things as tears about me, but somehow they have got into my voice, and, as I turn my head away, George takes my hand with a gentleness that Jack never knew, and keeps it.

"I wish you were my brother," I say, with a sob; "of course I could never have loved any one so well as Jack, but you would have been *kinder* to me!"

"If I had had a little sister," he says (how soothing his voice is! how quiet his ways are! He is not like any one I have ever known before. Can it be because he has no brothers and sisters?), "I should have liked her to be just like you, and I should have loved her beyond everything; but it is too late to think of that *now.*"

"Yes, it is too late," I say, releasing my hand to pluck a sorrel-leaf that is close to my elbow (we are sitting down on the warm, burnt grass; "but if you had only thought of it before, say ten years ago, you could have asked your father to marry again, could you not?"

"Yes?" says George, looking rather puzzled.

"And then you know you would very likely have had a sister. Step-brothers and sisters are not the same as one's *own* though; sometimes they quarrel dreadfully!"

"Nell," says George, bending his fair head to look me straight in the face, "do you like me?"

"Very much," I answer, promptly; "next to mother, Jack, Alice, and Dolly, I don't know any one I like so much." His face falls a little.

"I can't expect you to have much room in your heart for me," he says, "you have so many to fill it, while I have —nobody."

"You have the Mummy."

"Yes" (laughing), "but I have room for plenty more."

"So have I! Now I should not wonder if, in a year or two, when I get to know you better, you know, I were to like you very much indeed, almost as well as Jack; you are always so good to me!"

"Dear little Nell," he says, heartily, "I only hope you will. You'll have plenty of opportunity of getting better acquainted with me, for my father talks of going to Silverbridge next midsummer, to live at The Chace."

"How delightful!" I say, clapping my hands, "but why not before midsummer?"

"We are going on our usual wild-goose expedition round the Continent," he says, disgustedly, "and a lively time I shall have of it!"

"It will be such fun," I say, following my own train of thought, "when I am grown up and come home for good, you and Jack and I will be such friends!"

"Nell," says the young man, leaning over toward me, "do you think you will ever care for me as much as Jack?"

"It is not likely!" I say, smiling into his bright, eager, beautiful young face; "you are not my brother, you know!"

"And I am very glad of it," he says, decidedly.

"Glad?" I say, opening my eyes, "and you said just now you should like a sister just like me!"

"Just like you, perhaps, but not you. Nell, do you think you will ever be married?"

"Oh! I suppose so," I answer indifferently; "everybody is sooner or later. It is wretched to be an old maid, with no one to stand up for you, is it not?"

"Very! Have you any notion of what your husband ought to be like, Nell?"

"My husband!" I repeat, breaking into a peal of laughter. "How droll it sounds! it is like playing at a feast; and yet mother knew a lady who was married at sixteen, her mother at fifteen, and her grandmother at fourteen!"

"Then it is high time you were married! But you have not told me what he must be like?"

"Dark," I say, pursing up my mouth, and looking at the sun who is passing away to his rest in such gorgeous pomp with his bright children, the clouds, thronging about him. "Very dark; and he must have black or very dark eyes, and a long black mustache that sweeps, but is not waxed."

"Yes."

"He must keep me in rare good order, and not let me get my own way, for, though I love to have it, it is bad for me; but he must never slap me or call me names."

"Good Heavens!" exclaims George, "does a gentleman ever do that?"

"Sometimes! And he must be very fond of my people, and have them to stay with us very often, and let me go and stop with them."

"And you are quite sure he must be dark?"

"I think so; but if he were very nice and kind, I should not mind so much about his complexion."

"Do you think that I should do, Nell?" asked the young man, half eagerly, half jestingly, "when you are quite grown up, eighteen or thereabouts?"

"You!" I say, staring at him. "O George! do you mean it; are you joking?"

"Not a bit of it! You are the dearest

little girl, and the nicest little girl, and the prettiest little girl I ever saw, and you'll only be dearer and nicer and prettier as you grow older, and I'm fonder of you than anything or anybody under the sun."

"Including the Mummy?" I ask, rallying from the shock his calling me pretty has caused me.

"Including him!"

"George!" I say, beginning to cackle again. "Don't think me very rude, but is it, is it a *real* offer you have made me?"

"I suppose so," he says, beginning to laugh too; "why?"

"Because not one of us, not even Alice, had an offer made her at the age of fourteen before. I'm certain no one ever asked Milly to marry, and I don't think any one ever did Jack?"

"Highly improbable! But you have not answered my question yet."

"Papa could not send me to bed if I were married, could he? or set me chapters in the Bible, or box my ears?"

"Certainly not."

"And you would always live at Silverbridge, close to the Manor House, so that I could run in and out every day?"

"If you liked."

"Then," I say, stretching out my hand, "if you are quite sure that you will always be polite to Jack, and never call me names, or make a row about the housekeeping bills, or keep the key of the kitchen garden, I will marry you! Not for years and years though, when I am twenty or so."

"That would be much too old to be married," says George. "It would be a pity not to come to The Chace while you are young and able to enjoy the fruit. Eighteen is the proper age!"

"Too soon," I say, shaking my head, "let us say eighteen and a half; but, of course, if I see any one I like better, you won't mind my having him?"

"Not mind," he says blankly; "but I shall mind very much indeed! However, I'll take care that you never have the chance!"

"You need not be afraid," I say, consolingly; "no living man is ever seen in Silverbridge who is not married or old or a fright! Besides, who would be likely to fall in love with me?"

"Everybody!" he says warmly, "they couldn't help it!"

"I think," I say, disregarding this pretty compliment (of course he does not expect me to notice it, he only does it to please me!), "that it would be safer to promise conditionally. Most likely you will see some one or other who would just suit you, and then you might feel uncomfortable about me; and though it is very unlikely that any one else will ever want to marry me, for at home we see nobody, it is just possible that I might run up against somebody I liked better, or I might not care about being married at all, you know; so we will leave it open until I am eighteen and a half!"

"And it is a promise?" he says, holding my hand between both his own and looking very kindly into my face. (How his mother would have loved him if she had lived, he has such lovable ways.) "You will not forget?"

"No," I say promptly, "I always keep my promises: ask Jack if I do not—that is one reason why he says I ought to have been a boy! But look, how dusk it is growing! I must go. Good-night!"

"Good-night," he says, standing over me, tall and fair in the gathering shadows. "Perhaps this is the last time I shall have a chance of speaking to you alone before you go, dear?"

"I suppose so."

"Then, Nell, as you're going to be my little wife some day, and I have no sister, you know—nobody to be good to me, won't you give me a kiss, just a little one, before you go?"

"Of course I will!" I say, touched to the heart by the allusion to his narrow, loveless home-life; then, as he stoops his head, I lift myself on tiptoe and kiss his cheek as heartily as though it were Jack's. "I wish you were my brother," I say warmly—"I do wish it with all my heart!"

CHAPTER XIII.

"Virtue! a fig! 'Tis ourselves that we are thus or thus. Our bodies are our gardens to the which our wills are gardeners . . . either to have it sterile with idleness, or manured with industry; why, the power and corrigible authority of this lies in our wills."

THE morning of my departure has arrived. The carriage is at the door, my boxes are on the roof, and if anything could console me at this trying moment, it would be the knowledge of the number of good things one bursting hamper contains. As it is, I am vaguely conscious of some pleasant morsel at the back of my mind that will by-and-by emerge to the front and comfort me. I have swallowed half an egg and a pint of salt tears for breakfast; I have wished papa good-by, or rather I have aimed a damp shot at his nose between the sheets (he is ill); and now I am standing in the hall, hugging my plentiful brothers and sisters all around, kissing them passionately with streaming cheeks and loud sobs that might melt the heart of a stone. Finally I bolt headlong into the carriage, where mother sits awaiting me, and burrow in the floor thereof. Charles Lovelace puts his head in at the window to squeeze a tiny packet into my hand. I cannot thank him, for my voice is attuned to nothing but howls; and away we go. I lift myself from my abased position to wave my dripping pocket-handkerchief at the group by the door, and find some small comfort in the fact that they are crying, every one, except Charles. The sight of their regret gives me a fresh access of grief, and I am just retiring behind my useless handkerchief to indulge in a storm of sobs when the carriage stops, and George Tempest comes to the window. "Good-by," he says,

taking my hand in his, and looking painedly at my blubbered, miserable face, "good-by!" That is all he says, and yet he conveys as much sorrow and sympathy in the homely word as though he had talked for an hour. As we drive on again I begin a fresh bout that includes the leaving *him* in its grievances; and by the time we reach the station I am damp enough to give any one near me a cold, if it were winter instead of summer time. Jack fishes me out, and puts me in the waiting-room with the rest of the light luggage, and, while the footman gets our tickets, he tries to revive my drooping spirits by sketches as to what we will do in the Christmas holidays. But oh! on this burning dog-day, Christmas seems a very, very long way off; besides, why should I not be having my holidays now instead of looking five months ahead? I ought not to be going at all.

The train comes snorting in—how sickeningly hot it looks!—and somehow I am bundled into it. As it is starting I lean out of the window, and, regardless of porters and his own disgust, I hug Jack round the neck with despairing energy and a splashing shower of tears. "Good-by!" I cry, waving my wet rag and scarlet nose out of the window as long as he is in sight; then I tumble back into the carriage, plump into the arms of a nervous, spindle-shanked, elderly gentleman, who shoots me off his knees with such vigor that I fly into a seat on the opposite side. It matters very little to me where I am, for my whole attention is taken up with hard crying—crying that is as unlike other people's tears as a floodgate is to a brooklet. I wonder if, when I am grown up, I shall get out of this habit of wasteful, exhaustive weeping? I always did save my troubles up into a lump and clear them all off at once. It takes me some time to begin, but when I do I don't stop in a hurry. We are half-way to our destination before my nose and cheeks have lost their first glossy shininess, and the elderly gentleman has shut his gaping mouth of amazement. Thank goodness, I have mother; and after a while she brings me to a tolerable state of composure.

Charteris, the place to which I am going, is eighty miles from home; so it is evening before we arrive there—the last six miles being performed by coach through scenery that would delight me were not my heart so heavy. We stop before a long, low building, with a great many windows in two level lines. It is approached by a handsome carriage-drive terminating in a species of court, and the house-door is entered by a porch. We are shown into a moderately large room, hung with maps. It has a stiff, schoolish air that chills me and prepares my soul for all manner of cold, barren, loveless laws and habits. What would I not give for our battered, noisy, disreputable old schoolroom at Silverbridge? The door opens, and Miss Tyburn enters, stately, imposing, grave. She scans me so closely as she takes my hand that I feel she is reading to the very bottom of my soul. While she talks to mother I study her face, which is an uncommon one: command sits on her forehead; intellect and power look out of her eyes; upon her lips passion and will have set their seal; over the whole countenance, and in the marvelously, perfectly formed head, is a remarkable air of penetration, determination, and clear common-sense. Presently she asks mother if she would like to see the dormitories and schools, and we follow her along a glass corridor and into a dining-room, vast and square, with three large windows. The walls are hung with busts of Homer, Aristotle, Cicero, and all the grand old poets, senators, and orators. Over the mantel-piece hangs a picture of St. John and the lamb painted in oils. We go through endless school and class rooms, filled with girls who look with some astonishment at me as I walk behind my elders, and so up-stairs to the dormitories, which are long and wide, with windows on both sides, and partitioned

off into narrow bedrooms just large enough to contain a bed and a small square box, while a curtained shelf runs across from one side to the other exactly above the bed, and a thick curtain closes in the room at the entrance. We go down-stairs again, and very soon mother takes her departure. She is going to sleep the night at the house of a friend who lives twenty miles away. O mother! mother! as you drive away, do you know what a wretched, *wretched* child you leave behind?

Ay! she knows, and her heart is every whit as heavy as mine. I am too much in awe of Miss Tyburn to do more than sniff noiselessly after mother goes; besides, I have literally no tears left. One can be sorrier, I am sure, when one's eyes are dry than when they are wet. Miss Tyburn speaks to me kindly—indeed, I am a spectacle that might move any one to compassion — and sends for "Mary Burns," who presently comes—a gentle, fair, slim girl of fifteen, and into her charge I am given and dismissed. She takes me up-stairs, and, having washed my face and smoothed my hair, I go down with her to the schoolroom, where (for it is a half-holiday) about fifty girls are reading, writing, talking, laughing, moving about, and buzzing like a hive of bees. The noise comforts and reassures me. What I have dreaded was the stillness, the stiff formality of the life of routine; clearly my notions of female school-life were mistaken ones.

On our arrival we are quickly surrounded, and I am chaffed, catechised, and overhauled in a sufficiently merciless fashion. Though somewhat taken aback, I prove, however, equal to the occasion; for I am not one of a large family for nothing—she who could retain any of that *mauvaise honte* yclept bashfulness, or to be unable to fight her own battles after the training I have had, would either be a vicious idiot or a solemn and self-satisfied prig. So I retort and *riposte* with a success that presently beats my assailants out of the field. They bear me no ill-will, though, any more than I do them; they do but seek to test the value of the metal, and small blame to them if on finding it to be a sham they cry out. I think they find I am not that, however; and, though some hard knocks are exchanged, no malice is borne. By supper-time I am feeling tolerably cheerful, but my heart sinks again as after prayers a chorus of "good-nights" echoes around me, and a storm of kisses, both deep and loud, beats on my astonished ears. There are about sixty females of all ages present, and they all kiss one another with a hearty vigor that sounds as if they liked it.

We are not a kissing family at home: there is much affection between us, but little sentiment. Save when we have quarreled, or are going on a journey, we rarely embrace each other. It is a matter of course to kiss mother whenever we can, but we never dream of indiscriminate caresses among ourselves—that must indeed be a wonderful gush of misery or affection that produces a hug. Therefore, lest I be pounced on and kissed in mistake for somebody else, I precipitately retire to my bed, where I sleep as soundly and well as though leaving home and going to school were a most regular, every-day affair.

An evil bell clanging through the pleasant tangle of a dream awakens me. Before I am half dressed it sounds again, but somehow or other I scramble down-stairs behind the rest to the schoolroom, where lessons are gone through for an hour, while I look on; then prayers, conducted in a widely different fashion from that prevailing at home; then breakfast —good tea, good bread, sweet butter; then to church, where the service lasts half an hour. The church is scarcely bigger than a chapel, quite lovely in its dainty smallness, and far more richly garnished than are many more imposing edifices. The seats are of carved oak, every window is of stained glass — (I wonder why those strange stiff figures of

saint and apostle, that violate every rule of art, impress us with the idea of a supernatural beauty that no amount of exquisite and correct drawing could afford?) —the east one, a soft blaze of color through which the light falls on the tessellated chancel-floor in glorious patches of amber, purple, green and gold. It looks very hushed, and quaint and solemn; and as I slip into my seat in the chancel, which is divided from the body of the church by a carved screen, a wonderfully strange, novel sensation steals over me. It seems so odd to be kneeling without papa's stern eye upon me, and all the dear brothers and sisters stretching out right and left, in goodly sober ranks. The thought of them nearly sets me off crying again, for I have given my eyes a good rest during the night; but I fight the tears back and make my responses with the rest.

The clergyman almost makes me jump as I look at him. I have seen the same face, only twenty years younger maybe, hanging up in papa's study between a print of Taglioni in her best days, and a sporting celebrity, name unknown. We have even studied this man's face with impertinent interest, thanks to a remark mother made one day to the effect that papa and he had been "old friends," and we have speculated often enough as to whether they ever kicked each other, or never fell out from sheer lack of opportunity.

I am sorry when the last "Amen" is spoken, and we step out of the dim cool church, into the gaudy brisk day. I am sorrier still when, at ten o'clock, I am summoned to the committee-room, and undergo at Miss Tyburn's hands a searching examination into the extent of my very limited mental capabilities, and to whatsoever questions are asked me on this, that, and t'other, write the answers down in a large volume that is called the committee-book, but is in reality a Book of Doom, in which in her time many and many a girl has written herself down an ass. That I do the same you may be very sure, and I presently retire with the proud conviction that in ignorance I have beaten all my predecessors, every one.

In the afternoon I begin my real school life with needlework, over which in very good sooth my trouble begins, for though well versed in the arts of climbing and jumping, I am utterly ignorant of the gentle accomplishments of "felling" and "stitching." And so the day wears away, and the morrow comes, and very soon I get into the ways of my new life, and, in spite of sundry homesick qualms and heart-sinkings, grow to love it very heartily. It has its ups and downs, its jealousies and bickerings, its hard lessons to be learned, and hard knocks submitted to; but none the less I find my school existence a wholesome, pleasant, happy one. There is no tyranny here. It is in a girl's own hands whether she gets on well or badly. She will not be censured for faults she has not committed, or praised without just reason. Her work is plain and clear before her, and she can pursue it without let or hinderance. Every hour is well filled, every pleasure well earned, and the sleep that each night brings is sound and deep. Now and again I am seized with a passionate longing to see them all at home. I shut my eyes and picture them to myself so strongly, that my spirit seems to go out of my body and stand in their midst; I wander in at the schoolroom door, and look on all their faces, one by one, and if they only knew I was there, if they spoke to me, I am sure I should hear them. . . .

I had a letter from mother this morning. She bids me use my time profitably and waste none, for it is more precious than gold. She need not be afraid: I know that now is my apprentice-time, now that breathing-space that is given to all young people, and which, once wasted, will come back to them nevermore. Somehow a girl's mind at school always makes me think of a field on which the seed is sown, which will either take root

and ripen abundantly, or wither away, leaving it bare and unadorned. I never knew how really ignorant I was till I came here. I don't remember ever thinking about the matter, but I had a vague idea that I was a good deal worse than Alice, but rather better than Jack. *Now* I stand forth a confessed ignoramus, and am beaten at all points by pert youngsters of twelve and thirteen. Fortunately, I know the nakedness of my mind, so there is a hope that at some future day it may be decently clad. It is curious that the more one knows the more acutely one feels one's bareness. Intensely thoroughly ignorant people attain to a height of self-esteem, that the man who has spent a lifetime in amassing knowledge, only to find that all he knows is but a drop in the full cup of knowledge, can never hope to reach. My studies do not prevent my getting into plenty of scrapes; often and often my madcap pranks get me into hot water, but good luck pulls me safely through. We go for wonderful walks through such lovely country as Silverbridge could never boast. The school is built on the top of a hill, and on three sides the ground slopes away to the valleys. Following the road you descend this hill, and, crossing a bridge on the left, pass through the flower-bright fields, and so to the valleys through which a brook runs, leaping, sparkling, widening, narrowing, with a dainty border of forget-me-nots, and reeds that stand up stiff and straight, like sentinels guarding the pretty flowers. On either side banks and woods rise steeply to a great height. In spring-time, the girls say, they are speckled all over with spring flowers, of which there are many curious and unknown species, never met with in flatter, duller regions. And oh, it must be a rare and delicate sight to see these picturesque slopes, putting on their thousand tints of green and yellow, and one for which my eyes look eagerly. These valleys are strangely cool, and deep, and silent; not a sound breaks the stillness save the fretting of the water against the stones, or the infrequent song of the birds—clearer, sweeter here, I always think, than anywhere else. To me these valleys always seem to have remained just as they left God's hand at the creation of the world, they are so fresh, so pure, so untrodden with their vernal shades and dim, cool alleys. A deep peace broods ever over them, and the weary, struggling, sinful world seems very far away. Walking in them one feels the faint echo of some such exquisite delight as Adam and Eve knew when they walked together in the garden of paradise for the first time, when it was all new, fresh from God's hand, and their souls were innocent and pure enough to taste its exceeding delicacy. I think none but the very young, or the very old, can enjoy Nature thoroughly; with the latter the heart and mind are dulled, and ordinary events and interests have little power over them, and they go back to that simplicity of mind that makes the treasures of the earth suffice, without the excitement of the passions of the heart; while the very young look on it with unjaded eyes, and no restless longing after things they do not know and have never dreamed of. The nightingale has made his home down here. He sings at night to the brook, to the silent glades, to his mistress; and I know by the rapture of his voice that he rejoices in the beauty around him as keenly as though he had a human soul. Often I softly open my window to listen to his deathless song, and wish that I were in the valley below standing on the moonlit sward alone with the night, the little brown bird, and my own delight. And I grow to love these hills and valleys, with an exceeding love that I never knew for Silverbridge; and I know that, some day when I lie a-dying, in fancy I shall go back to and visit them; I shall look with clear eyes on the purple brow of the hills, hear the running silver babble of the brook, and the trill of the nightingale will come to me out of the heart of the silence. . . .

CHAPTER XIV.

" . . . . Love all, trust a few,
Do wrong to none : be able for thine enemy,
Rather in power than use; and keep thy friend
Under thy own life's key; be checked for silence,
But never taxed for speech."

A NEW era in my existence has begun. All my life long I have hated petticoats, and longed for trousers as hopelessly as an old maid of sixty sighs for a sweetheart; and now, lo! and behold, Providence, who so rarely grants to any human being his heart's desire, drops them at my feet, and any day I may step into them, and enjoy the exquisite satisfaction of not only feeling a boy, but looking one. Up-stairs, in my box, lie two simple garments never yet worn, but which I may be called upon to don at any moment. Perhaps this very afternoon the summons may come, and I shall cast my incumbrances to the winds, and for once feel like Jack. If he could only see me! On the whole, though, I am rather glad he cannot, for I know he would laugh, and I have a sneaking conviction that my *tout ensemble* in my new gear is more likely to provoke derision than admiration. But oh, it is so comfortable! I have put it on behind my drawn curtain over and over again, for no earthly reason but to assure my eyes and touch that I am not dreaming, and that it is my very own, made for me.

We are all at work in the schoolroom, toiling at "seam, gusset, and band," and envying heartily the blackbird who is free as air, and knows it, singing at his ease as he swings on the apple-bough that looks in at the tall, narrow window! The sunbeams dance and flicker on the dull schoolbooks impudently, saying, as plain as they can speak, "We can play hide-and-seek all day if we please; we are not answerable to any one, and we have no lessons to learn or work to do."

Steps come down the corridor; no mincing feminine ones this time, but a

man's bold decided tread. I lay down
my stitching to listen. The door opens,
a head is popped in. "Cricket!" says a
voice like a trumpet, the door is shut
again, and down go work and thimbles,
a Babel of delighted cries bursts forth, and
in thirty seconds the room is cleared,
and we are all up-stairs, pulling off ribbons, gowns, crinolines, all our feminine
belongings, and pulling on knickerbockers and blouses! Yes, *knickerbockers!*
Let no one blush or look shocked, for
they are long and ample, and tied modestly in at the ankle; and as to the blouse,
which descends below the knee, and is
trimly belted in at the waist, it is as decent and uncompromising as that worn
by Dr. Mary Walker; our costume being
in short nothing more or less than that
which is designated by the somewhat
opprobrious title of "Bloomer." The
knickerbockers bring comfort, the tunic
confers respectability. It is a lovely
thought that I can kick up my heels to
my heart's content, and yet preserve de-
corum. As to what manner of female I
look, I care nothing; my feelings are
all I think about, and they are blissful. I
feel as light as a feather, and equal to
Jack at running, vaulting, or hurdle-jump-
ing.

On my way down-stairs I fall in with
the girls—shrunken, insignificant creatures, measured by the standard of half
an hour ago, when they boasted a circumference of from four to five yards of
petticoat. They even look meek; for it
is a fact that a large portion of a woman's
assurance lies in her tail. Shear her of
that and she is in no way superior to man.
Out in the cricket-field I scan the assemblage critically, and nothing but the consciousness of looking a greater guy than
any one present prevents me from going
off into a fit of convulsive laughter. If
only Charles Lovelace, George Tempest,
or Jack, could see us!

We have roly-poly girls and bean-
stalk girls, little girls, big girls, long girls,
short girls; girls whose plump proportions fit their garments as closely as a
kernel fits a shell; girls whose garments
hang upon them loose, as did the armor
on Don Quixote's gaunt form; girls who
waddle, amble, jig, trot, hurry, and stride
—their action plainly showed in the narrow, straight costume. Can an English
girl walk? I trow not. It is a pity the
time spent in needlework is not used in
drilling. Conspicuous, even among this
remarkable throng, is the German governess, short, square, stout, not over-
young, with large flat face, enormous feet
and hands, and that general look of a
Dutch doll that usually marks the Teu-
tonic race. She wears the regulation
trousers and blouse; but whether under
an impression that she is not sufficiently
clad, or whether she wishes to give a full-
dress air to a somewhat severe costume I
know not; at any rate, she has over and
above arrayed herself in a very large,
ample, white-muslin jacket, profusely
frilled and starched, and tightly belted in
at the waist, and these frills set straight
out from her sturdy form in a fashion that
would bring a smile to the face of a croco-
dile.

The wickets are pitched; the ball is
flying from hand to hand; we are all
waiting for Mr. Russell, the man who introduced the game of cricket at Charteris,
or rather, made it an institution, for it
has flourished many years, and many a
pretty young mother makes an excellent
long-stop or field to her sons, thanks to
the training she received at school. To
Mr. Russell, therefore, be our eternal
thanks due, in that he has, for a time at
least, emancipated us from the slavish
thraldom of our petticoats and enabled
us to stretch our limbs and use them.
He is coming over the grass from the
school with Miss Tyhurn now; tall, erect,
a little gray, his dress showing but little
of the clergyman about it (he is one of
the committee, and owns "The Charteris," the only big house in the place. His
grandfather built these schools.) How
my heart leaps as I look at him! Why

did he not come home sooner? His daughter is with him. And now sides are being chosen, the game begins, and as my side is in I have no opportunity for making myself look ridiculous as yet, I merely look on.

It is droll sight to see a girl walk up to the wicket and send her ball in, if not as powerfully as a man, wellnigh as straight; and to see another standing, bat in hand, with body slightly bent forward, awaiting it. Mr. Russell is against us, and in the next over his fast, round-arm bowling gives me an uneasy sense of fear, the ball hurtles along so swiftly that surely a slender ankle or arm might snap like sealing-wax at its onslaught; and something of that Frenchman's astonishment comes into my mind who could not conceive the reason of Englishmen being so fond of cricket, for where was the pleasure of standing up in a hot sun for a man to shy a hard ball at you, while a lot of other fellows stood round and looked on? If I do come to grief I hope that any amount of arms and legs will be broken, but not my teeth. I never could stand false ones, and I could not do without any, so it would be awkward.

How hot it is! We are all sitting and lying about under the trees; a little farther off are Miss Tyburn and Mr. Frere, who has just come over from the parsonage. In common mercy to our numbers he ought to play, and allow us to enjoy the distinction of having a man on each side; but apparently he is more careful of his shins than ambitious of honor, so sits in the shade at his ease, looking on. All too soon comes that terrible moment when "Helen Adair!" is called, and, bat in hand, I walk forth to my fate. I begin my illustrious career by hit-wicket, but in consideration of my extreme greenness and inexperience am permitted to take my innings, that is to say, if I can get it. The ground flies up into my face, the sky lies at my feet, as I stand awaiting my first ball, holding with stiff, nervous fingers my bat, in what may be called the "first position" of cricketers—bolt upright, with my person carefully curved out, and away from it, like Cupid's bow. In comes the ball, and I swipe wildly at it. Have I hit it or the wickets, or the wicket-keeper, or myself? I am still in doubt and undecided as to whether I ought to walk off to the shade of the friendly tree, when another ball comes creeping in, very insidiously this time, and somehow I give it a neat little tip that sends it straight into Fraulein's face; and while I am looking all about, and marveling where it has got to, she is led away, weeping bitterly, with a bleeding nose. Quite overpowered by this proof of my skill, I send the next ball, which somehow seems to run of its own accord against my bat, a tolerable distance; and being pleased at the circumstance, and engaged in looking round with a modest smirk for admiration, am amazed at being violently hustled by my fellow bats-woman, who wildly exhorts me to *run*. Ah! I had forgotten all about the runs, I was too much taken up in congratulating myself, but I set out with a will, and am considerably taken aback on arriving at my bourne to find that I am ignominiously run out.

Moral: stick to business. Back to the tree I go, as crestfallen, miserable, and ashamed a lass as the world contains. As I am seating myself disconsolately, Miss Tyburn calls me, and I jump up to obey her bidding.

"Mr. Frere knows your father, Helen Adair," she says; "he would like to talk to you," and she rises and sails away toward the house, for which I am thankful. How could I talk to any one before her?

"And so you are Alan Adair's daughter?" says Mr. Frere, stretching out a kind hand; "and I never found it out until to-day."

"I knew *you*, sir," I say, nodding. "I have seen you hanging up in the library, you know."

"Has you father still that old likeness?" he asks, smiling.

"Oh, yes! Were you and papa very great friends, sir?"

"Not very," he says, smiling again; "what made you think so?"

"He does not keep photographs or—or pictures, generally."

"I knew him when we were both young men at Silverbridge."

"At Silverbridge!" I exclaim, my eyes sparkling. "You know my old home, then?"

"Yes, but your father was not married then. I suppose he has several children by this time?"

"A few, sir; *twelve.*"

"Twelve!" he repeats, starting back. "You are joking?"

"No, it is quite true! and goodness knows—for I'm sure we don't—whether there won't be as many more! At home there is always a baby, and they mount up, you know."

"And I have not *one!*" he says in a voice that is cheerful, and yet has a faint undertone of regret.

"Oh! you need not wish you had any!" I say, shaking my head; "you would never be able to keep them in order—never. Papa often says that if he had his time over again he would not have half so many! And I am sure," I continue, looking at his kindly, gentle face, "that you would never have the heart to whip—"

"And does your father?" he asks, laughing.

"*Rather!* Only ask the fry! Shall you be likely to go to Silverbridge soon?" I ask suddenly and apprehensively.

"Not in the least. Why?"

"You might tell papa I was naughty—or—or something."

"I never tell tales," he says. "And now do you think Miss Tyburn would allow you to come over to the parsonage sometimes and make tea for me?"

"Delightful!" I say, clapping my hands. "Oh! it will be so nice to get away from all these girls sometimes!

They are all very well, sir, but I prefer *boys.*"

"I expect a nephew in a few days, but he is not a boy, unfortunately."

"Will he play cricket with us?" I ask with interest; "one black coat does look so lost among all these girls!"

"I am afraid Miss Tyburn would object," says Mr. Frere, laughing again (really he is not a bit like most elderly gentlemen); "he is coming for some shooting a friend has placed at his disposal near here. I shall not see much of him."

"Is he nice, sir?"

"I think so."

"Helen Adair! Helen Adair!" echoes on all sides. The time has come for me to field. Surely I cannot distinguish myself as lamentably in that duty as I did in the other? "Good-by!" I say in a violent hurry. "Good-by! But before I go I want to tell you that I like you *very much indeed!*"

By-and-by I am able to do my side some small service. Mr. Russell is in, and batting away with a determination and vigor that strike consternation to our feminine souls, and presently he sends a mighty ball straight over my head (who am standing long field on) straight across the cricket-field and into the next. "Six!" cry the Russellites; but six it shall not be, if I can help it. Laying my legs to the ground with a will, I have cleared the field and leaped the hedge beyond, before he has got *one.* I go plump into the midst of a stinging-nettle bed—but that is nothing, I espy the ball and send it home with all my might. And after all he only gets *two.* He casts an approving glance on me as I return; evidently he is not used to seeing girls jump. If he only knew how thoroughly Jack has grounded me in that doubtful accomplishment!

CHAPTER XV.

" . . . . Beauty's ensign yet,
¶s crimson on thy lips and in thy cheeks,
And death's pale flag is not advancèd there."

IT is three o'clock on Saturday afternoon, and I am making my toilet preparatory to setting out for the parsonage. I would rather be playing cricket, but Mr. Russell, after giving us a glorious week, has gone away again; however, he is coming back, and the sooner the better, say I. Meanwhile, let me arrange my clean and crackling gown, as gracefully as the inequalities of my form permit, and try and persuade my curly thick hair to lie flat.

"Good-by, Mary," I say, putting my head in at the classroom door, where she sits illuminating a text, "I'm going now."

I never did care about girls, or want to be great friends with any of them, but I like Mary.

The parsonage is only a few yards away; it is right before my eyes as I walk along the bit of road that divides it from the school. As I lift the latch of the gate, and go through the old-fashioned, sweet-smelling garden, I give a long sigh of content, it is all so peaceful, so dainty, so still. There is a faint suspicion of magnolia in the hall, a scent of roses abroad; and, when Mr. Frere himself comes out to greet me, I feel blessedly, delightedly, restfully happy.

"Run up-stairs and take off your things, my dear," he says, and Mrs. Pim, his housekeeper, shows me the way.

Coming down again, I find that he has vanished, but she pushes open the door of a room on the left, and I enter.

It is low and wide, like our Silverbridge rooms, and it is orderly and prim as an old maid's parlor, with great formal bowls of flowers planted about it, and a stiff bean-pot set in the hearthplace. The windows are open, and, though it is September, the late roses nod in at the windows. A big, deep armchair is pulled up to one of them with its back turned to me; approaching to seat myself in it, for a long course of upright chair-backs has made me hanker very seriously after something easy, I see the crown of a dark, smooth head resting against it. I am about to take a peep round the corner to see who it can be, when the occupant of the chair rises, stretches himself, and opens his mouth for a yawn, stopping midway as he descries me.

"I beg your pardon," he says, shutting his mouth with a snap, "I never heard you come in."

"You are Mr. Frere's nephew," I say, sitting down on the edge of a sofa, and looking at him; "why are you not out shooting?"

"I have been out all the morning. How do you know I am Mr. Frere's nephew?"

"There is no one in Charteris," I say, shaking my head; "no one ever comes here except to see the girls, or Miss Tyburn, or Mr. Russell."

"And are you one of the girls?"

"Of course."

"The biggest of them?"

"Oh, no! but there are much smaller ones than I. Do you think me so very little? At home, at Silverbridge, you know, they always thought me so *leggy*."

"You will shoot up some day," he says, passing his hand over his mustache, "perhaps be a giantess, who knows? And do you really live at Silverbridge?"

"Yes. I suppose you have heard a good deal about it from Mr. Frere?"

"I was born there," he says.

"But you have not been there lately?"

"I lived there until fifteen years ago. Have you never been to The Towers?"

"Yes, I have been there," I say slowly, remembering certain stolen afternoons spent under the shadow of the oaks in the grand old park; "and that is yours?"

"Yes, it is mine. My father died in Rome last year."

I don't think that Jack and I ever knew who it was that owned The Towers, not that we should ever have been any the wiser if we had heard the name.

"No. I went away before you were born."

"And yet you cannot be very old," I say, lifting my eyes to the dark, proud, somewhat worn face, that is as far removed from mere effeminate beauty as it is from ordinary every-day looks.

"Old enough!" he says, with something very like a sigh; "I am thirty years old!"

"More than double my age," I say, soberly. "Oh! it seems a great deal; but then you must have seen so much, been all about the world; it must be nice to have had experience."

"I would give it all," he says, looking into my eager face, "to have your youth and freshness and *belief*."

"Belief!" I repeat, "what is that?"

"I can hardly tell you," he says, "for you would not understand. Do you not look forward to having your life all your own way, meeting with the men and women you think heroic, having your ups and downs certainly, but also your rewards and pleasantnesses? I did when I was your age."

"And why should I not?" I ask, puzzled; "are all our hopes of future happiness illusions? I should hate to think that."

"Do not think it, then," he says, standing up with a quick, impatient shake of the shoulders; "let us go out into the garden. By-the-way, what am I to call you, little madam?"

"Helen Adair," I say, laughing; "at home they call me Nell."

"Then I shall call you Nell, too," he says, promptly. "I wonder where my uncle is?"

He goes to a door leading into a small inner room, that is, I think, Mr. Frere's study, but he is not there.

"Sent for to some old woman who thinks she is dying, I suppose," says his nephew; "he is always being imposed upon."

We go out into the kitchen-garden, which is not close locked as ours at home, but open to all comers; and, since there are no little thieves here to make busy work among the fruit, there is plenty and to spare.

"You are as good as a pair of steps," I say, watching him with much interest gathering the pears that grow on the sunny side of the wall; "how useful you would have been at Silverbridge!" He gives me a satin-smooth Marie Louise. How I wish Jack was here!

"And of what use should I have been?"

"You could have jumped the wall and thrown the fruit over to us."

"And supposing it was breakable?"

"We should not have minded," I say, laughing. "Have you a first-rate kitchen-garden at The Towers?"

"We used to have. I don't know whether the raspberry and gooseberry bushes have grown, like me, aged."

"I do so love gooseberries," I say, looking fondly at the bare bushes we are passing; "grapes never came up to them in my estimation."

"Then when I am at The Towers will you come and help strip my bushes?"

"That I will," I say heartily, "only I am afraid that, if you once let me into your garden, you would never get any dessert."

"I shall not want any for a long time. I am not going there for three years, except for a day or two to arrange matters."

"Three years!" I say, blankly. "Oh dear! I shall be past gooseberries by the time you come back!"

"There will be the peaches?"

"Yes, but they will never taste the same, you know, after I am grown up. Are you going very far?"

"To India, America, Siberia, Australia, China, and—I forget the names of the places almost."

"It is a pity," I say, shaking my head, "a very great pity! You should do a little at a time. You cannot enjoy all that at once! Why, when we went to Periwinkle-by-the-Sea we were worn out with the novelties. We felt that they were almost too much!"

"But supposing," he says, with a queer look upon his face, "that you wanted to be worn out, wanted to tire yourself, what then?"

"I never felt like that," I say, thoughtfully, "so I cannot tell."

"You have a blessedly blank memory, child," he says; "would to God I had!"

"My master is expecting you," says Mrs. Pim, appearing suddenly before us, so we go in and have dinner; a cool, quiet repast that is very unlike the one of which I partook at one o'clock to-day. I think Mr. Frere is fond of this nephew; Paul, he calls him, his other name, I find, is *Vasher*. We are out in the garden again by seven o'clock—at so primitive an hour does Mr. Frere dine—and smelling at the roses, the carnations, and those sweet last gifts that Summer leaves behind when she sweeps her bright skirts away to make room for Autumn, and I have gathered me a nosegay at Mr. Frere's request, and am tying it together with a wisp of dry grass. We have wandered to the gate that gives on the road, and, while Mr. Vasher smokes his cigar, and Mr. Frere talks from time to time, we watch the cows go past, making all the air "like the sweet south, that breathes upon a bank of violets," and half a dozen laborers, and a tipsy man; for, strange to say, even in this out-of-the-world corner people are as much inclined to be wicked as anywhere else. Mr. Frere has his eyes fixed on the portals of the shining city, through which the sun seems to have only just passed; his face is grave; perhaps he is thinking of the gold, and silver, and jewels of his youth that are stored away there, to be given back to him by God's hand maybe, when this life is overpast.

5

Mr. Vasher's face is so calm and still and indifferent as he leans over the gate, blowing a smoke-wreath up into the clear blue azure above us, that I inly marvel whether he were not joking a while ago when he spoke as though the past had proved more bitter than sweet to him.

The sound of hoofs strikes sharply upon my ears: looking up I see a horse-woman approaching at a foot-pace; her head is bent, the reins are hanging loosely from her hand, her face is almost hidden. At my side I feel a sudden leap, a stir, and a hoarse voice, deep and shaken, says, below its breath! "My God!" turning, I see Paul Vasher's face convulsed by love, hate, scorn, longing, loathing . . . . which is it of all these feelings that possesses and shakes him? I look at the girl—she is riding slowly by; she has not lifted her head, or moved one hair's breadth. I feel rather than hear the sigh of relief he gives (surely it is relief?) when she lifts her eyes, looks full in his face, then, it is all in a moment, the reins slip from her hands, she sways and falls headlong to the earth. She does not touch it though, for Paul Vasher has leaped the gate, has caught her in his arms, and is looking down on her with a strange expression, while the groom hastily dismounts and catches his mistress's horse.

"Bring her in!" says Mr. Frere, pale with alarm. (Are not old bachelors and old maids easily daunted?) And Paul brings her in, and lays her down in the big arm-chair, in which I found him sitting a few hours ago. I do not think she has fainted, but her eyes are shut, and she makes neither sigh nor moan, nor does she stir hand or foot. As I look at her, I hold my breath for wonder at her. Well might Shakespeare have said of her, "For the poor rude world hath not her fellow." She is all white and gold, like a pure lily, and as tall; for, though her little hands and feet might belong to a child, she is really of fair stature, and so softly, sensuously lovely at all points, in every dimple and curve of cheek, lip, chin, and body, that it is a feast of the eye to look upon her, while—

> " . . . . Here in her hair
> The painter plays the spider, and hath woven
> A golden mesh to entrap the hearts of men
> Faster than gnats in cobwebs."

Once I look at Mr. Vasher, then back again at her, for the face fascinates me. I do not like it, but oh! I love to look at what is rare and unusual; and is not this such a picture as a man might dream of, and sigh after, all his life long and never see? Mrs. Pim is trying to pour brandy down her throat, but the beautiful mouth does not unclose, the fast-set teeth do not unlock; and yet, somehow, she does not give me the idea of being an insensible woman. I am thinking this, when she opens her eyes with a long-drawn, shuddering sigh, and looks about her, first at one, then another. She does not see Paul, who is standing behind her.

"I hope you are better," says Mr. Frere, advancing, and looking at her very kindly. "We were afraid—"

"I thought," she says, glancing about with dilated sapphire blue eyes, "that I saw—"

Paul steps forward out of the shadow. "I am here," he says, quietly. "I hope you have received no hurt?"

I had thought these two were lovers, but they cannot be: his voice is as cold and indifferent as though he were speaking to Pim. She looks up at him, and her lips quiver, like a beautiful child that seeks love and is given a blow; under the look he winces and turns away. She is very young, not more than eighteen, I think; and somehow, down in my heart, though why or wherefore I cannot tell, I am sorry for her.

"My dear," says good Mr. Frere, "are you sure that you are quite recovered?"

"Quite!" she says, standing up and giving him such a bright, winsome smile that the middle-aged man blushes up to his ears, pleased as any schoolboy. "I

must have been very careless, for Dandy never gave me a fall before."

"It is fortunate we were at the gate," he says, "and that my nephew was able to be of some assistance."

"Your nephew!" she says, staring at him; "is Paul Vasher your nephew?"

"You know him?" exclaims Mr. Frere.—"My dear boy, why did you not tell me so?"

"We have met before," she says, looking at Paul; "that is all."

"I beg your pardon," says Paul, coming forward. "Allow me, Miss Fleming, to introduce my uncle, Mr. Frere, to you. —This young lady, sir, is Miss Fleming."

"Lady Flytton's niece?" asks Mr. Frere, as the girl lays her lovely slim hand in his; "then we are near neighbors!"

"I have heard my aunt speak of you," she says, gently, "and we are coming to hear you preach to-morrow."

"And you know Paul?" continues Mr. Frere; "how very odd! I suppose you did not know he was in this part of the world?"

"I thought he was in Scotland."

"You said you were going to Scarbro'," says Paul, "you changed your mind?"

"Yes, like you. It is not a difficult thing to do, to change one's mind, is it?"

Their eyes meet; ay, these two were hot lovers once, but what are they now?

"You have laid me under a great obligation, Mr. Vasher," she says, in her proud young voice. "Pray understand that I am grateful.—Good-night, Mr. Frere, and forgive me, if you can, for startling you so much!"

"Good-night! good-night!" he says, and so with a hand-shake she goes, and the two men accompany her to the gate.

Now if Mr. Frere had possessed the most rudimental idea of his duty on this occasion, he would have stopped behind with me. Clearly he has about as much notion of being a gooseberry as a cabbage; but my instinct is active enough if his is not, and a long course of sympathy with Alice and Charles has made me very tender-hearted on the subject of lovers; so as Mr. Frere passes the window with the two young people, I utter a dismal groan and call out to him that I have tumbled down and hurt myself very much. Back he comes in a twinkling and finds me nursing my leg on the floor, with a twisted ankle. "I tumbled over a footstool," I explain, "and will you assist me to the sofa?" He wants to call Mrs. Pim, and have it examined; but this I object to, giving it as my opinion that rest is all that is required.

"So odd," says the poor gentleman, as he brings me a book and some papers, "that there should be two accidents in one evening!"

On some pretext or another I keep him in the room for fully ten minutes; then he goes out into the garden after Paul.

I wonder if, when I am grown up and am quarreling with my lover, any good Samaritan will take as much trouble to serve me as I have taken to serve those two who are standing down by the gate yonder, looking into each other's faces with such a different expression on each? So much I see as I hop nimbly to the window as soon as Mr. Frere's back is turned to me.

CHAPTER XVI.

"HAMLET. I did love you once.
"OPHELIA. Indeed, my lord, you made me believe so."

"COME and pray! come and pray!" ring the sweet bells through the hushed peace of the Sabbath morning; and obedient to the call we rise up, and, ascending to the higher regions, proceed to cloak and bonnet ourselves after our schoolgirl lights and abilities. There must be a little fashion wandering about the world somewhere, but it has not yet found its way to Charteris; only in one respect do we follow the mode, and that is by wear-ing spoon bonnets. Very fresh and fair look some of the faces inside those absurd monstrosities, but unlovely folk are not improved by their shape, and of those hapless latter virgins I am one. I would not mind if the tiresome thing would keep straight; but it will not, and I usually reach church looking as though I had had a fight on the way and come off second best. I am in short frocks still, so that from a distance I look all legs and bonnet—"like a windmill," as one of my friends kindly remarked the other day.

We are out in the road now, winding along it like a dingy ribbon, and as we pass the parsonage, Mr. Vasher comes out, fresh, perfectly dressed, with a delicate buttonhole in his coat; altogether a pleasant and refreshing sight among this regiment of indifferently clothed young women. He scans our ranks as carelessly as though we were a show of azaleas or roses (not that we are those pretty flowers by any means—far more dandelions than beauty-blossoms grow in our parterre), and does not discover me; apparently my bonnet is as good a disguise as an entirely new body. He has passed us all, with his long, quick step, long before we turn in at the churchyard. I wonder why a black coat on any man's back who is not fifty sends such a twitter of excitement through a girls' school? A few years hence and a hundred men would not cause the excitement that a single one does now in the breast of a schoolgirl. And now we are in church; anon Mr. Frere is in his place, and "Dearly beloved" is half through, when a prodigious clatter outside makes all eyes turn to the door. A hand and arm coated in gray and scarlet livery open it, and a tall, fair, majestic woman sails in and rustles up the aisle, her bracelets clanking, her dress trailing behind her, looking uncommonly like a ship in full sail. Miss Fleming follows. She does not rustle and she does not clank; she sweeps noiselessly along in her cool white dress, and she is white from head to foot. The very church seems the brighter for her coming, as she kneels against the carven oak; she looks as sinless, and fair, and adorable, as Marguerite may have looked before Faust came, and yet—and yet—I wonder why with this lovely bit of porcelain I am always thinking of the outside, never of the nature and inner life? For the best of reasons: save for beauty her face is the merest blank; if she has a soul she keeps it mighty well hid, but in the teeth of such perfection who would ask anything more? No sensible man or woman. It is a pity to look at the mother and daughter side by side. Will the lovely red and white of the girl's cheek strengthen into the fixed color that the other wears? Will the dainty contour of brow, lip, and chin in the daughter's face become thickened, even lost in time, as in the mother's case? They are so alike in features, coloring, and proportion, that the doubt is natural. Paul Vasher sits in the chancel opposite me, the Flemings a little below in the body of the church; once he turns his head and their eyes meet, and are held fast and long. It is a difficult look to read, but, though no change passes over his face,

"... makes her blood look out:
Good sooth she is the queen of curds and
  cream."

Now the benediction is spoken, and we rise and go our ways, standing aside in the road as Lady Flytton's carriage goes by. The girls are buzzing in low tones of the stranger, of her beauty, her bonnet, her gown; she has even astonished them into forgetting Mr. Vasher. We have dinner, that liberal meal at Charteris, that does not stand godmother to resurrection pies, cold remains, and potato puddings, or any other abomination. Our parents pay for us to be well fed, and we *are;* therefore the school prospers. We are in the first classroom now, and—oh, wonder!—I am actually seated in the midst of the potent Buffs; for so the six head girls of the school are called, who wield an authority in the school second only to that of Miss Tyburn. By no virtue of my own am I

here, but Kate Lishaw, the head of them, has been pleased to take some small notice of me; therefore am I sitting cheek by jowl with my betters.

"Girls," says Kate, resting her charming dark-eyed *mignonne* face on her clasped hands, "I have some news; we are going to have a *party.*"

"Not really?" "How I hate them!" "A lot of trouble for nothing!" "We shall get some supper, though!" "And there will be at least *one* man!" "He won't be asked." These ejaculations burst out on all sides, I alone holding my tongue, for as yet a party at Charteris is a thing heard of but never seen by me.

"It is even so, my brethren," continues Kate, "and the edict has gone forth that our quarterly, low-necked, manless, partnerless, full-dress ball is to take place on Thursday week. But do not be downhearted, my friends, about this impending festivity; there is an unusual and beautiful halo of novelty, for at it will probably be present—*a man!* None of your miserable old rectors or half-penny hobbledehoys, but a downright well-dressed, presentable man. There is no knowing to whom he may throw his pocket-handkerchief; therefore my advice to all and sundry is, curl up your hair, starch up your skirts, put on your most ravishing ogle, your finest languish, and—every man for himself and devil take the hindmost."

"Only he cannot dance with more than a quarter of us," says Laura Fielding, a languid beauty of the Lydia Languish type, who is ripe for flirtation but doomed to bread-and-butter.

"I have thought of that," says Kate; "we will have a lottery with fifteen prizes, and whoever draws one shall pin it to the front of her dress, and walk up to Mr. Vasher, and making a courtesy say, '*My* dance, I think?' and then lead him away."

"I wonder what he would be doing all this time?" says Belle Linden. "He does not look like a man who would be made to do anything he does not choose."

"So much the better," says Dora; "I don't fancy the *coup d'œil* of our assembled charms will have the same effect upon him that they had on that little man who came to our last with Mr. Russell, and who gave one look at our hungry and awaiting ranks, *and ran*."

"Where did he go?" I ask, speaking for the first time.

"Nobody knows. Of one thing only are we certain—he never came back here."

"Perhaps Mr. Vasher will not come," says Kate; "men like girls, you know, but, I fancy, in moderation. He does not look like a universal lover of womankind —we want a diffusive man."

"If he does not come," says Belle, "to view our forlorn and piteous gambols, then all spring and *verve* will depart therefrom, and we shall be like apple-tart without the apples."

"If he only knew," says Emma, "that every petticoat, skirt, and tucker in this establishment will be washed to his glory, he could not choose but come. He could not be a man born of woman without feeling touched."

"Helen Adair, you shrimp! you have spoken to him, have you not?" asks Laura. "Is he made of gentle stuff, or likely to kick over the traces?"

"I don't know," I say, laughing; "shall I ask him when I see him?"

"Do," says Kate, impressively, laying her hand on my head; "go down on your knees to him, and refuse to get up again until he says he will come! There will be a *ragged* look on us all if he does not!"

A bell ringing in the distance calls us together like a flock of sheep, to go out for a walk.

It is Wednesday afternoon, and we are all, great and small, up-stairs unearthing our evening dresses and fishing up boots, gloves, and other minor appendages. To me this party is a brand novel-

ty. Never have I been to anything that bore the most ghostly resemblance to one; therefore my festive garment is not, like that belonging to some of my less fortunate schoolmates, grown too short, too tight, or too narrow. Nevertheless it is not much to boast of, being a species of Phœnix revived from the ashes of one of mother's dead and gone tails. It is rusty, it is musty, it is villainously bare of ornament and green of hue, but it comes decently down to my heels, and does not refuse to meet over my chest—a piece of good luck on which I may congratulate myself, seeing that on all sides I hear the popping of hooks and bursting of buttons, as "bodies" after undue pressure fly off at a tangent, and gape widely when they should close; while petticoats that ought modestly to touch the ground, display ankles that refuse to blush unseen.

The woes of one girl in particular might draw tears from a stone. Poor Emma's existence is one long struggle to get into her frocks; for Providence, who ever loves to serve mankind nasty tricks, has predisposed her to fat, with an ever-increasing solidity that sets dressmakers at defiance. Not that this fact in itself calls for pity; for are not the fat ones of the earth the happiest, the cheerfullest, the best-tempered people living? The sting of it lies in this, that Emma has a stepmother who objects to new dresses on principle, and will allow no more than a certain number a year, and has decreed that when she has had those let out to their extremest limits, if they will not accommodate themselves to her form, then her form must be brought down to the size of her gown. So when poor Emma shows signs of overgrowing, she is put on Banting, and made to eat the things that she hates and leave untouched those that she loves, and, over and above, to skip for an hour before breakfast every morning. The latter in hot weather is trying, but, nevertheless, she works her step-mother's will; and though her life is a

burden to her, by degrees her fat diminishes, and she comes down to the size of
her garments. If this is not a practical example of the triumph of mind over matter, then where shall one be found? Just
now she is in the increasing stage, and
efforts that would not disgrace a blacksmith are being made to "fasten" her
low blue-and-white silk frock; but, alas!
until Emma has returned to Banting the
glories of that frock are not for her!

Consultations, serious and profound as
those held with a court dressmaker over
a London beauty's first drawing-room,
are going on in all directions; baréges,
grenadines, and muslins, being the aristocratic subjects under discussion. It seems
a great waste of good starch and time, so
much preparation, so little to gain by it.
But though no strangers worth mentioning will be present to appraise all this
bravery at its true worth, will it not be
something for Rose Mary with her superior flounces to cut out Anna Maria with
her scanty ones, and are not the merits
of the rival beauties of the school on
these occasions of dress-parade afterward
discussed as fully and exhaustively as
any Almack beauty, by any group of
beaux and wits at White's? Hence these
puckered brows and weighty discussions.

I hang up my black bombazine to try
and get some of the creases out; then I
dig out a pair of very large, very baggy
old white kid boots, at least four sizes too
big for me—family heirlooms that were
originally worn (I think) by my grandmother, then by mother, now by me, and
will be handed down in turn to future
generations. They are as yellow as autumn leaves; surely their complexion
might be improved? Not unlikely! So
might my own, so might the bombazine's,
by upsetting a pot of ink over it. It
would then at least be black; but I am
not going to take the trouble.

I put my hat under my arm, and go
down-stairs with a pleased smile on my
face, for am I not going to clean it, and
is not this duty a real labor of love with

me? But half-way down I meet a servant, who says—

"If you please, miss, you may put on
your hat and go over to the parsonage,
Miss Tyburn says."

I put away my hat and fetch my hat,
nothing loath, and set out immediately.
Arrived at the house, I find no one visible, but after some search discover Mr.
Vasher in the orchard, swinging in a
hammock under an apple-tree. Very
cool, and lazy, and comfortable he looks,
with the September sun glinting through
the green leaves, and on the sides of the
rosy apples that hang over his head;
though I fancy a smart shower of them
upon his face would not improve the
flavor of his "Balzac." He looks rather
astonished as my head suddenly appears
at his elbow, and lays down his book.

"How do you do?" I say, quickly.
"Do not try to shake hands, you will
only tumble out; I have come to ask you
something very particular."

"Well, what is it?"

"You like to do kind things, do you
not? You like to please people?"

"That depends on who they are."

"Oh, these are rather nice," I say,
nodding; "they can't help being only
girls, you know."

"Oh! girls," says Mr. Vasher; "and
how can I please them?"

"We are going to have a party," I
say, seriously, "and you are going to be
invited, and the Buffs were talking about
it on Sunday, taking it as a matter of
course that you would come; but somehow I felt in my bones that it was not the
sort of thing you would care about, and
I made up my mind to ask you to come
as a great favor to us all."

"And why did you think I should
not come?" he asks, amusedly.

"Because," I say, confidentially, "I
know that, as a rule, men do not care for
girls in a lump; they do not mind a few,
but they can't stand *fifty*."

"Only fifty? I thought I saw over a
hundred on Sunday."

"Oh no!" I say, laughing; "do not make us out worse than we are. And so —and so I thought I would just tell you how anxious we are for you to come, because I thought that, however much you disliked the idea, you would come as a matter of duty."

"You must think me a good-tempered sort of fellow," says Mr. Vasher, scrambling out of his hammock somewhat inelegantly (the handsomest man alive could hardly perform that feat gracefully); "before I promise, tell me what my duties will be."

"There will be fifty girls," I say, walking by his side, "without teachers, and you will have them all to yourself to pick and choose from, and you need not hurry yourself in the least about a partner, or be afraid of any one saying No, for you will be the only young man there."

"Delightful privilege!" says my companion.

"You will not be expected to dance with us all," I say, reassuringly; "not more than fifteen at most! The other girls dance with each other."

"And what are you going to do?"

"I never dance," I say, shaking my head; "I have never learned, and it is better not to make a spectacle of myself."

"Then you will not dance with me?"

"Oh no!" I say, "I could not think of such a thing. Even if I knew, how I should be ashamed to deprive the other girls of you! I see you sometimes, you know, and they do not, and they would think it so *mean* of me!"

CHAPTER XVII.

". . . . O thou weed,
Who art so lovely fair, and smell'st so sweet,
That the sense aches at thee."

THURSDAY evening has arrived, and eight o'clock is striking. We are all assembled in the big dining-room, and our petticoats are so voluminous and our bodies so pranked forth, that, instead of fifty souls, we look as though we numbered two hundred at the very least. If a Frenchman were let loose among us, he would clasp his hands in speechless admiration at the amount of raw material before him, the fine eyes, the abundant hair, fair skins, and perfect teeth; but he would also deplore, from the bottom of his soul, our *chaussures*, *coiffures*, and choice of colors —he would lament the total absence of style, *tournure*, *chic*, whatever it may be called, that in England is so conspicuous by its absence, and, while he hankered after our red and white charms, would console himself with the recollection of his sallow spouse's matchless taste and costume, perfect in every detail.

We each have a little card, or at least everybody has but me, upon which are inscribed the partners selected for the dances, although it is an understood thing that if a man should miraculously appear and request the honor, the former engagement is to be considered null and void.

After all, we have not had a lottery on Paul Vasher's account, and he will be free to go where he lists, although I privately entertain very grave doubts whether he will trot out one-half of the damsels who confidently expect to be asked.

The door opens and our little musicmaster appears, followed by his son bearing a fiddle, out of which he will presently harrow up our souls with shrieks that might wake the dead.

Miss Tyburn comes in. She wears maize silk and black lace; very imposing she looks as she bends in answer to the crackling bows every one makes all round the room. And now enters the Rev. Thomas Shrubb (rector of an adjacent parish) with his wife, who wears a blue gown and a green-and-gold cap. Their son follows, a dyspeptic, parboiled youth of eighteen, who looks like a beast led to the slaughter, and while he gazes fatuously about him, seems dimly to understand that he has fallen among thieves. We are not proud, we school-girls; anything in the shape of a man is comely in our eyes, but we scorn to reckon this fat youth as a man, or anything approaching to one.

At a sign from Miss Tyburn the fiddle strikes up, the little music-master thumps at the piano, and a quadrille is formed. Mr. Shrubb leads out Miss Tyburn with tottering steps (at his time of life he ought to know better), his wife sinks into an easy-chair; the fat boy advances a step, apparently meditating a plunge into the sea of white muslin before him, gasps, blinks, ruminates, thinks better of it, and finally sits down, puffing apoplectically. "Gentlemen" girls fetch out their lady partners, and lead them to their places.

"If there is anything I hate," says Laura Fielding, as she sweeps her pale pink skirts over my feet, "it is having a girl's arm round my waist!"

The room is one struggling mass of tarlatan, muslin, and barége; every now and then a hitch occurs, and half a dozen young women get firmly wedged together by their hoops, and are disentangled with great difficulty. In the ladies' chain, too, there is some confusion, but one can't expect everything. The old vicar sets, bows, and shuffles with the rest most valiantly; like the Shaker of Artemus Ward memory. The dance over, every one who can sits down and drinks negus; which might be better, but then, on the other hand, might be worse. The fiddler is just executing a preparatory scrape that seems to take his hearers into the very bowels of the earth, when the door opens and enter Mr. Frere and Mr. Vasher. As the latter stands talking to Miss Tyburn, I see him glance about him with a keen amusement; then, as the music strikes up, he leaves her and comes straight to the corner where I lie *perdue.*

"This is our dance," he says, placing my hand under his arm, disregarding my murmurs of dissent with masculine *sang-froid.*

I feel my shortcomings very grievously as he leads me forth. How I wish my gown were not so rusty, and that my boots did not curl up at the toes quite so much, seeming to require chains, as did those of our ancestors long ago. He puts his strong arm about my waist, and away we go; but, alas! if a lamp-post and a bottle elected to dance a jig together, they would bear about the same proportion to each other that Mr. Vasher does to me.

"Stop!" I cry, when we have taken one round and a half; "it is no good."

So he stops, laughing, and takes me to a seat.

"Long and short," he says, "and decidedly too much long!"

"I told you how it would be," I say, ruefully; "you see, I am only a little above your elbow! If one could only roll one's self out!"

"Supposing you grew up like that?" he says, glancing almost imperceptibly at a May-pole of a girl who is standing near, and who measures five feet ten in her stockings.

"One can always avenge one's injuries when one is that size; and, after all, must it not be nice to be able to snub people?" I say, laughing.

"That is a pretty little girl," he says, looking at Kate Lishaw, who has paused for a moment in her dancing near us.

"She is a duck," I say, quickly; "do ask her to dance."

In a moment I have fetched her, and they go off together, he looking with real admiration at her fresh, bright young face. I leave my place and go to the top of the room; hard by Miss Tyburn is speaking to Mrs. Shrubb, and as her voice is raised in rivalry with the fiddle, I cannot avoid hearing what she says.

"Remarkably lovely; but you will be able to judge for yourself, she is coming to-night with her aunt, Lady Flytton. I was calling there yesterday, and happened to mention Mr. Vasher's name; she said she knew him very well, and seemed to like the idea of seeing him again, so I asked her to come."

"Miss Fleming is coming! I wonder what Paul will say?"

The music ceases in a *crescendo* of shrieks that might well make Weber, whose waltz it is, stir in his coffin. The room is scarcely clear again when the door opens, and a little withered, bent old woman in a pearl-gray satin, half covered with lace, totters in. Behind her comes her niece, Miss Fleming. More than ever like a white-and-gold lily does she look as she advances by the side of that brown old witch, and pays her *devoirs* to Miss Tyburn. She wears white garments that sweep in great soft folds to the ground; they are bordered with a Greek pattern of gold, and about her neck, arms, and waist, are clasped heavy dead gold coins. She looks all white and gold, from the crown of her head to the tips of her embroidered *brodequins*. The scanty folds of the Greek bodice fall away exquisitely from the gleaming ripe shoulders and bosom; the arms bare from shoulder to wrist taper divinely, and are softly nicked at elbow and wrist like a baby's. We all hold our breath as we look at her; and Paul Vasher, standing hard by, marks every matchless point of face and figure as no feminine eyes ever could, and—does not go near her. On the contrary, he says something to Kate, who leads him up to Mary Burns—comely, gentle, honest Mary—and she goes off with him, looking hugely flattered. Miss Fleming is seated in a low chair talking to Mrs. Shrubb, fanning herself slowly with a quaint fan of crimson feathers. The fat boy on seeing her has gasped once and never got his breath back. His father is sitting with a hand grasping each knee, surveying her with senile admiration. Why is not 'Mr. Vasher by her side? Why is she sitting there alone? She looks as though she did not care, and yet I am sure she does: not often can it fall to her lot to be slighted and set aside for schoolgirls.

He goes up to her by-and-by though, when the evening is wearing away; and surely she is not proud, for she lays her hand upon his arm, and they waltz together, melting into the long gliding step that each possesses in such perfection. For a time I sit still and look at them, at the dark, magnificent looks of the man and the fair, luxuriant beauty of the girl, and think that never surely did a more splendid couple stand up together; they seem to be made for each other. Presently I leave my seat and go out into the corridor, which is bright as noonday in the clear, pale beams of the September moon.

The hall-door stands widely, invitingly open. Beyond its lintel lies the broad, sleeping, moon-washed earth, and down below—oh, so sweet!—gurgle up the glad notes of the nightingale. For a moment I hesitate—over that threshold I am forbidden to go; then, as the tread of many feet comes down the corridor, I snatch up one of the wraps lying about, and step forth into the silver peace and beauty of the night. Just outside the door is a dark corner, formed by the projection of the porch, and into this I slip, lest a teacher or Buff should come to the door and discover my unlawful whereabouts.

The flowers are all fast asleep; they look ghostly and weird in the glistening light. I wonder if they will wake up by-and-by, as Hans Andersen's flowers did, and trip a dainty measure to the music the nightingale yonder furnishes? Somehow I never can believe that these flowers are but colored shapes: they seem to me to be so much more worthy of souls and nerves than the ugly, stupid folks that walk about the world. There is not a breath of air abroad; the land is as still and unruffled as the dark-blue vault overhead, in which the stars glitter countless and brilliant, as though a royal hand had strewed them. We think queer thoughts sometimes, when we stand perfectly alone and in utter silence, face to face with the great mystery of Nature: the common, prosaic, every-day life falls from us, habit fades away, and custom is not; the thousand ways and words and thoughts that lie as a screen between us and her great truths, vanish like thin air; the coil does not press so heavily upon us at these times as at others, and some dim perception of the universal law that governs God's earth breathes itself imperceptibly into our souls.

I think I must have been out here a long while, for I am growing cold. Time to go in. I am just emerging, when, down the corridor, click, clack! click, clack! come the taps of high-heeled shoes and I hastily draw back into my corner as the new-comer steps over the threshold and stands, face and form and robe, bathed in a flood of pure silvery light. It is Miss Fleming, and she stands quite motionless, looking up steadfastly at the sky overhead. All the soft beauty of her face is gone; in its place there reigns a cold, still determination, that contrasts almost violently with the youth of her lineaments. As she slowly lifts her arm and right hand to heaven, her lips move, and she looks like some relentless goddess, who had been turned to stone in the act of calling down confusion and curses upon her enemy. More footsteps—a man's this time—come down the passage and approach the door, pause for a moment, then come on again.

"Had you not better have a shawl, Miss Fleming?" inquires Mr. Vasher's voice. "You will take cold."

At his polite, chill words she neither turns nor looks; she stands motionless, with her eyes fixed upon the ground, looking with her straight brow and antique raiment like a Greek slave standing before her master. He looks at her with a keen, devouring scrutiny from head to foot, and turns to go. He is within the house, when she calls to him—

"*Paul!*"

"Do you want me?" he says, pausing; but she does not answer, and he comes back slowly and stands a little apart from her. "Is there anything more to be said between us?" he asks. "Is it not all finished—done with?"

"To you, perhaps," she says; "but not to me—not while my life lasts!"

"You will forget," he says, looking down with a dark and bitter frown; "you are young yet."

"Have you forgotten?" she asks, below her breath. "Do you find it so easy?"

"God knows!" he says, lifting his head and staring up at the sky, that is so "thick inlaid with patines of bright gold." "Women can't feel things as men do."

"Do they not?" she cries, with a fierce jangle in her sweet voice. "Have you forgotten that it is the one who sins, not the one who is sinned against, that suffers the most keenly? Do you think that if it had been through your fault or folly I lost my happiness I should have mourned half as heavily as I do now, knowing that it is *my own doing?*"

"Why did you do it?" he says, looking down on her with an infinite yearning in his eyes, an infinite agony in his voice. "We could have been so happy, child."

"You were too hard upon me," she says, with a shuddering moan. "Any other man would have forgiven me if he had loved me."

"And did not I love you?" he asks, quietly.

"You cast me off," she says, lifting her lovely face to his; "I did not you."

"I never loved, never wanted any woman but you," he says, slowly. "I chose you out of the whole world for my wife. I would have worn you as my fairest honor, my priceless pearl; and how did you reward me?"

"I was never unfaithful to you," she says, drearily. "If ever I did anything wrong it was before I knew you."

"And there it was that you deceived me," he says, with a heavy sigh. "You had seemed so pure, and honest, and true."

"And so I was to you," she says, swiftly—"always true to you!"

"Heavens!" he says, throwing back his head with a quick, sudden gesture, "when I think of it all! It was much such a night as this three months ago—only three months—that you and I stood together in that garden, and I asked you to be my wife, and you put your arms about my neck; and, as we stood together, your lover came toward us and looked first on one, then on another, and went away. You never said, 'That is my betrothed husband, whom I have kissed and betrayed, as I will kiss and betray you if I have the chance.' When he rode that steeple-chase next morning so madly, so recklessly, that all saw the goal he strove to reach was death, and a quarter of an hour later was carried back to his mother's carriage *dead*, did you feel no remorse—no sorrow? You gave no sign. You were shocked; but he might have been a common acquaintance, no more; only later, in looking over the poor lad's papers (for I was a friend of his mother's), I came upon a packet of your letters, and, you being my promised wife, I thought no shame of reading one." He pauses, and she droops her head in the moonlight and shivers. Is she cold or shamed? "You know the story," he says, wearily, "and how we parted. I loved you then; I love you now, but differently—and it is all over."

"You love me," she says, in her low, passionate voice, "and I—my God! do I not love *you?* And yet are we to live apart! *Must* it be so, beloved—must it be so?"

"It must be," he says, very gently. "We can never be anything to each other —never any more!" She lifts her head, and the agony on her face shows clear and strong in the moonlight, as they stand looking at each other, she so surpassingly fair, he so lofty of stature and dark of face; it seems sad, unnatural, that they should suffer so. As she turns away he puts out his hand and draws her back.

"Silvia," he says, hoarsely, and in the September evening he shivers like a reed, "I would have gone to the world's end rather than have met you here to-night. What evil fate has brought us together again so soon—so terribly soon? Since we parted I have been trying with all my strength of body and soul to forget you, and it seemed as though I were beginning to succeed; and now you have appeared before me, to dash my hard-won peace from my hand, and give me all the raging pain and misery over again. If I were differently made—if I could forget everything and love you in the old fashion, I would do it; but I cannot. . . . I love you still, but with the worse half of my heart, not the better. Something has gone from you in my eyes that will never come back. Though I married you I should have no respect for you; in my eyes you would be no more than a beautiful toy. The old worship is dead, and it will never come back. And though you think you love me now, a woman who betrays one man will betray another; and it would not please me to see my wife's eyes roving among my friends in search of admiration."

"I would have been faithful to you," she says, very low.

"No, you would not," he says, with a heavy sigh; "it is not in you to be true to any man. You only care for me because I am out of your reach. If I were your husband you would not rest till you had played me false."

"And I have loved you so well, so well!" she says, with a sob, lifting the pale, lovely face that has so changed during the past minutes to his.

"God help us both!" he cries, passionately, pale as she through his bronzed darkness. He takes the soft face between his two brown hands and gazes into it eagerly, devouringly, as a man may look his last on his heart's delight, lying in the envious coffin that will by-and-by hide her from his sight forever. "Kiss me once, love, before we part, and then pray

God that on earth we may never meet
again."

She lays her arms, white as any lilies,
about his brown throat; she lifts the
beautiful lips, out of which all color has
fled, and kisses him — once. And he
snatches her in his embrace, and kisses
her, not once but many times, on lip and
brow, and shoulder, with a strength that
seems to crush her. Then he sets her
down abruptly, and strides away into the
night, and the girl stands breathless, pant-
ing, with a deadly pallor upon her face,
a wild agony in her eyes. "My love,"
. . . . she says, "my love." . . . She
puts her hand suddenly to her heart, as
though a knife had struck her newly,
then she turns and steps over the threshold.

CHAPTER XVIII.

'But mine and mine I loved, and mine I
    praised,
And mine that I was proud on; mine so
    much
That I myself was to myself not mine
Valuing of her; why, she—oh! she is fallen
Into a pit of ink, that the wide sea
Hath drops too few to wash her clean again."

"Most extraordinary!" says Laura
Fielding, resting her chin on her hands
and her elbows on her desk. "He actually left his hat behind!"

"Does any one know what became of
it?" asks Kate Lishaw.

"It was put in a bandbox," says Dora,
"and carried to the parsonage by a maid-
servant, who made him a courtesy, and
said, 'I've brought you something as you
dropped among our young ladies, sir!'"

"Nonsense!" says Kate; "but I
must confess I am disappointed in him!
After all, he proved a very little more
valiant than Mr. Russell's friend! He is
very nice, though," she adds, "and he
dances splendidly."

"He is magnificent," says Belle.

"Did you ever see such shoulders or
such a head? And then his style—unim-
peachable!"

"His mustache is—" says Laura,
"it has that long, bold sweep that you
never see on a plain man's face; and as
to his eyes—"

"Bravo! Laura," says Kate.

"He was a man— You know the rest.
I'll tell you one thing," says Belle, "that
I am sure of; that exquisite piece of white
and gold, Miss Fleming, was at the bottom
of his sudden departure; and I am certain
that if they are not lovers now, they were
once with a vengeance. They disappeared together that night. I would
have reconnoitred, but was curveting in
the Lancers. After that, you know, *he
went.*"

"I should not mind being you, Helen
Adair," says Kate, patting me on the
shoulder. "You do the visiting, while
we all stay at home."

I am sitting in my bonnet and jacket,
awaiting the carriage that is to take me
to Lady Flytton's.

"I don't want to go," I say, earnestly; "indeed, I do not. Why Lady Flytton asked me I cannot think, for she did
not know mother very well."

"What it is to have so many friends!"
says Belle; "I wish I had some!"

"And you are coming back on Monday, child?"

"Yes."

"I wonder if Mr. Vasher will go
there?" says Kate. "Keep your eyes
open, Helen Adair, and tell us all you
see when you come back. Hark! there
is the carriage."

We go out. Yes, there it is, and
the spirited black horses, with their scarlet rosettes, look far more fitted for a
drive in Hyde Park than to bowl along
these country lanes.

"Good-by! good-by!" say the Buffs.

The footman puts in my portmanteau,
and away I go, feeling like Cinderella
without the beauty. It is a lovely day,
but oh! I wish I had a companion, for it

is dull sitting all alone behind those two gorgeous-backed men-servants. How invitingly the nuts nod their brown faces at me from the hedge! I should be happier walking in the road with Jack, free to pick them, than perched up here with nothing to do. I wonder if I dare ask one of those men to gather me some? I cannot call them, for I do not know their names, so I uplift my voice in a "hem!" which I deliver point blank at the middle of the footman's back.

"Did you speak, miss?" he asks, touching his hat and turning.

"A—not exactly," I say; "but I want some of those nuts; can you pick them for me?"

"Certainly, miss," and in another minute he is in the road, and scrambling up the hedge; his long coat hampers his legs, the powder flies from his hair to his shoulders, but he is a man "for a' that;" and, finally, he brings me my nuts with an unruffled countenance. I fancy I hear him saying later in the servants' hall, "She's low, she is; she ate nuts out in the carriage, and cracked them with her own teeth, she did."

And now we have passed through the lodge-gates, and are rolling along between the avenue of tall trees that mark the approach to Flytton. It is a beautiful old place, and a footman ushers me through stately passages and anterooms to the drawing-room, in which I have some difficulty in discovering Lady Flytton—so little, so wizen, so shrunken is she. I make her out at last in a far corner. I think she is asleep, but she opens her eyes suddenly, and bids me welcome, very kindly desiring the footman to bring white wine and grapes; while I eat the latter, she chatters away, with the garrulity of old age, of mother, who was, she says, "a beautiful young woman;" of everything, in short, that her wandering thoughts hit upon. Presently she leans back in her chair, and, without the smallest sign or word, goes soundly to sleep. I am just wondering what I am going to do with myself, and thinking how lively it will be here, when the glass door leading to the garden swings back, and Silvia Fleming comes into the room, and, without looking about her, sits down with her back to me in a low chair. Her hair is hanging down her back in thick curls; she wears a plain white wrapper, that by its severity makes her beauty more than ever conspicuous. There is a listless droop about the whole figure as she leans back with her arms clasped under her head. She has not been seated there twenty seconds, when the door opens, and "Captain Chichester" is announced; he is tall, languid, *blasé*, but his steps and face quicken as he spies the recumbent figure in the red-velvet chair.

"How do you do?" he says, stooping over her and holding out his hand; but she does not put out hers; she only looks up at him with a lazy look of welcome, provocation, which is it?

"Too hot!" she says; "would not one think it August instead of September?"

He sits down beside her, and they talk in low voices. They do not seem to know any one is present; however, as I cannot hear what they are saying, it is somewhat unnecessary for me to announce myself, though indeed I am not anxious to play the degrading part of *eavesdropper* again, as I did a week ago.

Is yonder coquette the passionate, despairing woman that Paul Vasher kissed a while ago so hotly? Was it but a fine piece of acting—her love and her misery? For surely, surely she is acting her own proper character at this moment? No, she was not acting then, but she was taken out of herself for the time; and Paul's estimate of her is the right one, the taint of infidelity in her nature is too deep to permit her to be either a good or a faithful woman. Admiration is meat and drink to her, flattery the very air she breathes; no man could keep this woman straight any more than a rope can be made of sand. She does not love this man to whom she is talking, does not even admire him, but she will fool him to the top of his bent. A woman's vanity takes many lives to feed it. So much I guess randomly as I sit and watch her.

"*Little devil!*" says Lady Flytton, softly. Turning to look at the old woman, I find that she has come out of her sleep as suddenly as she entered it, and is surveying the couple yonder with an expression of countenance that is, to say the least of it, vicious.

"Good-afternoon, Captain Chichester!" she remarks, austerely.

The young man looks round with an astonishment that is ludicrous, rises and comes toward the old lady. Silvia, I observe, does not move an inch.

"I did not know any one was here," he says, holding out a hand that Lady Flytton altogether overlooks.

"I dare say you did not," she says, frostily; and he goes back to his charmer, looking somewhat red and decidedly snubbed. Tea is brought in and we partake of it apart. Oh, it is dull! If the little woman does not like her company, why does she not leave it? Anon Captain Chichester takes his departure, and, it being near the dinner-hour, I am shown to my room, where I array myself in my little all, and, modestly habited in the same, descend to the drawing-room. Silvia Fleming is there, and she speaks some half-words of greeting, giving me the contemptuous, indifferent regard that apparently she always bestows on her own sex. Mrs. Fleming comes in, fat and kind; I like her better than her daughter, last of all Lady Flytton; and we go in to dinner, where there is next to no conversation, for the hostess devotes herself to her knife and fork with the assiduity of a woman who knows her time for wielding the same is short, and the other two have little conversation. In the drawing-room later the two elders sit together, knitting and talking, while Silvia's restless figure paces up and down, up and down, the terraced walk outside, and I sit at a table,

turning over a photograph-book, and pitying myself from the very bottom of my soul.

"It is too ridiculous," says Mrs. Fleming's vexed voice, rising in her excitement, "and the offers and admiration she has had too!"

"She is a bad little cat," says Lady Flytton, shaking her ungodly, Madeira-warmed old head, "and she'll never come to any good, never! As to Paul Vasher, he'll never marry her; he knows her too well for that!"

I move quickly away before I hear more, and marvel for the ninety-ninth time why I was ever invited to Flytton

---

CHAPTER XIX.

"* . . . . Give me that man,
That is not passion's slave, and I will wear him
In my heart's core; ay, in my heart of hearts.*"

A TAP at the door. "Come in," I say, pausing in my wrestle with my bonnet-strings—which I am trying to settle in a bow that will not disgrace Lady Flytton's smart chariot—and enter Silvia. Apparently she is not going to church, for, although we start in five minutes' time, she wears a white morning-gown and slippers.

"Will you do something for me?" she asks, sitting down.

"Tell me what it is first," I say, cautiously.

"You know Mr. Vasher?"

"Yes!"

"Will you give him this note after church?"

I look at the held-out *billet*, and for a moment hesitate. I love to help lovers; but I like him, and I do not like her; shall I hurt him by taking it? He is strong enough to take care of himself. "Yes, I will give it him," I say, and put it in my pocket.

"You are a good child," she says, and goes away.

I wonder if he will be in church? Yes, he is there, as I discover twenty minutes later, and he gives me a friendly look as I go up the aisle behind Mrs. Fleming. That old heathen Lady Flytton never goes to church. The Buffs give me a smile or two, and I wink affectionately at Mary Burns at a favorable opportunity. In the porch outside, when the service is over, I find Mr. Vasher, which is lucky; for supposing I had been obliged to run after him?

"When are you coming back, little one!" he asks.

"Soon! To-morrow some time!" I say, flounderingly, then I thrust the note into his hand and flee.

"Did you give it him?" asks Silvia, as we are walking in the garden after luncheon.

"Yes."

"How hot it is!" she says, shrugging her shoulders; "there is a storm brewing."

She speaks truth, the morning was sultry, the afternoon is worse, the air is charged and heavy with heat, the skies are closing in black as night, the very birds have ceased singing; all creation seems to be holding its breath, awaiting one of Nature's fierce convulsions. With the same instinct that has sent all the animals to their hiding-places, I go in, leaving Silvia pacing up and down, with clasped hands, and an intent look of listening upon her face. I am not ashamed to confess it, I am horribly, terribly afraid of a thunderstorm; the dread crack of the awful, invisible hosts above always makes me shiver, and through my eyelids the lightning seems to strike and blind me. After all I must be a coward, for Jack does not mind it at all; he opens his eyes wide, and never puts his fingers in his ears. The sisters are fast asleep in a remote corner of the queer-shaped, many-angled room; every now and then a gentle snore attests their happy unconsciousness. When I am old, I dare say I shall consider it a godly and suitable employment to spend my Sabbath afternoons in slumber; being

young and broadly awake, I find the time hangs very heavily on my hands. I take a peep at "Good Words;" I look at the pictures in the "Sunday at Home;" finally I take up Lady Flytton's album, which I have indeed already explored, but still find intersting, thanks to the extraordinary unhandsomeness of her friends and relations; her defunct husband bearing the palm away from them all for general unsavoriness, imbecility, and grimace. I am just grinning at the photograph of a very short man, who has a most ferocious expression of countenance, and looks as though he were saying, "Laugh at me if you dare!" when the door opens, and Paul Vasher is announced. The sisters do not awake, and he does not see me. In another moment he is face to face with Silvia, who comes hastily through the glass door.

"You sent for me," he says, "and I have come."

"Come out into the garden," she says, abruptly.

And they go out together, along the terrace, and disappear among the trees. An hour slips away, the light fails strangely; the skies are of ink, save where a lurid-tipped cloud betokens mischief; every leaf and tree and flower stands stirless; there is not a living thing to be seen.

Steps come quickly along the terrace, and Paul Vasher comes in alone. I am half leaping up to speak to him, when something in his face checks me, and I fall back; in another moment he is gone. The closing door awakens Lady Flytton, who sits up, and asks sharply:

"Who was that just went out?"

"Mr. Vasher."

"Vasher here!" screams the old woman. "Has that little cat been up to some more of her tricks? Well, he didn't stay long!" And she composes herself to sleep again.

"Was I snoring, child?" asks Mrs. Fleming, with some anxiety.

"Not much!"

Hark! A few drops of rain, heavy

as lead, fall with a hissing sound upon the pavement; a low faint moan comes sweeping up over the land, and now, with an awful, shivering reverberation, the heavens are rent in twain, the forked lightning leaps out, the flood-gates of heaven are loosed, and the storm is upon us. I bury my head in my hands to shut out the glare of the lightning, but through the hideous discord I hear Mrs. Feming's voice ask, in sharp fear, "Where is Silvia?"

Out yonder; out in the fury and teeth of the storm, as reckless, as wild as the hurricane itself; and God only knows what depths of misery and shame she is sounding! Paul Vasher's face was not hard to read. And child as I am I know that she has played her last stake *and lost.*

In her present mood she will court death, if I know anything of her character. Some one must find her, and bring her back. But who? I will. My life out there is as much in God's hand as here; and though I do not love her, I would do this much for my worst enemy. I take my hands from my eyes, snatch up a shawl lying near, and, heedless of Mrs. Fleming's exclamations of horror, step out on to the terrace. Down comes the water-spout in its resistless strength, almost beating me to earth; blinded with lightning, deafened with thunder, bewildered by the hurly-burly, I push on, looking hither and thither, in every nook and corner, but I cannot find her. Stronger and fiercer grows the storm. At my side a tree, smitten in mid-air by an unseen hand, is whirled aloft, and hurled crashing to the ground; a rabbit struck dead by lightning lies in my path; overhead, from end to end, of heaven, echoes that long, hollow, shuddering peal that always sounds to me like the shrieks and wild laughter of lost souls in Hades. At last I come upon her, sitting under a tree, in a far-off corner, looking out at the storm as indifferently as though it were a pageant arranged for her especial amusement.

"Silvia!" I cry while yet I am a little way off, "Silvia!" But she never stirs, never lifts her head, or unclasps her hands, or seems to know my voice, while all about her lie the wrack and ruin of the wild hurricane, and a few yards away an oak struck with lightning stands bare and ghastly, stripped of its bark. I am stepping toward her, when—O my God!—the heavens above us open; a great light shines upon our faces, and, cleaving the air, there rushes toward us a great crimson ball of flame. I shut my eyes, and stand motionless: is not this death? and with a hiss and a swirl, and a burning breath that scorches my face, it smites the ground at my feet, and a great smoke belches forth, and hides everything from my eyes. Dimly I grope my way round to the other side; I am not killed, therefore Silvia must be! But there she sits looking just as she looked before the bolt fell.

"Alive and unharmed, thank God!" I cry, taking her cold hand in mine.

"If it had only killed me," she says, in a whisper, pointing her finger at the sullen flames; "if I had been only one step nearer—"

"Come away!" I say gently, and she does not resist, but lets me lead her away like a child. Her face is pale as the dead; her lovely eyes look straight before her, as though they beheld only one object; her hair hangs dank and heavy down her dripping back. An uncommonly nice couple we look as we reach the house, with pools of water running from our clothes; as beaten down and draggled as yonder poor flowers that lie with broken stalks in their churned-up beds.

Mrs. Fleming shrieks at her daughter's face—and, indeed, she might well have taken some grievous hurt out in the storm to judge by her looks—but the girl pulls herself wearily away.

"Leave me alone," she says, and goes slowly up the stairs, to the great embellishment of her aunt's carpeting, and

I follow. On the landing she turns round.

"Come into my room, by-and-by," she says.

I have slipped out of my wet clothes, and am almost attired in dry ones, when Mrs. Fleming comes in, bearing a tumbler of hot wine, which she makes me drink. It tastes very good, but surely it is rather strong.

She goes away and I proceed with my toilet; but somehow I don't seem to be quite mistress of my legs, and in crossing the room I have to tack a good deal. My ideas, too, are very hazy. I find myself surveying various articles of my attire with a benignant and fixed smile, instead of putting them on, and I am by-and-by distinctly conscious that, with no apparent volition of my own, I am standing before my looking-glass, swaying from side to side, and saying, in an indistinct voice, "My intentions is good, Jack, but my legs is weak." And after that I know nothing, save that I am blessedly, soundly asleep.

The clock is striking seven as I awake, and Mrs. Fleming is looking down on me with some anxiety.

"What does it all mean?" I say, rubbing my eyes; "I never went to sleep like this in the daytime before. Was it the thunderbolt?"

"No," says Mrs. Fleming, "I think it was the wine. I put brandy in it to keep the cold out, and forgot you were not used to it."

"And so I have been tipsy," I say, putting my hand to my head; "oh, what *would* papa say if he could see me?"

"Say it was my fault," says Mrs. Fleming, "and now, my dear, don't trouble about that; can you go to Silvia now? She has been asking for you."

"I will be ready in a minute; but, Mrs. Fleming, you will never tell any one about it, *will* you?"

"Never," she says, smiling, and goes away.

To my knock at Silvia's door, I re-

6

ceive no answer; pushing it open, I enter. She is standing by a window, looking at the smoke that rises from the spot where the bolt lies imbedded. She is talking to herself, and does not seem to see or hear me, although I am before her eyes.

"I was wrong to wish it had killed me," she mutters; "after all, it's a stupid thing to do—to die. Talk of the proud contempt of spirits risen, it is the living who have the best of it, and despise the dead. If I had died to-day, the women who hate me would have said, 'Poor creature!' *he* would have said, 'Poor Silvia.' I should have been *poor Silvia*, a weak loving fool to all eternity to him. I will live!—live to punish the scorn and coldness that has dared repay such love as mine—live to make him rue the day he made Silvia Fleming stoop to pray in vain. When he least expects me, I will be there; in the hour of his joy, I will stand by his side and strike the cup from his lips; in his night of sorrow, I will rejoice over him — and since I cannot have his love, I will work his misery—and this I will do, *so help me, God!*"

The last lurid gleam of the storm is on her set face, and in her wide eyes. Has the afternoon actually crazed her brain?

"Are you there, child?" she says, turning round sharply. "Have you heard all the nonsense I have been talking?"

"Some of it."

"Bah!" she says; "I have a bad habit of talking aloud. You were a good little thing to come out and find me like that; it would not have been pleasant to be killed by that bolt, eh?"

"No," I say, shuddering, "but it was very near, a narrow escape. Have you told Mrs. Fleming?"

"Not I! How that old woman, my aunt, would have hopped, if she had seen it all! That red thing coming through the air, you and I with our mouths wide open, at least yours was—" She goes off into a fit of laughter, that does not strike me as being particularly seemly.

"You can go now," she says; "will you send my mother up to me?"

Truly Silvia Fleming has somewhat odd manners. Down in the drawing-room I find the sisters looking out of a window at the desolation of the garden, and, having delivered my message to Mrs. Fleming, proceed to inform Lady Flytton of the shave we had, to which she listens with many upliftings of her hands and exclamations.

"And all that little cat's fault," she says. "Whatever will your mother say, when she hears that I took so little care of you? As to that Silvia, it's my belief that she is being saved up for something worse!"

CHAPTER XX.

"A heat full of coldness; a sweet full of bitters; a pain full of pleasantness which maketh thoughts have eyes and hearts and ears; bred by desire, nursed by delight, weaned by jealousy, killed by dissembling, turned by iogratitude—and this is love."

"I WONDER if Paul will come to-night?" says Mr. Frere, stirring the fire with a recklessness highly reprehensible in a godly man during these days of greedy coal merchants and champagne-drinking colliers.

It is rainy October now, and the nights are cold and frosty, and, without, Mother Earth is drawing the flowers, her darlings, down into her brown breast, as Hans Andersen tells us, away from the Frost-King's breath, which strikes chilly against the tender green stalks and late-tarrying fuchsias, myrtles, and magnolias.

"I don't think he is coming back at all!" I say, nodding; "he has been gone such a long, long time, you know—weeks!"

"Paul always keeps his word," says

Mr. Frere. "He is sure to come back. Besides, he left all his things here." That is conclusive, for, however heart-broken a man may be, he does not usually forget his dressing-case and his little comforts.

"The ground is good for walking just now," says Mr. Frere. "I dare say he has got as far as Devonshire."

Yes, the ground is good for walking, but I think all roads are pretty much alike to him just now. As I sit staring into the fire, I seem to see Mr. Vasher walking swift and fast, trying to escape from his restless thoughts; trying to quench a flame that will not be put out. Pshaw! Probably I see a myth and a fallacy, and at this very moment he is dancing a jig or—

"Are you asleep?" asks a cheerful voice behind me.

"You have come back!" I cry, starting up; "how glad I am! We were beginning to think you were lost!"

As the firelight falls on his face I see that it is pale and worn as that of a man who has fought a battle against fierce odds, and, though wounded and hard pressed in the conflict—won.

"Where is my uncle?" he says, looking round.

"He was here a minute ago, but Mrs. Pim fetched him to go to Sally Lane, who says she is dying."

"I wonder how long she will be about it?"

"She has been dying for twenty years," I say, laughing, "and she will probably be dying for twenty more! Dying with her means port."

"Does my uncle give her a bottle to soothe her last moments?"

"Always! About once a month, you know; and she is far too careful a body to go off until she has drunk the last drop; then the thought of the next bottle supports her."

Mr. Vasher laughs. "Do you know," he says, "that I have missed you, child, during these past weeks? Over and over again I have wished I had your saucy chatter to listen to. What have you been doing with yourself—anything particular?"

"Something very particular," I say, solemnly, "or at least—almost. It is a miracle you do not find Miss Fleming's pieces and mine laid out in baskets."

"What do you mean?" he asks sharply. "You have been in danger—and Silvia?"

"It was a thunderbolt," I explain; "she and I were only a few yards apart, and it fell between us."

"And you were out in the storm that day, you two?"

"I went to look for Silvia, she was out in it."

"Did she not come in after I left?"

"No!"

"Good Heavens!" he cries, striking his head with his clinched fist. "What a brute I was! Where is she now?"

"At Homburg."

"I wonder what she is doing?" he says, half to himself.

"Flirting!" I answer, almost before I know what I am saying; I have an unhappy knack of blurting out the thought that is uppermost in my mind.

"What makes you think so, child?" he asks, turning quickly to me.

"I did not mean to say that, Mr. Vasher. I was only thinking."

"And your opinion of her?" he says, looking at me. "I always like to have a very young person's opinion about another—it is always true; what is it?"

"She is young," I say, thoughtfully, "and well-born and rich and beautiful, and—I am sorry for her."

"Sorry!" he says, looking at me keenly, "and why are you sorry? What more does she want?"

"She is not happy," I say, turning my head away that he may not see how red my face is. If he only knew that I know the whole story, that I have been an eavesdropper!

"You have not told me what you think of her," he says; "I want an answer."

"I am not fond of her," I say, slowly.

"I would not trust her; she is rather cruel, but she could love well—"

"And never be faithful," says Paul. "Well! you will be a woman some day, little one; shall I give you some advice? But no, you would not take it; you will fall in love like the rest, some day!"

"And why should I not?" I ask; "everybody does!"

"Love," he says, "is made up of vanity and vexation, folly and bitterness; it turns to dust between the teeth."

"Your creed is a hard one," I say. "Now, I have seen some lovers" (I think of Alice and Charles) "who never have any of that; they are fair in each other's eyes, and, though they squabble sometimes, they never think of using any of those long words you do; they positively would not understand them."

"Perhaps they are worthy of each other," he says. "When two people trust one another, then their love is a pleasant thing, a jewel. But if a man loves a woman, and she proves unworthy, and he loves her still, cannot you guess something of the battle that is fought in that man's soul—the higher nature crying, 'Desist!' the lower, 'Yield!' The indomitable will and self-respect of the man fighting against the quenchless, passionate longing after the beauty of the woman he renounces . . . the integrity of the mind warring against the heart that rises in fierce revolt against such sacrifices . . . the lily of renunciation against the crimson blossom of love . . . and the crowning sin and shame if it all must be that, while he knows her worthlessness, he cannot forget her—her sweet words and ways . . . her veil of rippling hair, her clinging lips . . . in these memories must lie that man's chief tortures. . . ."

He passes his hand impatiently over his forehead and starts up. "Forgive me, child," he says, "I have been thinking aloud. Does my psychological study interest you? Poor devil! I hope he may reach the shore, don't you? A past error thoroughly repented of is the best basis for future good conduct! Can I take any message to Silverbridge for you to-morrow, little one?"

"You are going there?" I say, clasping my hands. "Oh! can you not put me in your pocket? Shall you stay long?"

"Only a couple of days. I am going abroad afterward; and when I come back you will be a grown-up young lady."

"Worse luck!" I say, dolefully. "I should like to put off 'tails' for another ten years!"

"Tell me," he says, leaning forward and taking my face in his hands, "how old are you?"

"Fourteen!"

"So much? you look about twelve; you have a dear little face, and a sweet— But I won't say I hope you will be pretty when I come back! If ever you pray heartily for anything, child, pray that you may never grow up beautiful."

"There is not much fear!" I say, ruefully. "I don't think any amount of praying would mend matters!"

"If you are good," he says, "that is all you want, and I think you will be."

"People like one so much better when one is pretty than when one is plain," I say, meditatively. "Plain people get all the leavings. Might not one be good and pretty too?"

"They might, but they very seldom are! No; when I come back, child, I hope I shall find you just as you are now."

"May I not grow, sir?"

"Grow as much as you please, child; but don't grow out of honesty!"

CHAPTER XXI.

" At Christmas I no more desire a rose
Than wish a snow in May's new-fangled
shows,
But like of each thing that in season grows."

CHRISTMAS has come with his garment of snow and crown of holly and icicles, with his jolly red face and lavishly-filled hands, and he has abode with us a little space, wielding his sceptre royally at feast and wassail; but now that the poor old year, the friend out of which he grew, is dying, and the new one in all its pride and pomp is dawning, he sweeps away from us sorrowfully, and we see his face no more. Jack and I, home for the holidays, have been very literally obeying the golden mandate that bids mankind "gather ye roses while ye may," and we have eaten plum-pudding and Christmas cates galore, reaping the punishment of our unholy gluttony in aches and pains that we have had to take upon our backs and bear in silence, venturing on no complaint; for in the somewhat unique rules of our family there is a stringent one— "Thou shalt not be sick." Ill or well, faint, pain-stricken or bilious, in our places at table we must appear; and if unkind Nature, refusing to be tutored, makes our faces pale and anxious, by angry looks and words are we made to feel the shamelessness and iniquity of our conduct. If either of us has a bout of real illness that refuses to be knocked on the head in deference to the governor's will, the culprit is placed under the ban of an awful and crushing displeasure below-stairs, that person's name is never mentioned, and when the convalescent makes his appearance in public, white and attenuated, his presence is ignored; he is considered to have disgraced himself past all forgiveness. To call in Æsculapius is a dangerous and most ticklish proceeding, and only ventured on in a case of extreme emergency; he knows his peril, and comes with reluctance and departs with alacrity. All things considered, we have had rather a stormy time of it lately. Over and above the perpetual little disasters that will occur in so tightly-managed a household (for every one knows that human nature if squeezed in at one place will burst out in another), the long-expected difficulty about Alice's and Charles's matrimonial affairs has appeared upon the scene. The six months of probation having expired, Captain Lovelace has pressed for a formal engagement, and hinted at a wedding-day, only to be met with contumely and dismissed with insult and mockery. He does not come here now—his place knows him no more, and the rebellious look on my sister's lovely face brings her many a bitter word and hard sneer; but outwardly, at least, she acquiesces in her lot, and says no word on the subject, good, bad, or indifferent. She is growing very thin, our pretty Alice. It might move any man's heart to see how her face pales day by day, how slender her little wrists and waist are. But papa never heeds, never looks; he lays hard burdens upon his children, and does not touch them with so much as the tip of his finger. I think we would deal him out greater mercy than he deals us.

Although I was so faithful a gooseberry to Alice, she never speaks of Charles Lovelace to me. ' Often I come upon her and Milly in close confabulation, and feel unreasonably vexed; for, after all, is not Milly sixteen, and old enough to understand, while I am but fourteen, and supposed to know nothing whatever on the subject of love and courtship? Ah! they don't know I have got a sweetheart too! That is a secret. I am a good deal puzzled by Miss Alice; I thought her so plucky, and good for any amount of fighting. Can she be going to "lay her down and dee" without a protest? On this point I am speedily disabused, making, in fact, a discovery so astounding and petrifying, that for a while I feel as though some one had rapped me on the head smartly and then run away, leaving me to recover as best I might.

It is in this wise. Diving under Alice and Milly's bed one day, after a slippery vagrant orange, I discover the ample space beneath the huge old four-poster to be filled with packed and corded trunks—Alice's all, from the imperial down to the bonnet-box.

Is she going away? She has nowhere to go to. An awful .thought strikes me, and I sit down on the floor, valance in hand, to follow it up. Can she be going to *run away?* She has no money. Ah! but Charles Lovelace has, and I read of a couple the other day who, after wasting away apart for six months, ran away and got married, and became fat directly. But then their governors weren't a patch upon ours! Alice never can be meditating anything so desperate as *that.*

As I sit ruminating, she herself comes in and sits down opposite me—a charming figure in her winter gown of dark blue, with the snowy Quakerish kerchief and apron of muslin.

"Alice," I say, lifting the valance and pointing at the assemblage of boxes, "are you *going away?*"

She looks at me, considering.

"I did not want you to know, Nell," she says, "but as you have found it out it can't be helped. I am going to be married."

"Married!" I repeat; "O Alice!"

She looks such a child, as she sits yonder, to wear a wedding-ring on her finger and be called Mrs., and order the dinner.

"It is all his fault," she says, nodding toward a distant field where we can see the governor harrying his work-people; "there is nothing else to be done!"

There is a clouded, sorrowful look in her blue eyes; lovely bits of color that *savants* say are becoming year by year more rare, the dark brown and slate slowly, but surely, hustling the saucy azure off the human countenance.

"Charles says it would have gone on like this forever, and that we may as well get it over now as in a year's time. If I staid here much longer, Nell, I should *die!*"

"Dear love!" I say, jumping up and running to her. "Well, it will be wretched without you, disgusting" (the tears trickle down my cheeks); "but I am not sorry, for you will be happy, dear! But, Alice, Alice—*papa!*"

"His capers, you mean?"

"He will kill us!" I say, with conviction. "Do not ever expect to receive any account of what happens after you leave, for there will not be one man left to tell the tale! You may look in the *Times* for the following announcement: 'At Silverbridge, the wife and eleven children of Colonel Adair, the sad result of domestic circumstances over which he had no control.'"

"Indeed, I do think of you all very much," says Alice; "it makes me very miserable."

"Don't fret, dear; we have weathered storms enough, and why not that? When are you going?"

"To-morrow!"

"O Alice! And you are going to Mr. Skipworth's to-night?"

"Yes; that was why we fixed to-morrow. Charles's man is going to get all the boxes out of the house, and Tabitha is going to help him."

"And would you have gone without telling me?" I ask, putting my arms round her neck, and raining down a steady drip of tears on to her pretty head.

"I should have wished you good-by, dear, but I did not mean to tell you, for fear he should ask you all round afterward, if you knew anything."

"Milly knows?"

"Yes."

"And mother?"

"Good Heavens, *no!* How shall I ever say good-by to her? She will see you have been crying, Nell."

"Do you think you will ever come back?" I ask, piteously. "Do you think you will go away forever?"

"No, no," she says; "we will come and see you at school, Charles and I, next half, and we shall stay somewhere near here, so as to see mother. Besides, sooner or later, it will be made up."

"Never!" I say, shaking my miserable head; "he will never forgive you for getting out of his clutches."

"Alice!" calls mother in the distance,

and with a warm hug and kiss she goes away.

"You *do* look a beauty!" says Jack, meeting me half an hour later. "Have you torn your last remaining frock to ribbons?"

"Preserved gooseberries," I say, determined to put as bold a face upon matters as I can; "they were very sour, you know, and they made my stomach ache, and I howled."

"Well, I never knew you to cry about such a trifle as *that* before," he says, loftily.

I should like to tell him, but I must not. Eight o'clock has struck. The governor and mother, Alice and Milly, set out for the parsonage an hour ago; scarcely within our memory has he been known to spend an evening out, but to-night he has really gone. It is to be hoped Charles's man and Tabitha will do their spiriting gently, and not be caught. I wonder if Charles Lovelace is wandering about among the flower-beds, keeping watch? We have supper, Amberly, Jack, Dolly, Alan, and I. I am just thinking of retiring to my couch, there to indulge in a good, comfortable roar, when Dolly appears bearing a small and elaborately-folded note, which she hands to me: "*I challenge you to a bolstering match.—*JACK." Now, if there is one thing on earth I love more than another, it is a hearty, no-quarter-given bolstering match round the house with Jack, and it is a treat I very seldom get, thanks to the governor's barnacle-like habit of sticking at home. To-night is a splendid opportunity, we are never likely to get such another; but with to-morrow's event impending over me, and with my heavy heart holding me down, I doubt if I should be able to give Jack those vigorous whacks to which he is accustomed, so I take a sheet of paper, write on it, "*Can't. I'm ill.—*NELL," and fold it as elaborately as his. Dolly goes away with it, but quickly returns with another. "*You are afraid; you ate enough supper* *for six.*—JACK;" to which I make answer, "*I ain't! I didn't! Come on,*" and then prepare for the conflict. I take off my dress and upper petticoats and shoes, put on my nightgown, tuck the sleeves well up over my arms; then, selecting my stoutest and strongest pillow, I sling it over my back and sally forth. The dimly-lit passage is empty, but I creep warily along, keeping a keen eye to right and left, for behind yonder chest the foe may lurk, or from out yonder half-shut door he may suddenly spring; and, if I am not prepared with my weapon, whack! upon my defenseless head will come a blow, heavy in proportion to the skill of the hand that aims it. Gingerly then I go, breathless with expectation, every nerve strung to its highest pitch; but the foe does not appear, and I am just wondering whether he is lazy or meditating a dishonorable attack from the rear, when, whir! from the oriel window comes a swift, well-directed blow that would smite me to earth did I not catch it midway with my pillow, which meets the other in a sounding crack that reverberates through the house. Now the engagement is opened, the exchange of compliments is brisk, and ducking, dodging, slashing, backing, retreating, advancing, we have a hand-to-hand encounter, until Amberley appears at the top of the stairs, candlestick in hand, meek, scandalized, open-mouthed. Down the corridor I flee, Jack in hot pursuit, showering liberal blows on my vanishing tail; past Amberly, who, being in the line of battle, receives a blow intended for my worthless back, which smites the candlestick from her hand and flattens her, a heap of ruins, against the wall; down the stairs like a flash of lightning; through the nurseries like a clap of thunder, where the nurse cries "Shame!" and the youngsters, "Go it!" out on the other side, down the lower staircase, across the hall into the dining-room . . . . but where is Jack? He was at my heels a moment ago; now he is neither to be heard nor seen . . . . Is he listening at the door, or creeping up behind me? The room is in total darkness, save for a tiny stream that shows under the half-opened door from the hall-lamp. I wonder what all that commotion in the hall is about? Can Jack have run against Simpkins in his pursuit, and upset the old thing? He is sure to be here in a minute . . . . I mount a chair behind the door . . . . As he comes in I will deal him a blow that will make him wink. Footsteps are approaching; he is coming . . . . I grasp my bolster convulsively, the door opens, and, bang! with all the strength of my body and soul, I bring it down on the head of—Jack? Scarcely. Does Jack swear like a trooper, and dance like a dervish? Does Jack rush madly hither and thither, vowing when he catches me to "break every bone in my skin?" My heart sinks like lead, the bolster drops from my limp fingers, my feet are glued to the chair, as the awful conviction strikes me that I have been bolstering *the governor!* Some instinct of self-preservation, as he comes near me in his furious search, makes me leave my perch and dodge him swiftly and noiselessly round and round. Finally, watching my opportunity, I bolt out of the door just as William appears with candles, shoot past him like a meteor, and am up the stairs before you could say "Jack Robinson." Papa, dashing out in hot pursuit, butts head foremost into the out-stretched arms of the footman, and they roll over and over and over, master, man, candles and all. A confused sound as of Wombwell's menagerie ascends to my ears, as I fly past the maids and fry who are hanging over the stairs anxiously watching the march of events, and, having locked myself into my chamber, I sit down on the side of my bed with my eyes fixed upon the door, expecting it every moment to fly asunder and admit my executioner. But, though I hear terrible sounds of devastation and fury in the distance, the minutes pass, and still he comes not. After a while, therefore, I am able to draw a deep breath, and contemplate the fact of my being still alive without any particular amazement.

By-and-by a gentle knock comes at the door. "Who is it?" I ask, trembling. Perhaps it is only a trick of my outraged parent?

"Me," says Jack's voice. Why will people persist in believing that "me" is known to everybody and requires no bush? I open the door and let him in, lock it again, then turn round and face him.

"*You sneak!*" I say, slowly; "you took good care to hide yourself, didn't you? And you took good care not to warn me, didn't you? *I'm ashamed of you!*"

"That's just like a girl," says Jack, sitting down. "Stow your heroics a bit, and listen to me. I followed you as far as the hall, and half-way across I caught my foot in a beast of a mat, and went head foremost. When I picked myself up you had vanished, and I was just wondering whether you had gone into the library or the dining-room, when a ring came at the front-door bell; and I had hardly got behind Venus, when in walked the governor! Quarreled with Skippy, I suppose, or yearned for his family; at any rate, *there he was*. He went into the dining-room, and the next thing I heard was a fearful *whack!* then noise enough to lift the hair from one's head. Then out you rushed, the governor at your heels, and bang he went into William's arms, and over they went. Oh! shall I ever forget it?" He stuffs a corner of the sheet into his mouth and rolls. "The candles were squashed as flat as pancakes, and the governor, only too glad to vent his rage on somebody, pommeled William like mad, who was underneath and offered no resistance, merely saying, 'Don't, sir! don't, sir! don't, sir!' without stopping for a single moment. I was behind Venus all the time, and I shook so that I nearly knocked the poor soul over. By the time the governor had

finished off William, Amberley appeared, bleating. The governor soon squashed her into a jelly; and, after shaking his fist at your door, and muttering darkly about to-morrow, he stormed himself into the library."

"Jack," I say, in a voice that I try hard to make "don't-carish," "do you—do you think he will *kill* me?"

"No," says Jack, judicially, "because he knows he would be hung if he did; but, if he was sure he wouldn't be, he'd do it like a shot! It's going rather far with him, you know, to bolster him!"

I shudder. Has this wretched hand of mine really dealt him a smashing blow on the head? Perhaps it will wither up.

"What a mercy it is there is a gallows in this country! I say, with a sigh. "It is such a protection!"

"Hard words break no bones," says Jack, cheerfully, "and he won't whip you, you're too big! Don't bother, Nell," he says, putting his arm round my shoulders; "you shall come and live with me some day, and we'll be as jolly as sand-boys."

"Dear old fellow!" I say, rubbing my miserable face against his cool red and white one. "You'll sit next to me at breakfast to-morrow, *won't you?*"

"All right," he says, and presently gives me a hug, and goes away.

Oh, if only to-morrow would never come! If I might go to sleep now, this minute, and not wake up again for five years! Papa would surely have forgotten then. If time would only step over breakfast, even, I should be safe; for by dinner-time Alice's elopement will be known, and the one overpowering fact will have cast all other misdemeanors into the shade. But, despite prayer and longing, the cold gray dawn comes at last. Groaning, I rise and attire myself for the slaughter. As in a dream, I go down-stairs and listen to prayers, and then —I will not write down the details of that breakfast. I must be a hardened sinner, indeed, for when it is over my spirit is not broken, nor my hair gray. I am even able to reflect with complacency on the fact that I still possess my full complement of arms, legs, teeth, etc.; for at one time I trembled for each and all of these valuables. And now I am watching Alice put on her cloak and hat. She is very pale, very trembling, but she does not cry; and when she is dressed, she goes into mother's room and kisses her, saying she is going to church.

Ay! she is going "to church," whence she will come out Alice Lovelace, and not Alice Adair—never our own pretty Alice any more. As this thought strikes me, I give a loud sob outside the door, which makes her turn apprehensively; so I cram my handkerchief into my mouth, and choke inwardly. And now we are walking with her across the sodden grass of the dismal, bare garden, toward the postern gate, where Charles Lovelace waits with a traveling-carriage and grays.

"Good-by," she says, looking into our faces and weeping passionately. Tears do not matter now; there are no more appearances to be kept up.

"Good-by," say Milly and I, weeping too, but with a difference. Through her present sorrow the gay bright future looks; we know what *we* are going back to.

"Good-by," says Charles Lovelace, kissing our dripping countenances.

"Good-by, good-by!" cries Alice, clinging about our necks in turn.

And now she is in the carriage, the valet jumps into the rumble and they are off, Alice's lovely pale face looking out of the window to the very last moment, away, away, through the cold winter morning. A couple of hundred yards away, papa is walking about, happy in the comfortable belief that he holds all our lives in his own hand, and that he can mete us out happiness or misery, according to his sovereign will. Well, one at least of his white slaves has turned a rebel; he will know it by twelve of the clock, and then—

"Dilly, Dilly, Dilly, come and be killed," I say to Milly as we go heavily back to the house. "After all, we can only be killed *once!*"

SUMMER.

CHAPTER I.

"LEAR. So young and so untender?
CORDELIA. So young, my lord, and true."

I AM eighteen years old. It sounds a good deal, does it not? It seems only yesterday that I was quite little, scrambling about in short frocks and leaving bits of the same on every railing, hedge, and gate the place contains: now I am in "tails," real downright tails; limited, it is true, as to length and width, but, still tails which come in useful when I want to snub Dorley or the boys; but, on the other hand, hamper me sadly when some forlorn remnant of my active youth prompts me to scale the trees, or go bird's-nesting. On the whole I am sorry to have reached that broad flat table-land of grown-upness that is so easy to ascend, but can be stepped down from never again. If one's young days might only be pushed farther, if we might be given thirty years of growing instead of sixteen, surely the forty beyond, that are allotted as the period of man's existence, would be enough for us to be grown-up, and steady, and sad in. I hate to part with my merry *insouciant* young years. I dread to let them go, and feel the old tastes and loves slipping away from me, and the new fancies and pursuits taking their place. I am sorry that I shall never grow any more—never measure my back against the schoolroom wall to see if my head is any nearer the notch that marks Jack's height—never look anxiously in the glass to see if Time brings me less ugliness as he brings more inches (for at

eighteen one is able to form a pretty tolerable estimate of what one is going to be like for the rest of one's days)—never go donkey-riding, or pig-nut-hunting, or shrimp-getting, any more—never love bulls'-eyes, blackberries, and treacle-tarts with the exceeding love that I knew for them of yore. I can even get over a gate without feeling my over-mastering impulse to vault or leap it. I can see Pepper taking an ecstatic roll in the grass without straightway longing to cast myself down and roll too. The kitchen-garden has lost some of its charm in my eyes, for, thanks to my being so old, other affairs than gooseberries and currants occupy my mind, very much against my will. I am the eldest daughter at home now, and obliged to mind my morals and manners to a maddening extent; for every sin of omission and commission of my brothers and sisters is laid to my charge, and said to be the fruit of my "example." It is dismal at the Manor House now so many are away. Jack is in London. He is going to be a barrister, and I call it *mean* of him; for if he had only elected to be a fat gentleman farmer, I could have gone and lived with him in a little house, and been as happy— Well! brothers never love their sisters quite as their sisters love them.

Milly has been "woo'd an' married an' a'" over a year and a half, and the family has not done gasping over the miraculous event yet. How it fell out that papa's unwilling consent was wrung from him; and how she never ran away at all, but stood up to be married, in a white-satin gown and trimmings; and how papa gave her away with an ineffable hitch of his nose; and how up to the very last moment every one believed that he did not mean her to be married at all, but intended to turn the whole affair into a joke; and how he disappointed us all, as he always does—are not these things writ in the chronicles of the house of Adair?

After so far forgetting himself as to make two people happy, he gave it to be understood in the family that nothing else of the kind would be permitted to take place for another century or so, and that this lapse of authority on his part was not to be taken as a precedent, but regarded in the light of a comet, a plague, or any other irresponsible appearance for which there is no accounting. About two years ago Alice was formally forgiven, and invited' to stay here, with her little son; but the sight of her perfect liberty of speech and action, the amplitude of her petticoats, the abundance of her pin-money, were too much for him, and the flag of truce came down with a run. If the governor could put his thoughts into rhyme, I think he would say:

"Oh! while my daughters with me staid,
    Would I had *whacked* them more!"

It must be hard to know that they have got safely out of his clutches; and that he may have nothing in the future to reproach himself with on my account, he makes my existence an uncommonly pleasant thing. Sometimes I feel that I must run away, or that it would be better to marry anything than live the life I lead. Common-sense, however, whispers that a spinster's troubles are but passing ones; but, once married, she must sit down under her misfortunes, and bear them to her life's end. For married folks have their troubles—have they not?—just like single ones. Oh! what a black, bitter hour that must be, when a woman lifts her eyes, and looking at her husband, sitting opposite her, realizes for the first time that she

has made *a mistake!* "Men," says Madame Scudéri, "should keep their eyes wide open before marriage, and half shut after." Surely women may very safely say the same?

I wonder why I have fallen on the subject of matrimony this afternoon? I am wandering alone through the garden, bright with its late July pomp of geraniums and verbenas, and across the orchard into the wide, hot fields. There is no shade anywhere, but my big sunbonnet is tipped over my nose, so I may defy sunstroke; and in "my mind's hi," as I once heard a man, of more worth than letters, remark, I see a cool, shady, green little chamber, of which the ceiling is woven branches, and the carpet of mossy grass, while the walls are made of the sturdy brown bodies of the oak and the beech. It is not far away, but it is shut in so deftly that a stranger might pass it by close and never see it, though he went through the field of rye that stretches out to its left in a whitely ruffled sea of light. "After all, " I say to myself, as I turn out of the last big field into a cool, shady alley through which a brook runs, "what does it matter if the governor *is* troublesome? He can't take away any of God's gifts from us; and all the tempers and hard words in creation could not take the glow out of this summer afternoon, or the color out of the sky, no, never!"

Thus moralizing, I sit down by the brook to rest for a moment before sallying forth into the sun-flooded fields of grain; and it seems to answer "Never!" as it hurries along over the clear stones, not knowing when it is well off, sighing to lose itself in the wide river. Its babble sounds very pretty, as though it were talking to the fragrant meadowsweet that borders its banks like foam, or the yellow milfoil that Jack and I call ladies'-slippers —a frivolous substitute for the grand old name of lotus, of which there are three species, and this common, unbeautiful yellow is one. Lotus! What an exquisite name it is! and what exquisite visions it brings up before us! The river is a rare sun-worshiper: almost all his flowers are either yellow or gold-colored: look at those brazen marigolds yonder, and those handsome irises a yard away; and farther down, where he deepens into a mimic lake, lie more yellow flowers, great, sleepy, languid lilies, to do him honor and deck his breast. It is a relief to look away at the forget-me-nots, with their innocent, candid eyes, that look straight into mine, saying as plain as they can speak, "Do not forget me!"

A bee-orchis lifts itself out of the hedge, straight and tall, with its absurd resemblance to the insect, as though it had alighted freshly on the flower, and been frozen there, retaining its exquisite colors. The hollyhocks, "emblem of cruelty and pride," stand stiff and stately. I wonder if ever at night their speckled bells ring out a dainty peal of music learned in Hollyhock land? The reed-mace stand round, tall and bare: with their long stalks and olive-brown spikes, they look too obstinate to shiver and shake; yet a curse lies upon them—for was not one of their number placed in the Victim's hand in direst mockery as a sceptre? Yonder, in the pale-blue blossoms of the ivy-leaved bell-flower, lies a naughty, sleepy little insect which Linnæus named Florissimus, from its love of sleeping in flowers. He must be a luxurious, dainty little Sybarite and a happy, to be able to choose his couch of red, white, pink, or blue, at will; while we, poor mortals, have to seek our dull four-posters night after night.

I pick up my sun-bonnet, put it on, and lean over the stile that lies between me and the cornfield, that is turning brighter and more golden day by day under the sun's fierce beams. The scarlet poppyheads, gorgeous vagrants, with their leaves as freshly crinkled as though they had but just left Nature's laundry, nod imperiously at me, saying, "Gather me! gather me!" The corn-cockle, pride of the harvest-field, and abomination of the farmer, cries, "I am handsomest, pick me!" The field-knautis lifts her insolent head high above the corn, seeming to say, "See how much higher a parasite can climb than her master!" The pheasant's-eye, or the flower of Adonis (over which, as the story runs, the life-blood of Adonis gushed, staining its white petals crimson), looks up invitingly; the pansies, "three faces under one hood," as the country-folk call them, from their lowly seat at the roots of the corn, please the eye with their modest, velvet-eyed beauty. And, since I know and love them every one, I dash in among the corn and gather my hands full. A scentless, bright-hued, vagabond cluster they make; for they are but saucy parasites, that love to creep about and hamper the knees of the strong, beneficent grain, as all useless, gaudy things ever do about the stalwart and brave. Already the scarlet pimpernel—the only wild flower that dares dispute the poppy's preëminence in color, has closed its leaves, for it is past three o'clock. I wonder how it always knows the time so exactly, when human people's watches are so often out of gear? The intolerable heat stops my somewhat unreasonable speculations, so I hastily retreat to the brook, and there weave my flowers into a garland, with many a nodding grass and leaf between, idly, carelessly, for no other reason than that my hands are idle and the flowers are pretty playthings. When I have finished it I turn it round and round and marvel whether Ophelia's could by any possibility have looked any madder? Poor lost Ophelia!—

" Larded all with sweet flowers
Which bewept to the grave did go,
With true-love showers "—

whose drowned face comes to us so freshly across the dead centuries, while the echo of her sweet voice singing, "Lord, we know what we are; but we know not what we may be," lives in our hearts with all our household words and treasures. I always think of Ophelia as a slender maiden, with far-away, dreamy, gray eyes, that saw Death beckoning to her, in strange and lovely guise, down among the rushes, and to whom she went gayly decked with flowers, as a bride to her bridegroom. I wonder if Ophelia had long hair, and whether it was golden, or yellow, or brown like mine? It ought to have been yellow — every woman should be fair, every man should be dark, in my opinion. I don't think many young women could drown themselves with decency nowadays; their locks are not ample enough, unless eked out with pilferings from the impecunious living and helpless dead. And if they tied any false curls and tails on for the occasion, it would somewhat take the edge off our pity to see the hapless maiden lying in one place, and her back hair in another. We Adairs are well off in the respect of head-coverings, rather too well off, in fact; for in hot weather our abundant manes are no joke, and we are inclined to envy our more lightly-crowned neighbors who appear at church in chignons that are the most innocent of deceptions, and provoke mirth, not admiration. Only last Sunday, a disastrous casualty occurred to a farmer's wife sitting in the pew exactly before us. Her chignon parted its moorings, and, suspended by a single wisp, hung down her back and over our pew, bobbing up and down in a horribly active manner, causing lively fear in our ranks; for in the too probable event of its falling into our midst, who among us would be found to possess sufficient *aplomb* to hand it to the denuded lady?

I pull off my sun-bonnet, for no one is likely to see me, and the cows yonder will tell no tales; and, putting my wreath upon my head, bend over the brook to try and see my own reflection. Close to the edge there is a little shallow, fenced about with sticks and stones, and in it I see my face, framed in its poppy-wreath and loose veil of brown hair.

"Not bad!" I say aloud. "Now if your nose were a little longer, and your mouth a little smaller, you wouldn't be an ill-looking young person, as girls go; but as it is, you are precisely what your amiable papa says—you are the—"

"Prettiest little girl in Christendom," says a man's voice behind me, making me start so violently that I nearly topple over into the brook.

"Did I not tell you," I say, without turning my head, "that I was tired to death of the very sight of you; and that you were not to come near me for three whole days?"

"The three whole days will be up to-morrow, Nell."

"To-morrow is not to-day," I say, turning round. "Now I wonder what you would say, if you were followed everywhere by a tiresome, teasing shadow, that never left you alone for a single moment, and the more you told it to go away the more it stopped?"

"Everybody has a shadow," he says, "I among the rest."

"Does your shadow make love to you?" I ask, stamping my foot on the soft grass. "Whether you will or not, does it?"

"No, it does not," he says, shortly. "Go on, Nell; don't be afraid of hurting my feelings!"

"Then you should not worry me so. Now I have had quite a little holiday the last two days, and of course you have come this afternoon to spoil it all! If you would only talk to me sensibly, as Jack does—"

"Only I am not Jack," he says—"worse luck. You would like me if I were."

"I like you now," I say, quickly; "next to mother, and the rest of them, I do not know any one I like so well. Why can't you be satisfied with that?"

"Nell," says the young man, standing before me, straight and tall and fair in the sunlight, with a vexed look in his blue eyes, and restless fingers that tug at his yellow mustache, "what did you promise me four years ago?"

"That when I was eighteen and six months old I would marry you, if I had not seen any one I liked better."

"And you are going to break your promise?"

"No," I say, looking up into his honest face. "Did I not tell you once that I never broke my promises? But you must give me time, George; you must not hurry me. I am not very old yet, you know; and love isn't easy to learn all at once. I wouldn't promise you anything I did not mean to stick to; but if I said to-day that I loved you, and would marry you, it would be wrong, for I do not think I am the least in the world in love with you, do you?"

"No," he says, with a rueful sigh, "there can't be very much doubt on that score!"

"So," I say, with alacrity, "I will wait till I am in love with you before we settle it all. Don't you think it would be much pleasanter?"

"For you, perhaps," he says, "but I know my own heart."

"Do you know," I say, diffidently, "that sometimes I think you don't go the right way to work to make me love you? If you were to be cross sometimes, or— or shake me—or something—I don't exactly know what. Perhaps if you made me jealous now, for a girl hates any one else to have her lover, even if she does not want him herself, you know—"

I pause. After all it is not easy to instruct a young man how to woo you; but I am so really anxious to fall in love with George, and so sorry for him, that I would take any pains to cultivate the gentle passion.

"I don't think you meant that," says George, with as much scorn as his manly, pleasant voice will borrow; "or if you did, I can't follow you. I know there are women who don't care a rap for a man as long as he is entirely their own, but directly he turns up his nose at them they are head over heels in love with him; but I never thought you were one of that sort, Nell. Now, when a man loves a girl he doesn't like her any the better, I can tell you, for staring at and hankering after this man and that. All her value is gone in his eyes if she does not stick to him in thought, word, and deed. Her flirtations with any one else provoke disgust, not love; and she makes him feel not so much piqued as *small*."

"And that a man hates to look," I say slyly. "Touch any man's or woman's self-conceit, and they never forgive you!"

"It is not self-conceit," he says, stoutly; "it is self-respect."

"I wish you were not so honest a man," I say, looking at him wistfully; "perhaps if you were not so good I should like you better."

I wonder what it is that George lacks, and which holds me back from acknowledging him lover and master? He is the best-bred, best-mannered, best-grown man I ever saw; he is likable, true, admirable in every way; and if he does not find favor in my eyes, it is hard to say who will. And yet I feel that I could love— ay, and well too, when the right man came, but I may never meet my Prince Charming, and as years go by dawdle into a comfortable, safe, friendly affection for my yellow-haired lover yonder. Perhaps if we had begun with "a little aversion" it might have been more hopeful, our exchange of words would have been heartier, brisker. In squabbles there is some heat, and I always think the people who quarrel the most fiercely love each other best; they must have power to move each other, or they would not bandy so many useless words.

Long ago I took off my poppy-wreath, and now I am swinging it slowly backward and forward.

"George," I say, looking at him thoughtfully, "were you ever very wicked?"

"Why?"

"Nothing," I say; "only to be wicked gives experience. I have heard experience is nice, is it not?"

"That depends on the sort a man gets."

"Did any one ever jilt you?" I ask. "Have you ever made love to any one before me?"

The young man looks at me with a queer kind of half shame on his face.

"And if I had," he asks, "would you mind?"

"I should be delighted!" I say, quickly. "If you had made love to people, and been thrown overboard, you know, and people had made love to you, you would be so much better qualified to make love to me! I should like to have a lover who had been in love hundreds of times, but considered me the nicest and liked me the best of all! That would be something to be proud of, would it not?"

"You don't understand about these things, dear," he says, sadly. "If you cared for me you would wish to be the first girl I had ever loved. You would grudge those other women having known me before you did."

"I wonder what it is to care?" I say, drawing a long tress of hair through my fingers, and looking down at the water flowing at our feet. "If to care for you is to like you very much when you are not making love to me, then I care for you very much indeed!"

But George does not answer; he is looking straight away over my head at the distant hills, thinking hard and deep, and the misery in his blue eyes hurts me. I never could bear to see anything, even a worm, suffer.

"George," I say, slipping my hand into his, "don't fret about it; perhaps it will come in time, you know, and—"

"Have you ever seen the man you *could* care about?" he asks, stroking my hand gently between his own.

"In my dreams, perhaps," I say, laughing. "Where else could I have met him?"

"You have never been away from home," he goes on, "save to school; and

you could not see any one there. But do you know, Nell, sometimes I have thought that the reason you don't love me is because you have a fancy for somebody else? A silly notion, is is not?"

"Very!" I say, taking my hand away. "Did you suspect me of an unlawful love of Skippy?'

"God forbid!" he says, laughing. "No! I did not suspect you of that misplaced tenderness! Do you know, Nell, that I think you are the coldest little thing I ever saw? I don't believe any one would ever move you."

"I am not tender," I say, making a grimace; "none of us are—we all had that nonsense knocked out of us in our youth; but I am true!"

"Are you?" he cries, eagerly. "Then when these six months are up—"

"I shall keep my promise," I say, my heart sinking; "only" (reviving) "don't make too sure of me, for six months is a long time, and there is no knowing whom I may see in it!"

"I am not afraid," says George, smiling. How happy he looks! "No one ever comes to Silverbridge, and you never go away, so how can any one see you?"

"Don't forget," I say, by way of damping his exhilaration, "that papa will have to be asked."

And for the first time in my life my parents' little prejudices on the subject of marriage commend themselves favorably to my eyes.

"That doesn't matter," says George. "Mrs. Lovelace ran away!"

"But there were exceptional circumstances in that case," I say, with dignity. "Besides, it would never do for that sort of thing to become a habit in the family. They were properly engaged for a long while!"

"And why may not you and I be?"

"Because he would never hear of it!" I say, looking forward with dismay to that dreadful engaged period of "pecking" that I have until now successfully evaded.

"Your governor and mine get on splendidly," says George, in a hopeful voice. "That would surely go for something?"

"That is one of those things no one can understand," I say, shaking my head. "My father has known your father for four years, and they have not quarrelled yet! Mr. Tempest must have the temper of an angel, or papa has never kicked him because he thought he was so little, and old, and frail!"

"Which redounds to Colonel Adair's credit," says George, laughing; "but I have often wondered he does not take a turn at me!"

"Don't be afraid," I say, nodding. "As soon as he knows you are anxious to have him for a father-in-law, he will be good for any amount of that. Is it not droll that parents should see things going on under their very noses, and then be so surprised and disgusted when anything comes of it?"

"I suppose their fathers were before them!" says George; "and some day we shall be the same! I say, Nell, what a little duck you look, to be sure!" he says, as, after stooping over the water, I turn round with my wreath set jauntily on my head.

"You have not half admired me yet!" I say, holding out my dress; "now do you know what I am going to do?"

"Stay with me."

"I am going to walk across the field of corn, and then the field of rye, just as I am, and then—"

"Well, and then?"

"—I am going to sit down," I say, guardedly. Not for worlds would I have George know of my little green parlor. He would spend half his days in it!

"And I shall come with you," he says, promptly, "in case you meet anybody with that wreath on your head."

"No, you will not," I say, decidedly. "What good would you be to me, pray? and whom am I likely to meet, except a ploughman, whose looks I should mind about as much as the stare of that cow yonder? I am going by myself."

"Very well," he says, sitting down on the stile; "I will wait here until you come back!"

Now, if there be anything harassing, it is to know that some one is waiting for you round the corner, and counting the minutes to your arrival. To enjoy one's self is impossible—some of his discomfort is passed on to you, and the result is nasty.

"I always thought," I say, with dignity, "that when a person was not wanted, he generally *went*."

"Thank you!" says George, jumping up with alacrity. "I won't require you to say that *twice*."

And away he stalks, his head well up, while I take the seat he has just left vacant and congratulate myself on the success of that last shot. Really I never saw him go away so quickly before! What a nice back he has! How well he walks! he ought to have been a soldier! He is really cross this time, for he does not turn his head once.

And now for a rush across that burning, broiling expanse of grain. I fly along so fast, my feet scarcely touch the ground, and as I go I sing a verse of the old, old song—

"Gin a body meet a body, comin' thro' the rye,
Gin a body kiss a body, need a body cry?"

I never could sing a bit, but there is no one by to hear me, and I feel so unaccountably joyously happy as though I *must* make a noise. With my head bent to avoid the level glare of the sun, I see nothing approaching me, and butt head foremost into a black something. . . . "I beg your pardon!" I say, as I hastily recoil, and put up my hand to tear off my ridiculous wreath. "I beg your pardon!" And then I lift my eyes and see that this *something* is Paul Vasher. And I stand staring at him with my poppy-wreath in my hand, mute as a stock-fish—I who have the longest, glibbest tongue in Christendom—with never a word to say for myself. Although I know him, he does not know me. There is no recognition in his glance, only an alert sort of surprise; but, thank Heaven, no amusement, which is under the circumstances simply angelic in him. My heart is crying over and over again, "He has come back! He has come back!" with a glad, breathless hurry that amazes me; but my lips are dumb, my hand does not steal out in friendly greeting, and if ever a young woman looked an awkward, gaping, silly bit of rusticity, that young woman am I. For the first time in all my life, perhaps, I do not take the first word, and he speaks.

"I am trying to find my way to the Manor-House, but I am not sure if I am in the right path. Can you direct me?"

His voice breaks the spell, my tongue begins to wag again.

"I am going that way, and will show you."

I turn my back upon him, for the path is narrow, wondering heartily whether he is relieving his feelings by having a good grin at my back? Such a figure as I look! though on the whole I fancy my back view is not quite so disreputable as my front. Shall I turn and ascertain? No, for it is always more bearable to suspect people are making fun of you than to *know* it. Arrived at the stile I find myself in a dilemma: to scramble over it anyhow by myself is one thing, to be delicately assisted over it by a gentleman another; for it consists of a single upright slab of stone that affords no foothold whatever, and the only legitimate means of surmounting it is to take it in your stride or vault it. In the present instance I can do neither, so I look in sore perplexity from Mr. Vasher to the stile, and from the stile to him, until, he probably seeing the difficulty, we catch each other's eye and go off into sudden laughter.

"I never saw anything in the least like that before," he says. "Was it erected for acrobats?"

"I think so!" I say, recovering.

"But please do not attempt to help me over, or we shall infallibly roll into the brook! Now, if you would not mind walking on and turning your back, I can manage it quite well by myself!" He walks on, for he is a man of sense—a fool would stand on the other side of the stile and argue the matter for half an hour—and I am over it, and after him like a shot.

"Do you know," he says, as I join him, "that when I saw you come dancing toward me I could not believe you were mortal? I thought" (laughing) "that you must be the goddess of joy dropped out of a cloud, you looked so happy."

"And may not one be happy?" I ask, looking at him in surprise. "Are not all folks sometimes?"

"Sometimes," he says; "but moderately, not so overflowingly as you were."

"Ah! if you only knew all my troubles," I say, shaking my head, "you would wonder I could ever laugh at all! And yet I do, morning, noon, and night. I often think I shall be punished some day for having such a light heart."

"Fuller says, 'An ounce of contentment is worth a pound of sadness to serve God with,' so I don't think you will be heavily judged!"

"By-the-by," I say, turning very red, and dropping my voice, "when you met me just now you did not hear me *singing*, did you?"

"Of course! Why?"

"And you did not laugh?"

"There was nothing to laugh at!"

"I will tell you a secret," I say, smiling. (May I not be confidential with him, since I knew him so many years ago, when I was quite little and childish?) "I would give the world to be able to sing, but I never could. It seems so natural to sing when one is happy, does it not? Just as a bird breaks out into song, because he feels that life is good and he loves it. I had singing-lessons at Pimpernel once, and the man did his very best with me, but at last he gave it up. One must be bad, must one not, before a singing-master washes his hands of you? About two years ago Milly (my sister, you know) and I were at a little party at the Vicarage, and I stood up to sing a duet with her. It was a foolhardy thing to do, but I had practised it for weeks; and when I opened my mouth there was not a sound to be heard—literally not a sound. Perhaps it was as well —but oh! I was so bitterly ashamed. I think I sat down and turned my face to the wall and wept."

"And did your sister sing it alone?" asks Mr. Vasher, laughing.

"She sang another instead!"

"It is very odd," says Paul, "but I know your voice quite well—I am sure I have heard it before; and your face seems familiar to me."

"People are so alike," I say, evasively, turning my head away from his keen regard. Somehow I do not want him to recollect me just yet. "Nature makes all her people in sets, and mine is a common pattern."

"I think not," he says, slowly; "for I never saw but one person a bit like you before, and that was Helen Adair."

I see his mind trembling on the brink of a discovery, so I hastily hold up my poppy-wreath for his inspection.

"Look!" I say, "is it not *bizarre*, extraordinary? Did not that make you smile?"

He takes it from my hand and turns it round. "It looked very pretty on," he says. "Did you make it yourself, Nell?"

"You know who I am: you knew it all along!" I say, starting back.

"Only since a moment ago," he says, smiling. "And now, after all these years, have you not a welcome for me?"

I hold out both my hands with a deep sigh. "If you only knew how glad I am you have come back!" I say—"how I have wished for you to come back! You have been away four whole years."

"And you remembered me all that while?" he says, looking down into my face eagerly—"you missed me?"

"So much," I say, gravely, "that often I have said to Jack, that if I knew where you, were I should write and ask you if you had forgotten your promise about the fruit-garden."

"And that was the only reason you wanted to see me back?"

"Oh, no! I wanted to see you too."

He seems to have forgotten he is holding my hands, so I take them away.

"Are you married?" I ask, looking up to the dark, strong face, that is altered no whit, save that the restless expression has fallen away from it, and a better, nobler look grown upon it.

"No."

"I am so glad," I say, clapping my hands; "so glad! Do not be angry with me, but after you went away I used always to think that when I saw you next you would be married to—"

I stop short, I had forgotten he does not know that I know that he loved Silvia Fleming; my cheeks turn scarlet as my poppies at my stupidity.

"Yes," he says, "and to whom?"

"No one in particular," I say, looking down at the grass; "it was only a ridiculous fancy of mine."

We walk on again, and there is a little pause in our brisk conversation; perhaps he is *remembering*, and I am recalling Silvia Fleming's vow, and marveling if she has tried to win him again, or forgotten her wild love in sober, respectable marriage.

"It was lucky I came through these fields," says Mr. Vasher, "for I was going to the Manor-House to see *you*."

"If you want to find me of afternoons," I say, laughing, "you must scour the country and look under every hedge and tree; I live out-of-doors in the summer. And were you coming to see me so soon? That was good of you."

"Will you believe," he says, looking down on me (my head barely reaches his shoulder, and yet I am a very decent height, five feet four inches), "that you were the first person I thought of when I came back to England? I only arrived at The Towers yesterday, and, as you see, have set out to see you to-day. And, after all, you are a disappointment," he says, with a queer smile. "Somehow I always thought of finding you a bright, frank-faced, honest little girl, just as I left you, and now—" (he scans me slowly from head to foot) "I find you grown up and—"

"I wish you had come back sooner," I say, interrupting, "for, do you know, I am getting beyond gooseberries, and can exist without apples?"

We are passing through the orchard now, and several of the fry are standing about in the distance, distinctly marveling whom on earth Sister Nell has got hold of. In the garden we meet the governor, and, to my amazement, instead of Mr. Vasher being ignominiously ordered off the premises, papa welcomes him with much politeness, speaks with respect of Mr. Vasher's defunct father, and finally floats him away in a stream of amicable conversation. Verily, this is a world of change!

CHAPTER II.

". . . . There is no woman's sides
Can bide the beating of so strong a passion
As love doth give my heart; no woman's heart
So big to hold so much. . . ."

It is nearly a month since Mr. Vasher paid his flying visit to Silverbridge, and we are drawing very near that illustrious First, which is the one day of the year to all Englishmen, from the keen sportsman and crack shot to the aimless booby who ever goes out with a gun save at the risk of his own and his neighbors' lives. Although the partridges on the Vasher estate may be supposed to have long ago taken to eating each other, as there is no one, save poachers, to shoot them, their owner will not be here to sally forth with his friends, and send them to kingdom come; on the contrary, he is bound over to appear in S———shire at that date, and will not be among his own stubble until the second week of the month. After that he is going to settle down in his own house, and become, he says, a respectable country gentleman. I wonder why the words "country gentleman" always bring up a vision of a red-faced, fox-hunting, ample-bodied, mutton-chop-whiskered, rather vulgar-looking man, who loves beer and doubtful jokes, and has a weakness for kissing the pretty Maries at roadside inns?

He seemed very sorry to go away, Paul Vasher. Papa says he was absolutely obliged to go, business affairs accumulated, etc., etc. He made a pleasant change; I hope he will come back soon! At the present moment I am walking along the passage that leads to mother's room, with a fresh nosegay of flowers in my hand, for her table.

"Come in!" she says, as I knock; and entering, I find her sitting by the open window, smoothing the primrose-colored locks of her youngest born with a brush as soft as swan's-down.

I have never written very much about mother, but she is as much the life of her children as the air they breathe; whomever or whatever we love we always place them 'after mother.' As I give her a hearty hug, I become aware of a pleased smile on her face, that not only lurks in every pretty corner, but covers it as a garment in a most unequivocal manner.

"*Jack*," I say, with a sudden leap of joy through my veins, "he is coming home?"

"No," says mother, "it is not Jack. It is an invitation."

"An invitation!" I repeat. "Are any of our neighbors mad enough, or forgiving enough, to try that on again?"

"It is from Milly. She wants you to go on the 30th to stay with her for a month."

"Lovely!" I say, with a deep gasp; "but he will not let me go."

"It is just possible that he may," says mother, "although he has refused all Alice's invitations for you. You would like it, dear?"

"Like it!" I say, sighing; "did not the country mouse love to go and stay with the town one, even though he came to terrible grief? But, mother, mother, I have no clothes. Running wild here is one thing, but footing it at Luttrell another."

"What have you got?" asks mother, setting down her darling, who speedily accomplishes his one object in life, which is to overturn himself.

"One black silk, which is skimpy and rusty, and tight and green; two decent white dresses, and one indecent one; a few prints that look passable enough in the dim vista of a woodland, but are not quite, ahem! the thing for visiting. Have you got anything at all left in the wardrobe?"

Mother's wardrobe is a kind of museum of dead-and-gone fashions and garments, among which she always rummages when any of us are particularly ragged or naked. Unfortunately, the rummaging of twenty years has left it very bald and miserable indeed; and, as everything of any value has been taken out long ago, I stand but a poor chance of fishing up a garment fit to go visiting in.

"There is the yellow satin," says, mother, "but then you don't like yellow satin."

"Especially when my great-grandmother upset a dish of gravy down its front," I say, grimacing. "Would you have me like the serving-man in 'L'Avare,' who was hidden by his master to hold his hat over his clothes, that the company might not see the rents and stains?"

"And there is the plum-colored paduasoy," says mother, unheeding my flippant interjections, "and you don't like that."

"No, I do not! If I can't have one or two moderately respectable gowns I must stay at home."

"I don't know what your papa will say," says mother, with a sigh.

"If he only says 'Yes,'" I say, kissing her, "I'll forgive all the rest. Is that other letter from Dolly?"

"Yes, she likes it very much at Charteris, but she seems rather homesick."

"Poor Dolly!" I say, "I wish she were back again. I do miss her so. Mother, mother, why did you not have more girls?"

"Nell," says the Bull of Bashan, rushing in, "the governor says you're to go down directly; the Tempests are in the garden."

"Bother!" I say, crossly; for would I not a hundred times rather be up here, talking of new gowns with mother, than trotting round the hot garden and fields with George, talking of love? I know those little morning walks round the estate well enough; and, as to the Mummy's being an invalid, I don't believe a word of it; his legs are made of cast-iron. I follow my sturdy young-brother, who has earned his nickname by the extraordinary power and volume of his bellow (when papa is out of the way), down-stairs very unwillingly.

The gentlemen are all standing together in the porch, and I say, "How do you do?" to the father, and lay my fingers in the warm grasp of the son; and, after that little formula we all stroll forth together, the two old souls in front, and we young ones behind.

"Do you know," I say, lowering my voice cautiously, for in our family we all firmly believe that papa has not only eyes but ears in the back of his head, "that perhaps something most delightful is going to happen to me? There is a chance of my *going away?*"

"Going away," he repeats, blankly, and a pale, dashed look comes over his face; "do you mean it, Nell?"

"Why should I not?" I ask in astonishment, tipping my sun-bonnet a little farther forward; "is there anything so very astonishing in that, pray?"

"It would not be in some people, but it is in you; I thought you never went away."

"That is just why I am so anxious to begin," I say, briskly. "Do you think he will let me go? do you *think* he will?"

"I don't know," says George, switching at the grass with his stick; "do you want to go so very much?"

"I think I should break my heart if I did not!" I say, with conviction. "You see I have never been anywhere really; and think of what it would be to go to, perhaps, a ball (do you think they will dance at Luttrell?), and have a real ball-dress, and a real—"

"Lover!" puts in George, with a pale smile; "for you 'are as sure to have the one as the other!"

"You silly boy!" I say, patting his coat-sleeve, "have you not got over that ridiculous notion yet? I wish you were coming too; yes I do, with all my heart!"

"Are you sure of that?" he asks, looking into my eyes with those blue ones that have never met mine yet without their warm love-light burning steadily.

"Quite sure!" I say, smitten with a quick compunction; for am I not devoutly glad at the prospect of going away from him? and when did he ever leave me without regret? "You ought to be there to take care of me, ought you not?"

"If you go away this time, Nell," he says, "some other man will fall in love with you, and you will never come back to me any more. I can see it all quite plainly. Will you not stay, dear, and try to put up with a poor, rough fellow *who loves you?*"

"There is no fear of any one I shall see there," I say, softly; "besides, who is likely to fall in love with me there or anywhere else? Every eye has its own

Naboth's vineyard" (did not some one or other say that?), "and I am yours, but I'm not likely to be anybody else's. I shall come back again like a bad penny, never fear." I stoop to pluck a handful of small bind-weed, whose pale pink cups are opening to the sunshine with a dim, faint fragrance.

"If only I were sure of you," says the young man; "if only these wretched months were up!"

"Poor George!" I say, gently. Alas! that I should have to say, poor George! When a woman pities her lover, she is a long, long way from loving him. I think he knows it, for he shakes his shoulders back impatiently; he looks as nearly wretched as his blond, sunny good looks permit; these fair men never manage to look as disconsolate and woe-begone over their misfortunes as do the black-eyed, black-haired, funereal lovers.

In these morning rambles we always visit every outbuilding and corner, clean or unclean. We have now arrived at the pigsty, and the two papas are inside, prodding the fat sides of the porkers, and disputing loudly over the superiority of this breed or that. "Poor chucky!" I say, resting my elbows on the top of the stone-wall that overlooks his unsweet dwelling, "you must have disagreed very seriously with our ancestors before they decided that your savory body was unfit for food.—Do you think," I ask, turning to George, "that they had trichinosis in those days?"

"Probably, only they called it by a less grand name!"

"The pigs must have had an excellent time of it when there was no one to eat them, you know; not that I will ever believe the Irish abjured the sweet creatures. I got into such a scrape here once," I continue, looking across to where the Mummy and the governor are waxing warm over their discussion. (After all, a pigsty is not a very dignified place to quarrel in.) Dorley used to milk a particularly vicious cow just in this corner; and one afternoon I popped my sun-bonneted head suddenly over the wall, and away went the cow, kicking over the stool, milk-pail, and Dorley, who lay on his back, with the milk all sweeling over him, never offering to move or get up, but just turned up the whites of his eyes, and murmured, "Ow could'ee do it, Miss Ullen? 'ow could'ee do it?' What a row there was about it, to be sure!"

I go off into a fit of laughter, in which George joins, and the two old people, having settled their dispute without coming to fisticuffs, move on, and we follow. How miserable it all is without Jack! Going over these old haunts without him I feel almost as ancient as the "oldest inhabitant" does when he toddles round the house where he was born. It seems quite a century since we sat, one at each end of yonder plank, see-sawing, and tumbling flat on our noses five times in every minute. "I wonder what poor, dear Jack is doing?" I say aloud; "working himself to death, I dare say! It was very inconsiderate of him, choosing a profession; there was no need, as he is the eldest son!"

"Jack is a lucky fellow," says George, with a quick envy in his voice, "don't be sorry that he is not here idling his time away! He is out in the world making his life, or marring it; he has the chance of proving himself to be of good stuff or bad; he is not laid on a shelf like an old maid's gown, with sprigs of lavender between. Pythagoras says that, 'in this theatre of man's life, it is reserved only for God and angels to be lookers-on;' and Arnold exclaims, 'Have we not all eternity to rest in?' Depend on it, Nell, every man ought to work."

"But what could you do?" I asked, gently, for do I not know how this purposeless, idle life chafes him? "I don't think you are clever enough to cut a good figure in Parliament, and you would not care to be a clergyman or a doctor? If you had gone into the army as you intended, your time would have been filled up, but it would only have been like play-

ing at being busy, for we never have any real fighting now, you know; we only make faces at our enemies, and show them that we are ready, and they never come on." George laughs.

"There are other things in the world besides fighting," he says, "plenty of good work to be done; but, however, it is no good talking about it. If ever I say. anything to my father, he asks me if I shall not have time enough to do as I please after he is dead? Pleasant that!"

"After a certain age," I say, gravely, "old people ought to go off; all that have any sense of propriety do, and make room for the young ones. They have had their day, cracked their jokes, drunk their wines; and when their lives are flat, stale, and unprofitable, they ought to make their bow and vanish."

"Only they don't think so," says George, laughing, "and Debrett chronicles many a depraved and inconsiderate old man, at a good deal past the orthodox threescore years and ten! and whose heir will have suffered the sickness of hope deferred, and have grown-up sons and a purple nose before he comes into his inheritance!"

"At any rate, George, you may be thankful that you are not a woman, shunted on to a siding, and bound to remain there for the rest of your life, unless some one has a fancy for murdering you, or you distinguished yourself in some discreditable way!"

"Women ought to be seen, but never heard of," says George, decidedly; "you don't want to scream on hustings, do you, Nell?"

"No, indeed, women possess far too much power to wish to wrest the semblance of it from man. A woman's rights! woman always seems to me to have lost all the privileges of her own sex, while obtaining none of the dignity of the other."

"Well done!" says George; "I'm glad you're not bitten like all the rest."

"That is because I am not clever," I

say, laughing. "I should cut but a sorry figure among those highly-cultivated females, and no one likes to look small!" (I turn aside to gather a spray or two of sweet woodruff that has no scent in life, but when dried possesses the fragrance of new-mown hay.) "Do you see that vervain, George? It is said to make the company it is in gay and jocund; had we not better take some home for our fathers?"

"I don't think *you* want any," he says, looking at me; "I never saw such a merry little soul as you are; and the way you laugh!"

"I read somewhere, the other day, that every laugh is a nail out of your coffin," I say, gayly; "if that is true there cannot be *one* left in mine, can there? Don't try and take from me my poor little cheerfulness; trouble will come fast enough; it always does to very happy people. It is the croaking, grumbling, ill-used folk who get through life comfortably and make other people bear their burdens!"

"You would never laugh as you do if you were in love," says George; "you couldn't."

"I do laugh very loud," I say, considering; "almost as loud as the Bull of Bashan?" George does not answer, he appears to be thinking; so, if I expect to be assured that my laughter is always low and sweet, I am mistaken.

"Do you know," I say, feeling rather ruffled, "that you never pay me any compliments now? No one ever paid me any but you, and, besides amusing me, I got quite to like them!"

"When a man is profoundly in love he does not make pretty speeches," says George; "he feels them, but he does not speak them. It would be like saying to the sun, 'How warm you are!' when he is warmed through and through with its rays. I don't think I ever paid you *compliments.*"

"George," I say presently, as we walk noiselessly over the close-cropped, sweet meadows, "do you not think that a woman may have several fancies, and only one heart? or do you believe her heart and her fancy always go together?"

"What put that into your head?" he asks, opening his eyes.

"Nothing!" I answer, dreamily, "only I can understand a man and woman falling out terribly, because he thought she loved some one better than she did him, when in reality her heart belonged perfectly to that man, although a fleeting fancy for some one else had, for the time being, obscured her vision: there would be misery and confusion come, would there not? But after all it is the heart that stands, the fancy dies away like a puff of summer wind."

"Have a fancy for whom you like, dear," says George; "only keep your heart for me!"

"If ever I had a fancy for any one," I say, looking out at the far-away, bloomy hills, "I think it must have been in dreamland. Bah! we are talking nonsense. Do you know that I shall look such an old guy, if I go away? Look at this frock!" And I hold out the skirt of my modest garment for his inspection.

"Well! and what is the matter with it?"

"Everything! material, fashion, cut, and age!"

"Never you mind!" he says, looking at my face, not my gown. "People will look at *you*, not your dress!"

"Not they!" I say, shaking my head. "Women look at your dress first and your face after; men look first at a woman's general turn-out; they would rather be seen with an ugly but perfectly-appointed woman, than ever such a pretty one in a bonnet out of date and ill gloved and booted."

"I should prefer the pretty woman with the out-of-date bonnet," says George; "but surely you can have everything you require for a visit?"

"I ought, but ought is an ill-used word that never gets its rights. Papa's daughters are never supposed to require anything so superfluous as *clothes*."

"If you would only marry *me*, you should have a new silk dress for every day in the year," says the young man, with masculine ignorance of the number of yards every well-brought-up young woman considers it necessary to cram into a skirt.

"You would not have me marry you for the sake of silk dresses, would you?" I ask, reproachfully, feeling somewhat allured, nevertheless, at the notion of trailing about in black, white, green, blue, lilac, cream-color, or pink attire, every day. I could not enjoy them all, though; and perhaps, after a bit, I should even get as used to them as I am to my cotton ones; and it would be no pleasure to choose a new one. "Heigho!" I sigh; "well, there is one comfort, I shall not have any of the women abusing me for my smart toilets; a woman will forgive another one for being better looking than herself—that is Nature's fault, not her own—but she will never forgive her for being better dressed!"

"That is true," says George, "and I believe that numbers of people do not dare to be stylish, or they would lose all their friends. There is to some folks a species of immorality in a perfectly-fitting dress or a becoming bonnet; it is a snare, a lust of the eye, and as such to be shunned by honest, sober people! I have often seen a man looking with positive pleasure at his dowdy, ill-dressed wife; it gives him a comfortable feeling of safety, to think that he can put her down in the middle of a crowded public room, and be certain to find her there unmolested when he comes back. In fact, too much style is the devil (they think), and men are often afraid to marry a very pretty or elegant girl, because they think her morals cannot be quite what they should be, or that she will take too much trouble in looking after!"

"And I have heard that a girl can have no higher compliment than the dis-

praise of her own sex, and that when you hear them abusing and picking to pieces some particular woman, and assuring each other that she has not a good feature in her face, that her figure is padded, her complexion kept in a box, and that not even her eyelashes are her own, you may be quite sure she is good-looking, or fascinating, or uncommon; on the other hand, if you hear them praising some girl to the skies, you may be perfectly sure that she is meek, insipid, and tame, too uninteresting to be a rival, and too vapid to attract the attention of any one's lover, husband, or brother. Is that true?"

"Perfectly."

"Well, I can't understand that feeling. When I see anything beautiful, I love to look at it. I never used to weary of looking at Alice or Silvia Fleming."

"Silvia Fleming!" he exclaims; "where did you ever see her?"

"At Charteris."

"At the time Vasher was there?"

"Yes."

"Whew!" whistles George; "why, he was in love with her; engaged to her some years ago; no one ever knew why, the match was broken off. Vasher must be getting an old fellow by now."

"Old!" I say, in astonishment. "Old! did you say? He cannot be much past thirty."

"That is a good deal," says George, with all a young man's impertinence; "why, you were only a child when you first knew him, Nell!"

"Yes, I was only a child!"

"And I can't imagine how you recollected him when you ran up against him in that field."

"It is not a face one could possibly forget," I say, rather tartly; "Paul Vasher is the handsomest man I ever saw!"

George stares at me blankly; he does not mind my not appreciating his good looks, but it cuts him for me to place another man before him.

"You always admired dark men," he says, with a fall in his voice.

"Always!" I say, beginning to laugh. "Do you know what I am laughing at?"

"No."

"I was thinking of that day when you were so angry, and walked off in a huff, and never turned your head once. I have so often thought since, that—that if you had only looked round, you would have seen how silly I looked when I ran into Mr. Vasher, and the moral I deduced was, 'Never turn your back on your friends, but keep your eyes wide open to see when they make fools of themselves?'" And I laugh heartily; I always had a bad knack of laughing more amusedly at my own small jokes than those of anybody else.

We are in the orchard now, and the Mummy is beckoning from afar to George to accompany him home to luncheon, for above all earthly considerations does he place his stomach and the comfort thereof.

"Good-by," says George, standing bareheaded under the trees, through which the sunlight flickers lovingly on to his fair, bright locks. "If you do go, which I devoutly hope you will not, Nell, there will be plenty of time for another nice long talk, will there not?"

"Plenty!" I say, my heart sinking, for I know he will try and win an unconditional promise from me before I go, and that I never will give. "Good-by, George!"

And so he goes away, through the light and shadow, a stalwart, knightly figure that many a proud woman might look after with glad eyes of love and pleasure.

"O love, love!" I say to myself as I go on toward the house, "that some people eat their hearts out in trying to win, and others take as thanklessly as though it were dirt; why do you not go where you would be welcomed with eager, grateful hands, instead of beating at a fast-shut door that can never be opened to you, never, ah! never!"

CHAPTER III.

"*. . . . If thou art rich, thou art poor;*
For, like an ass whose back with ingots bows,
Thou bear'st thy heavy riches but a journey,
And death unloads thee."

It is Saturday, the 30th of August, and I am speeding along through golden sun-flooded fields of wheat, and shorn brown-green meadows; not on my own two indifferently-shod feet, but in a carriage drawn by a puffing, snorting, hissing, dirty monster, who makes a prodigious noise, and hurry, and fuss, as he goes on his iron way rejoicing. I am off! Actually off! I am still doubtful as to whether it is really my veritable body that is seated on the hard blue cushions of the railway-carriage. I keep on rubbing my eyes to be quite sure that I am awake, that I shall not find myself sitting up in bed, bitterly sorry and wrathful that a mocking dream has made a fool of me again. I have pinched myself hard six times, and at the end of each nip have felt relieved on finding that the train, my *vis-à-vis*, and my novel, have not vanished into thin air. For a week I have been dancing like a cat on hot bricks, alternating between feverish hope and groveling despair; I have packed and unpacked my modest wardrobe at least twelve times, and only a short hour ago I was drowned in tears because the latest verdict had gone forth, "She shall not go!" Whether mother thereupon went down on her knees before her lord, as Philippa did to hers, and softened his flinty heart with her tears and prayers, I know not; at any rate his decision was reversed, and that delusive jade Hope spread her wings and vanished, leaving blessed and calm certainty in her place.

It is a quarter of an hour since I left Silverbridge station, and wished mother and George good-by. He did look so down in the mouth, and I always did hate to see a man miserable: all women whimper more or less, but men ought not to be bothered. Well, he'll get out into the world some day, I hope; and there's nothing puts a love-affair out of a man's head so quickly as having a lot to do: it is only the people who sit down and think, think, think, of one particular person, who take a disappointment so much to heart. I think most lunatics in love lived in the country. I wish I had a pleasant traveling-companion; some one who would not be afraid to open his or her lips, and with whom I could exchange a few reasonable remarks. There is small hope, however, of this lot. They belong, I can see at a glance, to that large class of people who look with horror on the smallest approach to conversation from a stranger; who are bound hard and fast by that ridiculous law of society which commands human beings to be in each other's company for hours, and yet give no more sign that they are aware of each other's presence and existence than if they were carrots or cabbages, or tables or chairs; you may know who they are, and they may know who you are, but until the magic words of introduction have been spoken over you—they are not. You are voiceless, eyeless, earless; so are they, and nothing short of your being all jumbled up together in a horrible accident would give any one back his faculties. To this class of people, the offer of the smallest civility, a newspaper, a book, or any other trifle, is regarded with grave doubt, and you are suspected of having designs on their purses, their bodies, or their acquaintance. "Nothing for nothing," is their motto. They never give without receiving a fair return, and why should *you?* It looks queer, to say the least. Therefore, when you are traveling, if you wish to be considered respectable, and neither an adventurer nor adventuress, put on a stony countenance; look at the ceiling or your boots—never at the countenances of your fellow-travelers; receive any offer of book, paper, etc., with a haughty "Sir!" or "Madam!" look down your nose if any one address you: but to be pleasant, to say "Thank

you!" and discuss the state of the weather, the state of the country, and the last new murder—then indeed you are low, hopelessly low, and you have yourself to thank if the silent ones dub you as something rather different from what you suppose yourself to be.

Now I should, above all things, like to ask one of those little virgins yonder to lend me the *Graphic;* there is a lovely picture in it, and I always did like pictures. I should like to announce publicly, that I am burningly, consumedly, unbearably hot; not but what my looks sufficiently attest the unwelcome fact, but it is always such a relief to talk over one's misfortunes; half mine always vanish when I can get any one to sympathize with me over them. In this case, however, I might be burnt to a cinder before I should dare to comment on the fact.

The two little people sitting opposite me are sisters, as alike as two peas, and I think as green; and the only difference that I can discern between them is that one has a permanent hitch in her nose, and the other has not. They are neither very young nor very old: they hover on that chilly, neutral-gray border-land that divides the young maid from the old one; they look as if they had never had a lover, or a sorrow, or a joy, or a hope, or a disappointment. I wonder what it feels like to have a torpid existence like that? Even the poor flies get wakened up and warmed by the sun sometimes.

A stolid British matron sits on my right, with a red account-book in her hand filled with rows of figures that should make her eyes ache. If ever I have a husband, I will take care of two things: that he keeps the accounts, and orders the dinner.

The only cheerful people present are two fat clergymen—comfortably dressed, happy, well-shaven souls, who are not only pleasantly provided for in this world, but are blessedly safe for the next. One is telling the other the latest *bonmot* of a certain witty bishop, and I strain my ears to catch the pregnant syllables; but he laughs so much over it, that the point is lost in successions of chuckles, and I feel unreasonably though distinctly cross. The other man says, "Hey?" at every tenth word. It strikes me he must spend a good half of his waking existence in saying, "Hey?"

What a small insignificant person a spinster traveling alone looks! She is a poor creature, compared with the "married woman," and all her smart paraphernalia, the footman, the lady's maid, the nurse, the baby, the husband. I place him last of all, advisedly; for, though he provided all the rest, he is often the meekest and most unimportant of all.

No wonder men call themselves lords of creation! It is not for what they are, but for what they give, that they are of so much importance: all good things come to a woman through a plain gold circlet, apparently!

There is no denying it—I like to feel important; or rather, I think I should if I ever got the chance—for I never had one yet. I do not want to be married for years and years; but if I could have all the nice, pleasant, dignified surroundings that married women have, without being obliged to take the husband, I should *like* it. Now, if I happen to get smashed-up to-day, there is no one to gather my pieces together, or acquaint my friends of my demise, or give me decent burial. I shall be simply an unattended, unappropriated female, and of no account whatever. I am proud to say that I do not bear a bandbox, a bag, and a sheaf of umbrellas and parasols, as is the wont of most unmarried females: I have only one bonnet, and that is in my box, and in a bad way, I fear; for, finding the trunk would not close, I sat down on the contents with much vigor, forgetting the bonnet in my excitement; and to-morrow morning I shall be a sorrowful sight to see. We wanted to buy a new one—mother and I; but an empty purse stared us sternly in the face, and

forbade the purchase. Next to being very hungry, I wonder if there is any misfortune, short of death, equal to that of an empty purse? To be ill in body is bad, to be ill in mind is worse, but for real downright, biting unpleasantness, and bitterness of soul, commend me to the empty pocket! I fancy Nick hates to see us penniless as heartily as we hate to see ourselves: he knows it is so easy for us to get into mischief when we have gold, so hard to distinguish ourselves in his court without it. I wonder how many extravagances and naughtinesses have been nipped in the bud for lack of the glittering dross? Well, if I do possess a sneaking love for smart clothes (is not love of dress one of his distinct and evil promptings? does he not ruin body and soul by hundreds every day, for the sheen that lies on a satin, the lustrous bloom on a silk, and the fairy cobwebs of a priceless lace?), it is pretty plain I cannot indulge it.

How hungry I am! In the breathless hurry-skurry of my departure, sherry and sandwiches found no place: I was too intent on conveying my person and box to the station (anticipating a revoke of the favorable sentence) to think of probable hunger: now, as the train slowly glides into Pringly Station, the sight of the refreshment-bar, with its fossil sandwiches, leaden buns, and orange-colored decanters, rejoices my heart.

"Guard," I say, jumping up as that individual goes past the carriage with his flag under his arm, "will you get me some sandwiches, and two buns, and a glass of ale, please?"

"Yes, miss"—and he vanishes.

In my hurry I have trodden heavily on the foot of one of the elderly young ladies, and she gives me a look as I make my apologies that quite revives me, it is so healthily vicious. They exchange glances of horror out of their pale eyes as I drink Bass's best or worst. In all their lives, if their complexions may be trusted to speak truth, they have never tasted anything stronger than barley - water. Now, why drinking a glass of ale in a railway-carriage when you are burnt up with dust and thirst, and scrammed with hunger, should be any worse than drinking ale at the family table when you do not particularly want it, I cannot understand; nevertheless, the British matron, the divines, and the little elderlies, all look at me with shocked eyes. If they only knew how I am inwardly laughing at them! for is not this one of those little affectations that make one smile at human nature?

Away we go again, tearing through the bright beautiful country as though it were the desert of Sahara, and we could not leave it behind fast enough. How the sun pours down on our devoted heads! Truly August is giving us some straight burning strokes before it goes. How I fuss, and fidget, and fan myself, and adopt the hundred-and-one flapping and fussy measures that mortals suffering under discomfort always affect, until they resign themselves to the inevitable, and learn that hardest of hard lessons—endurance! The little females sit white and silent: they are very warm, they are suffering horribly, but they make no complaint. Somehow they irresistibly remind me of little boiled hens with melted butter poured over them. They do not grumble even to each other. Now if Dolly were here, I should keep up a never-ending stream of nouns and adjectives, and grow cool over the comfort I received. The British matron has closed her eyes, the account-book has slipped from her fingers, and she is asleep, giving utterance now and again to a majestic snore, that once or twice wakes her up, when she looks round fiercely at us all as who should say, "Who made that noise? I did not," and then goes off again.

The fat parson is no longer saying "Hey?" aloud, though he may be shouting it in the land of Nod; his flabby cheeks are damp and unbeautiful, his mouth is a long, long way open. As a rule, human beings do not look well asleep: there is a startling resemblance between them and the ruminating animal world when the brain is dormant and the soul away.

After a while I think I fall off into a doze like the rest. I am conscious of making a deliberate effort to keep my mouth shut when "Luttrell! Luttrell!" comes sweetly to my ear. I start up in prodigious excitement, dancing up and down on both the little females' feet this time, but in too great a hurry to apologize; in fact, I am out of the carriage and across the platform almost before the train has stopped.

There is Milly in her carriage, but an ampler, grander, different Milly somehow from the bouncing, short-haired, handsome sister of the old days.

"How do you do?" I say, rushing up to her. "How glad I am to see you!" And I give her a hug, for I have not seen her for a long, long while.

"I am so glad you have come," she says; "but, good Heavens, Nell! *what a hat* you have got on!"

The gladness dies a little out of my face and voice; I feel ruffled and vaguely chilled. I have not seen her since her marriage, and she might have looked at my face, not my hat; besides, under the shadow of just such a one has Milly walked for all the years of her life before she married. As we drive away she asks for all at home kindly enough, but already I think her husband and child fill her heart, and the pomps, and vanities, and gands, and pleasures of her new life have shouldered away the memory of the old one at home. As I look at her I marvel greatly if she ever could have dodged papa round corners, and gone water-cressing, or worn a sun-bonnet and double skirts? And, although I shut my eyes tight and try to conjure up the vision, I cannot.

"Where is Alice?" I ask. "I thought she would have come with you?"

"Charles is driving her this afternoon,

but she will be in by the time we reach the Court."

"I am longing to see the babies," I say, looking at Milly's dress, and thinking what uncommonly fine birds fine feathers will make. (I am sure I could be made very presentable.)

"Mine is a splendid boy," says Milly, warming up directly; "he has the Luttrell skin and hair, and his eyes—" Words fail Milly at this point.

"And Alice's?"

"The youngest is a nice child."

How droll it seems to think of Alice as a mamma with two children! And I have never seen the last one yet.

"Have you many people staying with you?"

"Not many—a dozen or so. There is Fane!"

We are in the park now, and across the grass comes a tall, bonny, fair-haired young fellow, with a sunshiny face and a bright manner that makes every heart warm to him. It was but little that I saw of him at Milly's wedding; I am glad to have the chance of knowing him better.

"I am so glad you have come!" he says, heartily; "we were afraid that—"

A glance from Milly at the servants checks him, and he jumps into the carriage and we bowl away. I wonder if all married people behave as these do? There they sit face to face, hand locked in hand, gazing at each other with an absorbed spooniness that I do not know whether to smile at or admire. Well, I don't wonder at her loving him. In another minute we are at the house and in the hall. Through the half-opened drawing-room door comes a sound as of many tongues, a chinking as of many teacups ; evidently all the world is there.

"I will go to my room, thank you," I say, in answer to Milly's question. "Your maid will show me the way."

As I mount the wide staircase, shallow and wide enough to drive a coach and six down, I heave a deep sigh of relief. I am tired, hot, dusty; but oh! I am at my journey's end, and I am here, not at Silverbridge. My room is vast, and wide, and cool; it looks over garden and pleasaunce, hill and dale, fashioned after Nature's rarest and most lovely pattern; and away to the left glitters my splendid old friend, the sea, upon whose face I have not looked for many a long day. I have removed my traveling-dress and am drinking tea, when Alice comes in with a rush.

"How delighted I am to see you!" she says; and we fly toward each other and kiss heartily.

"You disgraceful young woman!" I say, holding her at arm's length; "so you have been and had another baby, have you?"

"Is it not shocking?" she says, laughing. "I have had my hands full, I can tell you."

"And what is the last one like?" I ask with interest; "as pretty as the first was?"

"Prettier!" says Alice, with emphasis.

"And what is Milly's like?" I ask, slyly.

"Oh, all very well; but he does not come up to mine."

(I expect some fun out of these babies.)

"And you are better looking than ever," I say, concluding my lengthened survey; "may I ask if you find any improvement visible in me?"

"Now I come to look at you," says Alice, "you are—yes—you decidedly are less plain than you used to be. There was a time, Nell, when I simply trembled for you, but your hair is lovely, your eyes are good, your dimples are charming. I think you'll do."

"Thank you," I say, meekly; "it is a case of 'it might have been worse,' is it not? Now would you believe it, but I know a young man who thinks me *very pretty indeed?*"

"A young man!" says Alice, opening her eyes; "not in Silverbridge, surely?

Did you advertise for him, or was he dropped out of a balloon?"

"Neither," I say, laughing; "but I am not going to tell you anything about him. I know so well how everything filters through to the husbands with married women, and I'm not going to have my heart's best affections made the theme of your unfeeling jokes. Did you think I should come, Alice?"

"Not in the least! Charles and Fane have been making bets on you. After this I shall expect you to come and stay with me at Lovelace Chace."

"I wish I could," I say, devoutly; "but, this 'outing' over, I expect to be shut up for the rest of my days."

"Marry," says my beautiful sister, resplendent in all the pride of her matronly young beauty; "you will be able to do as you please then. Now—about this young man—"

"I won't tell you now," I say, putting my fingers in my ears. "I am so glad to have got clean away from him, you know; another day I will. Are any nice people staying here, Alice—any one I am likely to fall in love with?"

"What a question!" says Alice, opening her eyes. "If you think of doing any such thing, there is no need to talk about it beforehand, is there?"

"In this case," I say, seriously, "there is a great deal of need, for if I do not fall in love with some one within the next five months—"

"What then?"

"What, indeed!" I say, gayly. "Come now, tell me, have you any Prince Charming staying here?"

"We have one handsome man," says Alice, "Sir George Vestris; but he is in love with somebody; and there is little Lord St. John, whose possessions are charming if he is not, but *he* is in love with me; there are two detrimentals looking out for heiresses, and there is some new man who arrived this afternoon, whom I have not yet seen. It is very odd, he lives near Silverbridge—I

can't remember his name. Fane and Milly knew him abroad. I am told he is good-looking."

"And this other man, the one you mentioned first, whom is he in love with? Any one here? I should fall quite naturally into my character of *gooseberry* again."

"With the loveliest woman I ever saw," says Alice, "and she has a pretty name—Silvia Fleming."

"Silvia Fleming!" I cry, starting up, "are you joking?"

"Why should I be?" asks Alice. "Why, the Flemings *live* only twenty miles from here, and it seems Luttrell *mère* and Fleming *mère* were old friends; Fane asks them here every year."

"What a little place the world is!" I say, sighing; "how one does run up against everybody!"

"But where did you ever meet with her, Nell?"

"Did I never speak of her? At Charteris."

"Ah! I remember. Well, she is a lovely bit of china, but I can't endure her."

"You are jealous," I say, looking at her proudly.

"Oh, no!" she says, laughing, and in her voice there is the ungrudging admiration that one very pretty woman can always afford to give another; it is only your half-and-half beauties who deny the existence of anything comely in their fair neighbors—"but somehow I can't like her. There is something so silent, so secret about her, one never feels sure of what she is up to."

"And she is engaged to this Sir George Vestris?"

Alice shrugs her shoulders. "They are inseparable, they behave like engaged lovers; she takes no notice of any other man, and he is quite in earnest; but she, I believe, is amusing herself. Milly is considerably scandalized, Fleming *mère* shakes her head and says nothing, the young woman keeps her own counsel, and we are all in the dark."

"I wish she was married to him," I say, heartily.

"Do you, indeed?" says Alice. "May I ask, Nell, if you have any intentions on any one who admires her?"

"No intentions," I say, turning my head away that she may not see how red my face has grown, "but I think she is dangerous—a man-trap!—and the sooner matrimony locks her up the better."

"I must go," says Alice, jumping up as the sound of a distant bell comes to our ears. "Come into my room on your way down-stairs, dear—it is the next but one on the right—and I will take you into the nursery to show you the baby."

"Wait a moment," I say, running after her. "I never was a gusher, you know, Alice; but oh, I am so glad to see your pretty face again!"

I put on my white-silk gown and twist a string of dim moonshiny pearls among my brown locks; I clasp about my throat and neck mother's pearl necklace and bracelets, and, when all is done, survey myself in the mirror with sneaking admiration. "You little fool!" I say, shaking my fist at my pleased face; "you don't look so much amiss there all by yourself, but wait till you get down-stairs among the rest—that'll take the conceit out of you!"

CHAPTER IV.

"A man that Fortune's buffets and rewards
Hast ta'en with equal thanks; and blessed
    are those
Whose blood and judgment are so well com-
    mingled,
That they are not a pipe for Fortune's finger
To sound what stop she pleases."

IN the Luttrell drawing-rooms, that open one out of the other, almost as lofty and wide as the aisles of a church, and which are darkly splendid with the pictures of the old masters and bright with glowing, brilliant flowers, that bloom in every nook and corner like jewels set in dull-brown leaves, are sitting a dozen or so of people, enduring that *mauvais quart d'heure* that precedes dinner. Silvia has not yet made her appearance, but all the other guests are present, I think, and I have bowed to so many, that my head feels like a pendulum that is bound to go on wagging by the force of its own momentum.

Mrs. Tempest reclines in an easy-chair, fatter, kinder, fairer than ever—an agreeable contrast to the lady to whom she is talking, who is sallow and lean and ill-favored. Her name is Lister, and she is mother to those two sweetly simpering young ladies who are frisking on yonder *causeuse* like lambkins, displaying an ostentatious affection for each other that speaks volumes for the encounters they have in private. Their nods and becks and wreathed smiles are evidently directed at two good-looking captains sitting near, who appear very insensible, and make no amative grimaces in return.

These latter are, I suppose, the detrimentals of whom Alice spoke. I like their clean, well-groomed looks much; they are the first "warriors bold" I ever saw, and they certainly seem to fulfill the whole duty of man, as understood by the youth of the present century, which is to be dressed to perfection and have the best manners compatible with the fewest possible ideas.

Talking to Alice is an ugly little fair man, who is looking at me through his eyeglasses with attention, for do I not live near the rose?

Charles Lovelace, handsome as ever, a trifle steadier than he was on that terrible day when he ran away with Alice (and we wretched left-behinds were left to pay the piper), lounges beside my chair, giving me little historiettes of the people present.

Leaning against the mantel-piece is a rather tall, very dark man, with a perfectly handsome face, that does not give me the impression of being particularly

sensible or wise. That is Silvia's lover.
She seems to have a rare taste for dark
men, but this one does not to me approach
or touch the grander, more masculine good
looks of that other, who could renounce
his heart's desire rather than forfeit his
own self-respect. How strong and kind
he looked when he said "Good-by" to
me under the porch at the Manor-House!
How surprised he would be if he knew
both Silvia and I are here! I wonder if
he has ever seen her since that Sunday
at Flytton? I wonder if he will ever see
her again?

I look up and see Paul Vasher coming
in at the open door. My heart seems to
stop beating as he comes forward. Are
my eyes playing me some trick? Am I
dreaming? No; for he comes straight
to my side after Milly has introduced him
to Alice (apparently he has seen all the
rest this afternoon), and holds out his
hand with a quick look of gladness.

"I had no idea I should see you here,
or that you were Mrs. Luttrell's sister!
Did you know that I should be here too?"
he says, as he takes a chair next me.

"No, indeed!" How small my voice
sounds! How tongue-tied I always am
before this man!

"I hope you left all well at home?"

"Quite well, thank you."

(Is Silvia ever coming? It only wants
one minute to eight.)

"Do you know," I say, rather nervously, "that you will see an old friend
presently—or perhaps you have seen her
already?"

"Do you mean Miss Fleming?" he
asks, quietly. "No, I have not seen her
yet."

The door opens and enter Silvia. As
she comes up the long rooms I see her
clearly enough, a thought larger, a shade
more voluptuous, than she used to be—a
woman now, not a girl. She wears dead-
white silk, with costly lace at breast and
elbow, and faint golden yellow roses in
her hair and the front of her gown. Her
beauty strikes me as freshly and sur-

prisedly as it did the first time I ever saw
her.

Sir George Vestris goes to meet her
with almost humble devotion, but she
looks around her seeking, I think, Paul
Vasher, and he rises and approaches her.
They are so near me that I could touch
either with my hand, and cannot choose
but hear their words.

"How do you do, Miss Fleming?"
says Paul.

"Quite well, thank you, Mr. Vasher."

"It is many years since we met," says
the gentleman, politely.

"It does not seem so long," says the
lady.

"Dinner is served," announces the
butler.

"Will you take in my sister, Mr. Vasher?" says Milly; and I put my hand under his arm.

So this is the meeting after long years
between these two once passionate and
despairing lovers. Cold and indifferent
as their words were, their looks matched
them; not a ray of excitement or interest
stirred Mr. Vasher's face, and she was no
whit behind him, and yet methinks there
must lurk some danger when two people
who parted so wildly meet so coldly.

Somehow or other we are all matched;
the stray men come out of their corners
and fall in with the rest, and we go across
the hall and into the dining-room, dim
with wax-lights, faint and subdued as a
room devoted to the worship of the palate
should be—or so gourmands tell us.

As yet, however, I am too young to
love my dinner very heartily. As yet I
"eat to live;" in the fullness of time I
may perhaps "live to eat," but not now,
not yet! I would rather be out in the
garden than sitting here watching un-
hungry people tempted with good things,
and I want to be able to think. It is all
so wonderful, that Silvia and Paul Vasher
should have met again. Will it be my
lot to see the last act played out, and the
lovers, after all their misunderstandings,
made happy?

"It is the oddest thing, my meeting you here," says Paul, as we sit down. "Did you know that you were coming, when I wished you good-by at Silverbridge?"

"I did not know it for certain myself until eleven o'clock this morning," I say, laughing. "When I saw you last I never thought any such dissipation was likely to befall me as paying a visit."

"You have left your color behind," he says, looking at me, "with the poppies."

"Those poppies!" I say, ruefully. "Oh, how good it was of you not to laugh!"

"I felt no inclination," he says; "the picture would not have been half so pretty without the flowers."

Here he betakes himself to his soup, for apparently he is hungry, if I am not. Across the table, and plainly visible (for Milly's servants understand the art of arranging a dinner-table, and no enormous épergnes and show-pieces of plate make a wall to block out our opposite neighbor, compelling us to look at our plates or our right and left companion for several hours), are Silvia and Sir George Vestris —she flirting as lightly as though the man sitting before her had never been any more to her than any other present; he, with his soul in his eyes and words, watching her exquisite face as though his life hung upon her favor.

"Do you think she is altered?" asks Paul's voice beside me; and I turn with a start.

"She is more lovely, I think. I see no other difference."

He is looking at her with a glance that is most coldly critical. It has none of the suppressed intensity of the unwilling lover, or the open admiration of the enamored one; it is simply and utterly indifferent. Verily a man's love passeth quickly. And yet I wrong Paul Vasher in this, for his love did not pass away; he wrestled with and cast it out.

"Do you know," he says, "that you

8

are the quietest young lady I ever took in to dinner in my life? I have not heard the sound of your voice for quite—"

"A minute!" I say, laughing, "and those at home would tell you that is an enormous time for me. But I know men hate to be talked to at dinner. You look upon women as a nuisance in that respect, and would abolish us from the table altogether if you could; now, would you not?"

"Not when they are as considerate as you," he says, "although I will confess that I have before now got up from dinner as hungry as I sat down, thanks to my companion's conversational talents."

"But if *she* talked, you were safe, surely? You need only have answered her in monosyllables."

"Only, unfortunately, she had the finest knack of interrogatory conversation that I ever heard. She would ask questions that could not be answered 'in russet yeas and honest kersey noes.'"

"I should have feigned deafness," I say, laughing. "She could not shout at you!"

There is a little pause while he helps himself to *vol-au-vent*, and I look round the room at the dark oak, at the massive sideboard, on which is carved the date 1690. How small and insignificant that date makes me feel, and how evanescent a thing life is! For how many generations has not that sideboard held food and drink? for how many more will it not hold the same? Just as those dead and gone Luttrells looking out from the canvas on the walls once sat here, jocund and happy, so will others fill up our places who are sitting here to-night, and these sober pictures will look down on them as benignly as they are looking on us. Stately old houses certainly lessen one's sense of self-importance. It is impossible in the face of the stored traditions and memories of many hundred years not to feel that these things remain, and *we go*.

I glance round the table. Mrs. Fleming is steadily laying the foundation for a fourth chin. Mrs. Lister is boring Fane to a pitch that almost brings tears into his eyes; he makes no secret of hating old women, and every night he is bound to take one in for his sins. Lord St. John is gazing at Alice, who is placidly eating her dinner; every one of us Adairs has a fine appetite, and is not ashamed of it. Miss Lister is worrying Captain Brabazon, who is trying, with secret wrath I am certain, to eat *his* dinner. The other sister looks sulky; apparently her squire is better skilled in the art of repelling unwelcome advances than the other poor captain.

Ah me! I wonder why it should be that when lovers do not come to look for Chloe, Chloe should invariably go to look for them?

"Can you tell me who that gentleman sitting next to my sister is?" I ask Mr. Vasher.

"Silvestre, of Melton. Do you like his looks?"

"He seems good-tempered," I say, smiling, "and he is very amusing to listen to. His ideas seem to sprawl all over the place, and he requires his companion to pick them up and put them before his eyes in a recognizable form! Is he not very lazy?"

"Very," he says; "and are not you rather sarcastic?"

"Sarcastic!" I repeat, staring. "Where could I have possibly picked up that trick? I only watch people, you know."

"And some day you will turn my character inside out, and hold it up for me to look at," says Paul.

"If you cannot hold your own against a village maid, I am sorry for you!" I say, slyly. "Does it not seem droll that Miss Fleming and you and I should all have met together again here? It reminds one of the witches' meetings in 'Macbeth'—does it not you?"

"Only I trust we shall not work such disasters as they did!" he says, laughing.

"Do you know that I was in such a hurry to get back to Silverbridge, that I only came here intending to remain until Wednesday, but now I shall stay."

"So he loves her still," I say to myself, glancing at Silvia.

"Will you be glad or sorry?" he says, looking at me.

"I am glad you are going to stay," I say, "very glad. I will even, if you like, play gooseberry for you. There!"

I have made another mistake. He never knew till this moment that I knew he was in love with Silvia. Having made the observation, however, I will not attempt to eat it; telling stories is so painful and hard, one had need to be so clever to fib successfully; and I never was clever, thank Heaven!

"Gooseberry!" he says, with a swift, amused gleam in his eyes; "for me and whom?"

I do not answer, for the sound of voices is ceasing, Milly is drawing on her gloves; and who cares to hear his or her witty or flattering remarks cut ignominiously short by a universal uprising of petticoats?

"And whom?" says Paul's eager voice in my ear, but I turn my head away with a mischievous smile. Milly is collecting the glances of her compeers now, and I leave my seat with the rest.

"You shall tell me by-and-by," says Paul, decidedly, as he holds the door open for me to pass out last of all, behind the bashaw-like tails of my elders and betters.

"Do not be too sure," I say, laughing. "And now," I think to myself, "for a time of penance. Women can be cozy enough together if they all know one another well, but a jumble of relations, friends, and acquaintances—never!"

Silvia has vanished when I reach the drawing-room. No one abhors her own sex more heartily than she, and I do not feel inclined to make friends with the sisters, who are sitting on a distant couch, chattering very earnestly, reporting progress no doubt. The matrons sit in a ring and discourse of babies and the extraordinary rascality of their servants, male and female. I am not married, and I have no servants, not even a lady's-maid; so I turn my back on the drawing-room and go up-stairs to the Lovelace and Luttrell nurseries, and look at the babies, happy little souls, with their perfectly blank memories, that enable them to sleep on, and on, and on, with nothing to awaken them save hunger. They look such soft, round little cherubs, with their tiny clinched fists touching their cheeks. I never can see a baby without pausing to dream over it, and recalling with an amazed wonder the fact that all our great heroes and statesmen and illustrious men were even thus once—yes, and our murderers, our felons, and our outlaws.

The young mothers and the others come up, and an enormous amount of baby-worship is gone through, during which I slip away, and going to my room look out at the night and promise myself a stroll by the sea on Monday. I wonder why people always eschew the sea on Sundays? On the same principle as they make themselves uncomfortable in every imaginable way, I suppose.

We all go down-stairs, and, as I cross the drawing-room, I see Silvia sitting by the window. She has not spoken to me yet, but then she has had no chance; I will go and speak to her.

"Have you forgotten me?" I say, putting out my hand. "I staid with your aunt once at Flytton, you know; I am Helen Adair."

She looks at me for a moment, considering; then she lays her hand in mine. "You are Helen Adair?" she says, with a kind of amazement. "I thought I had seen you somewhere before, but I did not know it was at Charteris."

And as we stand hand-in-hand, the door opens and Paul Vasher comes in, first of the advancing party of men, and looks at us with a quick and keen scrutiny. In another minute Sir George Vestris is beside her, and I am sitting on a velvet chair, professedly looking at Milly's album, in reality wasting a little malicious pity on the Misses Lister, who, having laid themselves out in shady corners with room beside them for one, are balked by Silvia, whose lovely face detains the captains on their enforced pilgrimage to those charmers. Has she not Sir George Vestris, and is it not mean of her to prevent those flies from walking into the parlors the spiders have so carefully prepared? Mr. Vasher comes and sits down beside me, taking half of the heavy book on his knee.

"Do not make fun of them," I say, laughing, "for nearly everybody here is a relation."

"Do relations love one another?" he asks. "If I wanted a real service done me, or had got into a scrape, I would go to a friend, not a man bound to me by blood. Relations give ton-loads of good advice, and there they stop."

"I never had any," I say; "and I always have been so sorry that I had not. Why should one always be getting into scrapes?"

"It is human nature," says Mr. Vasher. "Now, does she not look a little duck?"

The "little duck" is our queen, and the photograph represents her as she was in her beautiful youth, with the gentlest, prettiest, most lovable face in the world; looking upon it one's heart aches as one thinks of the long, dark, empty years that came to her after these blessed and happy early days. Her daughter-in-law looks from the opposite page with her exquisite tender smile. As Englishwomen beat all other women, does not our princess beat all empresses, queens, and princesses with her fair face? Our prince was in luck when he went a wooing.

"Are you loyal?" I ask, looking up at Paul Vasher; "I hope so, for I could never like you if you were not. Some people say rude things about royalty; they think it sounds grand, but I think it is simply very bad taste."

"Shall you think I am disrespectful if

I say that in my opinion kings and queens are not so good-looking as every-day people?" he asks.

"No, for that is often true. For instance," I say, looking across at Silvia and her lover, "where would you see such a pair as that?"

He does not wince in the very least as his eye falls upon them, and yet he is going to stay on here for her sake.

"So that is the couple for whom you are kindly going to act the part of gooseberry?" he asks, with a smile. "I thought you said you were going to play it for me?"

"So I was," I say, turning very red, but still looking him well in the face; "it was you I meant."

"And the lady?"

"Look at this photograph," I say, quickly; "is it not pretty?" In my hurry I have laid my finger down on a fat baby taken à la fig-leaf, so precipitately shift it and indicate a couple of Luttrell lovers, who look even more foolish than they feel.

"Very," says Mr. Vasher, with emphasis. "But where is the gooseberry?"

"I wonder," I say, raising my voice a little, that I may talk my color down, "why plain people have their photographs taken so much oftener than handsome ones? It is such a rare thing to find a pretty face in an album! Do you think those people *know* how ugly they are?"

We are looking at a man whose eyes, already well rolled by nature, have evidently acquired a distinct and supererogatory roll by long practice; he looks as if a smart rap on the back of his head would send them into his lap.

"No," says Paul, "for the plainest people always think themselves the handsomest. Have you ever had yours taken?"

"Once, at Pimpernel; it was a horrid experience, and I never wish to have another like it."

"What did he do?" asks Paul. "Did he, like the little fat photographer in *Punch*, say, 'Look at *me*, miss, and don't smile?'"

"No, but he did worse; he *wished* me to smile, but he would not let me do it my own way—he regulated it. When I had got up a moderate grin, he would say, 'A little more, miss!' but on trying to oblige him I showed a little of my teeth, which was strictly forbidden. Then, when I had nailed a painful smile to my countenance, and at his command made an arch grimace with my eyes, he took the cap off, and it was a horrible thing to feel my smile slipping away from me, though I held on to it with my eyelids, and to know that it was going—going—gone!"

"I am afraid the Pimpernel process is a long one," says Paul, laughing.

While he puts the book back I glance around me. The men look amiable and cheerful in the extreme, as all mankind has a way of doing after dinner; one or two of them sentimental, tears will stand in their eyes by-and-by, if a plaintive ballad is sung. It is not an ennobling reflection that the best of men is better after a good dinner than he was before; and that the hottest lover can be made hotter still by a choice vintage. Miss Lister is going to sing; she spreads out her green skirts, and takes off her bracelets and clears her throat. Do the birds make any preparations before bursting out in a rush of exquisite song? She sings "Only," and Jack's ridiculous verse comes into my mind as I listen—

"Only a face at the window,
  Only a face, nothing more;
  If ever it owned any legs,
  They must have walked out at the door."

Some songs move me, but this one never does. Give me "When Sparrows build," with the yearning cry of the girl's broken heart wailing through it, and "the faded bents o'erhead." Alice sits down and plays glorious "Tam O'Shanter." How the rollicking, dare-devil, spirited notes ring out! How we seem to see the hot pursuit, feel the witch fingers creeping nearer and nearer to the terrified galloping horse! An hour slips away. It has been a charming evening.

"Good - night!" says Paul Vasher, standing before me; "we are banished to billiards. Are you going to begin your duties as gooseberry to-morrow morning?"

CHAPTER V.

"He hath twice or thrice cut Cupid's bow-string, and the little hangman dare not shoot at him; he hath a heart as sound as a bell, and his tongue is the clapper; what his heart thinks his tongue speaks."

It is half-past eleven o'clock, and we are all in church (save Fane and Captain Oliver), confessing ourselves to be miserable sinners, although in our secret souls we think ourselves nothing of the sort. We are in a big pew that contains, besides hassocks and chairs, a carpet, a table, a cupboard, and red curtains, which latter hide us when sitting or kneeling from the open-mouthed, open-eyed gaze of the Luttrell hinds. In former and more unmannerly days the cupboard held good store of cake and wine, of which the squire, his wife and daughters, and the stranger within his gates, partook during the sermon. Rather trying for the poor parson overhead on a hot summer's day, with his parched throat, and secondly, thirdly, and fourthly, still before him.

And now we are all standing up, able to take our fill of staring at the well-washed, well-greased congregation, who are singing "Jerusalem the golden" with all the strength of their bucolic hearts and voices.

I wish they had a few H's among them, these good and bad people! They let them all go so recklessly, but with the universal law of compensation put them in again in the wrong place. How loud and clear presently sounds their

"Incline our 'arts to keep this law!" It is no use to struggle against overwhelming numbers; we may as well let ours go with the rest, for we can never leaven the lump. I think that whoever invented the letter H did not sufficiently take into consideration the prevailing tendency of mankind to ease. Aitch! It is a word in itself, and a hard one; in hot weather especially, how comfortably and easily does it disappear altogether!

The rector is very like Mr. Skipworth in appearance, voice, and manner. For an hour we sit under him and listen to his discursive ramblings, which, so far as I can make out, are about Jeremiah in the briers, though what on earth he did there and how he got into such an uncomfortable position we are not told. Could not a clever man say all he has to say to his congregation pithily and well in twenty minutes? Is there anything that damages the cause of Christianity so much as the incapacity of these servants of God to expound the Scriptures lucidly and well? In the Houses of Parliament, and wherever enlightened men are gathered together to hear clever, wise, or improving talk, would they sit silent for an hour listening to twaddle that is an insult to their understanding? A thousand times, no! They would walk out, or cry aloud, or silence the speaker quickly enough; but in the house of prayer that cannot be done, and so folks with starving souls go Sunday after Sunday seeking bread and having a stone offered to them. Surely men who stutter, men who speak indistinctly, men whose hearts may be pure and good enough, but whose words are weak; men who have no strong sympathy with their hearers, and cannot express themselves concisely and to the point—ought these men to be set up above their fellow-men, to preach the grandest, highest truths the world contains? A man should be proved to be a good and bold orator, a sound logician, and accomplished scholar, so that he may appeal as irresistibly to the mind and imagination as to the souls of his congregation, before he enters holy orders; for is not an enormous power put into his hands for good or evil?

When a fine preacher arises, how people flock from the north and from the south, from the east and from the west, to hear him! How his fiery, heart-searching words pierce his listeners' hearts. How he holds the mirror up to the bad, wicked soul, and cries, "Behold! to this you have fallen and are falling!" We almost see the gaping, bottomless pit, with the writhing scorpions and the worm that never dies; feel the licking fire of the curling flames; hear the voice of the Man of Sorrows calling us away from destruction. I heard such a man once in Pimpernel.

And now we are out again, and walking across the churchyard; and the sun flickers down gayly on the living who walk erect, and on the green shield of earth that lies heavy on the breast of those who have "fought their fight with the pale warrior," and been vanquished, as all men have been and must be. At the gate the carriages are waiting, for Luttrell Court is more than two miles away, and I find myself seated next to Mr. Vasher, and opposite Milly and Mrs. Lister.

"How well you behaved in church!" says Paul; "you never smiled once, not even when that fat lady tried to pass the fat man in the narrow pew, and they got wedged together!"

"Did I not?" I say, laughing. "I could not help thinking of a rhyme in one of the nursery-books at home—

' There was a young lady of Yarrow
  Who went up to church in a barrow.
  She said with a smile,
  As she stuck in the aisle,
  They build these here churches too narrow.'"

"The lady in church must have been a direct descendant of the one at Yarrow," says Paul, looking at me.

I hope he is not observing the crushed and forlorn appearance of my bonnet; in future I will, at all risks, carry a band-box. Milly's airy erection is quite faultless. How good-tempered people ought to feel when they are perfectly well-dressed! I could be quite angelic, I think, if I were. Mrs. Lister looks as prim and unapproachable as though she were made of buckram. Her lips are pursed up very tight; she grasps her prayer-book as though it were a pistol, and altogether she is not a pleasant object to contemplate.

"There is Fane!" says Milly, suddenly, as we roll smoothly along under the shadow of the giant trees that line the park; and there, sure enough, in the distance, sneakily dodging behind a tree, and looking very hot, dirty, and ashamed of himself, is her missing lord and master.

Did I ever say that Fane is only a few years older than Milly, and that they are a very young couple indeed? Every Sunday morning, regularly as clockwork, does Milly make Fane dress to go to church with her, and every Sunday morning at the very last moment does he succeed in making his escape, and she has to go without him. This morning he has seduced Captain Oliver from the path of duty, and the pair have evidently been up to some unlawful amusement, for they appear exceedingly anxious to hide their persons from our view. But Milly gets out of the carriage and majestically walks across the grass to where they lie *perdu* (where could she have learned that dignified swagger? I should like to see her try it on with the governor), and we all follow.

Fane and his companion, thus run to earth, emerge and present their disreputable persons to our gaze. Their light summer suits are all patched and stained with green, as though they had been rolling on the grass. The captain's face is scratched, and so is Fane's hand. Half a dozen dogs are tearing round and round a tree, at the top of which a piteous miau! sufficiently explains the nature of these gentlemen's Sunday morning amusements.

"I am disgusted with you, Fane," says Milly—"and as to you, Captain Oliver, I am *surprised* at you."

And she sails away with her lord, leaving Captain Oliver utterly squashed. He does not know that it is Milly's habit to visit all her husband's misdeeds upon his friends, and that nothing will ever make her believe that they do not lead him into every scrape—not he them.

"Poor Oliver!" says Paul, as we walk away, leaving that abased warrior to the tender mercies of Mrs. Lister. Very tender they will be too, as she wants him for a son-in-law. "How crestfallen he does look, to be sure! And he is considered to have more brass than any other man in his regiment."

"He is quickly routed, then; but it is impossible for a man to be rude to a lady, is it not?"

"Quite."

"Are fathers generally polite to their families?"

"If they are gentlemen."

"Oh!"

"I want to know," says Mr. Vasher, looking down on my tumbled bonnet, "what I am to call you. I won't call you Miss Adair; I don't like Helen. May I call you Nell?"

"Oh, no! What would Milly say? Besides, I was young when you used to call me that; I am grown up now."

"And no longer young?"

"Oh, yes; pretty well. When we have known each other a little longer, you know—"

"Yes, we shall be near neighbors," he says, with quite a sudden gladness in his voice; "we shall have plenty of time for getting to know each other better."

"I do not improve on acquaintance," I say, smiling. "Oh, you will find me out to be such a little wretch! If you saw me in a rage once you would not forget it."

"Who puts you out?"

"Dorley, or Bashan, or—or—another person."

"And supposing I do?"

"You will be frightened."

"I am not afraid," he says, looking deep into my laughing face with his brown, brown eyes, that are self-willed and strong and tender at one and the same time. "Did any one ever keep you in order, Nell?"

"Never!" I say, proudly.

And I smile to myself as I think of my lover and bond-slave George, who never swayed, never could sway me in will, or mind, or heart. No, certainly, I have never been managed by anybody yet.

"Women ought not to have their own way," says Mr. Vasher. "After a while they go in for Women's Rights, and at last it comes to the husbands standing on the platform and holding the baby, while they hold forth upon everything in heaven and earth."

"I don't think those sort of people ever have anything so frivolous as a baby," I say, considering. "Talking of babies, do you know that you will see two at luncheon to-day? They are coming down for certain."

"Horrible!" he says, shuddering. "If there is one sight more appetizing, clean, and savory than another, it is a baby at table."

"Take care the mothers do not hear you," I say, as we enter the house; "they would never speak to you again."

We have taken off our bonnets and pulled out our locks, have powdered or not powdered our hot faces as our habits or inclinations will, and we are sitting one and all, in the cool dining-room, eating cold lamb and salad. The griffins outside shadow themselves grotesquely on the drawn blinds; they seem to grin in upon us malevolently, with their great misshapen noses and curling wicked mouths. Everybody is talking at once, eagerly, alertly, as though the loss of his voice for two hours had been a severe trial, and he is determined to make up for lost time.

"I saw a man in church who was

even smaller than I am," says Lord St. John to me, "and I was so pleased. Not but what I always console myself with a couplet that I saw somewhere once; it began:

> ' Man wants but little here below,
> Nor wants that little long.' "

"I fancy that applies to things, not people," I say, doubtfully, "and I am nearly sure it is a hymn."

"St. John has lost himself among the Psalms," says Charles.

"The safest place he ever got into," says Mr. Silvestre.

"That comes of going to church," says Captain Brabazon.

Lord St. John smiles blandly at his friends and continues: "It may be that I am prejudiced, Miss Adair, for a man naturally likes to think that he ought to be exactly like what he is, but I like being little. There is a peculiar charm in the upsidedownness of being a lord of creation, and yet so much shorter than most ladies—to feel that they could take me up and horsewhip me without an effort, and yet that they do not! Delicious creatures! And it is a fact, Miss Adair, that if ladies cannot have a gigantic slashing fellow for a lover, who could crush them between his finger and thumb, they like to have something that they can protect, pet, and spoil. Women's love is divided into two classes, the adoring and the protective, and, upon my word, I think the dear souls enjoy the one as well as the other."

There is a chorus of laughter all round the table, in which Alice joins. I wonder if *she* pets the little man?

He betakes himself to claret-cup; so do I, and sit listening to the nonsense that is flying about. How very seldom Silvia's voice is heard! It is the rarest thing to hear her speak, and then it is only to Milly or Fane, or Sir George Vestris. Although she lives among us, she somehow seems to be set apart; if it were not for her perfect loveliness, one would

never know she was present. I have seen neither look nor word exchanged between her and Paul Vasher to-day. If he loves her still, how can he bear to see her appropriated by another man as he does? Lovers are kittle cattle. The butler is opening a bottle of Bass leisurely; but some imp of the weather has got inside it, and he shoots out the corkscrew in the man's face, hitting him severely on the nose, and deluging him in frothing, foamy liquid. To his credit be it spoken, however, there is not the ghost of a smile on his face, only ale, and he takes a cloth and wipes himself. Mr. Vasher catches my eye and laughs. I am glad he has some sense of the ridiculous; people are so difficult to get on with who have none! I wish he was on my side of the table, and not all that way off. Mrs. Lister is opposite me, and I make a discovery concerning her; she wears false teeth, and they do not fit her. She will choke herself some day. Perhaps if she were to return them to the dentist and say—

> "Take back the teeth that thou gavest—
> What is their use, sir, to me?"

he would give her a set that might fit her better.

"There's my precious," exclaims Alice, lifting her head and listening; and, sure enough, certain clucks and coos and chokes in the distance announce the advent of the olive-branches.

The door opens and enter two nurses bearing aloft a small Lovelace and a smaller Luttrell, who are deposited by the same on their mothers' laps. Milly's baby is very young yet, and has that peculiarly decrepit look that extreme youth and age seem to share equally. His wonderful little hands are shriveled and wrinkled as though he had taken in washing for a hundred years. He is too small to be troublesome, and lies flat on his back, staring about him and taking a meal off his fists. Alice's son is a different matter. He is eighteen months old, and of an inquiring, avaricious turn of mind. He drinks wine out of his mother's glass without winking; he smashes a plate or two, and nearly puts out his eyes with a fork. He takes a fancy to some bright, golden-colored jelly before him, but when he has some on a plate does not eat it; only churns it all up between his fingers, becoming so absorbed in his occupation that his voice is not heard for fully two minutes.

Little Lord St. John leaves his place, and goes round to look at the youngster, addressing it affectionately as " chucky, chucky, chucky!" whether under the mistaken notion that he is a species of young pig, I know not.

"Little angel!" murmurs Alice, gàzing at her son.

"Pretty king!" says Milly, as her infant sneezes in her face.

"Never makes a sound," says Alice, kissing the top of her baby's golden head.

"Never cries at strangers," says Milly, rubbing her cheeks against her heir's primrose down.

I never knew until to-day how mothers *drivel.* Lord St. John ventures his face too near Alice's boy, and he puts out his plump, jelly-covered little fingers, and firmly grasps that gentleman's mustaches with a solemn and delighted countenance. The more the poor man tries to get away, the harder the baby holds on, and not until tears of pain stand in Lord St. John's eyes is he released. At the top of the table there is a sort of a happy family show, that is calculated to fill all beholders with an insane desire to jump up and rush, all of us, to church and be married on the spot—the spectacle of connubial bliss is so beautiful. Fane looks at Milly, then at the baby; Milly looks at the baby, then at Fane. It is very touching, no doubt; but is it not rather public? Young Lovelace has struggled to the floor, and made friends with the dog. They are eating a biscuit between them. The dog takes a bit, then the baby does. It is very interesting, but rather dirty.

We go into the drawing-room, and stare at one another, and marvel, as everybody does every Sunday of their lives, what we are going to do with ourselves. If I were twenty years older I should retire to my bedroom and go comfortably to sleep, as Mesdames Fleming and Lister are going to do, I am morally certain. Alice and Milly have vanished after their babies; the Misses Lister are whispering together; Silvia is giving Sir George Vestris a liberal education at the window. A sound of merriment comes faintly from Fane's study; clearly men have a better notion of passing time than ladies. Reading novels on Sunday is forbidden, but it is no sin to *act* them. Spicy, full-flavored, exciting love-stories run through more quickly and easily on this day than any other, and more love-nonsense is talked on a Sunday than in all the remaining six days of the week.

"Are you going to church this afternoon?" asks Paul Vasher's voice behind me, as I stand drumming my fingers against the glass.

"It is too hot," I say, turning round. "Oh, I do feel so cross! Why may not one work, or dig, or do something useful, on Sunday afternoons?"

"We are going to church," says Miss Lister, appearing before us; "will you come, Miss Adair?"

"No, thanks," I say, looking up at the burning, cloudless vault overhead. "Is it not too far for you?"

They do not think it is, and go away to "put their things on," which means half an hour's hard labor before the looking-glass, trying to make a silk purse out of a sow's ear.

"Don't betray me if I tell you a secret," says Paul, laughing, "but I think the Listers expect Brabazon and Oliver to accompany them to church, and they are hiding."

"What cowards! Did they promise to go?"

"They temporized, I believe."

"Alas for the glory of the British

flag!" I say. "Is not that one of them peeping round the beech-tree?"

"It is."

"I have a great mind, a very great mind, to tell the Listers where he is; they would not stand on ceremony, they would *fetch* him."

"Brabazon and Oliver would run," says Paul, "and it is too hot for a chase, is it not? Here they are."

Yes, here are the young ladies freshly touzled, freshly repaired, with smart white veils that *now* stand out jauntily enough from their faces, but will by-and-by stick to them or melt imperceptibly into the same.

"Have you seen Captain Oliver?" asks the one.

"Have you seen Captain Brabazon?" asks the other, looking anxiously about.

They are not looking in the right direction, or they would see the whole of one gentleman's right boot and half of the other gentleman's left eye. They hunt about for a little while, poor souls, and at last, shame forbidding them to take their bonnets off, they set out across the park, quarreling fiercely as they go, if one may judge by their backs. When the coast is clear, the captains cautiously leave their hiding-place, and make off, looking as pleased as two schoolboys.

"When I look at those girls," says Paul, emphatically, "I feel thankful that I have no sisters."

"I am going out into the garden," says Milly, appearing with Fane; "will you come, Nell?"

I fetch my hat, and we all go out together. Husband and wife walk on in front. His arm is round her neck, her arm is half-way round his waist; they lean toward each other like a tall and short weeping willow. It is rather trying to one's gravity to walk behind them, and, catching Paul's eye, I go off into a fit of laughter.

"Do they always behave like that?" I ask. "I never saw them together be-

fore, except when they were engaged, and there was some excuse then."

"They always did abroad," says Paul, "or at least when I met them; they were the amazement of all beholders."

"I would rather get up early in the morning to do it," I say, energetically, "than have every one smiling at me, would not you?"

"Much rather!" he says, with emphasis; "it would pretty well take the bloom off to have any amount of people looking at one."

We are in the park now, where are cool shady paths and long pleasant glades, through which the hot tyrannical sun cannot pierce. In the distance Silvia and Sir George Vestris are walking; do they never, I wonder, grow tired of each other's society?

"There go the lovers," says Paul, looking toward them.

"Are they both pretending, do you think?" I say, speaking my thoughts, as I have a bad knack of doing since; for what are words given us, save to delicately disguise our meaning?

"Pretending!" he repeats, with real astonishment; "why should she? I did not know people ever pretended to be in love."

Evidently he has no suspicion that she loves him still; far less is there any of the quick eagerness in his voice that a lover should borrow.

"Nell," he says, looking down on me with a queer smile, "don't ever try to deceive any one, for your face will always betray you! Now, I know what you are thinking; pray, was it to me and *Silvia* that you meditated playing gooseberry?"

"Yes, it was," I say, turning my red face round. "I have always wanted to tell you. I knew all along that you *liked* her; I knew it at Charteris."

"And you think I *like* her now?"

"Do you not?" I say, lifting my eyes to his dark face. "Do you forget so quickly?"

"I do not forget," he says, "but that

old fancy is dead and buried, thank God!" (he throws out his arms with a gesture of freedom), "and it is as likely to be revived again as a body that has lain in the earth until it has fallen into dust."

"And she?" I ask, involuntarily.

"Has forgotten," he says; "why should she remember me? In fact, she seems positively to dislike me; never looks at or notices me, and I don't think we have exchanged twenty words."

"Yes," I say to myself, "and that is what makes me so sure. If she ever looked at or talked to you as to any one else—" But in him love is surely certainly dead, for jealousy is the very pith and marrow of the passion, and he does not feel a single twinge.

"She does not care for him!" I say, stoutly. "I have seen *real* lovers often: they are different. These are sham ones; to watch them is like looking at make-believe feasts, such as we used to have at home."

Paul is loyal even to his buried love. He does not say, "She is coquette to the heart's core; she can never really care for any one." And I honor him as he holds his peace and says nothing.

It is a glorious afternoon. The hum of insects and birds is all about us; the ripe earth seems to hold the year's full perfection in her lap, like a gold flower that is wrought to its uttermost beauty. All too soon, alas! will it tremble and fade and wither away, for does not decay tread ever on the heels of all absolutely fair and lovely things? It is the common, ugly, every-day belongings that are never taken from us.

"And to-morrow this time," I say, as we turn back toward the house, following the gracefully interwoven forms of my sister and brother-in-law, "you will be perfectly happy among the birds! I wonder if any instinct tells them that this is their last day on earth?"

"It is to be hoped not! And what will you be doing?"

"Oh, I am going to enjoy myself too," I say, brightly; "I shall have a long gossip with my sisters in the morning, and in the afternoon I shall go down by the sea."

"And take a book?"

"No. I have such heaps to think about!"

"People?"

"Plenty!—mother, and Jack, and Dolly, and—and others."

"And others?" he repeats, bending his head to look into my face. "Tell me, among these others is there—*a Lubin?*"

CHAPTER VI.

"In the indications of female poverty there can be no disguise. No woman dresses below herself from caprice."

At Luttrell our letters are brought up to us with our cup of early tea. Wise men tell us that our inveterate habit of tea-drinking is in reality but another form of dram-drinking, and that we are hardly less to be blamed than the poor gin-soddened wretches who reel hither and thither in our streets, a blot and a shame upon our country's manhood. They love their strong, coarse, deadly cups, and fly to them over ruined homes and women's broken hearts, and their own lost souls; and we who love our delicate, piquant, refreshing cup of tea, fly to it also, and reap our reward in the shattered nerves and a hundred and one of the intangible, irritable disorders that our grandmothers and great-grandmothers never knew, or so many of them had not lived to such a full and healthy old age. It is a habit of self-indulgence, no doubt; and, perhaps, if the liquid really intoxicated us, we should have a tough battle with our inclination and give it up. Fortunately, however, it does nothing of the sort.

I have only one letter, and it lies on the tray, staring me in the face. Letters! What a little word, and what a lot it means! Only a flimsy bit of paper to guard secrets that might set the whole world agog; only a few beaten-out rags between prying, jealous eyes and the written-down confirmation that, blared abroad, would carry wreck and ruin to many a proud and unblemished home.

Milord, reading his letters with a covert smile, on one side of the shallow breakfast-table, glances over to where miladi sits, reading hers, with a curious expression flitting over her features. Neither knows any more than the dead who are each other's correspondents; but if each were to make a snatch across the table and exchange notes, perhaps husband and wife would get a better idea of the real character, aims, and life of the other than they ever had before. I like this Luttrell fashion of receiving and reading one's letters alone. It must be trying to have your neighbor' watching your crestfallen countenance over unpleasant news, or your satisfied smile if you receive good. The face will sometimes expound the letter as clearly as though the writing were laid before the looker-on.

And now for George's epistle. I have heard that love-words written down are even sweeter than love-words spoken; if it be so, must not unwelcome love-making be even nastier on paper than when spoken? I break the seal and take out the sheet, which is written over in a bold, bright handwriting, very like his own looks. It is not very long or particularly eloquent, but it is manly and lover-like, and not sufficiently spoony, thank Heaven! to read ridiculously. I think a good, long course of such letters as these would impress me very favorably as regards him. If he only would be made to understand how much better I like him when he is sensible than when he is talking nonsense! A man should be firm, yet tender; strong to govern, yet easily led. A woman despises him when he grovels abjectly at her feet; but he chills her when he soars away in-

to the clouds. I wonder if I shall ever have a lover who will hit the happy mean?

This first of September has come upon us in kingly state, with mantle of azure and broad level sunbeams, with soft wooing breath and dew-spangled grass and leaf, and as I lean out of my window in the still, early freshness of the morning, and look abroad at the beauty of hill and valley, land and sea, I marvel to myself whether the pretty brown birds are up and about, preening themselves in the sunshine, tasting of the gleaming dew, as happy and careless and ignorant to-day as they have been all through their short, merry, pleasant young lives.

Breakfast is early this morning, to suit the sportsmen, and when I go down-stairs I find it well begun. The men are eating with a healthy vigor that nothing short of some prospective slaughter of bird or beast ever inspires in their manly breasts. They all look intensely awake, and upon their countenances is that satisfied, all-is-well expression that nothing on earth, save the first of September, ever brings there. Shorn of their nether garments, and clad in knickerbockers, they stand confessed—stalwart men of flesh and muscle, or weakly, miserable creatures, whose legs look as though a touch would break them. Fane, Charles Lovelace, Sir George Vestris, and Paul Vasher, stand the test well; but the others—ah, what a falling off was there!

The conversation is not particularly interesting; it is of "covers" and "coveys," "bags" and "beats," with many other phrases that convey small meaning to our ears, and once there is an indistinct murmur of "luncheon and ladies." Yes, ladies come last of all! For this is that day of days when women, with a certain sinking of the heart, or a sore smarting of their vanity, are forced to confess that they possess but a divided empire over the hearts of men, and that fairer than all the charms of his mistress, yea, sweeter even than the breath of her lips and the music of her voice, is to a man on this day the stubble under his feet, the feel of a gun in his hand, and the sight of a flock of little, soft, plump brown birds. The knowledge is degrading, and we all have a more or less hang-dog, neglected air. Alice looks as though she were going shooting too in her deft, womanlike Norfolk suit of gray. I wonder if, in the city of veiled women in Siam, shooting is practised by the gentler sex, as well as the calling of policeman, soldier, and blacksmith?

Breakfast is over, and we are all leaving the dining-room.

"Won't you wish me good luck?" asks Paul Vasher, standing before me, big and masterful in his cool, gray clothes. (What splendid legs he has got!)

"No, for you're bound on a bad errand. On the contrary, I hope you will miss everything, and that "—I cast about flounderingly for a suitable sporting phrase—"that your neighbor will *wipe your eye!*"

He laughs. "Who taught you that expression?"

"I forget. Jack, I think. It was quite right, was it not?"

We are at the hall-door now, where are gathered together sportsmen, keepers, and dogs, and a handful of young wives and maids. Milly is bidding her lord farewell for a whole day, with a fervor that many a death-bed parting lacks; Alice is standing on tiptoe to kiss Charles. It is as pretty a picture to my mind as any of Mr. Frith's.

"I hope," says Paul Vasher, "that you will enjoy your afternoon by the sea, and— You never answered my question yesterday—was it an impertinent one?"

"It was," I say, looking at him steadily through the burning red of my cheeks. "What if I had asked you if you had a Dulcinea?"

"What, indeed!" he says, looking down on me with an amused laughter in his eyes.

"Are you coming, Vasher?" calls Fane; and he goes with the rest.

The girls they leave behind them stand at the door and look after them, and, when the last pair of legs has vanished, turn and look at one another with somewhat lack-lustre eyes. Eight women left to each other's society for a whole day! Well may we look dull. I want to get Alice and Milly to myself for a bit, but how about these others? Silvia speaks first. No fear of *her* putting up with a morning with her own sex. She is going to write letters in her room, she says, if Mrs. Luttrell does not mind. Mrs. Luttrell does not mind, and she goes away. The Listers are going to spend the morning in the garden, if Mrs. Luttrell pleases, so *they* vanish likewise. Mesdames Fleming and Lister are still in bed, their morning toilets being affairs of some importance, so we are free of all incumbrances and able to follow our own devices. Having worshiped the babies on our knees for a full hour, we go into Milly's boudoir.

"Only to think," I say, executing a *pirouette* on the tips of my toes, "that we three should be all together again here, and that there is no one to send us to bed, or call us names, or insist on our *talking!*"

"Is he as bad as ever?" asks Milly.

"He is worse!" I say, with conviction. "When a person has got into a habit of making himself and everybody round him miserable, he does not stand still—he goes on improving. By the time he is sixty I cannot imagine what he will be!"

"Marry!" says Alice, encouragingly; "that is the only thing a spinster can do in self-defense!"

"You have been so lucky!" I say; "but how do you know I shall be the same? Besides, where is the husband to come from?" I add, laughing.

"But you have a lover," says Alice, "only you will not tell me anything about him."

"There cannot be much to tell yet, I should think," says Milly, with some sisterly rebuke in her tone. "Why, she has only known him since the day before yesterday!"

"Whom are you talking about?" asks Alice, looking puzzled. "Nell's lover is not here at all; he is at Silverbridge."

"Is he not?" says Milly, with a queer smile. "I suppose I was mistaken."

"How refreshing it is to see any one blush!" says Alice, meditatively "Now in London, or good society, you never see the ghost of a blush anywhere."

"But this Silverbridge lover," says Milly, with interest, "who is he—what is he—where did he come from?"

"He is a traveling packman," I say, gravely. "I met him in the fields, and he came from Glasgow. We won't talk about him. Tell me, Milly, do you think that while I am here you will have a ball?"

"Tell me about this young man first," says Milly, "and I will tell you about the ball afterward."

This is what I have been dreading—a long, comfortable, married women's conversation over my matrimonial prospects, with a calm and dispassionate balancing of *pros* and *cons*, in which my own heart will have no concern. For of all the strenuous advocates of two people marrying who are not particularly fitted for each other, commend me to a couple of young women who have married for love and are perfectly happy; they do not know what uncongenial wedlock means, and cannot be brought to understand its misery. I give a deep groan. With these inquisitors I know of no arts that will avail me save flight, and I do not wish to run away; for, judging by an intangible something in Milly's face just now, I have a shrewd suspicion that not only is there a ball, but that the day is fixed—so here goes.

"Alice—Milly, I won't deny it. I have got a lover, and his name is Tempest, and he lives at Silverbridge, and I don't mean to marry him if I can possibly help it; and I have told him so, and he is very good-looking, and—and that's all!" Here I stop, out of breath.

"Tempest!" says Milly. "I am sure I heard Fane talking about some Tempests the other day. Are they not very rich people?"

"I believe so."

"And why on earth don't you marry him?" asks Alice, warmly. "You will see nobody in Silverbridge; and as to living at home with papa— By-the-way, what does he say to your having a lover?"

"He does not know it, or at least he never says anything."

"Although it is all going on under his very nose!" says Milly. "Well, one of these days he will open his eyes very wide and be furious, and you will be sent to bed for a week."

"I expect he will make a great fuss," I say, cheerfully. "I only hope he will lock me up altogether, for then George Tempest will not be able to get at me."

"Nell," says Alice, with a serious disbelief in her voice, "have you kept back anything?"

"What, about Mr. Tempest?"

"Of course. Now, you said he was good-looking—is he short?"

"He is over six feet."

"And he has not a hump?"

"No."

"Does he talk through his nose?"

"No."

"Or wear large plaid suits?"

"No."

"Is he ignorant? Not that that signifies, for nowadays only the middle classes are well informed; well-born people are nearly always doubtful as to their spelling."

"No," I say again.

"Is there insanity in the family?" asks Milly.

"No! no! no!" I say, jumping up and going off into immoderate laughter. "He is nice, charming, desirable in every way; but—is it so very hard to understand?—I can't marry him, for I do not love him!"

"Then you are in love too with somebody else!" says Alice, scanning with broad-eyed candor my disturbed face, "though where you can have seen him I'm sure it is difficult to imagine."

"I am not in love!" I say, indignantly; "I never was in love! I would not do anything so silly, so—so ridiculous. If I had had any fancy that way I should have made a donkey of myself at Silverbridge long ago."

"And how long have you been sure that you do not care about Mr. Tempest? Since the day before yesterday?" asks Milly, saucy persistence in her blue eyes.

"I have known it all along," I say, steadily. "What should the day before yesterday have to do with it?"

"Nothing," says Milly, with a baffling glance at Alice. However, I will not notice their looks.

"And now for the ball," I say, fanning my heated countenance with the tail of my pannier. "Are you really going to have one?"

"On the 17th. Shall I send Mr. Tempest an invitation?"

"How delightful!" I say, drawing a deep breath. "I have never been to a dance in my life, you know, and—"

"What are you going to wear?" asks Alice, and her literal question brings me very suddenly down from the rose-colored clouds on which I am floating. My jaw drops, and I stare at her blankly.

"I never thought of that," I say, slowly; "I was thinking of the dancing and the fun, and—"

"Have you not a single ball-dress?" asks Milly, rather crnelly I think, for she knows as well as I do how the governor mulcts us in pin-money.

"A ball-dress!" I repeat, derisively. "Indeed, you may thank your stars that I have come in a gown at all, and not a petticoat body, for there is so much trouble to get any clothes at Silverbridge

that very soon, I believe, we shall have to do with none at all."

"Of course you must have a dress," says Milly, calmly; "had you not better write to Howell and James, and order one?"

Howell and James! When even that refuge of the destitute, William Whiteley, is far, far beyond me! Clearly Milly has forgotten the days of her youth.

"I shall not appear," I say, miserably; "I could not dance and enjoy myself with an awful bill hanging over me all the evening, and knowing what it would cost mother, so I shall be *ill* the night of the party, unless you think a costume *à la* squaw, consisting of a pearl necklace and a pair of boots, would be full dress enough."

"It would be quite full enough," says Alice, "and extremely well suited to the weather, only Mrs. Grundy might object."

"If you had only been at Silverbridge at the last bill row," I say, sinking into still deeper dejection, "you would not feel inclined to *laugh* at the prospect of another."

"Tell us about it," says my lovely sister; "those rows were terrifying things, but very amusing to think of after."

"The last *was* amusing," I say, laughing heartily, in spite of the dismal business of getting a gown that unpleasantly pervades my mind; "you remember Snooks, the draper?"

"Rather."

"You know the consternation his modest handwriting ever caused in our domestic circle? Well, at midsummer he sent in his account, and of course papa, instead of paying it, danced upon it as usual. I fancy he has a notion that after dancing a *pas seul* over bills they are, in fact, discharged, don't you? Well, times being bad with Snooks, he plucked up a spirit, and wrote a gentle request for his dues, but when it arrived no one could be found brave enough to present it to the governor; for two days it was handed round the house, everybody, servants and all, repudiating it, and then with one consent it was decided that something must be done. The Bull of Bashan proposed that we should lay it on the Prayer-Book, and receive in a body his overflowing wrath, but, after some consideration, that plan was rejected. Finally it was decided that we should place it in that little study at the top of the stairs, by his bedroom, where he often sits, and the time for putting it there was fixed at immediately after dinner, when he is always sitting in the library over his wine. Dinner over, Basan fetched the fatal epistle, and we set off, full speed, for the study, clattering up the stairs like mad, he first, I following. You know how narrow the staircase is, and that the door opens abruptly to the left, so that until you are right on the threshold you cannot see in at all; well, Bashan flung the door open and—stopped short: Alice! Milly! over his face came the most awful, indescribable, wonderful change: he looked as if he was turned to stone. Nothing short of the governor could produce that look on any of our faces, and *he* was down in the library.

"'What on earth is the matter?' I said, poking my grinning countenance round the corner; 'you look as if you had seen the dev—' There, within half a yard of my nose, stood *the governor!* The old gentleman would have been an agreeable apparition compared with that. Do you know the grin absolutely *froze* on my face; for a moment I started, then turned tail and ran, Bashan after me. Half-way down the stairs I remembered the bill.

"'You must go back and give it him!' I said in an agony, and I pushed him back.

"Meanwhile papa was capering at the top of the stairs in a perfect fury, asking how we dared go to his room, what we wanted there, did we mean to break the staircase in with our confounded boots, etc. When Bashan went back with the letter, he tore it out of his hand, saw what it was, and then threw it at him! Bashan never stopped to pick it up that time, he ran in good earnest, so did I! To this day

it is a mystery to us how he got up there, for we *saw* him go into the library."

"I know it all so well," says Alice, drying her eyes, "but we have had more amusing rows than that."

"Do you remember—" And here we slide off into a crowd of ludicrous reminiscences, that are very real and true, and ridiculous to us, but maybe would seem sad and unlikely enough to other people; perhaps they would not understand how we could laugh at all over such things, but, thank God, we have ever been able to find a silver lining to our clouds, and it is better to bear our ills with a smiling countenance, is it not, than to turn bitter, and hard, and cynical, and rail against Heaven?

CHAPTER VII.

'. . . . The best of rest is sleep,
And that thou oft provok'st; yet grossly fear'st
Thy death, which is no more."

WE are feeding the gold and silver fish in the pool before the drawing-room windows, Paul Vasher and I. He is providing for the silver ones, I for the gold, or at least am trying to, for the former, if they have duller backs, have far brighter wits than their orange-colored brethren, and get the crumbs oftenest. "Do you know," I say, as I drop my last bit deftly into the greedy maw for which it was intended, "that we are going to have something most charming and delightful?"

"And what is that?" he asks, as we pace along the terrace side by side.

"A ball!" I say, clapping my hands; "a *real* one, no make-believes this time! Will you ever forget that party at Charteris?"

As the words leave my lips, he looks across at Silvia, who is for a wonder sitting alone hard by, seemingly watching us with a listless indifference.

"I shall never forget that party," he

says, quietly; "and so you like the prospect of this ball?"

"Yes, indeed. Will you believe that I have never had a real partner in my life but once, and that was when I danced with you!"

"Have you not? Then, for the sake of that old dance, you will give me the first, will you not?"

"Yes, but you must not be angry if I bungle dreadfully; I never could dance well!"

"Then why are you so pleased at the prospect of this party?"

"I shall like the music, and the fun, and my partners, and all that."

"And I suppose you are full of delight at having to choose a new gown and wreath!"

"Full of delight!" I stare at him blankly for a moment, then look away; he little knows what a gnashing-of-teeth business having a new gown in our family is. "It is not much of a pleasure," I say, with an odd smile; "it is far more of a misfortune."

"You are afraid of its not being becoming?" says Paul, looking puzzled; "have you decided on what it is to be?"

"I have not thought much about it yet; anything."

"Wear white," he says, with a man's fixed belief in the perfectibility of that colorless color; black or white, or black *and* white, every man believes a woman to be well dressed when she is arrayed from top to toe in either, or both. Men have no notion of the innumerable little details that go to make up a perfectly-appointed toilet; they will say that a woman looks well or ill, but they can't pick her to pieces, and tell you in what part of her dress the fault lies. They will pronounce one of Worth's choicest confections to be "hideous," and a simply but gracefully attired girl to be "charming;" having no feminine admiration—the barbarians! —for the costly lace and exquisite trimmings that mark the former, while the

charming creature, poor soul, wears only ordinary muslin and ordinary silk.

"There are so many whites," I say, considering—"white silk, white satin, white brocade, white muslin—the materials are endless."

"And what had you on that day I met you among the rye?"

"A white cambric," I answer; adding mentally, "or a 'clean boiled rag,' as Jack calls it, and which the washerwoman knows as well as her own face!"

"If I tell you what to wear," says Mr. Vashér, "will you promise to have it?"

"So long as you do not put me in pink or yellow."

"Then you shall wear white of some glistening light fabric; and on one side you must have great bunches of gold wheat and scarlet poppies, with a little bunch of the same against your left shoulder, and a wreath in your hair."

"Not in my hair, please, Mr. Vasher! It is not so very long ago that it was almost red, and—"

"I don't think you need to be afraid of the poppies," he says, looking at my untidy, ruffled locks; "they looked well enough the other day."

"I only wore that wreath across the field out of sheer bravado," I say, laughing, "because I had been told not to."

"Who told you not to?" he asks, quickly; "who had the right to?"

"No one!" I say, turning my head away; "at least, no one in particular."

We walk in silence up the little steep path that leads toward the upper terraces. In front of us are Mrs. Fleming and Mr. Silvestre; following behind, Alice and Lord St. John: the men have returned from shooting early to-day. I am wondering what my dress will cost, and whether boughten poppies are expensive, also whether they are as handsome as their living sisters. After all I think I shall take Milly's advice. Papa could not possibly storm more over a big bill than he would over a little one, and, let the

9

cost be what it may, I am resolved that on the 17th I will for once in my life be not merely clothed but *dressed !*

"I have made up my mind," I say, briskly, "my gown shall be made of white *gauze*. It ought to be beautiful, ought it not ? "

"Very."

He is not looking at me, but straight before him, and there is a thwarted, vexed look in his face.

"Are you cross?" I ask. "Are you thinking how frivolous and senseless I am to be thinking so much aboùt my first ball ? "

"No, child! I was wondering if it were possible for one to meet with a girl who had never—"

"Never what ? "

"Nothing."

A silence falls between us as we pace along the gravel-walks, the coolness of the late afternoon all about us, the greenness of the earth at our feet, God's azure carpet hanging royally over our heads; only the faint pure smell of an occasional wild flower comes to us on the air, for we are high up on the cliff now, and the gay garden flowers are too proud or too lazy to climb so high.

"And how soon will you be going back to Silverbridge?" asks Paul, his voice disturbing me in the midst of an agonizing calculation of how many yards of stuff an orthodox ample ball-dress requires.

"Not until the end of the month." (Thirty, I should think. I wonder what gauze is a yard ?)

"I suppose you are in a great hurry to get back ? "

"Not at all ! why should I be ? Jack is in town, Dolly at school ; it is very dull at home just now. And I have not been here ten days yet."

"But you have other friends in Silverbridge ; there are some residents, are there not ? "

"One or two." (I must have a pair of white satin shoes at Marshall's, and long gloves with a great many buttons—I shall not stick at a button or two."

"Tell me their names, for they will be my neighbors too very shortly ? "

"We have neighbors, but do not visit them, nor they us. Papa does not like them. We know only one family, and their name is—Tempest," I say, turning aside to pluck a modest spray of euphrasy, and 'looking down on its purple-streaked petals.

"A large family ? "

"No; only a father and son."

Whether it is that I have really forgotten all about my absent lover, or that the thought of my new gown absorbs my faculties to such an extent that I am unable to entertain any other ideas, I do not, I am proud to say, blush in the very least, and am able to meet Paul's searching eyes without a ray of embarrassment or self-consciousness.

"And I suppose that it was because you had seen so few people that you recognized me when we met in the field of rye ? "

"Perhaps. I had never known but two men in all my life—young men I mean—until I came here, so I could not very well forget, could I ? "

"And I am very glad of it ! " he says, heartily.

"Are you ? I am not ! I do not think one is able to judge whether a man is admirable or the reverse until one has seen a great many ? "

"Women ought not to see too many men," he says, decidedly, "it is bad for them." Paul Vasher is like the rest of his sex, who value their privileges too highly to permit women to encroach the merest jot upon them, and would build so prickly a wall of propriety around us that we shall not even be able to climb up and see what is going on on the other side.

"That is very hard upon us," I say. "Is it not the author of 'Guy Livingstone' who says that 'a man must see and admire many roses before he plucks the fairest of them all, his Provence rose, to lay in his breast?' You are free to walk about, looking at this flower and that, critically surveying all, able to make your choice after mature deliberation, while we may not look around us or seek to judge for ourselves; on the contrary, we must accept the first flower that is offered to us, think it adorable, perfect, fall down before it in worship, and look at it contentedly to the end of our days!" Here I stop, somewhat out of breath and laughing.

"Is she always bound to take the first?" he asks, looking at me very keenly.

"Almost always," I say, with a heavy sigh. "Must it not be hard when some day, and all too late, a woman who has given away her life like that, ignorantly, meets with some other who would have suited her? Ah! what ugly words those are, 'too late!' They always make me think of Balzac and the dream that ran through his toiling, barren life; of the tender woman's hands that should one day smooth the hair back from his weary brow and say, 'Poor soul, thou hast suffered!' They came to him at last, too late."

"Do you know," says Paul, "that you have the saddest face sometimes, child, that I ever saw?"

"Do I look like a girl who is going to have a miserable story?" I ask, stopping short; "do I look like a girl who is going to die young?"

He takes my two hands in his, and looks down with infinite gentleness on my pale, scared face.

"God forbid!" he says, gently.

"Do not think me a very great coward; do not despise me," I say, shivering; "but I so fear death. I have such a bodily horror and shrinking away from it, not for what it brings, but because I so dread to go away, to be caught out of this warm, beautiful earth that I know, and away from all the people and things I love. I enjoy my life so keenly that I could not bear to let it go. Do you think

I shall be punished? Is it impious to feel like this?"

"You sweet little soul!" he says, in his strong, tender voice, "you be punished for aught in your fair young life? I wonder what God would reserve for sinners such as I, then?"

"You are not a sinner," I say, stoutly, looking into his noble face — a face that gives so much more promise of grand things than he has ever worked in his life yet. "You are *good.*"

I loose my hands from his, and we walk on again side by side.

"Do you know," I say, laughing (why does laughter often follow so quickly on the heels of sighs?), "that if I know you long I shall become the most egotistical, maundering little person in Christendom? You listen to my complainings, at home no one ever does! Who was it said that there were two people in the world one should never trust one's self to talk about —one's self and one's enemy?"

"A foolish man whoever he was," says Paul, "who knew nothing of human nature, for are not those two naturally the most interesting people under the sun?"

"I do not think I have an enemy!" I say, considering; "have you?"

"No particular one that I know of, though there are plenty of people who dislike me, no doubt. When you are back at Silverbridge, Nell, I shall see you very often, shall I not?"

"If papa does not take a dislike to you."

"I shall be glad to be back there," he says, with a hearty content in his voice. "After a bit, I suppose, I shall settle down and grow fat!"

"I don't think so," I said, glancing at his clean length of limb. "A man need never do that unless he pleases; he has so many active exercises by which he can ward off stoutness. Now, a woman has only got to sit down, and be free from worry of body or soul, to grow fat directly!"

"Then some day I may expect to see you of very comely proportions?"

"No, lean and haggard and ill-favored very likely, but stout never. I bother myself too much over everything for that."

"Your husband will take better care of you," he says; then, bending his head to look into my eyes with those splendid dark ones, that send so sharp and quick a pain through my heart, "has it never occurred to you, child, that some day you will marry?"

"All people marry at some time or another, do they not? It is a solid, heavy pudding of which all taste in turn!"

"Except the old maids?"

"I had forgotten them, but they have probably had lovers in their time; and after all, the courting must be so much pleasanter than the hard and fast wedlock!"

"I think your experience of married people cannot have been very fortunate," says Paul, looking amused. "Why should not people love each other after they are married as well as before?"

"They ought, but very often they do not! They begin very hot and end very cold; and I was wondering only yesterday whether, if one married somebody one did not care about, one would gradually get *warmer* toward him?"

"It would be rather a dangerous experiment," says Paul; "were you thinking of trying it?"

I do not answer, and, as at this moment we fall in with Fane and Milly, he has no opportunity of repeating his question.

CHAPTER VIII.

"Angelo. Nay, women are frail too."
"Isabella. Ay, as the glasses where they view themselves,
Which are as easy broke as they make forms."

It is high noon, and we are "six precious souls, and all agog," dashing along the dusty, hot, turnpike road toward Beecham Wood. The sun, knowing that his time is short, and that he will ere long sink from the proud, overbearing tyrant into a mild, benevolent, dull old luminary, is beating down upon us with broad level strokes, cleaving our parasols and tickling our faces, making us, in short, very uncomfortable, cross, and miserable. It is the sort of day when one longs instinctively for an open unoccupied space, no living being near to touch one, and nothing to do save imbibe cooling drinks; therefore pity us, O reader! in that I am shut up with three other females in Milly's landau. Behind us follows a carriage similarly filled, and we are *en route* for the vernal shades of Beecham and the society of the sportsmen, with whom we are going for the first time to take luncheon. They have several times asked humbly enough for our society, but with the first lust of slaughter upon them Milly judged wisely that they were best left to their own and the birds' company. They are somewhat sated by now, though, for to-day is the 16th of the month.

How fast the days have slipped away! How utterly pleasant and sweet they have been! Let me not begin to rejoice over them though, lest evil ones follow. Far away I see a little soft cloud of gray under the trees, with dogs lying about. As we approach nearer it resolves itself into the gentlemen, who are lounging about, cigar in mouth, looking as cool, and fresh, and comfortable, as we look precisely the reverse. We all tumble out of the carriages anyhow, and make a dash through the gate, only longing to get into the shady woodland beyond. In the general scrimmage Lord St. John is tossed up nearest to me.

"Have we much farther to go?" I ask, looking with affection at a big tree we are hurrying past.

"Not much!" he says; "two or three minutes' walk, perhaps."

I don't think he has done much shooting this morning: he looks as if he had come out of a bandbox, and his wicked little eyes are fixed with doting fondness on Alice's vanishing tail, for with all my haste I am somehow the very last of all.

Everybody seems to have got badly matched to-day: Alice is with Captain Brabazon, Milly with Mr. Silvestre; Fane's back expresses intense disgust as he walks by the side of Mrs. Lister, and her daughter's head has a sulky air as seen in the company of Charles Lovelace, while—oh, wonder of wonders—Silvia Fleming has fallen to the lot of Paul Vasher, and Sir George Vestris gloomily stalks with that young woman's mother.

I am casting my eyes about the wood, and thinking how pretty it is now, and how infinitely prettier it must be in spring-time, thickly powdered over with dainty forest flowers, when I put my foot into a rabbit hole and take a breathless header into space. Lord St. John picks me up without a smile, likewise my hat, which has ambitiously flown far beyond my head, like a rider who clears a fence while his horse remains behind. Goethe says men show their character in nothing more clearly than in what they think laughable. Now, Lord St. John does not even smile, whereas, if I had seen him meet with the same accident, I should have laughed immoderately for five minutes. There is no one behind to mark my confusion, so, as one's misfortunes are always bearable when there is no one by to observe them, I put on my hat with unruffled serenity and proceed on my way.

What a dull little lord this is! It is lucky that he does not, like other mortals, depend on "the quantity of sense, wit, or good manners he brings into society for the reception he meets with in it." He is neither handsome, nor wise, nor witty, yet he will never know the lack of good looks, wisdom, or sense; he will. pass over the heads of men better in every way than himself, only they are born with wooden ladles in their mouths, and he with a silver one.

Here we are at last! The white cloth

on the grass commends itself favorably to my. eyes, and the twinkling silken calves of the footmen, as they go hither and thither, look festive and cool. I sit down with a sigh of relief, and Paul Vasher comes to my side and sits down too. Sir George flies to Silvia, Milly to Fane; the sisters, alas! to the captains —it is a general post. I wonder what Paul and Silvia have been talking about? there is no expression on her face; on his there is a great deal, as he looks at me. I have hardly dared to seek to learn its meaning yet—hardly ventured to put out a trembling hand to touch the skirt of a mantle of great joy.

Everybody is sitting down now, and finding by painful experience that, though eating one's luncheon on the grass is a picturesque thing to look at, it is by no means a comfortable thing to do: one's back has an awkward trick of curving outward, and one's knees of encroaching on one's chin. Then the eating—whether is it better to bend two double over the plate on the damask, or permit it to reverse itself and its contents on our slippery laps? In spite of these drawbacks, however, the grateful shadow, gay voices, welcome champagne-cup, and the right companion, make the hour a pleasant one. If only these pleasant hours that come so rarely to us mortals would abide with us, not hurry so fleetly away!

"I think you must have snubbed St. John pretty well," says Paul; "he left you so precipitately just now."

"He is so stupid," I say, looking across at him; "and as I am not clever myself I like to be with amusing people: do not you?"

"Indeed, I do: but I don't think the cleverest people are the most amusing. They go too deep. It is the nonsense-talkers who are most companionable; just as you will laugh heartily at a book that you keep on saying to yourself over and over again is the silliest stuff imaginable."

"Then. there is some hope for me, is there not?"

The servants come and go, merry jests are born and die, the sunbeams flicker jubilantly down on our uncovered heads, the butterflies flutter idly by, the gnats swarm above us, there are a sleepiness in the air, a sense of comfort in our bodies.

"What have you been thinking about all this time?" asks Paul.

"You will laugh if I tell you," I say, "but just then I was ruminating about bread-sauce. Partridges grew and so did bread, but the man who wedded the two must have been a clever fellow, must he not?"

"And you were really thinking that?"

"Really! I suppose it was the sight of the birds yonder put it into my head."

He looks at me amusedly.

"I wonder if you could keep a secret if you had one?" he says. "I think you would bring it straight out. I always know when you are glad or sorry, vexed or pleased, in an instant; do you think you could be deceitful if you tried?"

"You don't know what stories I can tell at a pinch," I say, laughing; "and, if that is not being deceitful, what is?"

"You do not mean that you tell *lies?*"

"What a downright word! How ugly it makes the smallest deviation from truth look! No, my fibs are only harmless ones, extemporized to save the boys from getting into rows with papa, and so forth. I don't ever remember telling a real lie."

"And you have never deceived *anybody?*" he asks, with a strange persistence.

"Never!" I say, truly—for have I not told George the plain, unvarnished truth hundreds and hundreds of times?

Luncheon is over, and most of the men are not sitting but lounging at their ease, with a comfort very irritating to feminine eyes. Alice and Milly are making use of their respective lords by leaning against them *dos-à-dos;* the attitude is comfortable but not particularly elegant. A score of yards away a stalwart oak presents to our view a stout brown body that offers friendly support to an aching back, and toward it I turn my eyes.

"You are tired," says Paul; "shall we go and sit over there?"

He holds out his hand, pulls me up, and in another minute we are sitting against the old monarch.

"How tired that lord must have got who went on a tour round England without once leaning back in his carriage!" I say, laughing. "Don't you think he must have taken it out in a long course of easy-chairs afterward?"

"I don't fancy they had any worth mentioning in those days. What hardy old people they were, and to what an age they lived! Nowadays it is the old who bury the young. I think it was their leisurely way of taking things, their conversations, their journeys, their love-makings, that kept their bodies and souls so fresh. They were content to take life gradually: one emotion at a time was enough for them; they knew how to wait. Our generation is not satisfied with looking forward; it must desire, long for, possess, all in a breath. There is very little patience anywhere in this nineteenth century."

"I should have liked to live in those days," I say, thinking; "they lived such much grander, sweeter, honester lives than we do: they must have had so much more of eternity, so much less of the present, in their thoughts than we have!"

"Let me tell you, child," says Paul, "that there are girls in the world every bit as nice and honest and sweet as their grandmothers were. Do you remember," he asks, drawing nearer to me, "that once, years ago, I assured you it was much better to be good than pretty? And you disappointed me a good deal, by seeming to prefer the prettiness to the goodness!"

"It was not for beauty I wished it," I say, looking ashamed; "but because I had always thought it a great power, and because I saw handsome people treated far more kindly than plain ones!"

"Do you not know, child, that far more deeply rooted in a man's breast than the mere admiration of physical beauty is his veneration of what is pure, and not to be corrupted, something better than himself, in a word—good? Many women believe that they can hold an undivided empire over a lover's heart by being simply lovely to the eye, and charming: they trust to the comeliness of the body effectually preventing any search after the soul or mind, and their experience of a certain class of men justifies them in so believing. Of the far larger class, who put aside all the dazzle and beauty of the outside appearance to look beyond, they have no conception, little knowing that every sensible man, if he do admire the sparkling casket, always looks within to see if it contain a gem of value and purity, or a tawdry bit of colored glass."

"You are very hard upon us," I say, surprised. "Are all men so difficult to please as you?"

"Shall I tell you why we see the faults of women so freely?" he says. "Because we know how infinitely above us most of you are in purity, unselfishness, and goodness; it is because we hate to see you step off your pedestals and come down to our level, that we are so severe upon every failing and shadow of evil-doing. Do we not honor you more in setting you a high standard than a low one?".

"But do you not help to lower it?" I ask. "I have never been out into the world; I have only read and heard people talk: but I think, if girls are frivolous and vain, it is you who help to make them so. If you talked nobly and sensibly to them and tried to bring out, not the amusing weakness of their characters, but the hidden worth that lies in every nature, you would make less of toys, more of companions of them."

"You are right," he says; "men do incalculable harm in fostering the vanity and conceit of girls; but it is a fact that you may tell a woman she is virtuous, discreet, admirable in every way, and she will not say thank you; but tell her she is pretty—and smiles will break out all over her face. Fellows know this, and of course take advantage of the weakness, and so society becomes leavened with a general idea that beauty is the good and blessing on earth, and that all the other virtues and graces are set down second to it. There never was a greater fallacy. Now, if I had a wife, her good looks would be the last thing I should care to hear commented on. It would give me no pleasure to hear people exclaiming, 'How pretty she is!' 'How beautifully she dances!' but if they said, 'She is a thorough little lady,' 'She is sensible and charming,' 'She is good,' I should be proud of her, and in nothing so much as this, that no one would dare offer her the smallest liberty, in look or word."

"Are you reading me this homily on the beauty of goodness *versus* the goodness of beauty, to comfort my forlornness?" I ask, laughing. "Indeed, you need not: I have grown quite used to not being pretty like the rest."

"Pretty," he says, staring at my face, "can you be so——?" He checks himself, and breaks off. "I see your brothers are smoking," he says presently, "may I?"

"Yes."

I look around me. Mrs. Lister is fast asleep, propped up against a neighboring tree. Her mouth is wide open, and the flies are walking in and out of the same as seemeth good to them. Her daughters are pursuing their up-hill, one-sided flirtations; and the head of the elder is wobbling plaintively toward Captain Brabazon's shrinking shoulder in a manner that seems to say, "Let me lay it down, *and leave it.*" Mrs. Fleming is reading a letter, and her squire—Mr. Silvestre—lies on his back by her side, deeply, soundly, noisily asleep. Silvia is telling her fortune on a spike of grass, and looking with lovely, lazy eyes at Sir George, whose face is aflame with love, pleading, and God alone knows what. Fane's cheek rests contentedly on Milly's elaborate chignon ; and Alice, leaning against Charles's broad back, listens to Lord St. John's mild conversation and flatteries with half-shut eyes. The content on Paul's face is good to behold, when he has his cigar fairly between his lips. Was ever woman, I wonder, as true and faithful and kind a friend to man as tobacco ?

"Your sex ought to be better tempered than ours," I say ; "for you are able to smoke away all your troubles and disappointments and annoyances, while we can only sit down and think."

"You have one great resource that is denied to us—you can weep."

"That is so cowardly. I always look upon tears as a refuge only to be fled to when everything else fails (I mean, of course, when I am put out), and of the two I would far rather storm."

"And yet," says Paul, "utterly as you can rout us by the sight of your tears, I prefer even them to being reviled by you—a woman's power is pretty well gone when she takes to scolding."

"Cleopatra kept hers well enough," I say, half to myself. "Now, if I were you, I would far rather have a woman who was outrageous sometimes and sorry afterward, than a meek, obstinate, crying creature who never forgot herself—or a grudge."

"Then you prefer Katharine to Bianca ? "

"Infinitely ; and I am certain I should have slapped Bianca even harder than Katharine did. She only insisted on her own way until she found some one with a stronger will, then she gave in directly."

"And would you give in to any one ? "

"If I were quite sure his ways were better than mine, if not I should take my own."

"You ought to take his whether you are sure or not."

"Indeed! I see the race of tyrants is not quite extinct."

"Or that of rebels ! "

"There should be no question of 'giving in' or 'looking up,'" I say demurely. "Alfred de Musset says a woman should above all things be *bon camarade ;* and between comrades there is equality, is there not ? "

"The man should always rule," says Paul, in his masterful way ; "and you may say what you like, Nell, but you would love to be ruled, you would like to be kept in order."

"No, no," I say, gravely ; "that Frenchman's idea was a much better one. He went on broader grounds than you do. Yours is an English notion. He recognized the fact that, however pretty and amusing it may be to play at love, it cannot be made the business of a lifetime ; and that after a while a man grows tired of treating his mistress or wife like a goddess or a baby : he wants more solid stuff to live on, and the one everlasting dish palls then. If she will look the knowledge in the face that such is the case, and putting sentiment on one side enter heartily into his ambitions and aims, and hopes, and amusements, she becomes not only the beloved woman, but the bright pleasant comrade, who is bound to him by fifty ties of mutual inrest and support ; they are equals, and he considers her as capable of giving advice as taking it—"

I stop short in my serious disquisition on love and matrimony as I catch Paul's amused smile.

"Wait until you fall in love," he says ; "I shall see it some day, and I wonder where all your philosophy will be then ? "

"Where it is now," I answer, stoutly, through my blushes, "nothing will ever alter my opinion on that point. I think it is nothing but bad management that makes so many married people who begin

with so much love end up with so little.
Mr. Vasher!"

"Yes?"

"Do you think Silvia would ever have
been *bon camarade?*"

"No, she would keep a man to her
side by sheer fascination, but she could
never—"

"What do you call fascination?" I ask
as he pauses.

"I suppose the real essence of it lies in
the power a woman possesses of making
herself so delightful that every hour spent
away from her is an age."

"Do witty people fascinate?"

"In a different way. They amuse and
astonish more than they inspire respect."

"How I should like to be witty!" I
say, laughing. "It is a great power, is it
not, to be able to say clever, brilliant,
sparkling things?"

"Yes, but one not often to be coveted.
A very witty person is no one's enemy so
much as his own: he amuses people at the
expense of others, and the former have a
pleasant conviction that their turn will
come presently, and no one feels safe."

"Like Lady Hester Stanhope," I say,
"who lost all her friends through her
tongue, and was also known to boast that
no one could give such a slap on the face
as she could!"

"Yes, her wit worked her ruin," says
Paul, "as did poor Brummel's, although
indeed his was but barefaced effrontery!"

"I always admired that man," I say,
laughing; "he was so cool and his insolence was so splendidly audacious. I
wonder what master of ceremonies nowadays would dare say to a duchess, 'In
Heaven's name, my dear duchess, what is
the meaning of that extraordinary back
of yours? I declare I must put you on a
back-board. You must positively walk
out of the room backward that I mayn't
see it!'" We both laugh heartily.

"It makes one feel very small, does it
not," says Paul, "that people should feel
so much more angry at being made fun of,
than being called ugly, or wicked, or dis-
agreeable? Is it not Macaulay who says,
'Alas for human nature, that the wounds
of vanity should smart and bleed so much
longer than the wounds of affliction!'"

"One can forgive unkindness, ill-usage,
neglect even—but ridicule never!" I say,
laughing; "and yet it is curious, is it not,
to see how people like to make fools of
themselves comfortably, but hate to be
told of it? That, I suppose, is why you
men always like to marry stupid women,
who never find you out!"

"You are wrong," says Paul. "A
stupid woman, i. e., a fool, admires everything, and everybody, her husband
among the rest; a sensible woman looks
all about her, and, seeing nothing half as
good as the man she has married, admires
him!"

"A most delicate flattery; but supposing he is not wise?"

"Would a woman of sense marry a
man who had none?"

"She often does. Now, Mrs. Skipworth, at Silverbridge, she is sensible,
and she married a very prosy, foolish
man. And yet," I add, looking out at
the cool green shadows and gold patches
of sunlight that lie athwart the woodland, "I don't know that he is so foolish
as irritating. Did you ever know a man
who smiles when he tells you the day is
fine, smiles when he tells you your soul
is lost, and would smile over your new-
made grave, and say the funeral had
gone off beautifully? That is Mr. Skipworth!"

"Well," says Paul, "I shall see him
before long, and listen to his sermons,
which I suppose will be rather worse than
himself. Is your seat in church anywhere
near mine?"

"Oh, no! The Towers turns up its
nose at the Manor-House, and, while you
rejoice in a curtained pew under the pulpit, we occupy an abased position in the
aisle! The pew opposite yours was ours
once, but it would not hold us all, and
papa exchanged it for a big one; but there
is scarcely any one to sit in it now—there

are only nine of us altogether, babies and all!"

"Only nine!" he says. "Well, I shall come over to the Manor-House often, and you will—"

"Nell, Nell!" cries Milly's voice in the distance, and I jump up hastily. Everybody has left off sleeping, talking, laughing, and flirting; the men are repossessing themselves of their guns, and the ladies are standing about.

"At any rate," says Paul, "we have stolen two pleasant hours from the old thief Time, have we not?"

CHAPTER IX.

"Through tattered clothes small vices do appear ; robes and furred gowns hide all."

NINE o'clock is striking, and I am standing before a looking-glass, admiring myself with a hearty appreciation that it would be folly indeed to expect any one else to feel. For the first time in my life I am *en grande tenue*. With something of the recklessness of a man who decides that, if he must be hung, it may as well be for a sheep as a lamb, I am arrayed with a sublime disregard to such vulgar considerations as pounds, shillings, and pence, as might well set the governor dancing a *fandango* if he were but here to see ; not but what he will dance it safely enough over the bill. Out of my glistening dress of gauze poppies burn redly, in great bunches at my side, and on my shoulder, and in my hair ; they even twinkle cheerfully on my little white satin shoes, that look vastly pretty but pinch most horribly.

A tap at the door, and enter Milly's maid with a bouquet, "With Mr. Vasher's compliments." As she retires I take it in my hand. It is of blood-red and yellow-gold roses, with a few ferns, and they look out of place with my vagrant wild-flowers. I shall carry them though

for all that. A supremely happy, well-dressed, blessed young woman I look, as I take up my fan and gloves, and run lightly down the stairs.

My first ball! Will it be as disappointing, I wonder, as the fulfillment of most earthly wishes usually is? I make my way to the ballroom, wide, and cool, and lovely with the beauty of fair proportions, and delicate, brilliant dazzle of flowers.

The musicians are in their places, but nobody is visible, not even that mythical personage, the first arrival. Was ever any one known to confess that he or she arrived first anywhere? And yet somebody must, unless indeed several people race each other to the hall-door, and from the hall-door to the reception-room, and burst in on the host and hostess simultaneously, like "three jolly butcher-boys all of a row." I have laid down my bouquet, and am wrestling with the fourth button of my long gloves (I think I rather overdid them, they nearly reach to my elbow), when Milly sails in, majestic, gorgeous, with the value of the clothes of twenty ordinarily well-dressed females on her back.

"Good gracious!" she says, catching sight of me, "how — how decent you look!"

"Yes," I say with delight, "I had no idea so much virtue lay in a gown!"

"Upon my word!" says Alice's gay voice behind me. "Talk about the ugly duckling—"

I turn round to look at her, a dainty apparition in pale amber, with sapphires twinkling on her arms, neck, and hair. Alice is one of those fortunate people whom each color seems to suit better than the last. Dress her in blue, she is heavenly ; in pink, she is ravishing ; white sets her off to perfection ; and I have even known her emerge radiant from a bilious bottle-green serge that might have puzzled the fairness of Cytherea herself.

"Do not revive that stale, stale old

story," I say, entreatingly. "I know it is my clothes, not me; but let us try and shut our eyes to the fact. Let us for one evening indulge in the pious fiction that I am *good-looking!*"

"I don't know that it is altogether your dress," says Alice, considering. "I have seen you look astonishingly well once or twice lately. If I had not always been so used to the idea that you were plain, Nell, I should say you were rather pretty."

Much as I have been admiring myself, this unexpected praise makes me feel modest, and I turn the conversation with considerable haste.

"Has any one seen Silvia yet? I suppose she will be in something wonderful."

"Was Silvia Fleming ever known to waste her sweetness on the desert air?" asks Alice, seating herself. "When the company is assembled, and the music strikes up, she will appear, not before!"

"I do wish Fane would come down," says Milly, who is arranged in the expectant attitude of a hostess, on a high and ample crimson-velvet chair, that to the vulgar eye bears a wonderful resemblance to a throne. "He always behaves in this way; it is too bad."

Like other women, Milly likes to be supported when she is receiving her guests; but Fane, doting lover and obedient spouse that he is, distinctly objects to the process of standing still and saying, "How do you do?" for an hour at a stretch, and when it is his plain and bounden duty so to do—makes himself scarce. Here come the Listers! Lister *mère* in a low (save the mark!) black velvet, with uncommonly fine diamonds resting on her withered, brown, fleshless old collar-bones—I suppose mahogany is a better foil to the precious stones than alabaster, since it is so much oftener seen. Her daughters wear apple-green silk and apple-blossom flowers, harrowing contrast! and the eye aches as it rests on the inharmonious whole. Will our ma-

trons and maids ever, I wonder, learn to drape their garments, following the lines of the figure as a sallow Frenchwoman does, instead of breaking out all over in angles, tags, and excrescences?

A confused sound in the distance heralds an arrival.

"Nell," says Milly hastily, "will you find Fane, and make him come here at once?"

Rather a difficult matter that; I set out, however, with a bold front, and a regret that I have not been able after all to see the first people walk in. Ascending the stairs, I hear cackles and sounds of merriment above me. Looking up, I discover Fane and that other choice spirit, Captain Oliver, cutting capers on the landing, and evidently prepared to decamp at a moment's notice if any emissary from Milly appears upon the scene.

"Milly says—" I begin, rebukingly.

"I know," says Fane, swinging me round to his side in a manner that may be indicative of brotherly affection, but certainly is not good for my gauze trappings.

"Now, Nell, did you ever see so much *back* as that before?"

Following his example, I crane my head and body over the banisters until I nearly precipitate myself into the hall below, and am rewarded by the sight of a dowager who looks as though her enemy had assaulted her from the rear, and robbed her of half her clothes.

"The older she gets," says Fane, "the more she shows; and the Lord only knows what further revelations Time may have in store for us!"

"She couldn't go much further," I said, comfortingly. "I never knew before that middle-aged people's backs were of a rich *coffee* color, did you, Fane? Who is that shambling little man?"

"Bareback's husband. She might wear him as a bustle and never know he was there."

The stream below widens, swells, people come pouring past in tens and twenties, sleek and clean and glossy, freshly powdered, freshly crimped, freshly smiling. What a pity that they will all be so draggled, and hot, and frowzy in two hours time! Fat mammas, portly papas; pretty young girls, well-preserved old ones; young boys, old boys, middle-aged boys; women white-backed, yellow-backed, brown-backed; women dressed by Elise, women dressed by themselves, well-groomed, ill-groomed, overdressed, underdressed, and not dressed at all. Truly it is a "motley crowd," and from our vantage-ground we criticise them with the unripe sarcasm of our not over-wise youth.

I wonder why the young, and those who have only had the bright side of life turned to them, are so pitiless to the peculiarities, the faults, and the follies of others? It is only the old who are tolerant, and speak more kind words of their fellow-men than malicious ones.

After a quarter of an hour's impartial survey of the charms passing beneath us, "I think," says Fane, "I may venture down now without being let in by Milly for twenty-five duty dances."

Rum-tum-tum-tiddy! goes the music.

"Come along," cries Fane, "you and I will have the first together, Nell!"

"Miss Adair is engaged to me for this," says Paul's voice behind me. How long has he been there, I wonder? "I have been looking for you everywhere," he says, as Fane and Captain Oliver go down-stairs. "I thought your toilet must have proved a wonderfully complicated affair."

"Do you like me?" I ask, stepping back from him, and holding out my skirts in my hands. "You chose it for me, you know; and, to tell you a secret, to-night I am not Helen Adair at all: I am *Howell & James!*"

"Like you?" he says, coming a pace nearer and looking at me keenly from head to foot, and from foot back to head again; "no, I don't *like* you!"

"I am so sorry," I say disappointedly.

"I thought I looked so nice! I was so charmed with myself!"

"I like your poppies," he says, touching those upon my shoulder with the tip of his finger. "They make these things very well, do they not?"

"I will never ask you anything again as long as I live," I say, with dignity. "You might have tried, at any rate, to say something just a *little* polite;" and I march away.

But he catches my hand, flowers and all; and then I remember that I have not yet thanked him for his bouquet.

"Did I vex her?" he says, looking down on my flushed face. "Was she such a vain little soul after all? Nell, Nell! after all the times I have exhorted you not to care about being pretty?"

"I am not vain," I say, turning my head away; "I never had anything to be vain of! But when one has been quite ugly for a very long while, and been told so every day of one's life, it is very disheartening, just as one begins to think one can look decent, for a person to say your dress looks nice, not you."

"There will be plenty of men to tell you that when you get down-stairs, child," he says. "Can it make any difference to you what I think?"

"No, of course it does not!" I say magnanimously, and ashamed of my temporary fit of vanity. "I could not expect you to say what you did not think, could I?"

"If I were to tell you all I thought," he says, looking down on me, "I should frighten you, perhaps, and you would not understand. Perhaps you will let me tell you some day."

"Let us go down," I say, with a sudden shrinking away from him; "the first dance is already over."

Yes, it is over, and in the hall the people are pacing up and down, backward and forward, talking, laughing, flirting, in all the first gloss of their smartness; the men reduced to the smallest possible quantity of clothes, the women swelling forth in a lavish prodigality that mocks at "yards" and makes light of "breadths." Among them all I do not see any face I know; but a great many people nod and bow, and call acquaintance with Paul Vasher.

The haunting, matchless strains of "Blue Danube" come floating out to meet us as we enter the ballroom, and Paul puts his arm about my waist and we glide away, the first couple. After all it is not difficult to dance when one has a perfect partner: perhaps he adapts his step to mine—at any rate, we move in harmony. As the room becomes crowded we stop and sit down to look around us. Truly the scene is amusing enough, for everybody is revolving who has the means, without any question as to suitability in the age or size of that means: tall men dancing away from little partners, little men convulsively clutching tall women, old men and young maids, married women and young boys, fat girls dancing with Don Quixotes, Sancho Panzas puffing round with lean virgins. Everybody seems to have got the wrong partner, and not to mind it in the least. There are couples who rush round and round the room, crashing through every obstacle, and leaving overturned bodies, sore shins, and angry hearts behind; leisurely couples who tread their measures delicately, and are invariably overtaken and run down by the more bustling couples who come behind; couples who aimlessly drift about and are knocked to and fro by the rest. . . .

"I never saw myself dancing," I say to Paul, " but do you think I ever looked like that?" I glance at Miss Lister, whose head is wandering all over her partner's shirt-front, seeking rest and finding none.

"I will look at you presently when you are dancing with somebody else, and tell you," he says.

"How well she dances!" I exclaim, nodding toward a mountain of fat that is going by, held together by a whipper-snapper whose arm refuses to go any farther than the last hook and eye. "Can you tell me why those enormous women go round so sweetly? They seem to turn on a pivot! What a pity it is this one does not live in a place I once heard of, where women are sold by the pound —flesh, not good looks, being considered the most marketable commodity!"

"Only she might object to being sold," says Paul, laughing. "Shall we go on again?"

"Look at St. John," says Paul, as we pause to take breath. "However earnest his solicitations, do not be prevailed upon to dance with him: he has a knack of making spectacles of his partners."

"But I have promised," I say, with some dismay. "He asked me at dinner, and of course I was obliged to say yes. Do you not know that anything in the shape of a partner is better than none at all?"

"You will know plenty of people presently," he says. "Don't believe all the nonsense they will talk to you, child."

"But I like nonsense: it is far more amusing than heavy common-sense; besides, ballroom conversation is never expected to be very wise, is it?"

The music has ceased and we are walking down the room, past the wallflowers —prim and patient, with their white, white boots, that by-and-by will be their shame not their glory, and their sweet little smile that seems to say: "We are sitting down, certainly; but only because we much prefer doing so to dancing!"— past the portly, coffee-backed observant dowagers, and so to Milly, who is looking with real indignation at Fane's rapidly-vanishing heels, which he has been shaking with much agility ever since he came down-stairs. She is talking to a long, lean, liver-colored gentleman whose name I hear is Viscount Linley. We are all standing together when Silvia Fleming comes slowly past, the eye of every man and woman present following her. She is all white and crimson, and her fairness shows more dazzlingly than ever against Sir George Vestris's dark beauty.

"Are you not going to dance with Miss Fleming to-night?" I ask, as we move away. "If so, you had better be quick in asking her, for in five minutes her card will be full."

"Therefore I will not presume to ask so great an honor," he says. "And now, Nell, will you let me see your card?"

It is hanging at my side—an unmarked expanse as spotless as the wallflowers' boots; and I feel rather ashamed of it.

"You will keep all your waltzes for me?" he says, scribbling down his initials at somewhat short intervals.

"Yes; that is to say, if you do not meet with somebody whose waltzing you prefer to mine."

We walk about and make confidential remarks to each other concerning the company. We agree that those bare-necked, plumed old dowagers are unpleasant spectacles; but that the decorous, high-gowned, middle-aged folk who wear their own hair, and not too many fal-lals, are good to look upon, and by no means to be pitied, since they have had their fun, danced their jigs, and now, youth's fits and fevers, ups and downs past, they cannot be sorry to sit down in their comfortable prosperity, and rest. We agree that it would be a kindness on the part of any one present to fetch a shawl to cover Mrs. Lister's unveiled charms; but on my suggesting that Paul should take a neighboring antimacassar to her with his own compliments, he proves himself to be greater at discretion than valor. We think it would be a hard nut for a philosopher to crack if he were called on to decide why so many ancient, purblind, doting old people persist in going to balls, where they are neither useful nor ornamental, and are divided in opinion as to whether supper and scandal are the attractions, or an obstinate determination not to confess themselves too old for society and conviviality is at the root of the matter. We decide that the lack of

tournure in the girls present is appalling (although, for the matter of that, I am about as well qualified for giving an opinion on that point as a South-Sea Islander); and that whenever one sees a good figure it is generally capped by a plain face; and that the pretty-faced miss almost always has her head very ill set on her shoulders, and wears a badly-made gown.

"I have often wished I were a man," I say, as we turn back into the drawing-rooms, "but I never wished it as heartily as I do to-night. Even that silly-looking boy, propping himself up against the door yonder, is free to choose his partners, while I have to wait until some one or other condescendingly *fetches me out*."

"But you can always say 'No!'"

"Not in the face of this half-filled programme," I say, glancing down at it where it sprawls widely open across the front of my dress. "It looks very like an advertisement, does it not?"

"Shall I tell you something?" says Paul, looking down upon me with half-pleased, half-vexed eyes. "It is great nonsense; but then you like nonsense, do you not?"

"Yes."

"Well, then, I heard one man say to another, a moment ago, 'Does any one know who is that pretty little creature in the poppies?' And the other answered, 'No; but I'm determined to be introduced to her before I am half an hour older.'"

"You are making it up!" I say, quickly. "Did you think it would please me?"

"Nell," says Milly's voice beside me, "I have brought some gentlemen to introduce to you," and she goes through half a dozen introductions and sails away. My card is produced and duly written upon by them all, then they make their bows and retire.

"I should not know one of them again if it were to save my life, so it is to be hoped they will claim me all right," I say with some dismay as they vanish.

"I don't think they will forget," says

Paul, reassuringly. "And now here comes St. John to fetch you; it was the third round you promised him, was it not?"

"Our dance, I think, Miss Adair," says the little man, and I put my hand under his arm and go away, with a rueful look at Paul.

John Peel is ringing forth in glorious fashion as we enter the ballroom. Can anything be more maddening, I wonder, than good music and a bad partner? Lord St. John does not wait for an opening, but, gripping me round the waist, plunges wildly into the *mêlée*. On watching him I had been struck by the way in which he appeared to *run away* from his partner: on careering with him, I find that—proud and happy as I should be to be left out of his gyrations altogether—there is no such luck, for he holds on to me like grim death, "without any regard to my squalls or my kicks" (as a poet once wrote of a victim very little worse off than I), and that fast as he tears round me I am forced into a very similar and indecently-hasty appearance of likewise tearing round *him*. In vain I ask him to stop. . . . I am, indeed, too deeply engaged in the all-absorbing business of holding on, and praying that Providence will bring me out of this *galère* without the loss of my front-teeth, to say much; so on we rush, running full tilt at the company; dashing into the couples before us, recoiling violently on to those behind; landing with convulsive energy on the wallflowers' toes, taking headers into the wall or space, pelted with blows, harassed with return kicks, abraded with sharp elbows, verily we run a race as perilous as was that of Dick Turpin, but are not, like him, clothed with honor, but disgrace!

"Stop!" I cry loudly, when we have upset our fourth couple, and only saved ourselves from rolling upon their prostrate forms by a succession of aërial bounds that would not have done discredit to Taglioni. "Stop!" And, being tired by his exertions, he looses me, and I tumble into a chair, and go very near to weeping. There is a smile on the countenances of the lookers-on, the very wallflowers are grinning—nasty little wretches, who would not object to be twirled round like mops, rather than not dance at all! Examining into the extent of my injuries, I find that I have a lump on my forehead that will probably be black and blue to-morrow, a partially-skinned arm, and a tolerably severe cut over my left elbow, which I have indeed been using as an active weapon of offense and defense, as is the wont of womankind in a ballroom skirmish.

"Poor little soul!" says Paul's voice beside him, and, looking up with eyes that are filled partly with anger, partly with tears, I see that his face is dark with wrath, and that his glance at Lord St. John is of no very friendly character.

"You should have taken better care of Miss Adair," he says, sternly. "Do you see how you have hurt her?"

Poor little Lord St. John! He has no idea but that he has distinguished himself in a very spirited and successful manner, and is mopping his forehead preparatory to doing it all over again.

"Is she tired?" he asks, with genuine astonishment. "And we got on so well, too!"

"She is too tired to dance the rest of this galop," says Paul impatiently. "Miss Lister is not dancing, I see. Why do you not ask her?"

Lord St. John is essentially docile, he always does as he is bid, so he fetches the young lady and starts off again with much zeal if little discretion.

"I should like to thrash that little fool," says Paul, looking at my scratched arm, and making a sudden movement toward it that he as quickly checks. "Dairy-maids and cooks should be his partners, not delicate little things like you."

"I have one mercy to be thankful for," I say, sitting up and putting my hand to my head to see if my poppies still bloom there; "he did not let me down!"

"Miss Lister will not be so fortunate, then; for if they don't go down before they are five minutes older I am much mistaken. Look at them now!"

I do look. Lord St. John and his unhappy partner are taking a header straight down through the room; and another couple, equally daring and unconscious, are also taking a header from the opposite end; and, alas! before either couple has time to get out of the way of the other, they meet with a violent impetus that scatters all four to the winds of heaven, or rather to the polished oak shades of the earth below. They may be severely damaged—no doubt they are— but the laugh of the multitude is ever against those who cry out under misfortune, so they all jump up again in a trice —all, that is to say, but Miss Lister, who sits on the ground and weeps bitterly, displaying a good quarter of a yard of flat ankle, that considerably mars the effect of her pearly tears. In vain her unfortunate partner assures her of his sorrow in reducing her to such a plight—in vain her friends hold out friendly hands to help her up: there she sits and weeps.

"Perhaps if Oliver were to come to the rescue she would be persuaded," says Paul; and as he speaks that gallant warrior, attracted by the crowd, and not having seen the catastrophe, approaches with much interest and peeps over. At the sight that meets his gaze—to his shame be it spoken—he turns tail and runs. "It must have been her ankle," says Paul, in deep disgust. "I wonder they do not call in two stout footmen." She gets up at last, though, with unavailing tears running down her hot angry face, and her apple-blossom wreath cocked rakishly over one eye, as though it rather enjoyed her miserable condition than otherwise. "Let me see your card," says Paul, stooping over it; "ours is the second from this. I see your next is with Sir William Aldous."

"Was not he the man who was all nose and no legs?" I say, considering; "or the one with a big forehead and no chin?"

"You are very disrespectful to your admirers," says Paul, laughing, "considering your charms brought the assemblage together."

"My charms?" I say, laughing aloud. "Are they, then, un fait accompli? Are they placed beyond the region of doubt? Well, I am proud, really proud of the collection my charms brought together! Take me back to Milly, please, before my partner comes to fetch me."

On our way Silvia passes us on Viscount Linley's arm. His sallow face is alight with admiration.

"He seems to admire her very much," I say.

"He loves every pretty woman he sees," says Paul, with a queer smile, "whether she be white, brown, or black. If the love of woman is really a 'liberal education,' then he reflects great discredit on your sex, child; for the older he gets the worse he grows!"

I am scarcely by Milly's side when Sir William Aldous comes to claim me for the Lancers, and I find myself excellently well-amused, for he turns out to be a fool of the finest quality and most exquisite water. All through these sober, decorous old Lancers (how much longer will they be permitted, I wonder, in this age of breakdowns and fast dances? The nineteenth century stands them; but will the twentieth?) he amuses me charmingly; for fools may be divided into two classes —those who know it, and those who do not. My partner is of the latter class therefore, since his silly remarks are always uttered with a perfect air of good faith, and are neither recalled nor repented of, he is boundlessly fresh, inexhaustibly amusing, as no wise man could be with solid reason, admirable logic, and weighty *pro* and *con*. It is tolerably easy to guess at what a sensible man will do, under any given circumstances; but I defy any one to forecast the words and acts of a downright talking fool. He will unconsciously say things that are almost like flashes of genius, his words will be the very inspiration of folly, and he will scale heights and plumb depths before which wise men have stood silent and abashed.

The dance over, we go into the hall, and so to the refreshment-room, where he leaves me in a comfortable chair, and departs in search of claret-cup. Close to me a group of men are discussing the charms of their late partners, with a freedom that should delight those ladies, if they were by to hear.

"Give you my word of honor, Dalrymple," says one, "she had an entirely new set for this evening. Only had a very few teeth left—remaining stumps were taken out yesterday—new set put in this morning—here to-night!"

"Don't believe any mortal woman could stand it," says another.

"Then she's immortal, my dear fellow," says the first speaker, "for I know it to be a fact. She's engaged too. Rather awkward person to kiss—eh? Things may come to a dead lock."

"Or lock-jaw."

"I hope this is right," says Sir William, appearing before me. "I did not quite like the flavoring, so I have been showing the butler how to improve it."

So that accounts for the disgusted expression on Birkhead's face. Evidently he does not appreciate a fool as keenly as I do!

CHAPTER X.

" How sweet the moonlight sleeps upon this
        bank!
Look how the floor of heaven
Is thick inlaid with patines of bright gold."

SUPPER is over, and I have danced a great many dances with partners, good, bad, and indifferent; have been startled, amused, pleased at the pretty speeches

made to me, and which I have tried hard to convince myself are not meant in the very least, though in my secret soul I do believe that a few of them were not spoken in jest but earnest; and now we have stepped out of the crowded, noisy rooms, Paul and I, on to the terrace, where couples are walking up and down in the clear white light of the moon, making love, or the semblance of it, Corydon to Phillis, and sometimes—alas for the order of things!—Phillis to Corydon. Paul has stolen a warm white shawl from the back of a chair, where it had been left by an unsuspecting dowager; there will be a fine hue and cry after it by-and-by.

The night is very lovely, more like an August one than September, the air is so warm, and the perfume of the flowering myrtle wanders abroad so sweetly. Down yonder, by the trout-stream, the great masses of foliage lie dark and stirless; there is not a puff of wind to rock the pigeon-cotes hung aloft in the boughs; there is no sound of insect, bird, or beast, to ruffle the silence, only the far-off swish of the sea as it softly laps the shore. Turning the corner of the house, we come to a stone parapet, that overlooks the flower-garden dappled all over with flowers and melting imperceptibly into the woods, that in turn seem to merge themselves into the sea. From the bed of mignonette below comes up to us a pure, fresh breath, that recommends itself more favorably to me than any of the voluptuous heavy perfumes of the hot-house flowers we left in the room behind us.

"I wonder if Juliet had a bed of mignonette?" I say, looking out at the silver streak of sea beyond the dusky woods.

"I dare say. What made you think of her?"

"This parapet and the flower-garden stretched out below. I can almost fancy I hear Romeo calling—

' Call me but love, and I'll be new baptized;
Henceforth I never will be Romeo;'

and Juliet calling back—

'My bounty is as boundless as the sea,
My love as deep; the more I give to thee,
The more I have, for both are infinite.'"

"Do you think any girl could love like that nowadays, Nell?"

"Was she not very quick?" I ask, doubtfully; "do you not think it was strange she should have fallen in love with him all at once like that?"

"It is a poor love that is afraid to discover itself as soon as felt," he says, "and that beats about the bush until it is certain of the same being returned. I believe that the strongest and most enduring love is that which is sudden, or fallen into."

"I am glad they both died," I say; "perhaps if Romeo had lived he would have loved some one else and spoilt the whole story."

"Yes, I think he would have forgotten in time and loved again, as you say; why should he not? Do you believe that a man cannot care as much the second time as the first?"

"I do not know about men," I answered; "I only know that a woman could not. Juliet would have had no second lover, I am very sure."

"If you had been Juliet," he says, stooping his head to look into my face, "and Romeo had died, what would you have done?"

"I should not have killed myself, but I should have loved him dead as passionately as I had loved him living; and no word of love from another should ever have shamed his memory."

"I am going to ask you a question, child; an impertinent one you will no doubt consider it, but I will have an answer. *Have you ever had a lover?*"

My heart stands still as I lift my eyes to him, standing there by my side. For a moment I hesitate; then, for speaking the truth has always come more naturally to me than to tell lies, I answer, "Yes."

He turns away. "They are all alike," he mutters, half-aloud, "all alike!"

"And he makes love to you, I suppose?"

"Yes, indeed?" I say, with a rueful sigh, given to the memory of how bootless that love-making has proved.

"And do you like him?"

There is a confident, half-teasing ring in his voice as he asks the question, and I turn my head away ruffled and hurt. Shall I talk over George's true, honest love?

"Nell!" he says, coming round to the other side and looking into my averted face, "did you hear me?"

"Yes."

"Confess now that you do not care a straw for this—*this Lubin?*"

"Do I not!" I answer, roused by his tone and the slighting allusion to my absent lover, who is so leal to me, and to whom I— "There you are quite mistaken; I like him very much indeed; next to my own people I don't know any one whom—"

"Next to your own people!" he says, with a queer smile. "Would you not put the man you loved before?"

"That would entirely depend on who he was! If he were a selfish person—"

"If? Have you not made up your mind, then?"

But I do not answer him. I slip from his side and run fleetly away, and reach the ballroom before he can overtake me: certainly it was a narrow escape that time. My partner for the dance meets me as I enter, and I walk through the Lancers absently enough; fortunately, however, he has the gift of the gab in high perfection, and I am only required to throw in an occasional yes and no. We have for our *vis-à-vis* a very stout lady and a very active little gentleman, and, looking upon them, I am irresistibly reminded of an elephant laboring after a flea, she is so slow, he so spry; I am sure he takes a dozen steps to her one. On my left is a broad-faced young man, who wears a perpetual and uneasy smile, that seems neither able to expand into a grin nor depart in peace; I have a great mind to make a face at him as we advance in the figure, and see whether it deepens or vanishes.

It is growing very late, or early; daylight will soon be looking in upon us, but the fun of the ball is at its height. Supper has made shy men bold, bold men impudent, silent men garrulous, and cheerful men harlequins; prim young women relax into hearty laughter, fast young women wax faster; admiration degenerates into flirtation, and flirtation into downright love-making; love-making, that is to say, which is born of champagne, propinquity, and opportunity—a poor imitation of the genuine article. The dowagers beam unctuously over their double chins; there is not a wallflower left to grace the wall. Have they indeed risen and *touted* for partners? Several proposals are flying about, and the general appearance of everything points to the fact that time is scurrying with flying feet, and that they who would enjoy themselves must do so speedily, or not at all.

How the society masks drop off the faces! How the true ring of the voice comes out, and the real expression of lips and eyes reveals itself! If a physiognomist could stand in our midst, how easily he would read the relaxed countenances of those present! Of some, it is true, there is no evil or mischief to learn, but of others much. Many of the men and women here to-night bring into society faces as carefully prepared to meet the world's eye as the clothes they wear; it is not often one can get a peep at them as they really are.

We go into the supper-room, where are congregated a good many people, drinking, talking, fanning themselves, making love, and talking scandal. Scraps of conversation come fitfully to my ears. "What color eyes do you like best?" "Blue, like yours." "My dear Mrs. Backbite, I *saw* the man deliberately kiss her hand, and she actually looked as though she liked it!" "Yes, first-rate action. Is it true she is scratched for the Vasher stakes?" "Yes; and entered for the Vestris." "It was Vasher who sheered off, not the Fleming." "St. John says that Vasher is mad about that Miss—" (I do not catch the name). "Any one can see that." I do not hear the rest, for Paul himself stands before me.

"This is our waltz," he says. "Are you too tired to dance it?"

"No."

I put my hand in his arm, and go back to the ballroom. Already it is growing empty; some one or other has made a move, and like a flock of sheep every one is following. Willing mothers are running about after their unwilling daughters, who have, indeed, the advantage over their anxious parents, inasmuch as they can dance away from the same, "up the sides and down the middle."

Faster and faster goes the music, quicker and quicker go the flying feet; all are enjoying it with a zest that nothing, save the knowledge that it will be quickly over, could possibly give. Into the feet of some of the middle-aged waiting folk the music gets, and partners being forthcoming they essay a turn or two, at first with some shyness, much as Mr. Aminadab Sleek and Lady Creamly did in "Home," then with vigor; finally they revolve with much enjoyment, perfect in the steps of thirty years ago.

Oh, this last dance! The light, the music, the perfume of the flowers, the long harmonious movement, they are woven into one exquisite sensation that blooms for a little space and dies. And now all too soon the waltz ceases, and delivers over the girls to the custody of their mothers, and they go away torn, spoiled, draggled, with all the carefully built-up finery of a few hours ago in ruins. It is always wretched work seeing the last of everything—the lights put out, the daylight on weary faces, and the winding up. So at the foot of the stairs I say good-night to Paul. But he does not take my hand, and as I turn away he walks along by my side.

"Good-night, again," I say, wearily, as I reach my door. "Oh, I am so sleepy!"

"Good-night," he says; then pressing both my hands against his lips, "good-night, little Nell!"

CHAPTER XI.

"... . When Phœbus doth behold
His silver visage in the watery glass,
Decking with liquid light the bladed grass."

NINE o'clock is striking as I open my eyes, brightly, broadly awake, and rested. Sleep is a cunning fellow; he knows when his subjects have had enough of him, and when he strikes them with his fairy wand, crying, "Awake!" they only are wise who leap up and begin their day: it is the foolish ones, who do not know what is good for them, that turn away from the light, heavily courting the slumber that is not necessary, therefore will not refresh them.

Looking out of the window I discover that the morning is perfect; never did Nature wear a fairer robe than she has put on to-day; and I long to be out, assisting at her morning show, brushing the dew from her meadows with hurrying feet, smelling at her freshly-opened buds and flowers, taking a long draught of her beautiful, vigorous, healthy life. I have some difficulty in getting my breakfast, to which is added one welcome and one unwelcome addition in the shape of a letter from Jack and another from George. I read Jack's, the other will keep. The dear boy is coming home for a few days the end of October; he is very busy, he says, and will be very glad to see me again.

Down-stairs I meet nobody, save sleepy servants, who look, poor wretches! as though they had not been to bed at all.

As I open the glass door of the drawing-room, a cold, sweet breath of the sea comes faintly up to meet me, and seems to die pleasantly on this warmer air that creeps about the sunny terrace and south side of the house. The trees are still bravely clad, although the finger of decay has touched their greenness here and there into flaming scarlet and vivid yellow; the birds are singing loudly and jubilantly enough, but somehow their notes do not seem to be as sweet and joyous as they were a little while ago. To them the summer meant warmth and comfort, the fruits of the earth fed them, the nights gave them shelter, but with the first breath of the frost-king they see hunger and cold stretching out before them, and the iron hardships of the long winter, at least, so their song seems to say to me as I listen. On the upper terraces, and in the glades that the sun's eye cannot reach, since the screen of leaves above is so thickly woven, the hour might be six o'clock in the morning, not ten, and there is yet some of—

" That same dew that sometimes on the buds
    Was wont to swell with round and orient
        pearl."

And of the few scanty autumn flowers left I make myself a posy and fasten in my belt.

I wonder why one feels so much brisker, fresher, brighter, in time of autumn than in time of spring, which is so infinitely lovelier and more grateful to us? Somehow these trees, whose leaves are dying in such splendid livery of gold and sepia, crimson and brown, strike no pang to our hearts; they do not suggest unpleasant thoughts of our own decay; on the contrary, we walk erect, and cheat ourselves with the vain belief that, though all things fade, yet do not we; or, at least, not now. How we cling to our little atom of life, that is so small and yet so huge, and, placed directly before our eyes as it is, assumes grand proportions that block out the far-off and dimly seen plains of eternity—very misty, very vague, they look to our earthly, filmy eyes. Religion bids us hold ourselves ready to quit at any moment the world and every thing we value and love; and human hearts, recoiling, are called craven and sinful, as though a child would go willingly from the warm arms of the mother it trusts and is used to, into the unknown embrace of a veiled and shadowy stranger, that may be more tender, more loving, more satisfying, than the earthly mother; but, oh! the child cannot see its face, cannot hear its voice; it is all strange, and it turns back trembling to the face it *knows*, just as we who are grown up cling to life, with its sweetness and its sorrows, its love and its suffering, and hug it to our breasts, our very own and a most familiar friend. When my time for dying comes, and I know that surely—certainly it must come some day—that I shall lie straight and still, with blank eyes and heavy-shut lids, with ears into which no common call or every-day word can enter, I hope that all my dear ones, the few that I lay in my heart, will have gone before me; then, indeed, I shall not fear to die, for where they are there will be my home.

I have fallen on sad thoughts this bright morning. Am I not, indeed, becoming somewhat sentimental? a state of mind for which I have a most hearty contempt. I will go to the kitchen-garden and search for figs and pears. I have eaten three treacly-sweet figs, and am investigating the Marie Louise pears, when a voice behind me says, "Good-morning!" I turn round, and there stands Paul Vasher. Is he shod with the shoes of silence, or does he wear goloshes? for I never heard him coming.

"Good-morning!" I say, holding out my hand. "I thought you were still in bed, or out shooting!"

"Luttrell is lazy this morning," he says, "and nobody would turn out. Have you breakfasted?"

"An hour ago," I answer, looking at my watch; "it seemed a crime to stay in on such a morning as this, so I got out as quickly as I could."

"I hope you slept well!"

"I always do, always, that is to say, when I have nothing on my mind."

"Well, I did not sleep at all."

"Why did you not?"

"I began to think, and then it was all over."

"About bills?"

"No," he says, smiling; "what made you think of bills, of all things?"

"Because they keep—" I am about to add, "mother awake," when I stop short. "Is it not very odd," I continue, as we walk along between the cabbages, "how the merest trifles that we hardly notice by day assume *gigantic* proportions at night? Do you know that all the silly things I have said and done, and all the times I have made a fool of myself, rise up before me if I am awake, and seem to pelt me? and when daylight comes they appear quite small again, and I recover my self-respect; do you ever feel like that?"

"Often enough," he says, rather sadly. "Only the blows my sins deal me are somewhat heavier than those your little white misfortunes give you. I often think, though, that there is no exaggeration about those night thoughts; that things do but assume their real significance then; truer counsel comes to us in those silent hours than in the broad, garish day, with its thousand sights and sounds, and words to come as a screen between us and our souls."

"Let us take comfort in that our consciences are active and healthy!" I say, laughing; "it is when people do not feel their shortcomings at all that they may be considered to be in a bad way, is it not? I suppose all eminently wicked folk have no conscience at all?"

"Child," he says, looking down at me, "what a merry, heart-whole laugh you have! Any one could tell you had never lost yourself."

"Lost myself?" I repeat; "what is that?"

"Never been in love," he says slowly, and with an odd hesitation in his voice, odd by reason of his being usually so self-contained, proud, and cold.

I turn away my head that he may not see how the color goes out of my cheeks. I am glad he thinks me so safe and untouched. No woman should wear her heart upon her sleeve for every eye to look into. . . .

"Do people give up laughing when they fall in love?" I ask. "I should have thought it would be the very reason why they should be all the happier! My sisters never wore long faces when they were engaged. I do not think I ever saw any other lovers, unless indeed one can call Silvia and Sir George lovers."

"And are they not?"

"I don't know."

My thoughts go back to that moonlight night at Charteris four years ago, when a man and woman stood face to face and wished each other a bitter, long farewell—ay, *they* were lovers; and a hot sharp pain runs through my heart that I know well enough is jealousy.

"Mr. Vasher," I say, stopping short, while the blood leaps into my face and mounts to my very brow, "I have something to tell you—something I ought to have told you long ago." He does not answer, but I see him draw in his breath and set his lips hard, and in his eyes there is a look of strong, eager expectation. "That night, at Charteris, when you had that interview with Silvia, I was hidden close to you, and saw and heard everything."

"Is that all?" he cries, with a quick gesture of relief, and yet a certain shame in his face. "I thought you were going to tell me— So you heard our farewells, child; were you sorry, or did you laugh?"

"It was nothing to laugh at," I say, seriously; "but I have always wanted to tell you. I felt such a sneak, but it was not my fault, and I thought I should vex you so by walking out in the middle. I wish I had never been there."

"Do you?" he says. "Why?"

"Until then I had believed in love, and that it lasted. Now I know better; and that, however hotly a man may worship a woman to-day, he forgets her to-morrow."

"Not if she is worthy," he says. "Would you have him pour all his treasures into the sea? A man must be true to himself first, his love afterward."

"And I cannot understand this distinction," I say, looking down at my flowers. "If I ever loved any one, and afterward he proved unworthy, I should not let that turn me back. I should go on loving just the same."

"Because you have a sweet and unselfish nature, while I am selfish through and through," he says, slowly. "It is a cowardly thing, is it not, to be so careful to assure one's self against loss? But I have always felt that on the woman I married depended the making or marring of my life, and—still in my own interests, of course—watched natures as narrowly and carefully as a man would look to the joints of his armor before going into a battle, on the issue of which his life depended. Do you blame me that I will not sacrifice my life—I have only one, remember!—simply to gratify a woman's caprice? Can you show me a greater misery than to be bound to a person one can neither trust nor respect? With me worth ranks before beauty."

"I cannot argue," I say, slowly; "I can only feel; and it seems to me that lovers once, who love each other, should be lovers always; nothing but death ought to come between."

"Then Silvia and I should be lovers now?"

"If you had loved her really, I think you would be loving her still, faults and all."

"Faults?" he repeats. "You don't understand. What if I give you the key to the puzzle? What if I tell you why Silvia's beauty moves me no jot? Why it is as impossible to me to have any love for her as to breathe life into dry-as-dust bones? Shall I tell you a story? You may suppose it to be my own, or that of any one else, just as you please."

We have come to a gnarled old garden-seat, that is set where the eye can view the garden and woods and a glimpse of the sea below, and we sit down.

"Once," he says, leaning toward me and watching my face, " a man wandered over the world, searching in cultured gardens and wayside roads, at the gates of palaces and the doors of the poor, for a certain spotless, delicate flower. He saw many very like the particular blossom he was seeking, but there was always some trifling flaw, or speck, or stain, and he passed them all by, for he said to himself, 'I know that this flower exists, for other men have found it, and why should not I?' And at last to him also came the happy hour, and he found it. Long and carefully he watched it, lest after all it should be no more perfect and faultless than the rest; but at last he put out his hand and, with a great rejoicing in his heart, plucked it. It was but freshly in his hand, he had scarcely tasted of its sweetness, hardly felt his soul filled with its exceeding beauty, its petals had not withered with neglect or been scorched by the hot breath of passion, when a chance blow struck it; and, lo! the dazzling whiteness fell from it like a veil, and there it lay, robbed of its deceitful mantle, lovely still, but speckled, tainted, soiled. No one but God knows what that man felt then. He had sought for it so long, exulted in it so deeply; he could have laid his life on its perfect purity and soillessness, and now, broken and shamed as it was, he loved it still, though he knew he could never lay it in his breast, never wear it through life as his glory and pride; and, therefore, though it nearly cleft his heart in twain to leave it, he cast it from him, and went his way alone.

"Not long afterward, when he was in the very midst of his hard, fierce struggle to forget, he came by chance upon it, and though he knew its worthlessness, he longed after its beauty with a deep and passionate longing that nearly overcame him; and, after all, the speckled stains were faint and invisible to all eyes save his own, but his standard of purity was a high one, else had he not so long sought the one who should come up to it; and a second time he conquered this madness and went his way. Years after, when he was no longer seeking either good or evil, when his old search after anything perfect seemed faint and far away, he chanced upon a little flower that grew up sweet, and sturdy, and honest, in its quiet corner, past which the world never ran. It was not so gorgeous and stately as the tall white flower, but it had a fair, winsome face, and its clean, fresh sweetness came more gratefully to the weary, jaded man than had ever the voluptuous beauty of the other. And though his love of the first had long faded away, this fresher, healthier love took and cast out the last fragments of a lingering, haunting memory; and his heart was as empty of all feeling for it as though he had never loved and regretted so bitterly. And so —he was mad, you will say, for had not his experience been disastrous enough?— he longed for this little flower with a keen intensity that he had never known for the other." He pauses, and down-dropping into the silence come the exquisite notes of a bird, who seems to be singing miles above us, oh, so sweetly! in at God's gate.

"Was he quite sure this time?" I ask, watching a little snowy sail that is scudding across the bit of jasper that shines through the trees. "Was he not afraid that this was a deception like the other."

"He was not afraid of that; he knew its nature through and through, but sometimes he feared he was too late; that another man had set his mark on that flower, and that its treasures were not for him; at others, he felt sure it was his own, and, at last, he made up his mind that he would speak and find out the truth, *and know.*"

A rabbit scampering suddenly out of the bushes behind us startles me so violently that I leap up, and out of my shallow pocket fall two letters, and lie at my feet. Paul stoops, picks them up, turns to give them to me, when something in my face seems to arrest his attention, and he looks from me to George's big, bold handwriting, and from the letter back to me.

"Is either of these from your lover?" he asks, striking them with his fore finger.

"Yes."

"And he writes to you; you write to him?"

"Yes." (I have written George three bald epistles since I came to Luttrell.)

He does not speak again immediately, but his glance fell upon me heavy as a blow. Ah me! men are hard taskmasters. Do they love us women at all, save for their own pleasure? Are they not mercilessly cruel when we make them suffer passing pain or discomfort? I want to tell him that it is all a mistake; that, if George is my lover, I am not his; but somehow the words refuse to utter themselves. . . .

"I have not told you the end of my story," says Paul Vasher; "will you care to hear it?"

"If you please."

"I don't know how it was I came to tell it you, unless indeed it were to convince you that I do not love Miss Fleming. The ending is simple enough; some tales do end happily, you know."

"And it did end happily?" I ask, very low, while the dread that has for the past minutes been creeping about my heart, trembles and dies.

"Yes; I will show her to you some day."

Has the bird gone in at heaven's gate, or are my ears too deaf to hear him? What is this grayness that is creeping over land and sea? The little white sail has vanished, and the diamonds that bordered the ocean's breast have died dully out.

"I hope, sir," says a gentle voice, that sounds something like mine, "that you found her all you could wish."

Looking idly down at my lap, I see all my pretty flowers lying headless; did my fingers strip them from their stalks?

"It is cold," I say, shivering; "let us go in."

Side by side, down the green glade, we move in silence. "O fool!" the trees seem to whisper as I pass. "O fool!" cry the birds, in their mocking shrill voices. "O fool!" cries louder and deeper my heavy, heavy heart. If I could only laugh aloud, jest, speak carelessly. . . . About fifty paces from our seat we meet Alice, fresh and fair and blooming as the morning itself. Alice is one of those few people who can look as well by daylight as wax-light. After the usual salutation—

"How pale you are!" she says to me. "Why did you get up so early."

"You forget how I danced last night," I say, turning aside to pick up my small nephew, who is rendered the freak of fortune as much by reason of the length of his swallow-tailed pelisse as by the unsteadiness of his legs. How she ever got him so far up is a mystery; how to get him down again, I find by experience, is a work of time and difficulty.

Alice and Paul are talking about the ball; she with much spirit, he with a listlessness that makes me look at him once with shrinking, perplexed eyes. For a man who is successful in his second courtship, he does not look happy; there is a dull, disappointed expression upon his face.

"It seems to me," says Alice, "that you are two very lively people; have you been quarreling?"

A timely upset of her son takes up my attention at this moment; but I hear Paul's answer plainly enough.

"Quarreling, Mrs. Lovelace? I think not. I have been telling Miss Adair a story; that is all."

To Alice's sisterly looks and asides of inquiry, I turn blind eyes and a blank countenance, and presently, having guided the cherub's steps past the gold and silver fish, whose watery abode he evinces a rooted determination to share, I get away, and up-stairs to my own room, and lock the door. As I kneel down by my bedside, and press my knees hard against the floor, I do not say to myself that an exquisite hope that has sprung up, at unawares, in my heart is dead; slain by a sharp, swift death that, may be, is more merciful than a halting, lingering one. . . .

I am not conscious of thought, I only know that I thought myself rich, and that now my kingdom has passed away into other hands: my poor kingdom that was never anything but a fanciful one, and which I have seemed to see growing stately and beautiful day by day. . . . There are some miseries over which one may weep aloud with not only deep self-pity, but the pity of the world besides; there are others over which it is a shame to make one sigh, to drop one heavy tear, that can know of no relief, but must be carried about with us, like a burning cross that lies on the naked, bleeding heart.

"Luncheon is served," says Annette, entering half an hour later.

I have smoothed my untidy locks, put on fresh ribbons, rubbed my cheeks hard with a towel, and now I look no worse than any other country miss, who is not used to racketing, and who stood up for her first real ball, and danced twenty-one dances overnight.

"And now," I say to myself as I go down the broad stairs—

'Away! and mock the time with fairest show,
False face must hide what the false heart doth know.'

I dare say George would say my heart *was* false."

———

CHAPTER XII.

"Where fair is not, praise cannot mend the brow."

Out in the garden I am pacing up and down, up and down through the silver bars and the dark shadows, backward and forward as for a wager, trying to trample out the aching pain in my heart, as many a man and woman has tried before me, and will try after me in vain. And only a week ago at this hour I was so happy, so happy! And by this day twelve month I shall perhaps have got rid of this ugly ache, and be moderately happy again, but oh! I never knew the prospect of a cheerful to-morrow bring any comfort to a chilly to-day; it is the present hour that we hold fast between our hands that is our care. It is a pleasant thing, is it not, to find that your heart has slipped away out of your safe keeping, and knocked at the wrong door, and that your affections have set in a broad, liberal stream toward a man who wants none of them, who has been at the pains to tell you he is in love with somebody else? My cheeks burn, my foot presses deep into the grass as I wither under the shameful thought; taking all due blame to myself, has he not been somewhat in fault, did he not mislead me by his looks and words? Bah! it was all my own wretched vanity; could not a man be kind and friendly with me, but I must suppose he had lost his head, and fall in love-with him myself, a little fool! as though I had never had a lover, or heard a love-word in my life, and was ready to leap at the ghostliest shadow of man's light fancy!

I stand still to think, suddenly, of how thoroughly George is avenged, of how I have come to suffer all the pains that I laid on him; I can feel for him now, my poor fellow, as I never felt before; truly pity is sometimes a selfish thing. I think that, considering our youth and the few opportunities that we have had of gambling, George and I show as clean a sheet of bankruptcy in our heart-affairs as could be seen anywhere. We shall be able to mingle our sighs and groans in a pleasing duet by the river-side, for I know now very certainly that, difficult as I have always found it to look upon George as my future husband, when nothing more than a girl's idle fancy stood between, we are now as utterly separated as though either or both of us lay in our coffins.

His instinct warned him truly, when he stood before me, and entreated me not to come on this visit! had I not in truth done better to stay at Silverbridge? Might I not have come to love my yellow-haired laddie, and never had my heart wakened by the Prince Charming who came too late? My heart is sore as I think of the words I shall have to speak to him, sweet, pleasant-sounding words, bright with truth: " *I have fallen in love with somebody, George, who is in love with somebody else.*" That is plain enough at all events. I think I must have loved that other ever since the old Charteris days without knowing it. Was it his memory, I wonder, that made my eyes so fastidious when they rested on George? Was I ever unconsciously comparing my fair-browed lover with the dark, strong face that I had seen soften and pale under the lips of the woman he loved, and who loved him? Were George's sunny blue eyes but handsome, commonplace bits of color beside those splendid dark ones, that flash and burn and subjugate and sway my heart with their masterful will as none ever did or could?

We shall be a lovelorn assembly at Silverbridge: the thought of how everybody will be in love with everybody else provokes an unwilling smile from me. George is in love with me, I am in love with Paul, Paul is in love with somebody else: now, if *she* would only come to Silverbridge and fall in love with George, we would be the most amusing *partie carrée* of lovers that the world ever saw, and our united sighs would form a high wind wherever we went. In time of drought we might go out in a body and water the land, and at all the funerals in the neighborhood our looks would be far more grief-inspiring than any amount of well-fed, sober-faced mutes. I wonder if I shall always be able to see my misfortunes in a ludicrous light, no matter how painfully I smart under them?

Will Paul expect me to listen to the tale of his lady-love's perfections? I am puzzled to know why he should have told me of her at all, for clearly he has told no one else here. Probably he has favored me with his notice because he has all along had me in his eye as a nice, comfortable sort of person to whom he can maunder on by the hour about his charmer's perfections. I told him when I came here that I would be gooseberry to him : has he taken me at my word, and is he going to make a listening one of me? I have always been afraid that he would come under Silvia's influence again, but he has not.

Paul Vasher is neither a weak nor a forgiving man. I like these strong, deep natures : the impulsive, pleasant-mannered, facile folk may be twice as lovable, but they are like sand, and that which they receive quickly is as quickly effaced ; while the favor of the proud, reserved man or woman is precious and rare, since it is vouchsafed to but few. I should like to know what Silvia would say if she knew? For all her indifference, I have caught some strange glances shot at Paul's unconscious face, and several times lately perceived her watching me with a keen intentness that tells a different story to her idle, listless ways, and *nonchalant*, careless speech.

How the men are laughing in the dining-room! What guffaws and explosions and exhausted roars peal forth! Something vulgar is on the *tapis*, I am certain, for I have long since learned that anything broad appeals irresistibly to man, whether he be prince or potman, prelate or parson, learned sage or simple squire ; men's hearts warm to each other over a good joke, and

Shakespeare might as well have writtten, "A touch of *vulgarity* makes the whole world kin," as "nature." In the drawing-room the married ladies are holding up their hands, and relating to each other stories tending to the discredit of their men and maids in waiting, who are, strange to say, addicted to much the same vices and weaknesses as their masters and mistresses (such presumption!), only, poor souls! they are not delicate over them; and romance without an "h" to bless itself with does not appeal to the imagination as the more aristocratic failings of their betters do.

You, Sarah Ann, who have been discovered with Jeames's arm pressing your too adaptive form, are a bold-faced, abandoned hussy, and out you must pack without a character, and with a scanty wage; and you, Jeames, are a shameless varlet, who ought to be above such lowness, but as you are not, there is not much difficulty in prophesying your end. You neither of you seem to be aware that only rich people, high people, good people (so called from a polite fiction, for is not the best society the worst?) can be immoral with impunity, and embrace other men's wives and daughters when they please; to be wicked with safety you must roll in a carriage, and keep your unlawful assignations with a coachman and footman to vouch for your respectability. Sarah Ann is married and her husband has left her, and Jeames is married and his wife has left him, but as neither of them is rich enough to procure a divorce, and since (as I have said before) they are not in that state of life where their flirtations would be pleasantly winked at, I fear the poor woman will go down, down, down!

Birkhead was drunk the other night; could anything be more disgusting? All his life he has seen gentlemen with hard heads drinking a great deal more than is good for them; he has a weak one, but is indecent enough to wish to be convivial "below-stairs" too, and, of course, came to grief. Now drunkenness, sitting hiccoughing at the head of its table, and able to offer its guests the choicest wines, is one thing, and drunkenness in low life, without a cellar to bless itself with, is another. Faugh! send him away, and let him not come 'twixt the air and our nobility; that man will die in a workhouse.

Silvia comes stepping across the grass all in white; is she restless, I wonder, like me? Bad as my thoughts are, I would rather have them than her company, so I move away toward the terrace, but she calls to me—

"Helen Adair! Helen Adair!"

She has that most excellent thing in woman, a low, sweet voice.

"I wonder what she wants with me?" I say to myself, as I go slowly toward the seat she has taken. Our conversation has always been of the baldest; if, indeed, she can ever be said to converse with any woman.

"Did you call me?"

"Yes; sit down here for a few minutes, it is miserable out here alone. How long have you had a fancy for moonlight walks?" she asks, leaning her shapely head against the wooden seat; "for my part I always hated the moon, a great empty, bare splendor that chills one."

She shivers and draws her shawl closely about her—and, indeed, these September nights are growing treacherous. Looking down at her feet, I see that she has adopted the sensible precaution of thick boots, as I have done.

"How those men are laughing!" she says—"at some racy story, no doubt. Paul Vasher's lungs seem to be in a satisfactory state. Have you and he been quarreling?" she says, turning her head till her eyes rest on my face.

"I did not know it."

"Sir George and I have both remarked it. Until a week ago you were inseparable, now you are conspicuous by your absence from each other."

Some slight intangible insolence in her tone gives flavor to her words, and warns me that she means mischief; and, indeed, I might have known her better than to suppose that she would take the trouble to come out here to talk commonplaces; but since she has thrown the gauntlet down, I will not fear to take it up.

"You do me too much honor," I say, quietly, "and him. We should never have taken the trouble to watch the affairs of you and Sir George Vestris so closely."

And as I meet her eyes full under the moonlight, I smile scornfully, securely. How heavy my heart is she shall not know, and of her pity I shall have none; therefore, rally to my side, coolness, disdain, indifference. As I look into her face with a fuller knowledge of the truth than she possesses, I can see clearly enough that she believes me to be *her rival*, that she is jealous; I see that the love Paul believed to be long dead lives as fiercely and hotly in her as ever, and at this moment we read each other's hearts, see each other as we really are— henceforth no shams or subterfuges will rise up between Silvia Fleming and me! She looks away.

"May I then be allowed to congratulate you on your felicity?"

With the intonation she gives these words, they sound more like a menace than a politeness.

"When you will condescend to explain yourself, I may possibly be able to answer you, Miss Fleming." (How I must have disliked this girl all my life, to flare up so heartily at a moment's notice!)

"You are rather slow of comprehension to-night! I allude, of course, to your engagement with Paul Vasher."

A smile parts my lips as I listen to her. How sweet those words sound, spoken even by an enemy's tongue! For a moment I forget the woman by my side, and that she waits my answer; I am looking at a happy, far-away picture, that makes my eyes ache with longing;

only in dreamland does it exist, in reality it never will.

"And it is so," says a low, breathless voice by my side. "You sit there smiling; you dare to mock me with your gladness." . . .

Her words come hurrying out as though past her control. For the second time in her life, Silvia drops the mask before me; for the second time in my life I see her as she is.

"Let me tell you this, Helen Adair, that you will never be Paul Vasher's wife, never!"

"I have not aspired to that honor," I answer, quietly; "do you? I should not, were I you!"

"You have such faith in your powers of keeping him?" she asks, scoffingly.

"I have much faith in the power of the woman he loves. Pray, do not put yourself out! I say, looking away from her pale face to the pearly sea beyond; "we need not quarrel over Paul Vasher, since he is neither yours nor mine."

"Not yours?" she repeats, staring at me, while a swift surprise dashes all the triumphant scorn out of her face; "whose is he then?"

"Some stranger's."

"And her name?

"I do not know it."

"And so he was amusing himself with you all that time?" she says.

"You can call it that, if it so pleases you."

"And he told you this himself?" she says.

But I do not answer, and she goes on like one who is thinking hard and deep.

"I do not believe it. It is you whom he loves. . . . I have watched him—"

I turn my head away, that she may not see the pallor that has crept over my face. Others were deceived by his manner to me, then; I have not been the only mistaken one.

"It is all the same," she says, indifferently. "I told you that you should never be Paul's wife, and you never shall, but neither shall any other woman."

"Are you mad?" I ask, contemptuously, for the shameless, godless selfishness of the creature angers me deeply. Does she give one thought to him? She would trample his life beneath her feet rather than see another woman take the place she once filled; that which she calls love is one corrupt, foul adoration of self.

"I am glad you love him," she says, with a malicious cruelty of look and word that sets ill upon her fair, innocent-looking beauty. (No wonder Paul thought he had found his spotless white flower at last when he beheld her; no angel could boast a more perfectly fair face!) "Glad that there is some one who will suffer as I have suffered, endure what I have endured, weary for him as I have wearied."

"Hush!" I say, rising and lifting my hand; "do not dare to link my name with yours, or call your wicked passion for Paul Vasher *love!* You, who would sacrifice his whole life to grasp your own paltry, pitiful wish—you dare to call that loving him? No wonder you never kept him! Thank God, I can love him better than that! I wish I had been lovely, for his sake. . . . I should have liked to be good, for his sake. . . . He might have loved me then, but even as it is, and though he never loved me, while he loved you once (you should never forget that), my love for him has only taught me sweet and tender and sorrowful things; it has not set a flood of wild, impious passion ravening through my heart, as it has done through yours. If I could have my empty heart back again I would not, for if he has brought me pain he has also given me an exquisite happiness. And since you never truly loved him, or as he ought to be loved, I tell you now that, however low you stoop, you will never win him back, though Satan were your bondsman and delivered Paul Vasher's body over to you; you could not touch his soul, his mind, or his heart; they are dead to you now and always. And now go your way,

fight your fight, do your worst—win him if you can, Silvia, but if the memory of the girl he loves do not protect him from your unwomanly pursuit, believe me when I say that in his integrity you have an enemy that will never yield to you. By fair means you will never win him; from foul ones may God protect him!"

And I move away and leave her with that faint, wintry, strange smile on her face that I have so often tried to read and cannot. How cool and peaceful the sleeping garden looks! how fair the silver-braided sky! how hot and angry is my passionate, indignant, outraged heart! It was hard enough to bear my shame of lovelessness in my own eyes; it is something harder to have that sneering, evil woman speak openly of it. For she is wicked, I know it now, and that the intangible dislike and distrust I have always had for her is a well-grounded one, and that she means mischief to the man she professes to love. Does she love him, though? There was more of hate than tenderness in her voice just now. How can she reach or do him harm? A woman is so bound by the trammels of society, she cannot watch and balk him in life as a man might do; perhaps after all it is mere empty talk and babble; and, granted that she has the wish to cross him, she is not likely to have the power. She seemed in earnest, but she was jealous; I saw it in her eyes, and that threw her off her guard and made her talk wildly.

We must have looked very nice just now—two women quarreling over one man! There is an intense vulgarity in the situation, whether the actors be clad in silk and velvet, or homespun and duffle-gray; perhaps, though, the fact of his being not in the least in love with either of us somewhat lessens the disgrace. And all through my night dreams, ringing now near, now far away, sometimes in my ears, sometimes seeming to call faintly across the long years, comes a bitter, silvern voice, saying, "*You will never be Paul Vasher's wife—never!*"

CHAPTER XIII.

" . . . . Sir, the year growing ancient,
Nor yet on Summer's death, nor on the birth
Of trembling Winter—the fairest flowers of
　　the season
Are our carnations and streaked gillyflowers."

"WHAT is that?" says Milly, pausing on her way up-stairs.

"Can it be the ghost?" I ask, standing still to listen likewise.

Luttrell Court, like all other respectable family mansions, possesses its ghost; and an exceedingly ill-conditioned one this particular spirit is: given to heaving up beds (and their occupants) in the dead of night, dashing down cart-loads of crockery outside chamber-doors, beating members of the family with invisible whips, and boxing the ears of trembling footmen in dark corners, or so those gentlemen aver.

"I don't think a ghost could give such a substantial groan as that," I say; and indeed, as we ascend, a succession of wails, sighs, and squeaks, float out to meet us, that could not reasonably be supposed to proceed from the throat of that uncanny, fleshless, bony, counterfeit of a human being, that we call a ghost. The mysterious sounds issue from the yellow room, and Milly pushes the door open, and stands on the threshold. No poor daylight spirit is answerable for the hullabaloo; but on a stool, before an open harmonium, sits a real, tangible human being, who is rolling from side to side, in an ecstasy of delight at the hideous discord he is evoking. He wears a smart gray and scarlet livery, his silk calves are *en évidence;* he is, in short, one of the footmen, who has apparently a taste for music, and who believes Milly to be miles away at the present moment.

Some terrible instinct makes him turn his head, and standing behind him, he sees —his mistress.

"May I ask," inquires Mrs. Luttrell, "if I hired you to act as my servant, or to play on my harmonium?"

The man gazes wildly at the ceilin and the floor alternately, as though l prays Heaven to either draw him up l the hair of his head, or pull him dow out of sight by his heels.

"I thought you were out, madam," l stutters, casting his eyes wildly to and fr

"Another time," says Milly, "wl you make sure? Go."

He vanishes like a stone shot from catapult.

I look at Milly in amazement at he moderation, but suddenly recollect the the detected performer is devotedly a tached to the small heir of the house, an carries him about by the hour: a roy: road, that, to his mistress's favor.

"That man is a character," she say as we go away.

"He certainly has a soul above h station," I answer, laughing, as I tur into my room to lay aside my hat. Sha I lay it aside, though? It is only fiv o'clock. I can do without my tea an the clack of tongues in the drawing room; besides, the gentlemen have com in early, and I have no mind to spend a hour in trying to run away from Par Vasher. Why does he seek me so per sistently, I wonder? To make a conf dante of me, I suppose; but, at any rat I have never given him the chance; an during the last week I have become s adroit at dodging and avoiding him, tha I am sure I shall find my experience use ful when I go home, and have to circun vent the governor.

As I stand before the table consider ing, my eye catches the reflection of m face in the looking-glass, and startles me it is so pale, so sad, so dull. I used t have such a merry, saucy face, folks said but now, there are dark shadows unde my eyes, and a close, folded look abou my mouth, as though it rarely knew smile or laughter now. Verily my story is wri upon my face, people will begin to pity m next, O heavens! and I must bear it, sinc there is no means of forcing the body int subjection, even if one can the spirit.

At the end of the corridor is a door by which the grounds can be reached, and I leave the house, and climb to the upper walks and terraces. I should like to go down to the sea, but it is too late to go alone; and upon its shore I could not be more lonely than I am up here. I come to the seat where Paul Vasher and I sat a week ago—only a week! And it seems a year. Everything looks different from what it did on that morning: a faint chill bleakness lies over the landscape, the trees shiver a little as the leaves fall rustling to the ground, the bit of sea in the distance is not blue at all, but a dull grayish-green; the birds are all cross, or asleep, and there is no pleasant hum of insects on the evening air. Perhaps it is I who am out of sorts, not Nature. When we begin to study the passions, can we indeed go hand-in-hand with her as when her gentle lore and tender secrets were all the wisdom we sought, when her peaceful voice seemed satisfying and sweet to us? We cannot hear it clearly when louder and more selfish voices are beating at our ears and echoing in our hearts. Some day I shall come back to you, O nurse-mother! but not now, not to-day. Give me a little while to strive with this passionate, restless heart. It will wear itself out quickly enough, never fear.

On my way, I have pulled a handful of late carnations, and some of Shakespeare's streaked gillyflowers, and I am smelling at them idly, when a fragrant whiff of another sort floats up to me—that of a cigar. This is a remote corner, and people rarely come up so high as this, so I give it no thought, and have closed my tired eyes, and am looking inward at the vista stretching out before me of endless, empty, dull to-morrows, when footsteps, brushing through the short grass, make me open them suddenly, and there stands Paul Vasher.

For a moment I stare at him without speaking, then—"I think I have been asleep!" I say, starting up; "and it must be quite tea-time—time to go in!" As I turn to go he puts out his hand and lays it on my arm.

"Is this game of hide-and-seek to go on forever?" he asks sternly (a moment ago his face was overspread with a swift gladness). "Am I always to be avoided by you in this way, morning, noon, and night?" (I am in for it!—he is determined to make a listening gooseberry of me, willy-nilly.)

"If you call drinking tea—" I begin; then, looking up by accident and catching his eye, I stop short: evasions are always worse than useless with him.

"Your tea can wait," he says; "and you shall not go until you have answered me."

"Shall not! Who will prevent me?"

"I will."

For a moment I look straight at his resolute face and bent brows; then I sit down again and wait for him to begin.

"I want to know," he says, standing before me, "what you mean by behaving in this way to me?"

My hands are locked fast together, my gillyflowers lie in my lap, my cheeks could grow no paler than they were before: if only my lips will keep steady, and my eyes tell no secrets—

"In what way, Mr. Vasher?"

"In never speaking to or looking at me; in never giving me a single chance of a few words alone with you—though Heaven knows I have worked hard enough to compass it. Could you have treated an enemy with more coldness and disdain? And I have been your friend, child, for so many long years."

Yes, I have been wrong, as usual. I ought to have met him just the same as I did before he told me his story; instead of which, I have left him to guess the miserable truth; and now, no doubt, he pities me. . . . But I could not do the other: my strength did not go so far as that.

"You have always been my friend," I say, gently. "I know it, but—you will not be angry with me?"

"Angry? No!"

"When you told me that you loved somebody, I thought you would always want to be talking about her, like other lovers, and that you would expect me to listen; and I always was a bad listener; any one who talks as much as I do, must be; and so—and so I avoided you. Besides, you can always think of her, you know; and that must be better than praising her to me, who never saw her."

"And this is the truth, the whole truth, and nothing but the truth?" he says. Then, as I do not answer, for his searching voice arraigns me before my own conscience as having answered disingenuously: "Would it bore us so much if we were to exchange confidences—you about *him*, I about *her?*"

"Make as many as you please to me," I answer, steadily, "and I will listen; but I have none to give you in return."

"None?"

"None."

"You used not to be so secret."

"Am I bound to give an account of myself to you?"

"I will have no more of this miserable uncertainty," he says, suddenly. "Tell me, child, are you engaged to that man at Silverbridge?"

"That is a matter that concerns myself only."

"Are you, or are you not?" he asks again, while the veins rise in his forehead like cords, and his hand clinches.

I may as well tell him after all: why should there be any mystery over it? It can make no possible difference to him or any one else.

"No. But there is a kind of promise between us."

"A *kind* of promise! Tell me what it is?"

"When I was fourteen I gave him my word of honor that when I was eighteen years old and six months I would marry him if—"

"If!" he repeats quickly. "Go on!"

"I did not see any one I liked better."

"Indeed! And are the six months up?"

"No."

He draws a deep breath; and then in the voice of a man who puts a strong restraint upon himself, says: "Tell me one thing now. Do you love him?"

"You ask too much," I answer, turning my pale face away. "What is it to you whether I love him or not?"

And then, against my will, I lift my eyes to his, which are deep and tender with a warm love-light . . . though he is speaking to me, he is thinking of her; and somehow the thought of her riches and my heart-bareness unnerves me, and, my lips quiver, and slow, painful tears fill my eyes.

"You poor little white blossom," he says, casting himself down on the seat beside me. "Nell, Nell! are you fretting after that Silverbridge man?"

He is looking into my face with a passion of eagerness that startles me, still thinking of her, I suppose.

"I will be good," I say, as two big tears fall with a heavy splash on my clasped hands. "Do not be afraid, I am not going to cry any more. . . . I will listen to you patiently, if you would like to have a comfortable talk about her."

"I shall keep you to your word presently," he says; "meanwhile you have not answered my question."

"I will not," I answer, with spirit. (How dare he torment me in this way?)

"Will you make me a promise then?"

"Tell me what it is first."

"I cannot. Will you promise?"

There is nothing more to tell—he knows about George; is it worth while to bandy words about a trifle? And I am longing to get away.

"I promise," I say, listlessly.

"Then, when we are both at Silverbridge—for I have a fancy for hearing you tell me where I met you first, in the field of rye—you will tell me the name of the man you love."

I sit silent, pale as death. Is it kind, or manly, or fair of him, to trap me thus?

"I break my promise," I say, firmly, "although I never broke one before."

"It is too late, now," he says; "you are bound. You never failed in truth yet, child; are you going to begin now?"

But I do not answer.

"I think I never told you the name of my little girl? I will tell it you when you keep your promise to me—when we stand face to face in the place where I saw you first."

Ay! I see the scene clearly enough, the two figures, the shamed confession, the truth uttered as before God, the cart before the horse—the amazement of the man, who, with all his faults, was never vain or a coxcomb. But that hour shall never come to either him or me.

"Although I have asked you so many questions," he says, "you have never asked me one about my sweetheart. Why do you not?"

"How tall is she?" I ask, looking up at the chilly leaves as they rustle softly down—down—down, like silk, to the ground. Since he wishes to talk, I will put him through a whole catechism of questions, and, by haphazard, I begin with the one that loveless Elizabeth asked of her beautiful rival Mary.

"Just as high as my heart."

"Of what color is her hair?"

"Brown, with a warm, ruddy golden tinge running through it; it is all over little billows and cunning waves and ripples—the softest and prettiest head!"

"And her eyes?"

"She has two sweet, serious, saucy, tender gray eyes; they tell a different story every minute, but they are always true to her thoughts, which are honest; her face is the mirror of her heart, which is pure."

"Is she fair?"

"She has the whitest, softest neck and throat and hands I ever saw. She looks as though she were made to be kissed and spoiled."

11

"And her mouth?"

"Not very little, but the sweetest I ever saw; and she has a dimple set at each corner."

"Is she merry?"

"You should hear her laugh! But she can be sober; sometimes I watch her face with fear, it is so sad."

And so this is why he has taken notice of me; this is why he has sought my society—because I am a plain likeness of, because I reminded him of, her. My hair, too, is rich brown; and I have green eyes, while hers are gray—not much difference there; and I used to have some dimples, I think, not so very long ago.

"And does she love you?"

"I will tell you that when you tell me what you have promised to tell."

"And you love her?" I ask, while a bitter, jealous pain creeps about my heart, and stabs it through and through while every pulse of my body seems to stand still awaiting his answer. . . .

"Do I not? God knows!"

"You are a brave man," I say, smiling with pale lips. "Are you not afraid to risk your life's happiness so utterly?"

"Is any man wise who loves? But I am not afraid: she is honest to the core, and could no more play one false than she could alter her innocent face."

"God send you happiness with her!" I say gently, and rising I go away through the silent glades, and leave him sitting there alone, with his pleasant thoughts for company, and, maybe, a pictured girl-face to murmur fond love-words over—to press close kisses on, with a chafed, angry impatience that the warm living lips are not under his own instead of the silent painted ones.

CHAPTER XIV.

"If he would despise me I would forgive
him; for if he love me to madness I shall never
requite him."

"Good-by!" says Paul Vasher, as he
stands on the step of the railway-carriage
with my hand in his. "I am coming home
in a day or two, and I shall then keep you
to your promise."

I do not answer or look at him, although I feel his eyes searching my face.
The guard waves his flag; Alice kisses her
hand from the distant carriage—"Good-
by! good-by!" a swift glance at Paul's
dark face, a wave of the hand to Alice,
and I am off, either to render up my value-
less body at Silverbridge Station at 5.25,
or make an unsightly corpse on the top of
the engine boiler or thereabouts.

There was a horrible railway accident
a little while ago, and following that
another and another. They have come
hurrying after each other so fast that men
going on a journey wear sober faces, and
enter a railway-carriage with an ugly
presentiment of its being a probable tomb,
and are haunted with dread visions of a
fast train dashing up behind, or a slow one
right in the path in front, and cannot
settle to their newspapers and slumbers as
usual. What a pity it is bridges are not
built higher and people cannot travel outside trains as they do on coaches! we
would at least be able to keep a lookout
and see if Nemesis were overtaking us,
and have a chance for our lives, instead
of sitting stived up, blind as moles, helpless as infants, awaiting the crash that
shoots us in one awful moment into eternity. If I come to grief to-day it will be
alone, for I have a compartment all to
myself, and can walk about, yawn, stretch,
lounge, even laugh or cry, if it so please
me.

Can it be only a month ago that I sped
past those prim hedgerows and fields, with
the ruminating cows and insensate children, who wave their dirty bits of rag at
the train as it rushes by? It is thirty-one
days by the almanac; but when I last came
this way I was eighteen years old, and
young for my age; now I feel fifty at the
very least, and old for my age. By the
time I really am fifty, I suppose I shall
feel a hundred, and by the time I reach
threescore and ten—bah! It is a nasty
thought that I may possibly live to that
age, and live without teeth, taste, hearing,
seeing, enjoying, without memory even.

As the day goes on a thought that has
been lurking in some back lumber-room of
my memory, forced thither by my will,
steps nimbly out and stares me evilly in
the face: I have to tell George. I know
what I have to say to him well enough,
but that does not make it any the better;
and even when that terrible wrench is
over, there will be the long, inevitable
afterward. If only there were some city
of refuge to which rejected lovers might
flee, and be kept there until they had made
up their minds it was no good to sigh after
what they could not get! It is bad enough
to say no over and over again to a man
without having the word crystallized into
a two-legged illustration who struts up
and down your little stage an image of
despair, and never for a moment permits
you to forget that your being such a
wretch to him has brought him to this
miserable pass! I can feel for him now,
poor George! as I little thought I ever
should. Some men might be glad that I
should know something of the pangs they
had suffered; but George is not one of
those—there never was any selfishness in
him: I should have cared for him more,
perhaps, if there had been. I am glad
that I know the truth about Paul; that I
can take my lot and look it fairly in the
face, and know that if no better, still no
worse can befall me. Oh! it is easier to
endure the long, barren bondage from
which there is no escape than to exist
trembling on the frail support of a hope
that may vanish and leave the horizon
more utterly dark than it was before. I
wonder how soon he will bring his wife

home to Silverbridge? I wonder how soon he will call upon me to fulfill my promise? He may call upon me, but I will not go: in the field of rye alone he vowed to receive it, and thither to meet him my steps shall never turn.

I walk restlessly up and down the swerving carriage—for the train is express, and we are racing against time—then sit down and pull out my letters received this morning. That from mother contains news that a month ago would have driven me wild with excitement, that a few years ago would have made Jack and me happy as king and queen, but now brings no shock of surprise, pleasure, or expectation; indeed, until the present moment, I have scarcely thought about it. The news is this: papa is going away, a long, long journey to Australia, and he will be away many months. I do not quite understand why he is going; it is something about money, and perhaps he is tired of staying quietly at home (he was a great traveler in his youth); at any rate he is going in about three weeks, mother says. What a time the young ones will have of it! To Jack and me this gift of the gods comes too late. Now if such a chance as this had only been given to us while we were young, we would have got into every bit of mischief the place contained, and possessed consciences clear of ever having missed a single opportunity of evil-doing when he returned! As it is, with no one to harry and vituperate me, with no one to drive me out for walks, or compel me to overlook the morals and manners of the boys, or labor daily at the dry pump of conversation, I shall become a driveling, willow-wearing, lack-lustre-eyed damsel for folks to mock at. I shall hang out all the forlorn insignia of the lovelorn maiden—shall I? never! If the roses will not come back to my cheeks, the smiles shall to my lips; I will be as merry and noisy and saucy as ever I was, before people; I will defy any one to pry into my heart

and see what is there; and that peace will come to me after a while I doubt not.

I wonder where Silvia is now, and what she is doing? She left the day after our conversation in the garden, and we never met again. Sir George Vestris remained one day after her departure. If she cast him on one side, as report says she casts all her other lovers, he took his punishment quietly and gave no sign.

Alice goes to-morrow. She has asked me to go and stay at her country-house for Christmas; and perhaps, as papa will be away, I may be able to go. My sisters have pressed me hard with their questions about Paul, but I have managed to keep them off. They are puzzled, I think, as well they may be.

My journey's end comes at last, and at 5.35, reasonably punctual, according to the notions of country station-masters, the train reaches Silverbridge. There is mother in the pony-carriage; and on the platform, broader, bigger, more swaggering than ever, is the Bull of Bashan; but Corydon, where is he? Invisible, thank Heaven! I jump out quite briskly. If young men whose attentions are unwelcome only knew how they endeared themselves to the objects of their affection by their absence, they would surely practise the virtue much oftener! I gave mother and Bashan a vigorous hug; and then, my box having been duly produced and handed over to the dog-cart in waiting, we set out, mother and I, side by side, Bashan occupying an abased and harassing position between the reins.

"My eye! How white you are!" he remarks at once.—"Just look at her, mother!"

She looks at me with the anxious perfect love that no earthly face save a mother's ever wears, and says: "So she is.—The dissipations have not agreed with you, dear. We must nurse you up now you have come home." And I know that in her gentle heart she is meditating a course of port wine and rum-and-milk.

"I say, Nell, have you heard the news?" asks Bashan, dodging an insinuating irruption of leather into his right eye. "Won't we have a time of it—eh, Nell?" But mother shakes her head a little sadly.

"Poor papa!" she says; "he is very sorry to go away and leave us all." I stare at mother. Can she be *joking?* Can she mean (oh, the idea is too ridiculous!) that he *likes* us, that he is sorry to go away from us? I look at Bashan. His mouth and eyes are as round as mine. We have the two longest tongues in the family, but the notion has sobered him as well as me. Papa sorry to leave us! The idea is so amazing that it literally strikes us dumb. "And how are Alice and Milly and the babies?" asks mother; and for the rest of the drive our talk is nothing but question and answer.

At the house-door are drawn up the young ones, whose shouts of welcome attest, without any need of inquiry, that at the present moment papa does not pervade these parts; and as I embrace them all round, I find it in my heart to wish there were even more of them, that Jack stood near for me to put my arm round his neck, that pretty Dolly was "finished" and sent home from school. They escort me to my room in a body, and make themselves very happy and busy until nurse appears to welcome me, and sweep them all away.

"Eh! but your stay has done you but little good, Miss Nell!" she says, as she stands before me. "Maybe you've been fretting after your lover, honey?"

"No, no," I answer, pressing my lips to her brown wrinkled cheek. "I have been gay, nurse, amusing myself."

"And if that's amusing yourself, my dearie, you had better have staid at home," she says as she goes away.

I have removed my dusty traveling-dress, and am drinking tea and eating chicken, when the trot of horses' hoofs comes up the avenue, and in another moment George and my father appear on horseback. Already! I had hoped for a little grace—just a little time to draw breath and gather up my strength. He evidently knows I am here, for he is casting his eyes over the house in the aggressively eager manner all unfavored swains affect. It is your lover who knows he is kindly welcome that walks in lightly and easily, sure of seeing his lady-love in good time. Although I have precipitately rolled off the window-seat, teacup and all, I have an uneasy feeling that he is looking at me through the bricks and mortar, and that his importunity will *compel* me into his presence whether I will or not.

When papa appears upon the scene it is one of the rules of the family for everybody to turn out and see what he will do next. From the force of habit, therefore, I go to the top of the stairs and peep over. He is in the hall, inquiring how many hours I intend to spend in "figging" myself up. Reassured at finding him in his normal state of temper and character —for that other phase, as suggested by mamma, is too horribly subversive of all our traditions to make me feel anything but uneasy—I return to my room to finish my toilet, and in another minute am in the dining-room, standing before the gentlemen.

My peck at papa's cheek is soon made; and then George takes my hand with a gladness in his face that I turn away my eyes from beholding. After all, he only says, "How do you do?" and when I have answered, "Quite well, thank you," and told him that my journey was tolerably pleasant, our exchange of words ceases, and the conversation is sustained by him and the governor. The latter going away shortly, however, on some (probable) deed of vengeance, the young man comes quickly over to me. How frank, and fearless, and handsome he looks!—a better-looking man than Paul, the world would say.

Can you tell me, George, why you never made me love you?—why, when my heart was empty, you could not fill it? Was the fault yours, or mine?

"How I have missed you!" he says, looking into every line of my face with greedy love. "How pale you are, Nell, and how pretty—prettier .than when you went away, I think!"

"No, no" I say, while a pained, miserable flush creeps slowly up to my brow; 'I never was anything to look at, George; no one ever thought so but you."

"Did they not?" he says, quickly. "I am glad of that. I grudge every admiring look a man casts on you, Nell. I wish you could not be fair in any one's eyes but mine, then they would not want to take you away from me."

"That is kind to me," I say, smiling. 'However, you have your wish; *no one* ever wanted to take me away from you."

"Thank God!" he says, with a deep thanksgiving in his voice that is almost solemn. "And so you have come back to me, my own little sweetheart, never to go away from me any more!"

"Hush!" I say, turning deadly pale. "Is not that papa?"

"I don't care if it is—Nell—"

"I am going now," I say, starting back. "I cannot stay now. To-morrow afternoon at four I will be by the brook."

"To-morrow!" he says, below his breath; and the rapture in his eyes makes me shiver. "I have waited so long, dear, and now—" and on his face is a look of such utter, pure content as makes his beauty something to marvel at.

Ay, to-morrow! and ere the sun has set a few words will have dashed it all out —all the sweetness of his hope's fruition —all the reward of his long, faithful service; and never, I wis, on this side of the grave, will my lover's face again wear the look it wears to-night. . . . Somehow I creep away and up to my own room, where a bitter anguish tears and rends me, heavier than all the pain I have suffered in this task set to my hand; and

until to-night I have thought almost lightly of his misery, wearily and continually of my own. Human beings are very selfish—the pain they do not see they do not believe in or heed; it must be placed before their eyes for them to feel the mournfulness and pity of it in their hearts. If only I had hearkened to George's words that day when he stood under the trees and entreated me not to go away, or, if I went, to bind myself by a promise, there would be two miserable people less on God's earth to-night.

"Supper is ready!" cries Bashan, bursting wildly in an hour later; and I lift my head from the window-sill, and smooth my hair, and go down to a meal that fills me with a blank sense of amazement, it is so constrained, so unnatural. The sociable freedom of the Luttrell table, and to which I have grown accustomed, opens my eyes to the wretched discomfort here: the few and forced words, the abuse of the servants, the perpetual looking out for imaginary faults in dishes and attendance, the unmannerly manners. Toward the end of supper, a slight *contre-temps* occurs, for, Bashan being ordered in a voice of thunder to ring the bell, he starts up, poor willing youth, with extraordinary celerity, and, not spying a large silver dish-cover lying near him, plants a well directed kick in the centre of its hollow body, which sends it flying across the room into the fireplace, where it lodges amid a crash of falling irons.

"Dolt! booby! fool!" yells papa, bounding in his chair; and Bashan returns to the table covered with shame and confusion.

I wonder if papa will pay some family in Australia so much a week for permission to call them names? It would be hard upon him to have all his little comforts cut off at once. Supper over, poor Bashan goes to bed (I wish I might), mother works, papa smokes his pipe, and I make spills, a suitable and becoming occupation for a young woman in his estimation, but one that I never excelled at, for, laboriously as I roll and roll at them, they never have nice taper points or strong backs. Jack's are as stiff as pokers. How I hate these silent, dreadful after-supper hours! How Alice and Milly hated them in their turn! How the young ones look forward to them with dread! In summer-time it is not so bad —we are out till supper; but in autumn and winter our evil days begin, for immediately after tea we all have to take our work and sit round the table, while papa reads his newspaper; or rather, we used to, for they are all away now, the married sisters, and Jack, and Alan, and Dolly. As I look round the empty table, I seem to see us all as we sat night after night, mute as fish, but engaged in twenty reprehensible modes of passing the time.

How difficult we sometimes found it to restrain our hysterical giggles! Is there anything on earth more irrepressible or catching than a giggle?—and never so irresistible as when one knows that it is as much as one's life is worth to indulge it. Once out of the room, and free to laugh as much as we pleased, we felt no inclination to do so; it was only down there, when our spirits were so tightly bottled up, and we were denied all natural vent for them, that we felt so riotous. Making faces was a favorite amusement, and in the art we all attained a fine proficiency; and quick as lightning we often had to be in regaining our personality when papa turned his head to look at us. Pinches, tweaks, and nips, were given and exchanged with a Spartan fortitude, that should prepare us in some measure for the hardships of life. But our great and mighty temptation was to throw paper pellets at the place where the hair grows thin on papa's head. How often have we sat round the table, pellets in hand, and longed to launch them, certain that we could hit that little patch with a most delicate precision! . . . .

Well! I am likely to sit here making spills for a very, very long while. By the time I am an old maid I suppose I shall have made *millions*. Papa asks no questions about his daughters and their spouses; so when I have told him that they are all well, and that Luttrel Court is a fine place, my stock of conversation is exhausted. At half-past ten I say good-night, and take my bedroom candle thankfully; but oh! there is little rest for me, for does not a bitter task await me on the morrow? and in the long days to come is there so much as a shadow of any pleasant thing that is likely to befall me?

CHAPTER XV.

"Shall I command thy love? I may:
Shall I enforce thy love? I could:
Shall I entreat thy love? I will."

FOUR o'clock struck ten minutes ago; but I am not at the rendezvous. I am loitering slowly along the meadows that lead to the running brook, and I am possessed by a keen, overmastering inclination to turn round and run home again as fast as ever I can pelt. As yet, however, I have not forfeited my claim to valor, and as I go along, scarcely dragging one foot after the other, I look idly about me. This last September day is very different from that one little more than two months ago, when I wore my wreath of flowers, and later when I told George, with such grand triumph, that I was "going away." Then the world was all quivering lights and dancing shadows. Nature was gay and *débonnaire* with her full summer's smile; now she seems to have unfolded her arms to let autumn's chill breath steal over her warm, beautiful breast. The sunlight does not brood over the earth as it did then; rather it seems woven into a dainty network that hovers over the distant woods; and through the still, clear air, the far-off beeches gleam like jewels of gold and amber. Over all there is that nameless silence that spring and summer with their warm, bustling life never know; and the few remaining flowers seem to be dying sorrowfully, while the fallen and falling leaves cast their impalpable scent of decay abroad. And now my heavy feet have brought me within sight of the brook, and of a man who stands by its side waiting; and once again the irresistible inclination to take flight, even at this eleventh hour, possesses me; but remembering that if I do shirk my evil task now, I cannot get out of fulfilling it in the future, I walk quickly on, and he, spying my approach, comes forward to greet me.

"My darling," he says, and takes my two bare hands and kisses them; and I look up into his face, without a smile, without a word. But he is very blind, he does not see, does not heed. "You have come to tell me that you will make a happy fellow of me at last?"

But I draw my hands out of his, and hide my face in them, shivering.

"Are you sorry, dear?" he asks, gently. "Are you afraid? It must seem strange to you to promise yourself to any one—to a stranger; you have always been so fond of your own people; but I will be as careful over you, Nell, as gentle— You do not doubt that I can make you happy?"

Then, as I do not answer or lift my face, he goes on: "I have waited so long for this hour, Nell, for so many weary, weary years, sometimes I thought it would never come. If any one wants anything as badly as I want you, he rarely gets it; and you know I have never had any one to care for but you—neither mother, sister, nor brother, and I have often noticed that when a man centres his whole happiness in one object it is taken from him. That is why I have always so feared, Nell, that some one would come and take you away from me. That was why I hated your going to Luttrell; for I thought all men must love you as I did, and perhaps a stranger would take your fancy.

But when you told me yesterday that no one loved you but me, when I knew that my darling had come back to me safely, then, Nell, my heart was at rest, and I knew a perfect happiness, than which earth could give me no better, not if you were my own true wife, love, and bore my name. . . . I believe I thanked God." The reverent, simple voice ceases for a moment. "And now," he says, drawing my hands gently away from my eyes with one hand, while he gathers me to him with the other, "I have my reward; have I not, my darling?"

Ay! he has his reward, as I recoil from his embrace, slip away out of his arms, and stand looking at him with a measureless suffering in my eyes, with a deadly pallor on lips and cheek. A faint dread comes into his face, and dashes the surpassing brightness out; a terrible suspicion grows in his eyes, and dwells there. With that look upon him I can tell him better than I could a moment ago, when his beautiful face was all transfigured with its great happiness.

"I do not love you," I say in a whisper; "but love has come to my heart." . . . And then I cover up my face that I may not see his, and turn away.

For a moment there is a deadly waiting silence; then—

"Some one has stolen her from me!" he cries, in a voice like a trumpet. "God!"—and he falls downward like a dead man on the grass.

He does not speak or move, not even when I go and kneel down by his side and entreat him to answer my voice, to make some sign.

"George, George!" I cry, through my shuddering sobs; and then, for he may be dead, I say to myself in my wretchedness, I lay my hand upon the golden tressed head that lies so stirlessly on his folded arms.

"Do not touch me," he cries; "do not dare!" . . .

Oh! the relief it is to me to hear his hoarse voice!

"I might have borne it yesterday; but not to-day—not to-day . . . the joy I have been hugging to my heart is all a myth—a sham. . . . I was putting myself in *his* place." . . .

A tremor shakes him; he buries his face deeper in his arms.

"In whose place?" I ask, gently. "No one loves me but you, George!"

"No one but me?" he repeats, lifting his haggard face, all blotted and marred with grief and passion. "The man you love does not love you?"

"No," I say, subsiding into a tumbled, miserable heap by his side, while the tears trickle slowly down my pale cheeks. "You love me, George, and he loves somebody else, that is all!"

"Don't cry, darling," he says; "I can't bear it."

Even in this hour of supreme suffering my true, brave lover sets his own bitter grief aside to comfort mine.

"So that is the reason you look so pale and thin? Nell, you are quite sure you love him?"

"Quite—quite sure, George!"

"It is not an idle fancy; you will hold to it?"

"Do you love me?" I ask. "Do you think that you will ever love any one else?"

"You know that I love you; and I am quite certain I shall never love any one else."

"Then, George," I say piteously, "as you feel for me, so I feel for him, and—"

"I understand," he says; "I know." And a bitter heavy silence falls between us.

"And this man?" he says, waking out of it with a fiery anger that somehow comforts me. Who would not rather see a man swell with rage than bow his head in grief? "Who has worked this misery to you? Who has made you suffer like this? Who has dared?"

"It is not his fault," I say, slowly; "it was all a mistake, George; all my own doing and vanity."

"I don't believe it," he cries, with flashing eyes. "*You* make love to any one? *you* let your heart go before it ever was asked for? Never! I have known you long enough, and well enough; and you could not have cared for this man without his having given you good reason."

"There was no reason," I say. "He told me he was in love with some one else. Could anything be plainer?"

"Did he tell you that at first—at the very beginning?"

"Not quite," I say, in a troubled voice; "but he did not know, he could not guess, that I should—"

A burning, shameful blush covers my cheeks, and dries up the salt pricking tears.

"By Heaven! he shall answer for it!" says George, between his teeth; and in his blue eyes is a fixed resolve that makes me tremble. "I will find him out, whoever or wherever he may be, and—"

"My poor fellow," I say, with a faint smile, "are you the one to seek redress for my imaginary wrongs? You are not my brother."

"For once I wish I were," he says, quietly; "I should then have the right to punish the scoundrel who has dared to trifle with you. Nell, won't you tell me about it? We are not lovers now, you know—we are friends; and, dear, you need never fear my pestering you with unwelcome words and attentions: I thought no shame of entreating your love when there was a hope of my winning it; but now that I know how irrevocably it is given to another, and judging your heart by my own, I accept my fate and will bear it, please God, like a man. So could you not trust me, Nell?"

"I could trust you," I say, very gently, for the tender pity of his voice almost breaks my heart; "but I cannot tell you, George. I have never spoken to any one living of it save you, and more than I have told you I shall never tell."

We have risen, and are now standing

by the brook that leaps, and chatters, and froths, and fusses as it goes, pausing not a moment to look at the old, old sight of a miserable man and girl who have wrecked their lives for love.

"Do not suppose that I do not care," I say, passionately; "do not suppose that I do not *know*, George." . . .

"Yes, yes," he says; "but you must not fret about me. Think of yourself, my poor little darling. If I could only bear it for you!"

He breaks off, tries to speak again—fails; then, without a word or sign, goes quickly away, and I stand still looking after him, with aching, burning eyes, and the heaviest heart woman ever had. Have I passed the pure gold by, to covet the baser metal? Could Paul Vasher ever love a woman as purely, as truly, and as unselfishly as George loves me? There is a stronger, more selfish grit about Paul; he will have his own way, and no one shall balk him of it; he will be master, and no one shall say him nay. He will assure his own happiness first, that of the woman he loves after; and while George would look up to his idol, Paul would look down.

George is quite out of sight now, and with weary steps I go to the stile that divides the meadow from the field of rye and lean over it, thinking dully of that day two months ago, when I made my wreath and sent George away cross, and ran against Paul Vasher in the midst of the ripe grain.

"History repeats itself," I say, half aloud, as I watch those cunning workmen —the ants, scurrying about at the base of the primitive stone stile; "but only up to a certain point, and there it always fails. Now there is no Paul to come over the field to-day; he is probably shooting with the rest at Luttrell. I shall never have a chance of seeing him here either, for after to-day I will not come this way."

I lift my eyes, and see Paul Vasher coming across the field of rye to meet me. I do not speak or stir; the hour has come,

and must be met; and somehow, perhaps it is because my heart is so filled with George's misery as to leave no room for pity of my own, I feel a kind of indifference. "Nothing matters much now," I say to myself, as Paul stands before me. He makes me no greeting, nor do I him; he only looks into my pale, tear-stained face with a quick triumphant gladness that vaguely surprises me. Why should he look so eager and happy when his true-love is nowhere near?

"I have come to claim the fulfillment of your promise," he says; then as I lift my eyes to his, he catches and holds them fast to his; and lo! my listlessness falls from me like a garment, and a living, writhing pain stirs and leaps in my dull heart, and I know that the old glamour is upon me, that all the world has faded away, and that in all my past, present, and future, naught has place save the dark, beloved face that is looking so intently into mine.

"You never broke your word yet," he says, and his hands tighten their hold upon mine. "You will keep your promise, Nell."

With his eyes upon mine, with the resistless power he ever wielded over me compelling me, I open my lips to speak the truth as before my God; then I tear my hands out of his, my eyes from his.

"I cannot," I say with a bitter cry, "oh, I cannot!"

"Is it Paul?" he asks, folding his arms about me, and pressing my head down against his breast; "tell me, sweetheart."

"Tell me her name," I ask in a whisper; "tell me quick."

"*Nell*, do you understand *now?*"

As he lifts my arms and lays them about his neck, as he bends his dark head and seeks my lips with all the unsated hunger of the first kiss, I turn my head quickly away and hide it on his breast. Shall I receive the kisses of this new lover while the words uttered by the old one have scarcely ceased to echo in my ears?

"What is this?" asks Paul, holding me away from him to look keenly into my face; "after all, do you not love me, child? I should have waited for an answer to my question. Do you love me, my sweetheart, my flower?" he asks, looking into my face with a passion of tenderness.

"Love you?" I answer with a long, long sigh. "What is love? But let me go now, Paul; let me go!"

"Let you go?" he says, smoothing my hair back from my face, "now that I have just got my little witch? No! I will keep you safe enough, love, never fear!"

"But you do not know," I say, anxiously; "you do not understand; it is so quick, so soon."

"Soon! and you have kept me at arm's-length for more than a month! Ah! child, if you had known the restraint I had to put upon myself over and over again! I almost broke down."

"Did you love me all that time?" I ask softly; "are you sure you did?"

"Loved you!" he says; "I think I have loved you ever since the Silverbridge days; I know I have loved you ever since the day I met you in yonder field. I never was so sorry to say good-by to any one as when I said it to you under the porch at the Manor-House, and all the while I was getting through that confounded business in town, I was fidgeting to get back to Silverbridge, and, if it had not been for the absurdity of the thing, I should have come back just to get an hour's glimpse of you. Then I was obliged to go to the Luttrells, never dreaming they were relations of yours, and there I found you; and, sweet, I had not known you a week before I lost my head completely. Living as quietly as you did, I never supposed for a moment that you could have a lover; but very early in the day, from one or two chance remarks of yours, I gathered that you had; and never did a man chafe more under the knowledge than I. You would neither deny nor corroborate anything, and sometimes I felt certain you were beginning to care for me; sometimes, I believed, you were hankering after that man at Silverbridge; and at last—"

"You told stories," I say, laughing gently; "you told me you were in love with somebody."

"So I was."

"And that you would show her to me."

"So I will."

"And your behavior was inexcusable."

"I know it; but why, you little minx, did you rout me so utterly that morning in the garden? I was telling you my love-story full sail, on the point of asking you if you would try and love me, when out you tumbled a letter from your precious lover, with whom you told me, with inimitable *sang-froid*, you corresponded. And I had fondly imagined (after getting over the first unpleasant shock of your having a lover at all) that you cared nothing about him, flouted his attentions, and would none of them! In self-defense I invented a fiction; and even then, so stubborn you are, madam, I could not gather from your face any more than that you were disturbed, though whether on his account or mine, I could not for the life of me tell. I caught you by a promise, child, and made up my mind that here, where we first met, I would ask you a plain question, receive a plain answer."

"It is a plain answer," I say, ruefully; "for your sake I wish it were a prettier one!"

"Little sweetheart!" he says, devouring my face with his eyes, "do you remember how I told you years and years ago to pray that you might never grow up good-looking? Well, I am glad you did not, for I could not bear to lose a single one, not the very smallest, of your charms—your lovely hair, your sweet eyes, and sweeter lips. Nell, what do you suppose I am made of?"

"Flesh and blood, I suppose," I answer, giving him a soft pinch.

"Well, then, I can't stand this; do you know that we have been here more than ten minutes, and that I have not had a single kiss; do you think I am so patient?"

"Not to-day, Paul," I say, trembling; "some day perhaps, or to-morrow, but not to-day, I cannot because of—of him, you know."

"*Him!* there should be only one man in the world to you now, Nell."

"George Tempest," then I say, turning crimson; "*Lubin*, you know."

"What of him?" asks Paul, in surprise; "surely you are not bothering your head about him? Poor devil! he must be cut up at losing a little pet like you; but it is not your fault, you can't help it. I have a notion"—he goes on, smoothing my cheek with his hand—"that this admirer of yours is a great, awkward, country-looking fellow, who does not know what to do with his arms and legs; in short, just what I first called him to you, a Lubin?"

"Perhaps you will see him some day," I answer, smiling a little to myself at Paul's notion of George; it must be a source of small wonder, then, that I fell in love with himself. "Paul," I say, gently, "do you know why I have been fretting to-day? do you know why I have been crying so bitterly?"

"Well," he says, looking down on me with a whimsical air of pride and amusement, "I thought that you might have been thinking a little bit about me, perhaps?"

"No, no," I answer, smiling rather sadly, "it was not of you I was thinking just then, but of Mr. Tempest, who had scarcely left me when you came; he was so wretched, and it seemed so soon, so indecently soon, for you to make love to me."

"And you care so much as that?" he asks, with a sudden jealousy in his voice that startles me; "you could be sorry for him; could think of him at such a time as this? Heaven knows I had no other woman in my thoughts when I told you that I loved you."

"Yes, I can," I answer steadily; "and

I should not be worthy of your love if I could fling away all memory of his great misery in one moment to lose myself in happiness with another lover the next."

"Did you ever care for that man?" he asks, coldly, but he does not loose me out of his arms. "Did you ever have the smallest fancy for him?"

"Never!" I answer, gravely; "if I had I should be with him, not you, at the present moment, should I not?"

He looks deeply into my eyes, and what he reads there must satisfy him, for he murmurs fond, mad love-words over my drooped head, calls me his queen, his heart's delight, his idol.

"Papa may come this way," I say nervously; "he does not often, but he might; let us go and sit down in my parlor."

We cross the bare brown field, and reach my little green chamber, where a big log of wood affords us a seat, and sit down side by side.

"And now," he says, "I am going to show you my little girl;" and out of his breast-pocket he brings a velvet case, touches a spring, the lid flies back, and there, looking out at us from under a veil of hair and a wreath of poppies, is—me!

"How did you get it?" I ask, staring hard at it. (Surely, surely, I never was so pretty as that!)

"I asked an artist, who was at the Luttrells' ball, to study your face, and paint you with loose hair, and here it is."

(So it was my face that I left Paul to muse over that day on the terrace.)

"I have kissed this painted thing very often," he says, drawing me gently to his breast; "now the real lips are my own, do you deny them to me, Nell? I could take a hundred if I would, but I am too proud to do that; have you not one to give me, love?"

For a moment I tremble and hesitate; it is so soon, so terribly soon, if that other only knew! then, for my duty is to this my lord, I lift my lips to his, and as he folds me in his arms, he kisses me as I kiss him for the first time. Across that perfect kiss, than which the earth can give me no such other, why does a picture rise up before me, of a man and woman standing in the moonlight, wishing each other a passionate, last good-by?

"If you were not so strong," I say, stroking his hand with my slim fingers, "I would keep you in such order, banish you to such a distance; you would sue so meekly for ever such a little favor!"

"If you were like that," he says, kissing me passionately on cheek and brow, and eyes and lips (verily, one salute leads to a great many more!) "you would never have me at your feet. It is the soft, adorable, bewitching little creatures like you who get into a man's heart and stop there, though, Heaven knows, you kept me at a distance long enough!"

"I suffered for it enough!" I say, sighing. "Oh!·I shall always consider you treated me very badly! It is a wonder my hair is not gray with all the misery I have had."

"My sweetheart!" he·says.

Here there is a long and ridiculous pause, that people may fill up as they please.

"Do you know that I felt glad sometimes to see you looking sad? I thought you were fretting after Lubin; and I said to myself, 'Now she will know a little of what I am enduring.'"

Yes, he loves differently from George, not half as well; and I worship the very ground Paul walks on, and I esteem and like George as a brother.

It grows late, time has passed with such hurrying swiftness; through the dark stems of the trees before us shows the pale blue-green of the evening sky, cold and pure and beautiful exceedingly. Nature is robing herself in her cool twilight garment of silver gray, shrouding the trees and fields softly, as though preparing them for sleep; the sun has gone down, leaving a rack of amber and crimson clouds behind him; the leaves rustle

gently in the autumn wind that wanders over the face of the land.

"I must go home now," I say, springing up. "But, Paul, Paul—*papa!*"

"What of him?" asks my lover, pinching my cheek.

"He is furious at the notion of any of his daughters thinking of such a thing as being married."

"And he married himself, and had twelve children," says Paul, "which points the moral. Well, I am going to call on him to-morrow, and I shall tell him that you and I—"

"Do not!" I say, with much concern.

"He would, first of all, kick you, or try to," I add, mentally measuring Paul's stalwart proportions; "then he would lock me up, and, as he is going away in a fortnight for some months, it would be a serious business, for no one would dare to let me out."

"Poor little woman!" he says; "they shall not treat her like that while I am anywhere near!"

"If you would not mind waiting," I say wistfully; "if you would not say anything till he comes back (it would not be very deceitful, would it?), we could have such a glorious time while he is away! I have been looking forward to such a dull one too," I add, thoughtfully; "but now I shall be able to get into *heaps* of mischief."

"And do you think I am going to wait for you all that time, child?" he asks; "are you not afraid that my patience will wear out, and that I shall fall in love with somebody else?"

"No!" I answer, saucily, "I am not in the least afraid! Will you wait, Paul?"

"He must not be away too long," says Paul, significantly, "or he won't find his daughter Nell waiting for him when he gets back. For your sake, though, what would I not do for your sweet sake? I will not speak to him about our marriage before he goes."

"Our marriage!" how sweet the

words sound! As I muse on their good-ness, like a chime of jingled silver bells sweep Silvia's words across my memory, " *You will never be Paul Vasher's wife, never !* "

Ah! but I am Paul Vasher's love, and that is what you are not, never will be, Silvia. Your wild words are very far away, very puerile and empty to me, as I stand with my lover's arms around me; harm can be worked between two lovers apart and misunderstanding each other, but what between two who are to-gether in the first flush of acknowledged love and without a shadow between them ?

We take a long while to make our adieux to our parlor and to cross the field, but now we are standing in the meadow arguing; *he* wants to see me safely in at the home gates, *I* want him to go back to The Towers, lest we meet any one. Where we now stand is perfectly retired, save in harvest-time or seed-time people rarely come this way, but, the meadow once left, there is a chance of seeing any-body.

As we stand close together in the gloaming, talking our half-earnest, half-jesting nonsense, out of the gray shadow a man's figure emerges, and comes slowly toward us—George Tempest! He is look-ing down and walking heavily, with un-strung limbs and bent head; he does not see us until he almost brushes our gar-ments, then he lifts his eyes, and, oh heavens! I could cry aloud at the dull misery of their regard—the set, fixed stupor of his face, with not a glint of hope or peace or every-day indifference in it—and my face is radiant with my new-found joy.

At first, although we are in his path, he does not seem to see us, and is about to pass on, when some gleam of conscious-ness comes across his face, his ordinary bearing comes back to him, his eyes brighten.

" George ! " I say, stretching out my hand involuntarily; " George ! "

He takes it as gently as if it were a flower.

" Is that you, Nell ? " he asks in his natural voice; and then he looks at Paul, and, by some subtile intuition, *he knows :* I feel it in the sudden shock that passes from his hand to mine.

" You have not introduced me to your friend," he says.

Stumblingly I go through the form of introduction between the man I love and the man who loves me; then, I do not know how it comes to pass, we go on, and George passes on his way alone.

It is Paul who speaks first.

" And that is the man who loved you, Nell ? " he says, slowly, " whom I have sneered at, pitied—I! Heavens, that I should dare! Sweetheart, are you sure that you love me—not him ? He is noble, unselfish, grand, as I never was, never could be. It is not too late now; do you repent of the bad bargain you have made ? "

" I love you," I answer, clasping my arms, of my own free-will, about his neck; " I love you, my darling; what is any man in the world to me but a shadow save you ? "

" What is any woman on earth, what was one ever ? " he asks, peering into my face through the closing darkness, " com-pared with what you are to me, my love, my idol, my wife ? "

CHAPTER XVI.

" Think you I can a resolution fetch
  From flowery tenderness ? "

" NELL! Nell ! " cries the Bull of Bashan, rushing headlong into my room, " come down, quick! The governor is chasing Larry ! "

Anything more exciting than a race between papa and one of his offspring could not well be imagined. So I fly down-stairs in Bashan's wake, as eager for the fray as himself. It appears that five minutes ago the governor discovered Larry—aged eleven—seated in the kitchen, on a three-legged stool, eating bread-and-cheese; and, of course, made a dash at him as a terrier does at a neighbor's cat. But Larry, instead of dutifully yielding himself up to condign punishment, showed a most unexpected spirit, dropped his eatables and bolted out of the back-kitchen door, and into a paved walk that runs parallel with the kitchen-windows, and about as bad a place as he could well get into, for the only outlet from it is by an entrance to the house higher up, or a re-turn to the same through the kitchen-door. The governor is well aware of this fact, and, instead of giving a straight chase after the culprit, gravitates between the staircase and the back-kitchen, Larry outside, he in ; pursuer and pursued plainly visible to each other through the windows. When I arrive upon the scene I find papa, his face purple with rage and amazement, doubling, dodging, swearing, dancing, I see a pale but obstinate little face peeping in at the window, and then shooting back ; I see the youngsters posted about, evidently divided between delight at Larry's pluck and awful speculations as to his probable fate, one or two servants looking on, who are too much alarmed to offer the assistance the governor thinks it beneath his dignity to ask, though I am much mistaken if a certain hem ! from Bridget, the cook, does not warn Larry of his danger, when his gentle parent nearly catches him round the water-butt outside the back-door. Father and son are so well matched in agility and acuteness, that it seems as unlikely Larry will be caught as that the governor will permit him to escape. Unhappy Larry ! he must have been mad to begin the contest. What would his sin of eating bread-and-cheese at eleven o'clock in the morning have been compared with leading the governor this impious dance? No doubt he knows his foolhardiness by now, and repents him of it. But, per-

haps, he reflects that life is sweet, and the longer he can put off the evil hour of being caught the better, so he doubles and dodges with renewed vigor.

"What is the matter ? " asks mother, coming in, and glancing with amazement from papa's infuriated countenance to that of her miserable son, who is just peeping in with a ludicrous mixture of fear and bravado on his small face.

"Do you see that little devil, madam ? " asks my father. "Do you know that he has been dodging me, *me*, for the last two hours? (Ten minutes he means.) I'll break every bone in his skin when I catch him! and not one of these boobies (he points to us all standing about) can put out a hand to stop him! Stand at the foot of the staircase, and hold on to him when he comes past. Do you hear ? "

And off he dashes through the kitchen, and *round* the water-butt this time. Poor mother, she is in a quandary ! She is as utterly incapable of delivering the least deserving of her children up to the slaughter, as she is of disobeying her lord. So she meekly takes up her position where she was bid, and when Larry comes pelting in at the door, and hits her a smart blow with his head " below the belt," she puts out no detaining hand, but subsides into a comfortable heap on the mat; while the governor, entering in hot pursuit, catches his foot in her petticoats, and turns an energetic somersault over her prostrate form ! *Tableau vivant!* One can scarcely look on such sacrilege and live ; so I retire up-stairs precipitately in search of Larry, who, evidently, not valuing his life at a brass farthing, if he remain under the roof that shelters his parent, has escaped by some upper window and got away. In the midst of the wrathful clamor below, comes a shrill tinkle from our rusty front door-bell, and straightway papa retires to the library, and is plainly audible to something more than the ear of faith, taking it out of the furniture.

"It is only Tempest," says Bashan, who has followed me, peeping round the big leaves of the magnolia-tree that clothes the outside of our house with glossy green in winter, and creamy, fainting flower-cups in summer.

"Only George! It could not well be much more!" I say.

"He looks so queer," says Bashan, stretching his neck again. "He has on a long gray overcoat and a boxer; and his face is as long as my arm."

"Does he look as though he were going away?" I ask, anxiously. "Does he look as though he had come to say good-by?" then, recollecting myself, "Go down-stairs, there's a good Bashan, and make as much noise as you can, so as to drown the row the governor is making!"

I have been "fetched" twice, and now I am standing outside the drawing-room with my hand on the knob of the door, fearing to turn it. A crash of amazing magnitude from the library hard by suggests the desirability of my immediately hiding somewhere, so I enter the room with some haste to find George standing with his back to me, stooping over something that instinct tells me is a little ugly, disreputable photograph that the sun and a Silverbridge photographer worked between them to my eternal discredit. He has on a traveling-coat, just as Bashan said; and there is about him that brushed-up, stiff, touch-me-not air that Englishmen mostly put on when they go abroad, and take off when they stay at home. He turns at the sound of my steps, and comes toward me.

"May I have this, Nell?" he asks, holding up the poor little picture.

"It is mother's," I say, gently; "but I dare say she would let you have it. It was only yesterday papa said that, if he found any more of his daughter's likenesses littering up the mantel-piece, he would put them all in the fire!"

He does not join in my uneasy laugh; and we stand side by side looking out at the gay dahlia-beds, whose gorgeous colors will ere long be nipped and dulled by the chill night frosts. I have looked at him once and turned my eyes away. In all my misery at Luttrell did I ever look for one single hour like that?

"You will guess why I am here, Nell," he says. "I have come to say good-by to you for a time." And it was only yesterday that I was selfishly wishing he would take himself and his disappointments away out of my sight; well, to-day I have my wish.

"You will come back soon?" I ask, wistfully. "You will not stay away long?"

"I shall come back," he says, quietly. "There is my father to be considered, you know. Promise me one thing," he says, turning his haggard face away, "that you will be *married* before I come back."

"Married!" I repeat. "O George! and it was only yesterday that I told you— I have not *thought* about such a thing!"

"But Vasher will. How came you to suppose he did not love you?"

"It was all a mistake!"

"When I met you last night," he says, slowly, "I was picturing you with a heart as wild and unsatisfied as my own; I was thinking that I would bear twice my own burden if I could but lift some of the trouble from your weak shoulders, and all at once something stood in my path; I looked up and saw your face, Nell, passionate, tender, transfigured, with a look upon it that had never through all these years grown under word of mine, and, almost before I looked at the man by your side, I *knew*, Nell, I knew. . . . When I come back I shall find it easier, please God. After all," he says, with an attempt at cheerfulness that does not deceive me, "it is only now; it will not be so hard after a bit. But I did not come here to whine over my misfortunes. Good-by, dear." He holds out his hand, and I put mine in his without a word, without a tear, and so we look hard at each other's pallid faces for a moment, then—"God bless you!" he says. "God bless you!" I echo, and he is gone.

When the door has closed, I sit down on the floor, and, heedless of the fact that tears are a thrice-forbidden luxury in the house of Adair, cry long and bitterly, with no sneaking reservations as to quantity, quality, or the state of my appearance after it. Bitter and sweet, sweet and bitter, how have you not been mingled in my cup yesterday and to-day! and there should be only sweets in these my early, freshest days of happy, assured love. Perhaps this heavy-heartedness about George will wear away after a while, but just now my thoughts seem to go out more constantly to the lover who has gone away from me than to him with whom I shall be face to face in a few hours' time; nay, in my keen burst of sorrow for George's misery, I can find it in my heart to wish it was to-morrow, not to-day, I was going to see Paul. And the hours slip away so quickly, four o'clock has even struck, and I am still standing before my looking-glass, gazing blankly at my puffy eyelids and red nose. It is quite certain that Mr. Paul will discover that he has made a shockingly bad bargain, for he does not strike me as being a man likely to look at his lady-love through rose-colored spectacles—not but what that has its advantages though, for when a man like that pays a compliment he means it, and he has paid me one or two lovely ones. By the time my foot is on the first stair, the smiles have come back to my mouth, the gladness to my heart; is not my lover waiting for me? am I not going to him now, this minute?

All along the garden and orchard I go with hurrying steps. The convolvuli, hanging their marble vases over the hedge, blow out their faintly-scented welcome to me as I pass; the pale bramble-blossom hanging on the bough whispers, "He is waiting! he is waiting!" the brook, as it hastens along, mutters "Time is short, do not linger!" and very soon I have

reached the trysting-place, where he stands erect, impatient, watch in hand.

"How late you are!" he says; then, holding me away from him to look into my face, "Why, little one, you have been crying!"

"Yes," I say, rubbing my cheek against his hand, and feeling that now I am here it does not much matter whether I begin to cry again or laugh; by his side all is well with me.

"Who has been vexing you?" he asks, with an unamiable frown.

"No one! It is about George."

"George," he repeats, and his arms slacken their hold upon me; "why, this is the *second* time within the last twenty-four hours that you have been crying over Tempest! You must have liked him very much!"

"I did like him," I answer, stoutly, "*I do!* He is the truest, noblest, most unselfish lover a girl ever had, only— (I lift my eyes to Paul's jealous face) *I like you best!*"

"Do you, indeed?" he asks, with a queer upward twist of his brows. "And have you no such word in your vocabulary as love?"

"Perhaps."

"At any rate you are quite sure that you do like me?"

"Quite sure, Mr Paul Vasher; quite sure!"

Here our conversation becomes indistinct and ridiculous. And in our little green parlor leave us, O reader! to our idiocy, and cast your memory back to the days when you loved and were beloved and your happiness was but freshly born to you; remembering that time, you will, while smiling at our folly, understand it. . . .

———

CHAPTER XVII.

*" That is the true season of love, when we
believe that we alone can love; that no one
could ever have loved so before us, and that
no one will love in the same way after us."*

NOVEMBER has come upon us with a
garment of rain and fog, with leaden skies
and sodden earth; and the land looks
like one vast, mournful burying-ground,
with its fallen leaves, dead plants, and
flowerless brown stalks. Nature is shroud-
ed, motionless, bound hand and foot beneath her covering of decay; and looking
abroad it is hard to believe that spring
will ever come back, that green shoots
will thrust their way through the sullen
earth, tender buds spring out of yonder
bare brown trees. The gloominess of
the weather has its outcome in the newspapers, where murder succeeds murder
with sinister rapidity, and the heavy,
deathly air seems to prompt the souls of
men to deeds of rapine, crime, and slaughter. But to me these sluggish days bring
no sense of dullness and oppression; I am
not even longing for spring, with the passion of longing I used to know all through
the dead, silent, winter months. I have
Paul now, and he is life and home and
love and seasons bound up in one; and
since he is mine I lack nothing. The
chill winds have shaken every leaf from
the trees in our green parlor; the ground
is all dank and dripping, it knows our
faces no more; but we do not care, we
are cozier in-doors than we ever were out.

We have been playing at a foolish
game this past month, Paul and I. We
made a bad beginning in being so much
in love with each other, and we have
gone steadily down, deeper and deeper;
every day we go a little further, for love
either increases or diminishes; passionately as one may care for a thing to-day,
one can love it even better to-morrow;
there is no standing still. And as besottedly fond as Paul is of me, so I am of
him, and an uncommonly pretty pair of

12

fools we make. At the present moment
there is no one to take heed of us, fortunately, no one, that is to say, but Venus, who is shaking an uncommonly loose
leg in the distance, and as she is hanging
on the wall without any visual power, save
that given by cobalt blue badly laid on,
we may be said to be tolerably secure
from unkind criticism.

We are in the old schoolroom, whence
Amberley's rule has forever departed;
the curtains are drawn, and we are
sitting before the fire. It is our favorite haunt, for the boys are far too well-
bred to intrude upon us; indeed, they
avert their jolly faces if they happen
to meet us, as though a recognized pair
of lovers were the most immoral spectacle
in the world; and there is no chance here,
as in the drawing-room, of Simpkins or
the footman walking in every five minutes
or so, on some trifling pretext or errand.

" Have you heard from your father
yet ? " asks Paul.

" No. Paul ! "

" Yes."

" Do you know, that I really think he
was sorry when he went away—"

" Well, darling ? "

" Nothing ! only I don't think I can
ever feel comfortably rebellious with him
again ; I shall have a sort of half-and-half
feeling, that will make me a detestable
mixture."

" You won't be here very long, little
one," he says; " you will be at The
Towers before he has been back very
long."

" Shall I ? " I ask, doubtfully. Somehow it seems natural to me that Paul
should be my lover, but I never look
ahead or fancy myself his wife.

(A pause, which we fill up.)

" I want to ask you a few questions,"
I say presently. " Will you ever swear
at me when we are married ? "

" Good Heavens, no ! I never was a
very good temper, but I hope I know
how to behave like a man." '

" And do not all men ? " I ask, meditatively. "I always thought they did, at home, you know; it's very nice to find they don't. You had better never put me out," I add, pinching his brown cheek; "for I have a command of language that would frighten you. Tell me, do you ever shy dish-covers at people?"

"Never."

"Would you ever call me a peacock, a dummy, a mummy, a gawk, a mawk, or a beast?"

"I won't promise. They are pretty names, Nell—some of his?"

"Of course! but when he wishes to be especially withering he calls me 'that beauty.'"

"Lucky little woman," says Paul, fondly, "for both her lover and her father to have such a high opinion of her good looks!"

"Yes, indeed!" I say, laughing; "only, you see, he means it rather differently from the way you do!"

Here our conversation becomes too ridiculous for repetition.

"It is my turn now," says Paul, presently, "to ask you a few questions; it may be as well that we should know each other's little weaknesses before marriage as after. Do you ever go into hysterics?"

"It is like poor Martha Snell's staying," I say, laughing; "'who would if her could, but her couldn't.' I would if I could, but I don't know the way. Hysterics is a luxury papa would never have permitted."

"Do you nag?"

"I despise a nagging woman!" I say, sitting suddenly upright; "it's so intensely mean! No, Paul, I shall get into a boiling rage, and then I shall have done with it."

"Well spoken!" he says, heartily. "Get into as many passions as you like, my pet, but never nag, and don't sulk; more love is worn out that way than by any other. Now for another question. Will you ever flirt? I could stand a good deal from you, child, but I would never stand that."

"Are you afraid?" I ask, proudly. "Is your opinion of me so bad as that?"

"There is only one man I should ever be afraid of your taking too much notice of," he says. "You know who that is; some day, perhaps, you will compare me unfavorably with him, and—"

"Have you not lost that old madness? Paul, Paul! is there not a wide difference between pity and love?"

"There is, but I hate to think that any man ever uttered a word of love to you save me, and—confess now," he goes on half jestingly, half earnestly, "that you don't think me half as good as he is?"

"You will not get me to say that you are, for you are not," I say, shaking my head. "You are too masterful and determined; you will have your own way, and you are more than a little bit selfish, and—"

"A jealous fool!" he says, finishing my sentence in a different way than I had intended. "Well, you have taught me one vice I never knew before, and that's jealousy."

"Is it a vice? I think the very pith and marrow of love must be gone when lovers grow careless about each other's likes and dislikes. Paul," I ask, suddenly, "do you think that by any possibility, under any circumstances, you could fall in love with Silvia again?"

"Can a man be in love with two women at once? Could you be in love with two men, Nell?"

. "I suppose not; only you loved her first, you know."

"And I love you now, you know."

"Are you as fond of me as you ever were of her?"

"What do you think?"

"That you like me best."

"Well, I'm inclined to think the same. For one thing, I have a respect for you."

"That is a funny idea! I never heard of lovers doing that before."

"Nevertheless, it is 'the sweet-marjoram of the salad,' the very salt of real love. The divine passion, as it is inaptly called, may burn brightly and hotly enough for a time, but it does not last unless it has something more substantial to go upon than sheer love and admiration."

"And did you respect Silvia?"

"Until I found her out."

I do not think I am jealous now of Paul's first love; I might be if she were here in her real flesh-and-blood beauty, but out of sight is very truly out of mind, and she is to me, in my warm, living, every-day happiness, no more than a half-forgotten shadow. Paul's thoughts are mine, and since he never thinks of her, neither do I. I have never repeated to him her wild words at Luttrell; somehow it has seemed to me needless and, in a certain sense, dishonorable—she has lost, I have won; would there not be a species of cowardice in holding her impotent boasts up to ridicule?

"I wonder what she would say if she knew about us?" I say aloud.

"It would not interest her," says Paul, carelessly; "her own affairs are far more engrossing, no doubt. I say, Nell, when is your father coming back?"

"In March."

"Three whole months and part of another. If you think my patience will hold out till then, little woman, you are mistaken. I shall make you marry me before he comes back, to make all sure."

"No, you will not!" I say, quickly; "just think of mother! And she has been such an angel to us. Only think of what it would be if he came back and found me gone! Supposing she had refused to hear of our being engaged or let you come here, save as an ordinary visitor, what should we have done then, pray?"

"Fitted up a cow-house, my dear, and sat in it from ' rosy morn till dewy eve.'"

"And quarreled when we grew hungry," I say, laughing; "but mother really is frightened out of her wits. It is all

very fine for us, you know, but *we* dance and she pays the piper."

"Sweet soul!" says Paul. "How, if all mothers-in-law were like her—"

"Wait until she is yours," I say, slyly; "you don't seem to know half the difficulties that lie in our path!"

"If he is very bad," says Paul, "it's easy enough to run away. Alice did."

"Yes; but The Towers is not far to run away to."

"I should like," he says, tightening his clasp on me, "to walk into a church one morning (you could put on a white bonnet and a clean print), without a gaping crowd of people looking on, and a pack of idiotic children throwing flowers for us to tumble over, and you and I be made man and wife; then eat a good breakfast, and set out for Paris, without being spattered with salt and pelted with slippers."

"You would take me to Paris?" I say, in delight.

"Rather! you have never been abroad, have you?"

"Never!"

"I wish I could take you with me to Rome next month."

"To Rome! next month!" I repeat, sitting up and pushing the hair back from my eyes. "You are *going away*, Paul?"

"Yes, little one, for a few days. I have to settle poor Lennox's affairs; and it is a thing that cannot be got out of. I have been putting it off as long as possible, but I shall be back by Christmas."

"I have only just found you," I say, my lips quivering; "and are you going to leave me so soon?"

"My flower," he says, taking me in his arms, "it is worse to me than to you, this separation; don't make it any the harder, for I *must go*."

But I only clasp my arms close about his neck and shiver; somehow this going away seems to lay a cold finger upon my heart, and change all my safe, glad trust in Paul's love to a trembling, miserable fever of unrest.

"Paul!" I say in a low voice; "when two people love each other beyond everything, don't you think something or other generally happens to them?"

"They get married."

"No! one or other of them dies, or they get separated, or—or—*something*."

"Who could possibly separate us?" he asks, almost sternly; "are you not sure of yourself, Nell?"

"I was thinking of you, Paul; you will see so many people."

"Are you judging me out of your own heart?" he asks, still gravely; "would any amount of *seeing people* make you forget me for a moment?"

I do not answer; I am struggling against the unreasonable feeling of dread that the mention of this short absence has brought me. I have been living in a fool's paradise lately; every day, every hour, he has been close at hand, under my very eyes, and it smites me with a bitter, desolate pang to think that for a space he will be gone, his place stand empty; be out of reach of the sound of my voice, the touch of my hand.

I think Paul sees the misery of my face, for he takes it between his two hands, and looks at me with passionate love and tenderness.

"Is it not worth the pain of parting, sweetheart, to come back to each other again? Shall we not love even better for the days spent apart?"

"'Absence makes the heart grow fonder,'" I quote ruefully; "but we don't want to grow any fonder than we are now; and, as to that hateful word good-by, I wish I had never, *never*, got to say it to you!"

"When I come back," he says, "I will never leave you again until you are my wife; never any more, little Nell! "I shall miss you horribly," he says, with a falter in his strong voice, as he winds a long tress of my hair round his neck; I shall weary for a sight of your soft face, for a touch of your sweet lips! Will you long for *me*, Nell?"

I look up into his dangerous, passionate, proud eyes—the eyes that have swayed me so absolutely from the beginning, and which, if they beckoned me over flood and flame and yawning pit, I must needs follow, never recking where my feet trod.

"*I love you*," I say, with a long-drawn, quivering sigh; "do you know what that means?"

"Never desert me, my angel," he says, looking down with almost fierce worship into my upturned face; "for if you do—better far had it been that I died before I met you."

CHAPTER XVIII.

"....Love's voice doth sing
As sweetly in a beggar as a king."

Do what I will, I cannot get used to the fact that I may run up and down stairs, sing, laugh, talk at the top of my voice, not only in the school-room, but in the passages and in the drawing-room; sit nose and knees into the fire if I please, instead of looking at it from afar off with blue cheeks and pinched nose; give my opinion with a pleasant conviction that it will be treated with consideration; in short, conduct myself generally as a human being and independent member of society, whereas, until now, I have been but a miserable and insignificant atom gravitating round that tremendous magnet, the governor.

I don't suppose that he would be considered a very great man out of his family. Folks might call him a handsome little man, or a cross little man; and if he tried on his pranks in society no doubt society would show him the door. (Happy thought! perhaps that is why he has eschewed it; and unhappy we, who are made to act as buffers between him and the outer world.) But to us he is Queen Victoria and the Emperor of all the Russias, and anything else that can be suggested as important, awe-inspiring, and not to be set at naught.

It is all very different now. The house echoes from morning to night with gay young voices, doors bang, not compelled thereto by a wrathful hand, but naturally; dogs bark, the parrot struts about at its leisure, conversation goes on briskly and evenly " up-stairs, down-stairs, and in my lady's chamber; " our meals are no longer served up and eaten by steam.

Simpkins has made a long farewell to all his greatness in impromptu slides and races against time, subsiding into a dignified demeanor that is far more *convenable* in a man of his years and size.

And Paul Vasher comes and goes. Never were two such lucky lovers as we are. Mother is the most absent of duennas, the children the most invisible of pickles (Bashan is at school), and we have the garden and schoolroom to ourselves; and oh! we are not unthankful for our good luck! Life can give us no fairer, sweeter days than she gives us now. Are we not more fortunate than our fellows, in that we can gather up so many precious hours, and say, "They were wholly satisfying; there was no speck of alloy mixed with their pure gold?" Perhaps, if we only knew it, this is the one green spot in our lives, to which, in days to come, we shall look back with a keen longing. If only this golden time might remain with us a little! But it may not.

"Move on!" cries the inexorable voice, "move on! Take up your chain or your garland where you laid it down, and go your way; life gives no time for dallying or sitting still." It is moving on until we reach the grave; and, O spirits! can you tell me this? Is it not moving on *after?*

The desolate old Persian proverb comes into my mind: "It is better to kneel than to stand, it is better to sit than to kneel, it is better to lie than to sit, and it is better to be dead than lying." I think the man who wrote that must have been a cowardly, half-hearted fellow, who had not enough pluck to take up his burden and bear it. It is an ignoble longing to wish to lay down the weapons of life, and rust away in stirless, helpless sleep.

My thought seems to be taking a dismal turn; but I feel dismal. For the first time in my life I am waiting for Paul. He is delayed, I suppose, by some more of those tiresome people who have been flocking to call upon him since his return has been made known. He has seen a few, escaped a great many, but this morning, I imagine, he has been fairly caught, to his own disgust, no doubt, as much as to mine. I have not seen his home yet; mother would not allow me to go there, and he does not want me to see it just directly; he is getting a surprise ready for me, he says. I have not told Alice and Milly a word about him. Mother did not wish it until papa's return; neither have I mentioned Paul's name to Jack, who did not come home in October after all. Christmas he is to spend with the Lovelaces, and Alice thinks I am going to accompany him too. But indeed I am not; Paul is going to be here, and where he is I shall be.

"It is quite certain," I say aloud, " that he is not coming for ages; he will very likely not be here till luncheon-time, and then, of course, mamma and Simpkins will be there, and I shall not be able to speak to him, and—" Here my fortitude gives way, and tears run down my cheeks. "How *wasted* every minute does seem that I spend away from him! "

"They're something worse than wasted to Paul," says my lover's voice behind me; and, as I turn my forlorn countenance to him, he catches me up in his arms, and lifts me from the ground.

When he has wiped my tears away— and it takes a very long while, although I have not shed a single one since he came in—he puts my hat straight, and we go out into the garden, and stroll up and down the graveled walks, talking the silly, selfish stuff that is vastly entertaining, important, and absorbing to *us*, but would be flat enough to anybody else.

The world (say Alice and Milly) calls Paul Vasher haughty, cold, proud; if they could only see him now, planning out our married life with all the zest and *abandon* of a schoolboy out for a holiday!

He is going to teach me to ride, he says; it is to be hoped that his efforts will be crowned with more success than were those of the governor. Not that he took any pains with me; he used to gallop away, and leave me to follow as best I might; and follow I did—over my animal's nose. How often have I not sat at my ease on a dusty road, weeping plentifully, while my steed refreshed himself from the hedge, waiting till Providence should send somebody to put me into the saddle again! Altogether it was a failure; and after my pony had walked me in at the open door of the village public, and was forced to be backed therefrom, to papa's rage and disgust, he washed his hands of me, and I was left in peace. "You won't be very angry if I break the horse's knees," I ask, anxiously; "that was what unnerved me so when I was out with the governor; my own would not have mattered half as much!"

"Poor little sweetheart!" he says; "well, I don't know that I should care particularly for a stable of broken-kneed horses, but I would far rather they came to grief than you did."

"I can stick on pretty well," I say, with modest pride, "but you will never be able to teach me to *trot!* You will be so ashamed of me when you see me shaking up and down in the saddle, with my hat at the back of my neck and my hair tumbling down—you should only hear Jack talk about it! Poor fellow! how I have forgotten him lately! All your fault, sir."

We stand still among the cabbages to make ourselves ridiculous, and then go on again.

"Do you know, Paul, that there is one thing I shall not like at The Towers?"

"What is that?"

"The visitors! Don't you think it would be much better to quarrel with our neighbors all around, as papa does? We never should have had this glorious time here, if callers had been popping in at all hours! Now, if visitors only came when they were asked, or when they had something nice to say, or because they knew they were welcome, there would be some sense in their coming; but when they only call as a duty, and don't care twopence for you, and *you* only receive them as a duty, and do not care twopence for them, is it not a great waste of time and trouble?"

"I don't think it would do to quarrel with them all," says Paul, laughing, "but we will keep as clear of them as we can. You won't be always here; we shall go to town in May, for you to be presented."

"Presented!" I repeat, stopping short, and staring at him, "do you *mean* it?"

"Of course I do, child, why not?"

"Why not?" I repeat again; "oh! the very idea! why—why—" I say, going off into a hearty roar, "the queen would laugh in my face! Oh dear! oh dear! only think of *me*, in a tail three yards long; *me*, in white feathers; *me*, walking out of a room backward—why, I should turn a somersault as sure as fate!" And I go off again into a louder explosion than the first. "Papa would never get over it," I say, wiping my eyes; "he always called me a peacock, and if I went to court, I should be—*be* one; tail, feathers, strut, and all!"

"Nell," says Paul, gravely, "I am afraid you will not make a very dignified Mrs. Vasher."

"Do you mind my being so noisy?" I ask, suddenly sobered. "Would you rather I were quieter? Only I am so happy, you know, and I never was quiet over that! And if you really mean me to go to court, Paul" (I check myself on the edge of another outburst), "I will promise you not to smile even, or turn a somersault—or anything else; I will be as sober as a judge!"

"Will you?" he asks; "I don't think I should know my Nell if she moved slowly and spoke seldom."

"Did you ever think your wife would ever be a bit like me, dear?"

"Did you ever think your husband would be a bit like me, Nell?"

"No," I say, absently; "for I always thought I should have to marry George."

"Don't say that," he says, frowning; "it sounds as though it did not matter much to you whether you married him or me; and I suppose if I had not come you *would* have married him?"

"I suppose so, sooner or later!"

"You are very cool over it," he says, giving me a little impatient shake; "I do believe that after a while you would have got a comfortable sort of a liking for him, and never found out that you were capable of feeling anything different."

"Of course I should! And, when you came back to The Towers later on, we should have looked upon you as a sort of benevolent, elderly gentlemen, whom we should have prevailed on to intercede with the governor to obtain his consent to our marriage, and we should have become very fond of you."

"Would you, indeed?" he says. "Let me tell you, child, that, if you had been betrothed wife or wedded wife when I came back, it would have been just the same, you would have loved me as I should have loved you—instinctively."

"Would you?" I ask, slowly.

"Ay! that would I! And your heart would have come to me as mine would have gone to you, across everything."

"No, Paul, it would not. If I had belonged to George, and, too late, met and loved you, you should never have known it. You praised me once for being honest."

We are in a remote corner of the garden now, and we stand still with the dull, sodden ground at our feet, and the gray, blank skies overhead, and he takes me in his arms.

"Sweet and honest, fair and true!" he says; "was ever any one like my sweetheart? Thank God that no other man has a shadow of right over you, child; who is there indeed, of all the living world, that could come between us and make our love a sin?"

And the chill, wintry wind that is moaning and creeping about the leafless trees echoes eerily, "Who?"

"If you plese, Miss Ullen," says Dorley, appearing, "I've got a nosegay for 'ee."

I take the scanty little bouquet with a very red face, and a not very gracious "Thank you."

"Mebbe that's your young man, Miss Ullen?" he says, in a stage-whisper. "An' it seems ony yesterday I saw you a-dangling from that quarinder-tree with yer pantaloons—"

"That will do, Dorley!" I say, hastily, and he shuffles away.

"What was the end of the story?" asks Paul, inquisitively; "your—"

"Dorley does not know his manners!" I say, with dignity; "we will not talk about him!"

We go and look at the rabbits, Bashan's now, not Jack's, soft, helpless, pretty creatures, whose bodies, alas! we too often nourish to feed our greedy cat.

"I should like a good many pets at The Towers," I say, as we move on again. "Will you read prayers, Paul?"

"I!" says my lover, looking considerably astonished; "well, no, I think not, Nell."

"Then I must. What made me think of it was the canaries."

"The canaries! what on earth have they got to do with it?"

"When papa begins to read they begin to sing, and then he gets in a rage, and altogether—"

"Hum!" says Paul, "prayers and

temper seem to go together. Don't you think we had better do without both?"

"O Paul!"

"Look here, little woman!" he says, "I may as well tell you now, to save bother hereafter, that I don't believe any amount of praying by rote does a man a vestige of good. Let him set to work to mend his morals and weed his heart first, and keep the outward observances of religion *after*. Many a man who makes a great parade of religion is at heart ten times more sinful than he whom the world calls infidel, yet has throughout his whole life been true to every generous, noble instinct, doing his duty to his neighbor without shrinking, asking and expecting no approval, save that which is given by his own conscience. Such a man's life is, to my thinking, a far truer worship of his Creator than any amount of empty prayer ascending daily from a selfish, presumptuous soul, that glorifies self in his Maker, and believes that words, not acts, are reckoned up above."

"Then you would abolish prayer?" I ask; "you would do away with a man's going to church?"

"No," he says; "I believe in the efficacy of the one and the good of the other, if he seeks them because he feels the need of them; not from custom or habit, or because the omission will be observed of his fellow-men. Do you believe that prayer is of any use to a man who takes his every-day thoughts with him to worship and, outwardly observant, hugs himself in the consciousness that he is doing something at once pleasant and profitable, making his peace with God and mankind at the same moment?"

I shake my head. "You would sweep away all the old landmarks, Paul. How would you teach a child to understand this?"

"I would say, 'Be good, for goodness' own sake, and because it is honest and right,' not 'Be good, and you shall go to heaven; be naughty, and you shall go to hell.' I call that plan one of lollipops

and terrorism. The child is too young to take in all the things that are poured into its mind; it gets a vague idea that being good is a very hard thing, but to be rewarded by something nice, and that to be naughty is very pleasant, but will be followed in due course by something uncommonly nasty; and, between the two, the poor little wretch loses its head and gets an entirely false idea of religion. Now, if the instinct of right were implanted in that child's mind, and it were taught to follow after good and reject evil, not because it would be rewarded for the one and punished for the other, but because goodness and virtue were beautiful and to be worshiped, while vice and sin were ugly and hateful, and to be shunned for the sake of their own deformity, then would be laid the foundation for a race of men who would be neither free-thinkers nor Pharisees—'

"If you please, miss," says Simpkins, in a patient voice, that signifies he has made the announcement more than once to us, "luncheon is served!"

CHAPTER XIX.

"ROSALIND. Oh! how full of brier is the working-day world!

"CELIA. They are but burs, cousin, thrown upon us in holiday foolery."

WE have never quarreled before, Paul and I, never. We have had little disputes about this, that, and t'other; he has been jealous, I provoking, but we have never actually quarreled till to-day. We are at it at this very moment, and oh! what dull, dull work I find it! We are not saying bitter things to each other shrilly and fast, with angry tears in our voices and treacherously soft hearts. (When one is having a good downright quarrel with a person one loves, does not the tongue wax the bitterer in proportion as the heart grows softer? Mine does.) We are in the sulky, dignified, silent stage, each waiting for the other to speak, and each grimly determined not to be first. Paul is in one arm-chair, I am in another —we are *yards* apart; and on the hearth-rug, sprawling on their backs, as though they had alighted in a hurry, lie two books. I shall not say what the quarrel began about. I was certainly very rude; but what business had he to take up a newspaper, and read it right before me, after I had said what I did? I lost my temper then—always an easy matter with me—and my manners along with it, and threw a thin little book at him, and it just shaved his nose.

He looked up and said, "Don't do that again, Nell!" And his cold voice so provoked me that I threw another one, and could have wept for shame when it struck his newspaper, and then fell down beside the first; for he neither spoke, nor moved, nor looked at me.

How different a man is to quarrel with from a woman! Now, if I were falling out with the latter, she would be so amazed at my holding my tongue instead of going at her, hammer and tongs, that she would be thoroughly nonplussed, and suspect me of possessing some weapon against her of which she knew nothing; in short, to thoroughly rout and overcome a female opponent, nothing answers like a stolid silence, whereas, a man considers a woman who holds her tongue instead of storming at him, a good, sensible little soul, worthy of his best consideration. Therefore I am harassed by fears that he will think I am meek and sorry; and, *indeed*, I am neither.

I always thought men remained on their knees until they married. I know a good many of them hop up pretty quickly afterward, for, the cold plunge of matrimony once taken, they have an awkward knack of remembering Byron's words—

"Love is of man's life a thing apart,
'Tis woman's whole existence,"

though I never heard before of a *lover* behaving as Paul is doing.

In novels, if Amanda is offended with her Adolphus (although she may be entirely in the wrong), Adolphus always tears his hair and beats his breast, and does everything but walk on his head to restore serenity to her ruffled brow. I am sure George would never have sat in my presence mute as a fish for five whole minutes. I wonder if I should have cared so intensely if he had? not that I do care *much*.

How the minutes drag—the ugly, empty, dull minutes! The hands of the clock are surely standing still, for I am sure that it is hours that Paul and I have been sitting apart, with this leaden silence between us. I was very rude to him just now, and when he held out his hand to me and said, "Nell, did you mean what you said just now?" why did I not jump out of my chair and say, "No, no, *no*," instead of answering, "Yes, certainly!" in the confident expectation that he would cross over to me the very next moment and fetch me. But he is sitting in his chair and I am in mine; and, if he will not come to me nor I swallow my pride and go to him, shall we sit on and on in this old school-room till doomsday? I shut my eyes and count sixty seconds at a smart gallop, then sixty more; then I unlatch one eye cautiously to see what he is doing.

The newspaper hangs from his hand; he is staring into the fire rather wearily; suddenly he looks full at me, but, as my one open optic is more suggestive of mirthful winking than penitence, he looks away again. It is full a minute before I take another peep and discover that he is, to all appearances, following my example, and courting slumber—or pretending to. I had no idea Paul was so sulky! He looks very handsome with his head lying back upon the cushion, and I am just thinking so, when he opens his eyes and looks at me as I hastily shut mine. After all it is very like a game of bo-peep, and if it goes on much longer I shall burst out laughing, which would be dreadful, for how could I dictate terms of surrender in the midst of breathless giggles?

I wonder what will bring him into a state of repentance quickest—reproaches? It would be very *infra dig.* to speak to him. Hysterics? I don't know the way, and he hates them. Faint away? He would not know when I began unless I made a series of horrible faces; and he might consider them purely vicious, and take no notice. Tears? The very thing. Decent, touching, non-compromising tears, that may mean anything or nothing. If only I could get them up, there's the rub; tears never came easy to me at any time. Joy or sorrow must prick me pretty sharply before the salt fount is unsealed. I sit bolt upright, take out my handkerchief, and, with the heartiness with which I always set about all my undertakings, I try hard to "weep a little weep." I think of my own tomb, and nobody to weep over it—always a subject of dismal contemplation with me; of the end of the world, and the sorry figure that I shall cut; of Jack, cut off in the flower of his youth; of George, a victim to my charms, standing on his head, with his heels sticking out the Thames mud; of every dismal picture, in short, that I can conjure up before my mind, but all in vain. My tears come not; and, though I scrub my eyes and nose and cheeks into a high state of refulgency, they remain dry as bones.   .

I am putting away my handkerchief, feeling that my last weapon has broken in my hand, and that nothing is left to me but dignified flight, when I catch Paul's eye, and discover that he is absolutely—yes, absolutely *laughing.* I stare at him for a minute in amazed silence: is this his way of going down on his knees?

"Have you quite finished trying to pump up those tears?" he asks, passing his hand over his face. "I have been watching you for some time, and I am sure you must have hurt yourself with that piece of cambric.

"I am going," I say, jumping up. "Oh, I had no idea you could behave so ill; I thought you *liked* me."

He snatches at my skirts as I pass him, and in a second has perched me on his knee, holding me there with a firm grasp that I cannot shake off. Tears, real tears, are in my eyes now, but they do not fall; he shall not think that what is a laughing matter with him is a crying one with me.

"Now, Nell," he says, and there is no laughter in his voice, it is very grave, "I want to know what you mean by this stupid behavior?"

Stupid behavior! I never heard of a man saying such a thing as that to his lady-love before; and I thought Paul was so hopelessly, drivelingly, besottedly in love with me.

"I think it is you who have been stupid," I say, blankly.

"What did you say to me when I asked you to—?"

"That will do," I say hastily; "we have discussed all that before."

"And do you call that a proper way to speak to me?"

No answer.

"Do you call it a proper thing to throw books at my head?"

"Do you call it a proper thing to read a newspaper before me?"

"Certainly; if you are sulky and will not speak to me."

"You were sulky too."

"I spoke to you."

"And I answered you."

"In a nice manner."

"I had better not speak to you at all," I say, with dignity; "perhaps you will allow me to leave you, Mr. Vasher?"

"Presently. Now, Nell, do you think that because we are lovers we are to be careless of each other's feelings? The most passionate love that ever existed between man and woman would make neither happy if consideration did not form a part of it. Do you think I would wound you as you did me ten minutes ago; do you think I could ever make such a speech to you as you did to me?"

"Is it only ten minutes ago?" I say, looking at the clock; "it seems like ten hours."

"Are you sorry that you made it, Nell?"

I lift my head and look him in the face silently, and, for a minute I have a sharp, short struggle with myself, then, for I love him very dearly, I say "Yes."

"Little darling!" he says, clasping me tighter; but—oh, wonder of wonders!—he does not kiss me; does not even try to. "What a deal of time we have wasted, to be sure! But that is not all; there are the books."

"The books," I repeat; "what of them?"

"You have not picked them up yet."

"Did you suppose I was going to?" I ask, smiling at his joke, which is excellent.

"I am sure you will."

I look at him quickly, fancying my ears have played me false, but he is grave enough.

"Do you mean it?" I ask, slowly.

"Most certainly,"

"Then I never will," I say, with spirit. "Oh! I did not think you were so mean, after I had said I was sorry too."

"What did I say to you after you had thrown the first one?" he asks.

"That I was not to do that again."

"And you threw another the next moment; so you were not only rude but disobedient."

"Am I your daughter?" I ask, turning round to look at him with a hovering smile.

"No, miss, but I am your lord and master, and you are bound to obey me."

"Don't be so sure of that," I say, putting my head on one side to look at my smart engagement ring of big opals and diamonds—the "jewels of calamity," as folks say. "If you are such a tyrant now, when we are only courting, what would you be if we were married?"

I don't feel a bit miserable now, or sorry, or ashamed. He is talking to me; there is not a dreadful wall of silence built up between us.

"Do you expect me to tell you I am pleased with you when I am not?" he asks, gravely.. "Would you like me to be a hypocrite? I cannot say one thing and mean another, and the same with you; when you are vexed I should like you to speak out and have done with it."

"I am very much vexed with you now," I say, with alacrity; "I wish to get off your knee this very minute and you will not let me."

"You shall go when you have picked up those books."

"Then we shall stay here until we are fossils," I say, swinging my foot. "Simpkins will be here presently to say dinner is ready; are we to eat it as we are?"

"The dinner can wait."

"Only I can't wait for my dinner," I say.

There is a little pause, during which I look into the red-hot heart of the fire and take counsel with myself. Clearly he is not to be managed by dignity, and I don't mean to give in. Nevertheless, I have no mind to sit here mumchance till we turn into fossils. I will try coaxing, and see if that will bring him to a proper frame of mind. I steal my arms round his neck and hold up my mouth to be kissed, but he does not bring his face a jot nearer to mine; and, for the first time in my life, my offered caress is repressed. If he had slapped me he could not have astonished me more.

"Nell," he says, "Nell," and he looks into my eyes with a vexed and strong pain in his own, "could you not give up your willfulness for once to please me?"

For a little space I look at him; then I slip out of his arms and sit down on the hearth-rug. There the books lie, nasty little toads! How I hate the man that wrote, the printer that printed, and the person that brought them here! I turn them over with the point of my shoe, and take a covert look at Paul; his head is turned away, thank Heaven! or I could never pick them up, never. A thought strikes me; and I smile to myself as I scramble up and into a chair, and lift up one of the volumes between my two feet and hold it toward him. .

"Paul," I say, in a very small voice, "Paul, here it is!" He turns quickly, but, on seeing the fashion in which my offering is made, he reseats himself.

"That is not the way, Nell," he says; and is it fancy, or is there a keen disappointment in his voice? I lower the book to the ground and consider for a little while; then I jump up and kneel by his side.

"Paul," I say, wistfully, "won't you let me off, dear? I'll never throw any more at you, big or little, never!"

He turns and looks at me.

"I misunderstood you, child," he says; "I thought you would have done it; but never mind."

"And so I will," I say, heartily. "I would pick up a whole *library* full rather than you should look at me like that."

And I stoop down to gather up those nasty, nasty little volumes; but Paul snatches me in his arms. .

"My plucky little girl!" he cries; "after all she has not disappointed me. Do you know, child, that I had made up my mind just now that, with all our love for each other, we should never hit it off if you were too proud to own yourself in the wrong?" .

"Only I did not pick them up after all," I say, slyly. "How do you know I ever intended to?"

"Did you not?" he asks, pinching my cheek; "I know better!"

"If I have come out of the ordeal well, sir, so have not you! A more pigheaded, self-willed, obstinate person I never met; and how you could bring yourself to behave in such a way to a lady—"

"Why did you provoke me so, then?" he asks, quickly; "have you forgotten what it was that you said?"

"Hush!" I say putting my hand over his mouth. "At any rate, I will kiss you now."

"If you please," says Simpkins the ubiquitous, "hem! dinner is waiting!"

HARVEST.

CHAPTER I.

"Hermia. Why, get you gone; who is't
that hinders you!
"Helena. A foolish heart that I leave here
behind."

The 10th of December has come and
the hour of Paul's departure—a black and
bitter day—and I am bidding him farewell; not in the old schoolroom, or by
a warm fireside, but out here in the cold,
raw winter's day, with the wind blowing
wildly, dismally in our faces; with the
dead leaves whirling about our feet like
a host of restless spirits; with a dull,
hard, cold sky above, and a desolate sweep
of barren landscape stretching out before
us. We are standing by the old stile
where we first met, and our faces are not
gay and warm as they were then, but
pale and cold; his with the sorriness of
a man who hates to part with the thing
he loves best on earth; I with the restless
misery that only a woman's heart knows
who sees her treasure go forth into the
world, and knows not if it will come safely back to her. It is such a little while
that he purposes to be gone—only ten
days, a mere nothing—why, therefore, do
I feel such a dragging, heavy foreboding
at my heart? why do I hold his hand in
both mine, and look at him as though I
were taking my last fill of gazing on him
for years? Why do I kiss him again and
again, with a passion that I never knew
until to-day; as I could kiss him no more
tenderly if he lay dying in my arms?
Ah! why, indeed! I have had a dream,
but that is nothing; I have an instinct,

but that is nothing—something above and
beyond these seems to tell me that our
parting to-day is for evil: there is sorrow
in the air, there is dread in the rustling
leaves, a keening of mortal anguish in the
sobbing wind, a dark shadow passing like
a doom betwixt my lover and me.

"My sweetheart," he says, "how pale
you are! I should not have let you come
out in this cold—"

"Only you promised," I say, button-
ing his coat closer about his throat with
trembling fingers. "You will come back,
Paul; you are sure you will come back?"

"Come back to my pearl, my darling?
Ay, that I will! You are not yourself,"
he says, looking into my face; "you are
ill, suffering; I cannot leave you like this,
dear, I shall take you back to the house."

"No, no," I say, faintly; "but you
are quite sure that you must go?"

"Quite sure, little one; if it had been
possible to get out of it, you may be sure
I should have done so. But it is such a
little while, you will scarcely have real-
ized that I am gone before I shall be back,
and then, Nell—"

"We shall be very happy if you come
back," I say, dreamily. "Take care of
yourself, Paul; do not forget that any
harm to you passes straight through me,
and that every hour you are away I shall
be wearying for you. Do not let any one
put me out of your head; do not forget
me."

"Forget thee!" he cries, kissing my
pale lips again and again; "who could
forget thee? not Paul. Write to me twice
or thrice, darling; it will pass the time

more quickly to you, and I will write too; but I never was a good scribe, pet, so you must not expect much. Of course I shall scrawl you a line from Marseilles."

"Ten days!" I say to myself, as he smooths the hair back from my forehead with his brown hand. "Only ten days!" what could happen in that time? Yesterday I seemed to have no fear; to-day I see into shadow-land. What has happened to me between the days that has shaken me so horribly? Only a dream! a silly, mocking, intangible dream, that Paul would laugh to scorn—shall I tell him of it before he goes? shall I warn him?

"Don't flirt with George while I am away," he says, jealously; "you will have lots of opportunities, you know."

"Poor George!" I say, sadly; "I don't think there is much fear."

"Darling," he says, "I shall give up this train, and take you back to the Manor-House."

"No, you will not, Paul; for where would be the good? If you missed that you would have to catch the next. I should only have to say good-by to you at home instead of here, and you promised me that I should say it here, dear, and nowhere else."

"I did promise," he says; "but I can't let you go like this."

"Yes, you will go," I say, gently; "you will kiss me once, Paul, and then you will go."

And so he takes me in his arms and kisses me many times. "Good-by, little sweetheart, good-by," he says, and at last goes away.

Half-way across the field he turns and looks at me. All unconsciously I hold out my arms to him, and he comes back.

"Do not forget," I whisper, "that here, where I kissed you first, I kissed you last."

There is one more swift embrace, a passionate clinging of hands, and he is gone; and I stand staring after him, with aching, burning eyeballs, and a heart heavy as lead. Why do I feel so certainly, desperately sure that he is going away from me to-day—for evil, not good? I watch him over the brow of the hill, turning often as he goes. Then I go along the meadow with halting, lagging steps, and presently meet George with his dogs at his heels.

"Is that you, Nell?" he asks, and mechanically I put my hand in his and look dully into his face.

"You are ill," he exclaims; "had you not better go home at once?"

"I am going. He is gone," I say, looking up into my companion's face with a chilly smile, "and I think my heart is broken."

"He will come back," says George, soothingly; "it is only for a little while. Can't you live these few days without him, Nell?"

"He will never come back," I say, standing still. "Do you not hear the fairies and spirits whispering it—'He will never return to you, never, never!' That is what they are saying quite plainly; and I—O God!" I cry, standing still, "He will never be my Paul any more, never any more. I can see it—the dream!" I shudder from head to foot, and stagger. George holds me for a moment, then I shake the blindness from my eyes, the lassitude from my limbs, and break away from him. "Hark!" I cry, holding up my hand; "surely that was his step—listen!" But no sound comes to us, and, though I run to the bend of the meadow and look around, there is no one to be seen; all is blank and bare and chill.

"It is too cold for you here," says George; "come away home, Nell!" And he puts my hand under his arm and takes me away.

"It sounded just like his step," I say over and over again; "could he have come back?"

"George," I say, looking up into his worn, kind face, "do you think I am mad? I am not—only I feel strange, as though I had had a bad blow. Do you think a person could die in ten days, or that any one who hated him could do him a mischief in that time?"

"Do not think of such things," says the young man; "your nerves are unstrung, dear. You will feel differently to-morrow."

"Do you know," I say in a whisper, "that when he was saying good-by to me, I seemed to see as clearly as the daylight that we were saying good-by to each other, not for a little while, but for ever? It was second-sight."

"It was fancy," he says, decidedly. "Who could possibly come between you? Who has the power to do it?"

"A woman," I say, dreaming; "her words sounded empty enough to me once —they have a different meaning to-day."

"But how can she do you mischief," asks George, "if you and Vasher thoroughly understand each other?"

"I will tell you my dream first," I say slowly—"about her afterward.

"I thought I was in a church crowded with people. Among them I saw the faces of mother, and Jack, and Alice, and you, and Dolly, and many others that I knew. Before the alter-rails were standing a man and woman; the marriage service was being read, and he was putting a marriage-ring upon the woman's finger. Both the figures seemed familiar to me, but something seemed to hold me back and prevent my seeing distinctly. No one heeded me, although I was standing at the foot of the altar-steps. When the service was over the two turned and descended the steps; and as they stood face to face with me, the cloud lifted, and I saw Silvia Fleming in her marriage-robe of white, and her marriage-ring of gold, and on her beautiful face as she looked at me was that slow, faint, dawning smile that I knew so well. . . . I turned my eyes away from her to look at the bridegroom, and there, with a terrible face of shame and horror, stood

Paul Vasher. 'Nell!' he cried, and held out his arms to me; and though I knew he was that woman's husband, I strove to get to him as madly as he was striving to get to me, but we could not reach each other. Then church and crowd, and bride and bridegroom, faded away, and in their place I saw the field of rye, and Paul coming quickly across it to meet me, and I seemed to know that the picture of the wedding had been a hideous dream and that now I was awake, and the familiar trysting-place looked so natural and familiar, that all my misery fell from me like a veil, and the blood leaped in my veins for joy. And he came nearer and nearer with his dark glad face, and we were but a hand's breadth apart, when between us there came a woman, fair as a rose, with a marriage-ring upon her finger; and though we tried to grope round her, we could not find each other, for between us she stood smiling, always smiling—and in calling madly upon him I awoke."

"And that is what has made you so fearful?" he asks. "Nell, Nell! it is not like you to believe in such folly—you always were such a sensible little thing!" His cheerful, robust philosophy heartens me. Does he not know more about everything than I do? But, oh! he does not know the whole story. "I know Vasher was engaged to Miss Fleming once," he goes on, "but it is sheer folly to suppose that, loving you as he does, he can ever come under her influence again. Why, Nell, are you afraid he will *flirt* with her?"

"No," I say, thoughtfully, "I can't picture him doing that; but I always had a vague, intangible feeling that she would do him a mischief, and that dream confirmed and strengthened the belief. I cannot say positively what it is I dread, but it is something bad."

"And are you really so silly, Nell, as to suppose for a moment that he will marry her?" says George, smiling.

"No," I say, slowly; "a woman

can't *make* a man marry her—can she?
It is not that; as I told you before, I do
not know *what* it is I fear."

"Comfortably indefinite," he says,
cheerfully; "but you have not told me
why you think she is so ill-inclined toward Vasher."

"Because he would not fall in love
with her again," I say, smiling, "and I
heard her vow that she would be revenged.
Then, at Luttrell, when she thought he
cared for me, she told me that I should
never be his wife—no woman should be
but herself."

"Pretty cool that," says George; "but
a jealous woman will say anything. And
so you have put yourself into this state,
Nell, because of a few spiteful words?"

"No, it was the dream. It was so
real—so vivid—"

"As mine have often been," says
George; "when I dreamed I was falling
down a bottomless well, for instance."

"Nonsense! Do you never have bad,
ugly, haunting dreams?"

"The realities of life are about enough
for me," says the young man, with a
quiver in his voice that pierces through
my selfish, complaining sorrow, and reminds me that all this while he has been
soothing and listening to me when his
own heart is heavier even than mine.
These ten weeks of absence that have
sped so gayly with me have left their
mark on his face. Neither heart-broken,
nor complaining, nor preoccupied does
he look; but something has gone out of
it that will never come back in this life,
though he bears his lot like a man, and
never speaks of the past—never gives a
sign that he remembers, save when a
chance break in his voice betrays him.

"George," I say, wistfully, "if you
only knew how much happier you have
made me! When I met you I was so
wretched."

"Whenever you are in trouble, dear,"
he says, "I hope you will always let me
be of use to you. Try and think that I
am Jack."

"You are better than Jack," I say,
heartily, "for he never gave me much
sympathy; he would not understand—"

"Sister Nell's hitched up with young
Mr. Tempest!" says Larry, thrusting his
head out of the schoolroom window as
we pass. "I say, Geoff, what would the
other one say if he could see them?"

The hours go by very slowly; and
now George is gone my forebodings creep
upon me, strong and vigorous as ever.
They haunt me all through the night,
waking and dreaming; but with the
morrow they wax fainter and duller—
already I have the inevitably blunted
memory that attends things that happened
yesterday, not to-day. I hurry down-
stairs quickly, and scramble through my
breakfast, for am I not going to do something most charming and delightful this
morning, and can I possibly begin it a
moment too soon?

It is barely half-past nine when, with
a sigh of delight, I fetch my desk and sit
down at the schoolroom table to write
my first love-letter. How Paul laughed
at my writing-paper the other day, as
well he might, for it is mysterious and
wonderful indeed! The color is a sort of
bilious yellow, and the monogram (of
Pimpernel manufacture) is eccentric, the
H being so very little and the A so very
big; while the whirligigs of flourishes
that surround it remind one of a loose
bundle of snakes. It is not an easy
matter to find a pen that is good enough
for addressing my sweetheart, and the
ink is not what it should be; but at last
I begin, with many a smile and pause
between; and what I say to him I shall
not tell you, for that is a secret between
Paul and me. The mere touch of the
paper sends a swift delight and comfort
to my heart: is it not going from me to
him, and if he holds it in his hand and
sends me an answer, shall I not know
then that all my miserable fears are vain
and idle as a breath of summer wind?
He does not seem so far away from me
now; I am speaking to him, and I know

that the words written on this paltry bit of paper will cleave to him, straight as an arrow, over moor and field, and town and sea. And as I write it seems to me that now—not days later, but *now*—he is listening to me and replying. It is not a very long letter, saucy and loving, with none of my doubts in it. They are silly enough spoken; they would look more ridiculous still on paper.

I lay my letter down inside my desk and go out into the garden, for I am going to put in a tiny nosegay; he will like it, I know. I can fancy how a lover sees a tender meaning in every flower . . . the girl's face stooping over them, the slender fingers binding them together, the kiss given to every blossom, the lingering care with which she lays them down for the last time upon the written love-words—they must be like spiritual tokens of her presence. So they would be to me if Paul sent me any; but men do not often think of those things, least of all he, who is so strong and proud and manly—something to hold on by and look up to. No, I do not think he has enough sentiment in him for that. After all, I get but a sorry bunch—a few honey-sweet violets, a spray or two of scarlet geranium, a bit of late-flowering mignonette, one or two brightly-tinted leaves, and that is all.

Entering the schoolroom I meet Jane, the under housemaid, coming out—a pale, unhealthy, evil-looking young woman, whom I have heartily disliked ever since she came to us, two months ago, on Milly's recommendation. I tie my flowers together with a scarlet thread, I lay them in my letter with a foolish, foolish pantomime, and then look about for sealing-wax and seal. The former is here, but the latter I cannot find. Perhaps mother has taken it. So I seal my letter with a trumpery little beehive affair, instead of my own large one, with "Nell" cut on it in old-English letters. I should like to go and post it myself, but the rain is coming down in torrents, and Simpkins (who looks as if he knew what was in

my letter quite as well as I do myself) is waiting to put it in the post-bag, for it is going by the morning post, not the evening. So with a sigh I hand it over to him, and wish that I had not been in such a hurry to write it; for what am I to do with myself the rest of this long, dull, empty day?

"Come quick, to-morrow!" I say, looking out of the blurred window-panes at the driving sleet and rain, "and bring me a letter from you know whom."

CHAPTER II.

" . . . . Come what may,
Time and the hour run through the roughest day."

PAUL will have been gone a week to-morrow, and I have not had a single letter from him, or tidings of any kind, good or bad. I know now that my presentiments were true ones, and that all is not well with him. If I could only think him careless, or neglectful, or busy, or that the letters have miscarried, I should not care; it is this deadly conviction of evil that makes my heart so full of fear. Is he dead? He said he would write, and he never broke his word yet; he knows how eagerly I must be looking out for his letters day by day, and he always hated to disappoint me of the smallest thing. The letter from Marseilles might have missed, but not the one from Rome, though indeed it is unlikely enough that either should be mislaid, for when letters are posted safely they usually come safe to hand, unless indeed they contain postage-stamps, to tempt unvirtuous postmen to their ruin. If I could only be angry with him, if I could give him a good downright scolding in my heart, and call him hard names, I should be so much easier; but I cannot. I feel like a mother who is looking for a naughty little truant child, who has strayed away from its home and wandered into danger,

13

seeking for it in fear and trembling. She forbears to blame it—for what if she find her darling dead, will not her angry words rise up and strike her as she looks on the silent, still, defenseless face? So I, who have lost sight of my lover, will not blame him until I know whether the fault be his or not, only if he comes back to me safe I shall be so angry with him, so angry. . . .

"That's the first smile I've seen on your face for a week, Miss Nell," says nurse; "do it again, dearie, for it makes my heart ache to look at you!"

"I was thinking how I would tease Mr. Vasher when he comes back," I say, looking at her; "he is quite sure to come back, is he not, nurse?"

"Quite sure, Miss Nell. Never was a gentleman who set more store by a young lady than he do by you."

"But I have not heard from him yet," I say, wistfully. "You don't think anything has happened to him, nurse dear?"

"No, no, honey! Maybe he's busy or bothered; 'tis not the man who loves warmest that is the best hand at writing, many a man as is a fine fellow at his pen is a poor hand at courting. There was a young fellow once came courting my sister Susan; his letters was beautiful, a perfect show, and when he came to see her, he was a miserable little sparrow of a creature that it 'ud make you smile to look at. Some does it well on paper and some does it well on their tongues, and I think your lover, Miss Nell, is one of them last."

"Nurse," I say, watching her as she sits darning the boys' socks, "do you remember you used to say I was certain to have a deal of trouble some day, because I am always so merry and laugh so much?"

"Did I?" she asks, peering anxiously at me over her spectacles; "I can't call it to mind, Miss Nell. Why should you be worse off than other folks? Rain and sunshine come pretty much alike to all, and you've got such a spirit 'twould take a great deal to make you give in. You're

terrible fond of Mr. Vasher," she says, shaking her head. "Father used to say 'twas wonderful the difference there was in people when they fell in love: with some it went to the head and was safe, for pride protected it; with others it went to the stomach, and, if things turned out contrary, got dangerous and sometimes killed. Now, I think yours is the last, Miss Nell. Not that you've any call to look out for sorrow that way; things'll go straight enough, never fear, for he loves you as the very apple of his eye."

"Does love keep off misfortune?" I ask, as I get up from my seat; "it seems to me that those who love least come off best."

My restless feet have brought me into the nursery, and now they carry me out again. All day long I wander hither and thither, to and fro, and can settle to nothing, think of nothing, save Paul. I go down-stairs and search the newspapers of the past week through and through, those useless, ugly papers that come every day regular as the clock, while my eagerly-looked-for letter comes never. How I dread the sound of the postman's knock and ring, how I shiver as Simpkins places the bag upon the table beside me, how plainly I see his alert look at me as he leaves the room (he knows what I am looking for as well as I know myself)! How my heart sinks as I unlock it and take out the letters, some for mother, one or two for me, welcome enough at any other time, but a hateful mockery to me now! Other people's letters come safely enough—why should not his?

In to-day's paper I come upon the account of an Englishman murdered at Florence. Perchance some woman looked out long and vainly for news of him, as I am looking now. Perhaps her soul sickened within her with dread, just as mine does, only God grant the awakening from my night of dread may not be even as hers! I wonder why, when our friends disappear from our ken in any unaccountable way, we always think they are dead!

That is always the dread boundary to which our thoughts fly; that, the only sure and certain thing that can come to us in this life, is the theme of our sharpest fear. Neglect, loss of love, illness, misfortune, all pale before the ghastly visage of the "king of terrors." "Take everything else," we cry; "leave us naked, sorry, maimed, and loverless; but leave us life!" I wonder why, when a man or woman is ugly, selfish, and unlovely in life and character, he or she nearly always lives to a good old age?—why the young, the beautiful, the beloved, should always be called away first? Death passes by the wicked, whose evil deeds increase and multiply, to take the adored husband, pillar of the house, the happy, loving wife, the tender house-mother; he spares the vicious, wretched cripple, to gather the beautiful, vigorous child. Oh, he has a rarely dainty taste, and there must be some sweet blossoms up above, since he takes our best from us so ruthlessly.

I fetch my hat and jacket and go out into the garden, leafless, sodden, miserable, that looked almost cheerful when Paul and I walked in it a week ago. Round and round I go, visiting every haunt in which he and I have sat together, pausing to recall the memories that hang about every nook and corner, standing still at last in the place where we stood that day Dorley came upon us with his untimely nosegay. Yes, it was just here, and I hold out my arms to the empty air, with a bitter yearning of body and soul. He was here only a few days ago, but where is he now? How lonely it is! If only Jack or Dolly could suddenly appear before me to fill up this deadly, drowsy silence! Even the echoes of papa's belligerent voice would be better than nothing, or Amberley's bleating monotone, which I disliked so heartily in the old careless school-days. One of the children has the chicken-pox, and mother is nursing him; she has no time to attend to me, and if she had I could not say much to her about Paul: it is never easy to talk to one's elders about one's lovers.

Steps come along the gravel-path behind me. I know whose they are—George Tempest's.

"You have heard?" he asks, eagerly.

I shake my head.

"Then he must be on his way back," he says, walking by my side. "No doubt the business has been concluded more quickly than he expected, and he did not think it worth while to write."

"It could not have been that, George, for he would not have known at Marseilles, and he promised to write from there."

"Do you know, Nell," he says, looking down into my wan face, "that you are making a mountain out of a mole-hill? Because you have had a dream, and because you have not received a letter, you have made up your mind that something dreadful has happened. I wonder what Vasher will say, when he walks in and finds you have been fretting yourself into a shadow?"

When Vasher walks in!—how comfortable and safe the words sound!

"I'll try and not be foolish," I say, my spirits rising, as they always do when I have some one to speak to, "but oh! George, this past week has been so wretched; I think if I had such another I should go mad. I have learned the length and breadth, and depth and height, of that ugly word 'endure.'"

"Have you, dear?" he says, and brave man that he is, he does not add, "and so have I."

It is a strange hap that makes my old lover my friend and consoler in the absence of my new one. Are there many men, I wonder, who could fill the post with such unselfishness, dignity, and single-heartedness, as he does? All too often I forget how he loved me, and in speaking of Paul say something that touches him to the quick. Noble George, for whom no woman that I ever saw was half good enough!

"How near Christmas is!" I say, looking at the flaming scarlet berries that close round the green stalks with such prim, glossy precision. "Only think that to-morrow week is the 25th! He is sure to be back then, is he not, George?"

"Quite sure!" says the young man; "he may come any day now."

"We meant to have such a merry Christmas-eve," I say, half aloud—"snap-dragon with the children, and— George, what are you going to do this Christmas? Will you be dull at the Chace? Come and spend it with us, do!" I add, laying my hand on his arm.

"No, no, dear!" he says, looking down on me, with no hidden bitterness of word and tone; "you will not want me. After all," he says, looking up at the sullen sky that has given over raining, but gives ample promise of plenty more dropping, "I am afraid we shall not have what you are so fond of, a white Christmas!"

CHAPTER III.

"No, no! 'tis all men's office to speak patience
To those that wring under the load of sorrow,
But no man's virtue or sufficiency
To be so moral, when he shall endure
The like himself."

GEORGE'S prophecies prove as falla-cious as those of most other people here on earth, and the night after his assur-ances of dirty weather the snow comes down, silently and delicately covering the face of the earth with a gleaming white mantle, that makes my eyes prick and burn with its exceeding purity, as I look out at it from the dining-room window. The postman is coming up the carriage-drive. How slowly he walks, and what ugly marks he makes on our soilless, dazzling carpet! I do not watch him with any interest; for it is not a letter I am looking for now, but the sound of a step in the hall, the sound of a voice in my ear.

Will they not be better a hundred-fold than a few hasty words on paper? And yet I should have loved to have a love-letter from him. I have flung all my foolish fears away in a bundle; smiles have crept back to my mouth, lightness to my footfall. Does not George say that Paul may come in any day, and would he like to find me pale and wretched-looking?

For the first time since he went away I have made myself look smart. I have put on the gown he liked me in best— Quaker gray, with crimson ribbons; and a cap which he liked too, though it never was straight when he was with me: and one day (we had both forgotten it) I gave Simpkins some orders with it perched rakishly on one side, and, alas! his breed-ing was not equal to the occasion, and he disgraced himself by a smile.

At present it is straight enough, but when he comes back— I am laughing softly to myself when Simpkins comes in bringing my breakfast, the post-bag, and the *Times*.

There are two letters, one from Alice, one from Dolly, both for mother. I send them up-stairs, and begin my breakfast. Then—for I have fallen into bad ways during my lonely morning meal, day after day—I open the paper, and proceed to look at the "Births, Marriages, and Deaths;" not that I know anybody who is likely to be married or dead, but be-cause they interest me. Many a sad sto-ry is told here in three lines; many a bitter tragedy chronicled that moves me far more than the fictitious woes of an imaginary man and woman, whose misery lasts through the regulation three vol-umes of a novel.

"Nothing in the papers," folks cry, and perhaps they are right; there is nothing new. Newspapers are but a faithful transcript of human nature, with its vices, sins, faults, and follies, and hu man nature is pretty much the same to-day as it was yesterday, and will be to-morrow.

I glance through the agony column, and find it in my heart to smile at its fustian pathos. I wonder is it true that most of these heart-broken maunderings are signals from the greatest thieves in London to each other? My eye traveling downward is caught by the announcement of the death of a Mrs. Waddell, who, after surviving her beloved spouse Thomas forty years, has gone to join him where he dwells, let us hope, in comfort. Thomas must have been about making up his mind *that she had gone somewhere else.* A poor young wife of nineteen is dead, "passionately regretted." Another announcement says three little children, aged two, four, and six, respectively, are dead of scarlet fever, all within one short week. An elderly gentleman of ninety is "deeply lamented," and has R. I. P. placed at the end, though surely if any one deserves to rest in peace he does.

Turning to the births (for I am reading in a purposeless, desultory fashion), I see that Lady Fatacres has a daughter, and the Rev. James Poorman a son. I observe that most of the happy fathers are either clergymen or officers, and I wonder for the fiftieth time why Providence sends such an abundance of children to the men who can barely fill their own mouths, and withholds them altogether from those who could bring up a dozen handsomely and never feel the shoe pinch.

Now for the marriages. How jolly that first one looks—two sisters married on the same day to two brothers! Douglas marries Ruby, and Donald marries Violet. What a big wedding it must have made, and what fun the four young people will have when they meet (as I dare say they will) on their wedding tour! Rather awkward, though, if the sisters ever quarrel; there will be a scrimmage, husbands and wives, all in a lump. This one looks more sober: plain John James marries Eliza Ann; her name is Prodgers, his Trimmins. I can fancy that they make a very decorous couple,

she in a gray-satin gown, he in a brown coat and a blue stock, and that the festivities are more of a funereal than a jovial character. (I wonder what my wedding-dress will be? It is odd, but I never thought of it till to-day. All things must be pretty much alike, though, on that day, when every woman who has a heart looks her worst.) Here is a male Brown married to a female Brown, which must have been very convenient in the matter of marking her clothes, though one would have thought that, when she did change her name, she would take a prettier one. In that respect we have a great advantage over the other sex, who, if they are born plain Higgins, Hodge, or Stubbs, must remain so to the end of their days, unless, indeed, they are guilty of the snobbery of being rechristened through the columns of the *Times;* while their sisters and daughters, if they are lucky or good-looking, may be metamorphosed by marriage into Fitz-Jameses, Fortescues, Sutherlands, and the Lord knows what.

I wonder why a familiar word, lying before one in a newspaper, always catches the eye so smartly, seeming to leap up into one's face? Thus, "Silverbridge," and the "Rev. Thomas Skipworth," look up at me in larger type, seemingly, than any of the other words. Who on earth could have been married in Silverbridge without my knowing it, or considered their admission into the holy state of matrimony sufficiently important to demand an advertisement of the same?

A scuffle in the court outside makes me turn my head. Larry and Walter are snowballing each other with admirable vigor and skill. No quarter is given or taken; and I watch them for some time with keen interest, remembering the days when Jack and I indulged in the same recreation, although we were not so fortunate in getting the court; we had to walk a mile or more before we got a nice quiet corner to shout in to our hearts' content. Presently they vanish in a whirlwind of snow and laughter, and I pick up my paper and sit down to read this marriage comfortably. It was near the Browns. Here it is: "On the 16th instant, at the parish church, Silverbridge, ——shire, by the Rev. Thomas Skipworth, George Dalrymple Tempest, only son of Laurence Temple, Esq., of the Chace, to Helen, third daughter of Colonel Adair, of the Manor-House, Silverbridge, ——shire. No cards."

Yes, there it is, word for word, line for line, and for a full minute I sit staring at the paper. The words are there, but my brain does not seem to be able to grasp its meaning; no, not even when my tongue repeats the announcement aloud, as though the sound of my voice might reassure and convince me. I am married, married! and here I give my head an impressive little nod, as much as to say: "You are a poor creature, Helen Adair, and you don't seem to know exactly what you are about; but one thing you may be sure of—you are married." I feel something like the old woman who left it to her little dog to decide whether she was herself or somebody else. The little dog decided against her; the paper decides against me. Here I sit, without the ghost of a wedding-ring on my finger, and yet I am George Tempest's wife; clearly there must be a slight hitch somewhere. My stiff hand relaxes, and the paper flutters to the ground. If it were only out of sight I might get my breath back, but with its respectable, commonplace front facing mine, how can I possibly treat it as a myth? I take my eyes away from it, and glance round the room. There is the breakfast-table; there are the canaries pecking at each other from contiguous cages; there is the old family Prayer-Book, high and dry, among Blair's sermons, on the bookcase; there is the cat asleep on the hearth-rug. It all looks familiar and real enough; but nevertheless I am asleep, and I know it, just as one may have a dream within a dream, and in the last one believe that one is awake. I lift my sleeve, and give my arm a good nipping, rousing pinch (not that people under the influence of bad dreams usually have the sense to bethink themselves of that homely remedy), and expect to see all my surroundings dissolve; but no, there they are still, and here am I, in a gray gown, not a *robe de nuit.* That I am broad awake there can be no reasonable doubt, and that the paper is a very evident fact there can be no doubt either. Oddly enough the first idea that now enters my head is, "What will the governor say?" The *Times* is read in New Zealand, I suppose; and a vision of his dumfoundered face, as he comes across the intelligence, tickles me into sudden laughter. I have heard of such tricks being played before, practical jokes people call them, but I never believed any one could do anything so foolish; where could be the good of it? Why did they do it, these other people? For fun? A sorrier jest, surely, neither man nor woman ever perpetrated. For mischief? It could not work any.

Let me try and think. I do not seem to be able to follow up any one thought. Did those other people ever do it—not in senseless wantonness of folly, but to try and work a girl harm? When her lover was away from her, was it ever done that he might see the paper, and believe her false to him? He would only laugh at it; it looks like a lie; he would know it is a lie. He would be angry at my name being coupled with George's, but of course he could not believe it. I wonder who wrote it? We have no friends, we Adairs, to trouble themselves about our affairs, or play us tricks; and no enemies, that I know of, who hate us heartily enough to try and do us a mischief.

A thought suddenly strikes me: *Silvia!* And yet, why should she? How can this absurd *ruse* benefit her in any way? My being married to George, even if it were true, could bring her no nearer to Paul. And yet how can it be Silvia, who has never been here in her life? How does she know about George Tempest, or Mr. Skipworth, and all the names? The traitor must be some one in our midst.

Well, I must go and tell mother; and I have just reached the door, when it opens, and George comes in.

"Good-morning!" I say, making him a courtesy. "And do you know that you are my bridegroom?"

But he does not smile; he looks very grave. He does not seem to see the joke in quite the same light that I do.

"Nell," he says, quickly, "this is a very serious matter. Can you guess at all who is at the bottom of it?"

"Serious!" I echo. "Pray how can it be that? Some one has taken a most insolent liberty with our names; but *serious*—"

"Vasher will probably see it," says George, uneasily, "and—"

"I thought," I say, indignantly, "that you said he was sure to be on his way home—that he might walk in *any minute*. He may come this morning, even, and probably he won't *see* the paper until I show it to him!"

"I did think he was on his way back; I think so still," says George; "but supposing that he has been delayed, and he does see this announcement, of course he will believe it."

"You mean to say, George, that he would really suppose you and I had *got married* the minute his back was turned?"

"I don't know. Tell me, Nell, was Vasher ever in the least jealous of me? God knows he need not have been!" he adds, half to himself.

"Yes, he was," I say, promptly; "and I always laughed at the idea!"

"Did you?"

There is a pause, in which my short, blessed span of two days' content slips away from me, and the old presentiments, doubts, and fears, creep upon me like living cruel shapes, grown rational by the sustenance of fact—for he has been gone nearly ten days; he has sent me no word of tidings if good or bad, since he set out;

he were alive and well and my own true lover, he would never have left me to watch and wait like this. God only knows what treachery has been worked between us. . . . Yes, I see it all now: it is Silvia's doing.

"Do you remember my telling you that he would never come back?" I say, trembling violently. "He never will!"

"Nonsense!" says George, hastily. "In all probability he is on his way back; but in case he has been detained in Rome, I shall set out at once—or at least as soon as I can get off."

"You will go?" I ask, taking his hand between both mine. "O George! but you will be too late. Something tells me that it is all over now. If you do find him, and he asks who did it all, tell him '*Silvia*.'"

"Impossible!" exclaims George, starting. "Can she be such a wretch as that?"

"She loves him. Women will do a great deal to get a man they love, will they not?"

"Of a very different sort to you, dear. Will you give me Vasher's address?"

I write it down for him—yes, I can actually write—and in no hour of my life have I known the breathless agony that I know in this one.

"If he arrives here in the next three days you will telegraph to me, Nell?"

"Yes. And if you come back—if you *both* come back, I mean—when will it be?"

"I cannot be quite sure, but I should think about Christmas-morning."

"Do not come back without him," I say, in my selfish misery; "only if he is dead you cannot bring him."

"Only he is nothing of the kind," says George, cheerfully. "Keep up your spirits, dear, and put all these fancies out of your head. As to that Silvia, he's no more likely to fall in love with her than I am."

In another minute he is gone, and I am standing at the window looking after him as he strides over the snow. This is his departure: I wonder what will his return be?

As in a dream, I go and tell mother; hear her exclamations of horror and anger; read the letter she writes to the editor of the *Times*, asking by whose authority the advertisement was inserted; as in a dream, fetch my hat and jacket, and wander out over the fields and meadows, walking stiffly and slowly through the deep snow-fall, on and on for miles and miles, my feet carrying me where they will. Why did I let him go without a warning? Why was I so mad as to leave him ignorant of Silvia's threats and vow to work him evil? For I know as surely as I am living that it is she who has done this thing. I was so confident, so sure, when he was with me it was so impossible to fear. I should have spoken when he went away. Did not my good angel call upon me to speak when I wished him good-by? Supposing George has an accident on the road! supposing Paul is not at Rome when he gets there! Somehow I feel in my heart that anyway he will get there too late. It was a sure hand and a strong that struck that bold and open blow through the newspaper. That the same hand has reached him in Rome in some different way I cannot doubt. And Paul was always a little jealous of George. But here I stand still to ask myself if it is likely that he will credit so monstrous a story. Granted that I had played him false, could I be so horribly quick in my treachery? Over hill and dale my feet leave their restless track; by frozen pool and ice-cold rill, by cheerful homestead and farm, through the wood and over the fir plantations I go; and the afternoon is closing in when I stand in my parlor and look up at the frosted trees overhead, and down the familiar walk, longing, with an intensity of longing that shakes me like a leaf, to see him coming down the path to meet me, to hear the sound of his step on the snow. But not a sound comes to me— not even the faint chirp of a bird. There

is not the ghostliest breath of air to ruffle the clear splendor of the boughs; Nature is pulseless, voiceless, without heart, a great glittering shell that estranges and chills me. I cross the field of rye, that was so bare and brown a week ago, and reach home, tired in body, but with my misery as keen and vigorous as when I walked out with it in the morning hours. In the drawing-room I find mother, and standing before her with a perturbed countenance is Simpkins.

"You should have told me this before," she is saying, with an unusual severity in her voice; and I sit down, idly wondering what that foolish old man has been doing now.

"I know it, ma'am," he stammers. "When I caught the young woman meddling with the post-bag, she said she only wanted to get out a letter of her own that she had written, but did not wish to have posted. I believed the story, ma'am, and did not tell you."

"What is all this about?" I ask. "Mother, who has been tampering with the post-bag?"

"Jane, the under-housemaid," says mother. "It seems she ran away from here this morning without a word, and Simpkins tells me that he caught her meddling—"

"She must have meddled with it more than once," I say, putting my hand to my head. "Why did you not speak of this before?" I cry, turning upon the man in a fury. "Do you know what you have done? Go out of my sight!"

He stares at me for a moment; then, as I stamp my foot, he turns and flees.

"Mother! mother!" I say, groping my way across the room to her, "I see it all now. He never got my letters. I never got his. That woman was Silvia's spy."

"Poor little daughter!" she says, and her tears fall fast and heavy on my uplifted face. If only *I* could weep! if only this terrible tightness about my heart would relax!

"Mr. Skipworth," announces Simpkins, tremblingly, half an hour later; and I escape by one door, as he enters by another. He has come to talk about my marriage, no doubt. In my present state of mind, his voice would send me straight into Bedlam. I wonder, I say to myself, as I go wearily up-stairs, why so many good and moral people irritate us so intensely? why we would rather be beaten by some hands than be stroked by others? Their very virtues make us feel vicious, and their pious and proper sentiments impel us to flatly contradict every word they say. In my bedroom I stand, looking out at the night, that seems to enwrap me like a cold, dark mantle, while the stars draw my soul up to them. I feel not so much a miserable, passionate, struggling speck of humanity, as a disembodied spirit, that is wandering abroad, searching after, crying after Paul, my darling—who will never be my lover any more.

All night long I lie awake, hearing ghostly steps coming up the carriage-drive; hearing ghostly hands beating against my window-pane—ghostly voices that whisper in my ear. My ears are strained to the faintest echo of sound in the world without. Shall I not hear him toward the morning coming lightly over the snow to tell me he has returned? I know that he is not dead, or he would have come to me in that supreme wrenching of soul from body, as I should go to him straight if I died to-night.

The morning breaks, gray and chill. "How shall I bear it!" I cry aloud, as I sit up in my bed, and rock myself to and fro in my restless agony—"with all these long days and nights to live through before Christmas-morning comes!"

CHAPTER IV.

"Oh! let me not be mad, not mad, sweet Heaven!
Keep me in temper: I would not be mad!"

IT is Christmas-morning, and I am leaning out of the open window of the dining-room into the cold clear air, looking at the clean white world, that during the night has been covered over freshly, so that she is fair and spotless for the great, high festival, as a bride coming out of her chamber to meet her bridegroom. It is splendid enough, but a little cruel, perhaps, if one happens to notice that little dead robin yonder, whose crimson breast shows prettily enough against the snow. He has struggled gallantly through the bleak days and bitter nights, but to-day —on Christmas-morning, the time of feasting and plenty—his poor, slender, starved little body has found death.

Behind me the house is all alive and merry, with bustle and noise. They are all at home now save Jack; and they have decorated the whole place with holly and mistletoe, which gleams brightly red and white from every corner and cranny. The church-clock strikes ten: in another hour church will begin, but I shall not go with the rest. I think I should stand here listening, though a year and a day passed before Paul came back.

What a noise the boys are making! I shall never be able to bear the sound of the carriage coming over the snow. Hark! What is that? My heart stands still, every pulse pauses, then bounds madly on, as a sound, a certain dulled, muffled sound, comes to my ears from a distance. It is the sound of wheels—it is coming this way. Is that a carriage coming toward me? the snow has blinded my eyes, I cannot see. . . . I look up *seeing*, and there is George, alone. I do not move or speak as he comes over to me and looks into my face.

"He is dead?" I say, gently, looking away from him to a bird perched on a bough near, who is *singing*, absolutely singing—starved and bitter cold as he is. Why do I not sing too?

"He is not dead," says George.

"Not dead!" I shriek, recoiling from him with parted lips and wide eyes— "*not dead*, did you say? Thank God!"

And the frozen blood in my body stirs nimbly in my veins, and circulates once again; and, whereas a minute ago I was a dead woman, now I am quick.

"But why did you not bring him?" I ask. "There could be nothing to detain him."

"He is here," says George; "he bade me tell you," he goes on slowly and painfully, "that he was waiting for you at the old place—yes, at the old place, and you were to go at once, he said."

"He will have to wait a little, then," I say, with a delicious, happy laughter bubbling straight up from my heart to my lips. "Oh, he has kept me waiting for him long enough! I don't seem to be able to take it all in at once," I add, putting my hand to my head; "but by-and-by, yes, by-and-by I shall be perfectly happy! How tired you look, George! how pale! How can I ever thank you enough for bringing him back to me? We shall never forget it, George—Paul and I—when we are so happy we shall never forget that we owe it all to you, for if you had not gone to Rome in time—"

"I know," he says, shivering. "Vasher is waiting for you, Nell."

"What a hurry you are in!" I say, as I tie the strings of my cloak. "Now do you know that I mean to scold him—perhaps he was afraid I should, so did not come up to the house? Perhaps! And I shall be able to see him whenever I please now, you know, for he has come to stay."

George groans.

"Are you ill?" I ask, turning round from the looking-glass, where I am putting on my hat. "I must try and make myself look nice now Paul has come back."

But George does not answer.

"And I have been so wretched," I say, laughing softly, "though you always told me there was nothing in that presentiment, or the dream! Do you know you have not wished me a merry Christ-

mas, sir? But never mind, you have brought me the best Christmas-gift of all."

He has turned his back to me, and is looking out of the window.

"Good-by," I say, pausing at the door. "I shall not go to church this morning."

In the hall Dolly and the children crowd about me; but I just tell them Paul has come back, and break away from them all.

I wave my hand to George through the window. How terribly pale and strange he looks! Then I go away over the snow with hurrying, dancing feet. Have I not got my Christmas-morning at last—real, golden, perfect? In the whole, wide world does there beat such a happy heart as mine? I have not asked George how it happened that Paul never wrote: he shall tell me that himself, and I will be so angry with him, lazy, naughty, careless fellow! As I turn the corner of the meadow, I see him standing with his back to me, leaning over the stile; and for a moment I stand still—the absolute delight of seeing him in the old familiar place is so keen, that it leaves me no immediate longing to touch his hand or hear his voice. Then I walk quickly on. He does not turn his head, and he used to hear my footfall quickly enough. Perhaps the snow dulls it. I am close upon him when he looks round and faces me.

"You have come back," I say, thrusting both my eager hands into his; "and I have been so frightened, so miserable. . . ."

He does not answer, only, as I lay my head down on his shoulder, he lifts his arms and folds them about me, pressing my head close against his breast.

"Do you know that I thought you would never come back, that you were dead, or that some one had come between us, and even now I cannot believe that you are here . . . . you ought to have written, darling. Did you not guess what a miserable time it would be to me? I am going to scold you for it by-

and-by, sir; but I shall have plenty of time for that—plenty of time! And I was wicked enough to doubt you, Paul—as though I might not have known better! I had all sorts of queer fancies. But I will never be afraid again, Paul—never again. I could even let you go away from me and be quite sure you would come back safely."

How silent Paul is! because he is so happy, I suppose; and how quickly he is breathing, as though he had been running hard!

"And you have come back to me on Christmas-morning," I say, dreamily, "to give me the whitest, happiest, merriest Christmas. Do you know I asked George Tempest to wish me a merry Christmas just now, and he turned away. I suppose he is very tired, as you must be, darling."

I lift my head to look at his face, but he presses my head back in its place, stroking my face with his hand with a passionate tenderness that fills to overflowing my hungry heart.

"How quiet you are! " I say; "but I do not want to hear you talk—it is quite enough for me to know that I have you so near me. What can come between us now that we are together? "

He draws my hand across his lips. How hot they are! how they quiver!

The church-bells ring out sweet and cheerful across the fields; the peal rises and falls gayly. Can any sound be sweeter than Christmas-bells when one is happy?

"Paul," I say in a whisper, "did you see that wicked paper? I might have known you would not believe it."

"It is cold here," he says; and I lift my head suddenly and look into his face.

Is this my Paul—gaunt and worn, and pale as death, with deep, burning eyes? He looks like a man just risen from a bed of illness.

"You have been ill!" I cry. "That was why you staid so long away and never wrote! "

"No," he says slowly, "not ill. We cannot talk here. Let us go to the old place."

But as we go I look at him again and again, and see plainly enough that he is ill. I should scarcely know him again for the man who went away from me a fortnight ago. As we cross the field I slip and stumble on the uneven, snow-covered ground, and hold out my hands to Paul to help me, but he does not seem to heed me: he walks forward, alone.

In our snow-parlor I sit down on the old log of wood; but he does not—he stretches himself out at my feet and lays his head against my shoulder. His face is hidden; he does not move or stir, or speak. Is he only weary, or in actual bodily pain? I have so much to tell him, he has so much to tell me, I think that if I were not so perfectly happy in merely knowing that he is with me I should be piqued, and a little angry. I never noticed until to-day that Paul's hair is streaked with gray—I always thought it was raven black; and it is full early for the color to change. He is but little past thirty. I pull the short locks out between my fingers, and he shivers under my touch. Yes, he is ill, and it is madness for him to be out here in the cold.

"Paul! " I say, stooping over him, "you must not stay out here; come with me to the house."

He lifts his eyes to my face painfully giddy; then his head falls heavily back and he clasps his arms tighter about me.

"Can you not wait a little while? " he says, and his voice is strange and harsh.

"Yes, I can wait," I say, gently, looking out at the wide stretching sweep of white, just as I looked at it a few days ago, when I came hither alone; only then my heart was heavy as lead, and now it beats under the head of my lover.

I fold my arms about his neck close and warm: it is such a new delight to me to know that he is all my own. If he had been given back to me from the dead I could not look at him with greater wonder and thankfulness. And yet it is altogether unaccountable. But though Paul has been with me all this time he has not kissed me once; no, nor seemed to think of such a thing! It never happened so before.

"Hark at the bells!" I say, as they ring out, now loud, now clear, across the fields. "I wonder will they ring as sweetly as that when you and I are wed, Paul? And I actually dreamed that you were married to somebody else, dear; was ever anything more foolish and senseless?"

He lifts his head, suddenly rises and stands before me. The minute-bell has almost done ringing as he begins to speak; it ceases, and with the last stroke every joy and good hope the world contains has died out to me for ever and ever . . . . and this is my white, merry Christmas-morning!

Not a sound breaks the silence as we look in each other's deathly faces; then his mouth opens, and a terrible curse breaks from his lips and wanders out over the desolate, stirless land; and my heart begins to move again, and sluggish life to creep into my body. His words do not shock me—do not even seem strange to me. I listen to them as idly as I used to hearken to the frozen brook yonder, when it ran its summer course between the green banks.

"And why did you come back?" I ask, and my voice is much the same as usual, only maybe a little slower. "Why are you not with your wife!"

"My wife!" The words leave his lips as though he cast a foul stain of leprosy from him. "Why did you let me go without a warning?" he cries, with clinched hands. "Did you know all the time that we had such a bitter enemy? Did you know that for years I have been spied on, dogged, followed, and that here, in your very home, lived one of that woman's spies to report our every word and act?"

"I knew we had an enemy," I say, sitting with stiffly-folded hands and eyes that never lift themselves from the blank, blinding carpet of my parlor, "but I thought she had no power to harm us."

"And that has undone us," he cries, with a despair and fury in his voice that make it sound like nothing human. "If you had only warned me that morning before I left you—" He stops. "God forgive me for blaming you when my own mad folly has brought us to this. And to think," he cries, smiting his brow with his clinched hand, "that I have lost you to get that vile—thing! After parting with you the day I set out for Rome, I walked some distance; and then, reproaching myself for having allowed you to return home alone, I retraced my steps. Turning the bend of the meadow, I saw you in George Tempest's arms, your head against his shoulder; and, acting under I don't know what impulse, instead of walking boldly forward, I turned sharply, and in another moment was out of sight. I returned to the Towers, just caught my train, and at Marseilles sat down to write to you. My first hot anger had passed by then: your parting words of love and sorrow had come back to me with the stamp of their own beautiful truth upon them; and, though I could not understand the situation in which I had found you, I felt sure you could explain it. And though I did not like it— what man would?—I was not at that time actively jealous of him or doubtful of you: that was to come after. In my letter I asked you how it was you came to be with him, and whether you had been ill or miserable when I saw him holding you. I reached Rome safely, and on the day after my arrival I looked for the letter that you had promised to post to me the day after I left Silverbridge; but there was none—no, nor on the next day, or the next. Can you wonder that by degrees there grew up in my heart a terrible fear, a sickening doubt, with my absence had your love grown so faint and lifeless? And if I could have hurried back I should not have done so: no word of mine should ever seek to determine your wandering allegiance. Only I could not yet suppose such a thing possible—you had seemed so honest, so true; your love-words were so freshly in my ears. But sometimes I remembered that so others had sounded, spoken to other men by women who had betrayed them."

"And did you never receive a letter from me?" I ask, slowly, remembering the dainty knot of flowers that I gathered so carefully and kissed so tenderly.

"I received one," he says, "later. Meanwhile I was detained by business beyond the time that I had fixed to return to Silverbridge; and on the 21st a letter and a newspaper were brought to me. The former was in your handwriting, and your seal, with your name 'Nell' on it, looked me in the face so naturally and sweetly, that my doubts forsook me on the spot, and I kissed it like a fool, child. I opened the letter, and out fell a tiny withered nosegay of flowers, that seemed to have been plucked many days and had little scent; and for your sweet sake, I kissed them too, Nell, many times. Then I read your first love-letter. I took it in my hand so carefully, remembering that it had touched yours, and started as I read the first words—'Dear Mr. Vasher.' With all your willful ways, I could not understand that. Well, it was a simple epistle enough. It was only to say that, after mature consideration, you had come to the conclusion that you would be happier as George Tempest's wife than as mine, and that you had already married him, and were going abroad immediately with him and his father. You sent a newspaper to corroborate your statement; you asked forgiveness from me for any disappointment you might cause me; and you signed yourself 'Helen Tempest.'"

"Have you it here?" I ask; and he takes it out of his pocket-book and hands it to me, and I sit looking at it much as a man may look at the knife that has stabbed his nearest and dearest to the heart. The writing on the envelope is mine, that on the sheet inside is not; but the forgery is so excellent that, were this letter a copy of one I had ever written, I should pronounce it to be my own. I give it back to him without a word.

"The sight of your handwriting," he goes on, "had so routed the jealous demons that had for the past ten days tormented me, that the letter itself came upon me like a rude, violent shock. Then I grew angry, and thought how unlike you it was to play me such a trick, and (knowing my weakness about Tempest) how unworthy of you! The joke seemed to me to be in the worst possible taste. I pushed your letter and the flowers aside, and mechanically opened the paper—not that I expected to find there the announcement you bade me look for, but because I thought some curious similarity of names to yours and Tempest's had suggested the sorry jest. And I found no less than the actual announcement of your marriage. I was still staring at it, incapable of any reasonable thought, when Mills knocked at the door, and asked for orders about something or other. As he was going out of the room I asked him if he had heard any Silverbridge news since he came away. He hesitated for a moment, then took from his pocket a letter which he laid on the table, then went away without a word. Like all the other servants, he knew pretty well how matters lay between you and me. The letter was addressed to him, and the inclosure was from a housemaid (apparently) living in your house. She said that you were married to young Mr. Tempest, to everybody's surprise; that people said it was like a stolen marriage, even though Mrs. Adair went to church to see you made man and wife, and Mr. Skipworth read the service. Nell, I had treated your letter as a bad joke, I had doubted the newspaper, for I know mistakes sometimes occur, but this third piece of evidence I could not and did not doubt; none but a madman would. The gross improbability of the whole thing; the unlikelihood that you should be in so indecent a hurry to marry another man the moment my back was turned; the strangeness of your mother's abetting your rash act by her presence, when she had countenanced your engagement to me; your father's absence, and the tacit disobedience displayed to him by the marriage in his absence—all these unnatural circumstances I recognized clearly enough, but they vanished before the one great fact that you were *married;* how, or why, or where, mattered little enough—you were Tempest's wife."

"And then?" I ask, lifting my dull eyes to his bleached, wild face.

"And then I went mad—as utterly mad for the time being as any wretch in Bedlam; as drunk with grief as any senseless beast on the pavement; as incapable as either of accounting for or guiding my actions. Well, I wandered about all that day; at night I found myself back again in my rooms; and, as I sat there, my despair at losing you gave way to a fierce fury—that you should have dared to so trick and shame me; you, who had known of the disappointment I had found in my first love; you, to stab me so surely to the heart, who knew how entirely my whole life and belief in all things rested on the trust I had in your honesty and faithfulness. In that hour my love for you seemed to pass away even more utterly than it had done for Silvia, when I found out her falsehood, for, be her sin what it might, she had been true to me, while you had deliberately left me without a pang, without a care.

"As I sat there, out of the darkness suddenly came clinging arms, and stole round my neck, drawing my burning head down to a soft embrace; a tender voice, gentle as a mother's, whispered words of comfort in my ear. I did not know whether I was actually mad or dreaming. Had an angel dropped from heaven to tend me, or was my unknown consoler some earthly creature, like myself, who could care for so heart-bare, desolate a man as I? And some touch of the hand, some tone in the whispering voice, by-and-by informed me that this woman, who could lay aside all pride and thought of self, to come to me in my hour of agony, was Silvia, to whom I had dealt out such bitter mercy, and who, it now appeared, had loved me through it all, ay! from the first day to the last, while you, whom I had loved a hundredfold more than I ever did her, had cast me from you as unhesitatingly, as coolly, as a withered flower or a soiled glove. I did not question how she knew my story. I asked no reasons for her coming; she gave none. She had only fled to me in my misery: recking, caring nothing for name or reputation—so I thought then—good God!

"The night wore on; her love, her tenderness, her clinging beauty, her great love worked in me like a charm. I have told you that in that hour I hated you for your falseness; well, in that hour I loved that woman for her truth. Had she not through good and evil report clung to me? Did not her own sin show white as snow beside your black, barefaced desertion? And remember that I was mad, child—utterly mad! My higher, better nature was dead within me. All reasoning, thinking power had gone out of me, and so—God knows the rest!—the maddening wiles of the woman, the rage that filled my heart against you . . . and the morning found us standing together before a priest, and, later on, at the British embassy man and wife.

"Even then the madness had not passed. I did not know what I had done, did not know what I had married. The darkness still lay upon my eyes. She was to me simply a woman who had been faithful; you a woman who had betrayed me. My thoughts never went any further than that. I did not love her, and did not hate her; I had simply no feeling for her whatever.

"We went to Florence immediately. Tempest was at that moment in the town, if we had known it. With the usual fatality where men's lives are concerned, there had been no less than three break-downs on the road, and he had arrived too late. Afterward I found that, half an hour after we set out, he reached my door, but no message had been left, and he had no clew to our whereabouts, so he had a long search before he found us. At that time I never *thought*. It did not occur to me strange that Silvia should be in there alone and unattended; I never asked myself or her how she knew of your marriage, or how she could care to marry me knowing what effect the news had had upon me. I felt something like a man under the influence of an opiate that has not made him perfectly unconscious—everything passes around him as in a dream, but he knows that by-and-by he will awake and see things as they really are.

"On the morning after we reached Florence, my senses came back to me; for the first time I saw face to face this thing that I had done; knew that, married though you were, I loved you as madly as ever; knew that the woman I had made my wife was less to me than one sound of your voice, one touch of your hand. And, strangely enough, you had not seemed so lost to me when I knew you to be the wife of another man, as now that I found myself the husband of another woman. I walked out of the house in the still early morning, and the first man I met was your husband, George Tempest. There must have been murder in my eyes as I looked at him, for he said at once, 'It is all a mistake.'

"I don't know what happened after that. In an hour we had set out for England. You know the rest."

Yes, I know the rest, as I look upon the face that is now no more than a shadow. The features are there, but where are the life, the glow, the spirit, that

filled it in bravely a fortnight ago—only a fortnight ago!

And we stand looking, looking into each other's haggard countenances, and dare not put out so much as the tips of our fingers to each other—'twixt him and me a great gulf lies. I wonder if I shall always be this dumb, senseless stone . . . will the spirit ever wake in me, and cry, and rend me?

"If I had to choose between dying now this minute and living over again the last hour, I would choose to die," he says, slowly. "I have suffered enough, God knows, since you and I stood here together, but never half of what I did when I heard your footsteps coming over the snow, and dared not turn to face you; and then, when you clasped your arm round my neck, and ran on in your loving welcome . . . when I think of the future, of how I shall never watch for your coming, never see you stepping across the rye to meet me; never, in summer or seed-time, or winter or harvest, listen to your steps and the sound of your gentle voice . . . we shall miss each other's morning kiss, child . . . at eventide we shall hold out despairing arms to each other—the days will be empty and dreary . . . we shall call upon each other across the silence that gives back no answer."

His words enter my ears, but do not stir my heart; by-and-by they will come back to me, perhaps. I shall have plenty of time after he is gone to muse over and be sorry for them—yes, all the rest of my life.

"We need not have quarreled about the books—need we?" I ask, with a faint smile. "I shall never have a chance of throwing any more at you."

"Don't," he says, sharply. "You were right, child, when you used to say we were too happy."

"Paul," I say, shivering, "when do you go back to your wife?"

"Go back to her?" he asks, frowning. "Did I hear you aright?"

"Yes. Of course you will go back to her—you are bound to."

"Am I?" he asks between his teeth. "I think not."

"She could not force you to marry her," I say, steadily; "you did it of your own free-will. What reason would you give to the world for casting her off?"

"What reason?" he asks, with a deep, steady blaze in his eyes. "She is no wife of mine, and it shall be my business to prove that she is not!"

"She loves you."

"Loves me!" he cries, with a fierce scorn in his voice. "She would have shown her love better by stabbing me to the heart! And you would send me back to her?"

"Yes, I would send you back."

"Ay!" he says below his breath, "I will go back to kill her!"

"Will you? Was Paul Vasher born to be a murderer?"

"Yes," he says doggedly, "even that!"

"No, you will not. That weak, sinful woman has no power to plunge your soul into guilt. She has ruined your life, but she can do no more. Shameful though she is, she is yours. You took her not for a day or a week, but *for better for worse*. You must bear the burden of the rash act you committed; and remember that any discredit you lay upon her will recoil upon yourself; for she is, in the eyes of the world, your wife and the bearer of your name."

"In the sight of God she is not! Did you ever love me?" he asks, bitterly. "After all, I do not think you can know what love means, to wish to send me back to that woman. Do you think that if you had been cheated into marrying another man, and you came to me, I would *send you back to him?* I would hold you —keep you—bind you in my arms so safely that no one should wrest you from me —my love, my darling!" He covers up his face, he trembles in a strong man's agony, and still, still I can look at him and feel absolutely nothing.

"As you will not take up your burden and bear it like a man," I say—and at my words he lifts his head—"I must take it up and bear it for you. I will never live to have people pointing at me and saying, 'That is the girl Paul Vasher loves, and who loves him—*the married man*. It is on her account that he does not live with his wife.' Do you think that I could bear it? If you will not go back to her, I will leave Silverbridge and go far away where the prying finger of scandal cannot reach me."

"And why should you? Who will know the story?"

"Every one. Do you think *she* will keep silence?"

"There can be no possible reproach to you in it."

"None if you are with her, much if you are apart. She who is known to stand between husband and wife receives but scant mercy from the world."

"Ask me something less hard," he says, and the veins in his forehead stand out like cords. "Even for you I cannot do this. Set me some task that body and soul do not utterly forbid. I am not mad, Nell; but I know my own strength, and I could not do it. What do you think I am made of, that I could see her fill your place, bear your name, stand by my side usurping your rights—*she!* Do you think I could ever let my eyes rest on her false face without yours rising up before me? ever hear her called *Mrs. Vasher* without longing to strike to earth the man that said it? ever endure to so much as touch her hand, when I was wearying, aching after you—you think that I could do all this and *live?* Sooner or later I should break down—and—"

"Paul," I say, and my voice is so hushed that I can scarcely hear it, "do you not see that there is no safety for either you or me if you are not by the side of your wife? For the sake of all the love you bore me, in recompense for all the misery you have brought me, I ask this one mercy of you! Live with her as a stranger if you will; but, in the eyes of the world, be man and wife."

A shamed streak of red comes into my cheek as I speak; then I bow my head and wait, and a terrible doubt crosses my mind as to whether I am acting for good or for evil in demanding this supreme expiation of a life. The silence is so long and unbroken that time seems to stand still; when he speaks his voice appears to come from a long way off. I lift my eyes and look at him, and in his there is the beaten, broken look that never comes into a man's face until the last hope is gone—the last stake lost.

"You have conquered," he says. "I will do it for your sake. Could any man do more? You must give me a little while to get used to the idea, a little while to get rid of some of my prejudices" (he laughs harshly), "then she shall be offered a place in my house as the mistress of it, to be treated by me as any other stranger within my gates; if she refuses, she can live alone."

A sick, jealous pain, the first that has begun to stir my dull heart, awakes as I look at him. What if he grow to love her again? Is she not fair as the day? and do men remember forever? And I am sending him back to her! There is a little bitter silence, and then Paul kneels down in the snow and looks into my face; but I do not look at him: my heart is waking from its torpor, and I dare not. Yesterday he was my lover, to-day he is Silvia's husband. Not in one moment can I pass from the familiar friendship to the new, unnatural position we hold toward each other

"You have fixed my lot, child; what is to be your own?"

"I shall live."

"Will ever any one fill my place?"

"Never."

"No one man more than another?"

"No man."

"I was always a selfish brute," he

14

says, slowly; "I am selfish still, and I tell you that I would rather see you lying in your coffin with violets in your pale hands than know you to be another man's wife. And that is my love for you, Nell. I would have you love me to the very last beat of your heart. I would have the last thought of your sweet soul, the last call from your lips; as your name will be on mine when I die, sweetheart; as I shall love you to the day of my death—and after. And when we meet, as we *shall* meet, in another world, where there are no marriages, will you come to my side with lips as pure and untouched as they have ever been, save to me? as on mine no touch of living woman shall rest between now and then—so help me, God!"

"I will come to you," I say, simply.

The calm that lay on me, heavy as the snow on the once throbbing earth at my feet, has broken up now, and a wild fever of agony possesses me—a breathless longing to touch his hand, to speak one word of love and comfort to him—and I may not, dare not, though we are young, loving, together, though not a yard of space lies between us. We are separated, not for a week or a year, but *forever*. Since he lifted his head from my shoulder when the bells were ringing, there has been space between us—Death himself could not set us farther from each other. I must get away soon—soon, or I shall break down utterly. I stand up. "Goodby," I say in a whisper; "I am going now."

"So soon?" he says, and his voice is almost as faint as mine; "shall we not be apart all the rest of our lives?"

"Will talking give us back our murdered happiness, Paul? will talking about our beautiful yesterday quicken our dead to-morrow? We can never be any more to each other than we are now; we can never be any less. Let me go now while I have the strength."

"Strength!" he repeats, hoarsely, as he peers into my face; "and I have brought you to this, my poor broken little white flower. It is my mad, senseless sin that has driven the color from your cheeks, the gladness from your sweet eyes. Nell, Nell! I cannot let you go; you are my real wife, not that other—my life, my lily!"

"Should I be your lily, then?" I ask tremblingly. But he who has been so chary of touching me since he has told me his evil tidings, comes closer; would fold his arms about me.

"Back!" I cry, springing aside; "what! would you be the falsest traitor on God's earth?"

"To her!" he cries, with a fierce gesture of loathing.

"To me!"

"To you," he mutters, then an ashen gray replaces the fire of a moment ago; his hands fall to his side; and so, with a hand's breadth between us, we stand looking on each other's wild faces, then—

"Good-by," I say, in faintest, dreadest whisper; but he does not move or answer, and noiselessly I step past him; but when I have gone a score or so of steps, I pause shuddering, for over the cold desolate fields sweeps the wild and bitter cry of a strong man in his pain: "*O God! O God!*"

CHAPTER V.

"When daisies pied and violets blue,
    And lady-smocks all silver white,
And cuckoo buds of yellow hue,
    Do paint the meadows with delight."

SPRING! The dainty, lovely guest has stolen upon us early this year, sweeping away the clinging mists and frosts of the dying winter with her warm, fragrant skirts; touching the sober brown hedges with her fairy wand, until, lo! they have bloomed forth into rarest tapestry of powdery green and downy delicatest spikes of yellow, starring the banks with faint pale primroses and purple-breasted violets, carpeting the woodlands with grayish wind-flowers and slender blue-bells, that sway all their dainty blossoms with every soft wind that steals about them. She has set all the young leaves waving, the birds singing, and her south wind blowing, and over the pulsing, throbbing, blossoming earth her light feet have skimmed, leaving beauty, life, and gladness everywhere. The poor, the sick, the lonely, the rich, the happy, the sad, love her equally, and welcome her with eager, smiling faces and outstretched loving arms.

She is a rare friend to the poor; to them she means respite from that black, bitter aching of the bones, known as *cold*. She means soft green food to put between their lips, weary and starved with the broken, dry morsels of bread; her fair bountiful bosom brings warmth to their chill bodies. Oh! Spring is comforting, Spring is faithful; she never yet failed her poor, but comes back to them year by year, ever young and fair and sweet, for she is one over whom time has no power. They look up at her azure ceiling; they look down at her emerald carpet; they take her delicate flowers reverently, gently in their hard, rough hands, and, remembering for one little moment—

"The days when were young, lads,
    The days when we were young"—

feel a softening, ennobling gleam of beauty strike across their rugged hearts, and go back to their toil and labor better, stronger men. The children rolling in the fields, golden with king-cups, forget the winter with all its hardships: in their beautiful to-day yesterday has no place. The poor drudge at her house-door looks out at the fields and sky, and gives a tender thought to the time when she and her goodman were young and took a long day's holiday together, and a quick gleam shines athwart her dull, care-worn face.

Ay! Spring brings a holy, softening influence with her, and jogs the memory of men and women alike to better things and better hopes. And she brings to me no more and no less than green leaves, blue skies, and gay flowers. No delight creeps through me as I see the first early blossom parting the brown earth; no thrill stirs me as the trees, one by one, each after other, don their varied livery. I think I shall soon be like that man of whom it was written that

> "A primrose by the river's brim
> A yellow primrose was to him,
> And it was nothing more."

I would give a year of my life—and that would be little enough as I value years just now—to know another such moment as I knew long ago; when Jack and I, searching in earliest spring for wild flowers, came upon the first delicate primrose of the year, nestling in its green leaves. How we stood before it breathless, entranced, and forbore to put out a hand to pluck it, with some strange, unknown reverence stirring at our hearts that we could not understand, and were only dimly conscious of. . . . I think it must have been our fresh, untried souls that made things, common to us now, so rare and lovely to us then.

Often I shut my eyes, that I may not see the flowers growing so bravely on their stalks. They were here last summer, they will be here next; they are but poor perishable little things, and yet they come back to us every year, unlike those human blossoms that we lay away from our sight with such bitter, passionate tears and cries.

We know that the flowers, pretty, soulless, lovely toys, have no future life; and we do know that our dead will rise again, immortal and incorruptible, to bloom forever fair and stately in the garden of the Great King. But oh! is not that far-away uprising shadowy and vague to the fleshly, eager eyes that would see and *know?* Here are the flowers, we cry, but where are they? And we fold our empty arms closely above our ravening hearts, that will never be satisfied on this side Jordan's wave. Never, ah! never!

What man or woman mourns his dead in the bitter, ice-bound winter as they do in the tender, warm, passionate spring, when every flower and bud and leaf and bird is quick and living, rioting in life, and praising God each after his kind? All things seem to *remember*.

The birds cry, "We are calling him, we are calling him!" The leaves rustle and whisper, "Where is he, where?" The flowers murmur, as they shake their bells, "He used to pass this way." Every tiny blade of grass, every thrill of the blackbird, brings the past quivering before us—the days when we had our beloved, and could look in his face, and put out our hands to touch him, that we seek to bridge and cannot, with a bitter, yearning pain that is the intenser by reason of its impotence. To some people forgetfulness comes naturally and unconsciously; day by day memory softly detaches first one link, then another, in the bustle and moving to and fro in the vigorous, working-day world, the lost or the parted from gradually become vague, impalpable, receding shadows, dear still but indistinct; unlike that first horrible sense of loss that was theirs when their darlings were snatched suddenly from their side, and, whereas, a minute before they had been face to face with them, now *they were not;* the full minute ago, the empty present standing side by side in bare and shocking contrast. Who that remembers has not a hurt anger at the quickness with which mortals forget? Do not our dead and absent ones seem to cry to us out of the darkness, "Speak for us, for we cannot speak for ourselves?" It is the noisy, selfish, living and present people who fill our ears with common, everyday talk, and shoulder the memory of those others away. "The proud contempt of spirits has risen," has been grandly sung; with more truth and less beauty has it been said that "a live dog is better than a dead lion." If any one doubts the fact, let him go to the funeral of a man who is not followed by any heavy-hearted relation or friend, and yet who is better a hundred-fold than the men who walk behind him. Through the mourners' regret may be detected a faint though certain under-current of self-complacency, as who should say; "Yes, there lies So-and-so, dead. He was a clever fellow. In life he made some stir; but his race is over, his day is done, his place in the world is empty, and he has no longer a voice in anything. He cannot avenge his injuries, or punish the man who assails his memory; he is no longer to be flattered, feared, or regarded; he is simply—*nil*. Let us thank God that we are upstanding, cake-eating, wine-drinking, vigorous men; able to walk about the earth, speak our minds, have a voice in the world's affairs, and hold our own against anybody, instead of being reduced to a helpless log like *that*." These men never put their thoughts into words; they are, indeed, scarcely conscious of them, but they are there.

I wonder why I am thinking so regretfully to-day of those poor, voiceless, eyeless, dead people? I have my dead, it is true, but they are not lying under the grass, but deep down in my heart. God has not yet come to the names of any of my people or the few strangers that I love.

There is some one of whom I always think as dead, though I know that he is numbered among the living. Only by thinking of him thus can I keep the high wall standing between us from falling and crushing beneath it my hard-won, icy composure. If I ever thought of him as living, breathing, sleeping, laughing, sorrowing, I could not bear my lot; every common sight and sound and act would send my thoughts leaping toward him; and, since I cannot forget, I will not think.

I will not stand in a fair garden and, lifting my eyes, behold him—far away, indeed, but still like unto me; subject as I am to God's sun and rain and snow and heat—rather do I set my feet on a barren shore, where no living thing can come; where I can look north, south, east, and west, and see not one speck of aught to break the dull, gray monotony. I did not come out to think dismal thoughts, though. The world looks very fair this morning, like a great, softly splendid emerald set about with sparkling precious stones. The

"Flowers purple, blue, and white,
Like sapphire, pearl, and rich embroidery,"

speckle the meadows and banks, exquisitely pure, and delicate, in their first robe of thousand, thousand shades of green and yellow; so young and fresh are the leaves yet that they look as though a rough hand would brush the bloom from their surface. The light quivers and plays hide-and-seek with them, the shadows dance on the grass, as though they were tripping a measure to music from unseen fairies, the bees and waters mingle in a low symphony, bearing up the exulting song of birds, who sing not because they are bid, or because they have anything in particular to say, but because they are happy—their little bodies are full of rapture, and it overflows in their voices. Down here in the woodland, the earth is carpeted with pale azure bluebells, that seem but a reflection of the sky overhead; and among them spring the wind-flowers swaying their pinkish white heads with every passing breeze; the celandine glistens like gold in the sunlight, and the frail stitchwort, pearliest of beauties, opens her snow-white breast to the soft air; the lords and ladies, stiff and tall, overlook all the little woodland flowers, like a proud king and queen set to watch over the revels of the humbler folk.

A clash of bells rings out across the fields, and I lift my hands to my ears, trembling violently. Since a certain

Christmas-morning, three years and more ago, the sound of those bells has been to me like the touch of a coarse hand on an unhealed wound, and I have to hear them so often. All through that desperate brain-fever I had, they jangled and pealed through my head; bells, bells, bells, that almost rang me out of this world and into the next.

I take my hands away from my ears; shall I not have to listen to the sound through all the years of my life, and think to myself how like wedding-bells they sound? There is a mad, exulting hurry in their peal, as though they could not utter themselves for joy; and yet no one is likely to be married at four of the clock in the afternoon. Poe's weird verses always come into my mind when I listen to bells. I wonder could any other man have caught their meaning so perfectly, and written it down so faithfully? That is a great gift to have, not only a beautiful idea, but to clothe it in the right words.

As I listen my thoughts go back to that day, just three years ago, when I looked in my glass and saw my hair just beginning to grow in short thick locks over my head; it has almost all come back to me now, but it is not so long as it used to be. When I began to get about, I made up a chignon out of all that had been cut off, and used to put it over my short curls, but I was always losing it, and at last Pepper found it and worried it to bits, and there was an end of my first unlawful adornment. I wonder if I look that popular object of ridicule, a blighted being, as I sit under the oak-tree in my smart print gown, with all the flowers creeping about my feet and the bonny blue sky over my head? I pull back my sleeve and look at my arm; it is not very fat, but it is not lean, and my fingers have dimples in them still—decidedly, grief has not altogether made a wreck and a ruin of me. That is the beauty of never having been particularly handsome; when there is so little to lose, the difference is not perceptible.

Dolly says that if I had more color I should look exactly as I did three years ago, and I believe that she and mother both think that I am beginning to *get over it.* Well, I live, it is true, and sleep, eat, drink, laugh even, much as I used to do, but I am like a body of which one half is paralyzed, while the other retains its vigor; the inevitable, every-day, common side is quick and capable; the other, God and my own heart only know about that. I never was one to keep up a running complaint about anything; when I was glad or sorry, I always made a great noise over it and had done with it; so in the fortnight that preceded my illness I think I exhausted all power of active suffering, and that for the rest of my life I can only endure passively.

I do not believe in any healthy man or woman dying for love, unless they set themselves deliberately to do so. They must be either vicious or weak to do so, for it is a little-minded nature that, possessing many good gifts, counts life as stale and worthless because the one thing he desires is withheld from him. Shame and disgrace may well kill, and do, but mere suffering never; the human heart must have something more than simple pain before it breaks. Folks do die of broken hearts most assuredly; or rather, it should be said, that a morbid and sinful indulgence in the luxury of grief, a dogged resolution to contemplate no subject save that of his own misery, causes remembrance to become a disease; the mind and heart consume themselves in unvarying regrets, the powers of both mind and body fall into disuse, and gradually, but surely, the silver bowl is broken at the fountain.

It is considered a poetical thing enough to die for love; surely men must know by this time how infinitely easier a thing it is than to *live* for love? The man who takes up his burden and bears it bravely has my honor, but he who lies down, and lets the waters of adversity swirl over his head, has my hearty contempt. Every man and woman too has work to do; the time for rest comes surely enough to all; let us wear out, say I, not rust out. And so I have tried, yes, from the very beginning, not to make my trouble a misery to those about me. I ask no pity, and, what is better still, no one ever offers me any. I make just as much hurry to be down in time for prayers as ever I did in my life; I still love that unlawful ten minutes in bed after being called, that has cost me so dear on many a terrible occasion; still, with a dexterity acquired by long practice, work at the rusty pump of daily conversation at the family table. I feel snubbed and miserable when the governor calls me by the time-honored title of a dummy, and distinctly indignant when he apostrophizes me as a peacock, when my tail does not even touch the ground, and, though I am growing as old as the hills, I have never yet relieved my feelings by making a good face at him *to* his face.

I can still see the absurd side of things as quickly as the sad, though for the matter of that the one frequently suggests the other. Now and then I feel a desperate distaste for my bright-colored dresses and *insouciant* ways, and lean severely toward sackcloth and ashes, while as to lamentation I doubt not I could lift up my voice in a dolorous howl with the best. These luxuries being denied me, I am garbed like any other Christian, and my voice is seldom raised in anything more distracted than a bellow across-country after one of the boys.

I wonder if I shall live to be an old woman? Perhaps, and take to flirting in my old age like Cleopatra, Helen of Troy, and the rest. Until the other day I never knew that Antony's goddess was thirty years old when she fell in love with him; that Helen of Troy was forty when she eloped with Paris, sixty when she returned to her long-suffering husband. Madame Récamier was reckoned the most beautiful woman in Europe from the age of thirty-eight to fifty-three; Aspasia ruled royally from the age of thirty-six to that of sixty;

and ever so many more of them; and to my thinking it is a miracle, with all these frisky matrons on record, that our mothers and grandmothers don't cast about their eyes among the neighboring squires for a Paris, an Antony, or anything else with a presentable name.

What silly thoughts I have fallen upon! I look at my watch; six o'clock; more than time for me to go home. I pick up my hat, almost as shabby and quite as unbecoming as the one I used to wear at the old trysting-place—that trysting-place that I have never passed, never looked at since that Christmas-morning. In our rambles at papa's heels, if he has gone that way I have dropped behind and struck across the fields by another path. My way back to the house lies very near it; from a hedge that I shall pass I can see it quite plainly, but I never have any wish to see it. I should even like an earthquake to come and swallow up the spot that has such bitter-sweet memories. I leave the woodland, thinking how pretty it is, and that I will bring Dolly with me to-morrow, and go along the narrow lane that leads homeward, and, coming to the place whence the field of rye is visible with the old stone stile, some overmastering impulse impels me to climb the bank and look over. I part the boughs, and see standing, with arms folded, on the top of the stone, Paul Vasher, looking out at the tender green and fresh spring beauty of gold and meadow and wood.

CHAPTER VI.

"Make me a willow cabin at your gate,
    And call upon my soul within the house."

"*You know?*" asks Dolly, swiftly, as she lays her two hands on my shoulders and looks into my face.

"Yes, I know;" and in the soft spring twilight I go up-stairs into my dusky pink-and-white chamber.

"When the bells rang out," says Dolly, with a certain anxious hesitation, "everybody wondered, and Larry went into the church to ask the reason. 'Mr. and Mrs. Vasher return this afternoon,' the ringers said; and ten minutes after they drove by. I looked for you everywhere, dear. Nell! Nell! do you *mind* so very much?"

"Mind!" I say, looking at the dimpled, fresh face of my eighteen-year-old sister, "I don't think I *mind*. I have seen him, Dolly."

"What! And spoken to him?"

"No. He did not see *me*."

"How long ago?"

"Perhaps an hour."

"Don't fret, darling," she says, putting her arm round my neck; "perhaps he won't stay long, and you need not meet him."

No, I need not; but will he not breathe the same air that I breathe—see the same people that I see? Is he not alive and quick, *here*, instead of a shadow moving somewhere out of my sight? Sooner or later, I have always known Paul must come to the house of his fathers; but not thus—not without warning. He should at least have given me time to get myself away, and now he is *here*. The whole world was not wide enough to lie between us: and now there is a patch of grass, a few trees and flowers, and that is all. And the woman is with him who took my life in her hand, and trampled it under her foot; and her son is here, hers and Paul's. Ay! she has triumphed over me in very truth, and she is not only Paul Vasher's wife, but the mother of this child. They must make a handsome family, the dark, strong-faced father, the exquisite mother, the pretty boy. I dare say I shall see it some day. No doubt he has grown to love her. Is she not bound to him by a closer, tenderer tie than he dreamed of, when he swore not to go back to her that Christmas-morning? and may not time, man's inconstancy, and her own maddening loveliness, have closed the wounds that gaped so wildly three years and more ago? Three years ago! Little enough to a woman, with her empty, uniform days: an eternity to a man who has a man's busy, eventful life to lead. He must have forgotten me, or he could never have borne to come back to a place which must remind him, at every turn, of the old days. And yet the man I saw looking out, over the field of rye, two hours ago, looked like anything rather than a man with his heart at rest. If he would only go away soon, and leave me in peace—or that dull refuge of apathy that I misname peace!—Mother comes in, and sits down beside me in the half-light.

"You know he has come back, dear?" she says.

"I know it, mother."

"He might have staid away," she says, with a quick anger in her tone; "he ought to have known better than to come."

She does not love him. Poor mother! to her, he is the man through whom her daughter's life has been spoiled. She thinks him weak and sinning, as many another would think him who did not know the man or his temptations.

"He has been away long enough, mother. He could not stay forever. You forget the estate. No doubt he was forced to come."

"Well!" says mother, sighing, "the misery of it all we know, the unpleasantnesses of it have now to be faced."

Yes, they have to be, surely enough. What mortal can remain on the mountain-tops of misery always, and is not obliged to descend to the valleys of commonplace consideration now and then?

"I don't know what to do," says mother. "As to calling on, and receiving that woman, I will not." (It must be a very bad female indeed that goads mother into calling her "that woman.") "And if I refuse to do so, your father will insist on knowing the reason, and you made me promise you that I would not tell him about you and Mr. Vasher."

"And you must not," I say, starting up, and sitting down again. "Tell the whole world, but never tell *him!*"

"Very well," says mother, sighing; "then you must put up with the chance of meeting her; and remember, Nell, that you lay a heavy burden upon me, not only of deceit toward your father, but great unpleasantness as regards myself. It is something, indeed, that I should have to take the hand of a woman who has done you such horrible injury!"

"She won't come here, mother, dear," I say, kneeling down by her side; "and you need only leave cards."

"It is such a pity," goes on mother, "that your father liked the Vashers always: if he were quarreling with them, as he does with everybody else, there would be no trouble. I am afraid you will have to meet him," she says, stroking my hair gently; then she adds, wistfully—"Is it so very hard to you, dear? It should not be by now."

Mother does not understand quite. My story seems a very long while ago to her.

"Don't be afraid, mother; if we do meet face to face, I dare say I shall know how to behave."

"Supper is waiting!" says Dolly, entering hurriedly; and we go down-stairs with much haste and more fear.

The governor's visit to New Zealand has not altered him in any way, neither have the added years made any perceptible change in his appearance. To-night he is in an amiable mood, and there are no desperate pauses and pregnant hiatuses in the conversation. How easy it is to amuse a man when he pulls with you, not *against* you!

"So Vasher has come back?" he says to mother, when he has got his pipe, and is blowing out long, comfortable clouds that make us all cough and wink again.

"Yes."

"High time he did, too: the estate's going to wrack and ruin. And he has brought his wife and son. There are queer stories abroad, I am told, about his relations with his wife."

Here the governor pauses, and gives an uneasy glance at Dolly and me, as fathers and mothers have a knack of doing when they find the conversation turning more to meat than to milk.

"What are they?" asks mother, with a certain curiosity in her voice; gentle as she is, I am sure it would not grieve her to hear evil spoken of Silvia Vasher.

"A pack of lies, no doubt; they always are where a handsome woman's concerned. I am told she is magnificent. They say he left her two days after he married her, and never returned to her for a year. I don't believe a word of it myself; for the Vashers were never hasty men, they always looked before they leaped, and I never heard of one of them marrying beneath them—which is more than can be said of most good families nowadays, where at least one cook, or housekeeper, or worse, moves in the family circle. Mrs. Vasher is one of the Flemings of ——shire."

Never before did I hear so long and peaceable an oration from the governor. Plainly the subject has a soothing effect upon his mind.

"If these reports are afloat," says mother, "will you wish me to call upon her? There are the girls, you know."

But this little diplomatic move avails her nothing.

"Vasher must not be slighted," says the governor; "so you will call upon her and take the girls."

Dolly turns red as a turkey-cock, and screws up her mouth in a form that says plainly enough, "*Never!*" I go on with my fox's nose without a word. Mother subsides: it is never easy to argue anything with the governor; to question the wisdom of any one of his edicts is to reduce his conversation to a highly-animated monologue of *one*. As he often says, "Let any one dare to cross me, or say this, that, or the other, to my face, there sha'n't be a *bit of him* left in two minutes!"

Now, though I can easily imagine him reducing any one to the condition of body that he mentions, it has always puzzled me as to what he would do with the remains; it certainly opens out a vast field of conjecture.

He gets up for some more tobacco, and, turning his back upon us, we perceive that a very ornamental antimacassar has caught in the buttons on his coat, and is dangling elegantly at his heels. It is quite out of the question to tell him it is there, equally out of the question to relieve him of it, so he will carry it to bed with him, and, on discovering it, will cast his mind backward to try and remember whether, during the evening, we showed any signs of unseemly levity.

Why am I noting, even smiling at, all these trifles, when brain, and heart, and mind, are aching and tense with the consciousness of a great fact? I thrust it away from me—I will not think of it: I shall be alone by-and-by, then I will look it in the face.

"The Tempests return next week," says papa, with a grateful change of subject. "What the old man can be thinking about to race about the world as he does—" Here he pauses expressively.

"Do you hear, Dolly?" I say to her. "George is coming back! Are you not glad?"

"Very," says Dolly.

As I look at her pretty, blooming face a happy thought strikes me. Why should not she and George make a match? She always liked him, and he would suit her far better than he ever would have suited *me*. I wonder what he has been doing with himself these last two years? distinguishing himself I hope.

It angers me sorely sometimes, when I think that neither of the men who loved me have ever done anything to lift himself above the ruck of men, being held back, in truth, as much by a superabundance of gold and lands as anything else.

What I should have liked, if I had my life to choose for myself, would have been to love and be loved by a moderately poor, ambitious man, who would fight his way up, step by step, taking me with him. Then, when we had reached the top, we should have loved each other so much better for having borne the burden and heat of the day together. He could never have fleered at me then by saying, "You married me because I was rich."

If women who openly, shamelessly marry for money only knew the despicable, degraded wretches they look, and are! Selling their bodies for what? Sensual material enjoyments, that none but a coarse, vulgar mind would set any great store by. Soft carriages, good food, rich habits, bodily comforts, that the beasts of the field might sigh after if they knew of them. And for the heart, the soul, what? Nothing. It is the gross shell that incloses those minor considerations that is the care of this class of women. And yet, can she be always eating choice meats, drinking choice wines? Can she spend her whole time lolling in her carriage and her gauds? Does she never find a time for looking upon her husband, who in his heart despises her, knowing that his money has bought and paid for, not only her body and allegiance, but also every look and embrace she gives him?

I hold that woman who deliberately marries for money as more utterly fallen than she who leaves husband, children, and home, to follow the man she loves through the world. The latter sins heinously, it is true; but is she not obeying the divine, though in this case erring, and self-sacrificing instinct of love, while the other hands herself over to a man she detests for lust of gold—the basest, most ignoble greed man or woman ever stained his or her soul with?

Bedtime comes. "Good-night! good-night!" At last I am in my chamber; the door is locked, and I am alone. I open my window wide, and the soft, moist air creeps in with the faint earthy smell that ever wanders abroad in early spring, whispering that Nature's forces are stirring at their sources, and preparing new and beautiful treasures for our eyes' delight.

There is no moon, and the darkness enfolds me in its softness, and seems to hide me away—body and soul, unborn thought and conscious feeling, anxious fear and trembling joy. Joy! What have I to do with it this night? As though it were a demon, I must send from me the heavenly visitor that has staid so long away from me, lest my soul perish.

Is it a sin that my eyes beholding him to-day have been blessed indeed? Is it a crime that my body is one ache to feel the merest friendliest touch of his hand, my ears one eager hearkening for the sound of his voice?

And this is my strength, this my composure, that I had built up so slowly and painfully, to melt away like snow before the sun at a mere glimpse of his unconscious face! Is it as another woman's husband that I think of him; or as my lost lover, who cleaves to me through time and space, and who is *mine* as I am his? Less of fear than delight moves me, I wis, at knowing he is close to me, that I have seen him, a living, breathing man, instead of a gray shadow in spiritland, divided from me by a river my feet shall never cross.

My mind contemplates the misery and bitter circumstances of the situation—the sight of my enemy filling my place, usurping my rights. My heart sweeps away all paltry, trivial considerations; and, looking the truth fairly in the face, sees and recognizes, trembling, the danger of the hour. It bids me put all my armor on, since love that is lawful strengthens, and love that is unlawful makes men and women alike weak as water—ay! better and stronger ones than are Paul and I.

And since I know my danger, and meet it, not hiding my countenance from it as a phantom that a lying spirit would tell me does not exist, I show a fairer courage than he who vaingloriously goes forth to battle trusting in his own strength, without sending up one prayer for safety.

This night, then, is my breathing-space, and in it I will struggle to convince myself that to disobey any natural beautiful instinct of my heart, is virtue—to indulge every irresistible impulse and longing, sin; to make my heart cold and hard as steel, my eyes blind and dull as those of a mole; to transform myself from a creature of flesh and blood, subject to human passions, to a chill, blank automaton. Then, maybe, I shall be able to meet him, not as my lost, lost lover, but as the husband of another woman. This is my task.

O Night, your hours are long and silent, and the faint daybreak of the morning comes not yet.

CHAPTER VII.

" . . . . Leave her to Heaven
And to those thorns that in her bosom lodge
To prick and sting her."

It is Sunday morning, and all Silverbridge that is not bedridden, infidel, and naked, is sitting in church listening to Mr. Skipworth's droning voice that makes up in sound what it lacks in sense. The chancel-door is open, and through it my eyes, weary of gazing at the vacuous rotundity of my pastor and master's countenance, wander, refreshed by the pale green of the young leaves on which the lights and shadows quiver and leap. A bird, alighted on the threshold, is sending his shrill, clear song straight into the church, and Mr. Skipworth shakes his head impatiently as though he said, "How dare that impudent bird lift up his voice while I am speaking?" But, oh! how much more sweetly does the voice of the ignorant bird inform our hearts and ears than that of the preaching, reasoning man!

The bucolic part of the congregation sits stolid and sleepy. They have listened to him Sunday after Sunday for the last twenty years, most of them will listen twenty more; and, if he were suddenly to awake out of his sloth and preach a good rousing sermon, it would probably disagree with them horribly and give them a moral indigestion, making them uncomfortable for weeks. If you put the question to them whether they would like to be spiritually awakened, they would tell you that they do very well as they are, and see no necessity whatever for a vigorous stirring up. To them, heaven is on the right hand, hell on the left, and church in the middle; to go to church is to be safe for the former, to stay away from church is to go to the latter sharp and sure. Church is church, and it does not much signify to them what they hear there—there's always the Bible and the Prayer-Book to fall back upon. They do not make any very strenuous efforts to unlock the gate that leads into the kingdom of heaven: they walk decorously and slowly according to their lights. There are certain well-known landmarks in sin that they steer clear of, for the rest it is out of all conscience to suppose that honest, industrious bodies, who say their responses and amens every Sunday of their lives, can be anything but safe for a comfortable place in the next world. Among these simple folks are some wolves in sheep's clothing; men who beat their wives, neglect their children, and spend their earnings in the alehouse, who are, in fact, veritable *mauvais sujets*. But mark the difference! These men come up to time every Sunday morning; in their places they sit with their pommeled wives and hungry children, with a decent coat, and a clean face, and steady legs—*respectable*. Let them commit one tithe of these misdemeanors and stop away from worship, and they are outcasts.

Under the pulpit, in the square red-curtained pew of the Vashers, sits Silvia, Paul Vasher's wife. I know she is there; but I have not glanced once in her direction. But now, as Mr. Skipworth closes his book and we all rise, I look across the church, and we meet each other's eyes fully and fairly, face to face at last. The dawning look of triumph wavers and dies before the cold, steady scorn of mine. Ay, Madam Silvia! though you stand there his wife, and I stand here lonely, forsaken —though your words have come true, and you have got your heart's desire—you are a cheat, an interloper; it is I who am conqueror, not you. You stole Paul's body and name from me; but his heart, his love, his life are mine, and you know it. He will not even be seen by your side on this your first appearance among his own people. All this my eyes say to her as we look upon each other, and then we kneel down. At the gate Mrs. Vasher's carriage awaits her, superbly appointed, as are all her surroundings at all times; and I think to myself of how small I should feel in spite of all the frippery and bravery of it if I had to get into it and drive away *alone*.

"Handsomest woman I ever saw in my life!" I hear the governor's voice saying as we cross the churchyard behind him; "and Vasher ought to have been with her."

I smile to myself as I listen. Will not every man who looks on Silvia's face condemn Paul as a selfish, cold-hearted wretch for his indifference? Talk about beauty being only-skin deep, "Handsome is as handsome does," and the rest of those worthless, lying sayings that man never spoke, which are rather the embodied spite of generations of plain women, who, finding the grapes denied them, declared them to be sour—it is no such thing. Beauty is power, love, influence, rank, and riches; beauty covers a multitude of sins for which the possessor will never be punished so long as she can ravish the eyes of men with her sweet looks and smiles. Ugly folks may starve and nobody cares, but Providence sends good things to fill the mouths of the beautiful. Who does not feel his heart turn warmly toward the joyous, winsome, lovely woman, as to a flower, a picture, or anything else delightful to the eye? The very sense of pleasure it communicates to us makes us grateful to the cause, therefore we love it.

Yes, Silvia will have consolation offered to her, enough and to spare. She is altered: there is more expression in her face. She has suffered keenly, I think, since that night at Luttrell when I saw her last. She has her wish, but, if her eyes speak truth, it has brought her little peace.

I pause in untying my bonnet-strings, to think of how Paul and I would have spent this Sabbath morning if I had been his wife, he my husband. We should have walked to church, I think, across the glistening, fresh park and fields; we should have paused now and again to gather a flower or two by the way. We should have given each other lectures as to our deportment when we got into church; he would have put my bonnet straight, and made me tidy in the porch before we went in. In the Litany I am sure he would have kissed me, and in the Ten Commandments I am sure I should have kissed him, and during the sermon—for there is nobody to see—I should have slipped my hand into his big brown one.

I catch the reflection of my face in the mirror, and start back: it warns me of what I am doing—*thinking ;* and I have vowed that I will never look back—that I will keep my eyes fixed straight and steady on the monotonous level of to-day.

"If you don't want to find the governor dancing a hornpipe on the dining-room table, come down!" says Dolly, rushing in, and I follow her in hot haste.

Heavy as my heart is, my heels are light enough. On Sundays, for some unknown reason, papa always seems to feel our numbers pressing more heavily upon him than any other day ; he, so to speak,

throws our existences in our faces as a fact of which we ought to be deeply and abidingly ashamed; although what finger we had in the pie, and why our presence in this life should be set down to our own determined and unaided obstinacy and vice, is rather more than we can understand. At these times the governor does not look upon us as decent responsible souls, but as so many *mouths* that he is bound to fill; and for my part I feel intensely ashamed of being obliged to eat at all, and that I should hold a very different position in his eyes if I could do without any such sublunary matters as food and drink and clothing. While he fulminates against the beef, the butcher, the carving-knife, the plates, and the round world and all that is therein, I speculate as to whom he might consider a suitable person to rear and maintain his family, reserving to himself the small rights of controlling our souls, bodies, looks, words, and actions. Clearly he thinks it no legitimate affair of his; but a man who will adopt ten children, and provide for them, is not to be met with every day. While as to Providence—whom he possibly regards as the person to blame—why, Providence, in providing us with a father, evidently considers it has done its duty, and there is an end o't. By the time the governor's plate is empty his angry mutters have ceased, and peace, dove-like and beef-inspired, broods mildly over us.

The best of men is better full than empty, and the most rampagious of men is ten degrees less rampagious when he has eaten a good dinner ; and, if I were going to keep house, I would not forget that the way to a man's heart is through his stomach. I will give Dolly excellent advice on the subject when she marries.

At dessert a remark of papa's strikes me like a blow.

"Vasher is coming here this afternoon ; I saw him yesterday, and made a point of it."

Fancy *papa* pressing anybody to enter

his hospitable house—it sounds wonderfully like the spider and fly!

"Did he seem unwilling to come, then?" asks mother.

"Not exactly, but he hesitated in a queer way—said he never went anywhere. He inquired for you!" continues the governor, nodding at me.

"Did he?" I say, with my eyes fixed on the apple I am peeling.

"You will call there to-morrow," he says to mother.

"Yes. And take the girls."

"I won't go," says Dolly in an angry aside to me; "not if I am *tied in a cart*, like a pig going to market!"

"Supposing he comes now," I say to myself, "before I can get away!" and I sit in a restless misery until the familiar chuck of papa's thumb releases us.

"Mother," I say, in the drawing-room, "I am going out at once. I shall not come in until I think the coast is safe."

"May I come with you?" asks Dolly.

"Not now, dear," I say, kissing the soft cheek that has never blushed or paled for love of any man living yet; "we will go out together to-morrow."

As I go through the garden I press my hands hard upon my heart, and a mist creeps over my eyes, blotting out the garden, the flowers, and the sky. He is coming, here where his feet trod every nook and corner beside mine, here where we had our one perfect day of happiness and content; but he is not coming to me —he will sit in the old familiar room where we sat together so often, and I shall be out here *alone*. We are both alive, and well, and strong, living in the same place; but between us lies a woman's plain gold wedding-ring.

I hurry away to the orchard, and sit down under the very same tree where Jack and I sat so many years ago with our beasts and birds all about us. I wonder if the time seems as long to him as it does to me? or if I look as old as I feel. (Jack's ridiculous old question of whether I would rather be a bigger fool than I look, or be a bigger fool than I am, here comes into my mind and provokes a smile.) Twenty-two next birthday is a considerable age; but, perhaps, if I were happy, it would not seem so much. How the bees are humming and buzzing all about the trees, as though they smelt the pink-and-white buds that are forcing their way through the dull brown boughs! How carelessly the birds are singing! O bees! O birds! can you not give me a little of your light-heartedness, O your forgetfulness? You have hardships, no doubt, but you do not seem to be able to *remember*. . . . God does well to make your memories blank ones.

I leave my place and saunter along to a belt of trees that girdles round a dark, sullen pool, set with dank weeds, and ugly henbane and nightshade, lying in the far corner of the orchard. It is, in fact, an outlet to the meadows beyond, for behind the pool rises a low stone-wall with a stile. I do not often come this way, for I hate the spot; and yet it fascinates me, and I pause to look down into the sluggish depths. A sudden tongue of sunlight pierces the close-set trees, and trembles on the black water, and in the momentary illumination I see strange, loathsome, misshapen horrors, that writhe, and turn, and wriggle away into dark corners. This pool typifies to me a foul heart that conceals many an ugly secret, and slinks away from the light that reveals its deformity.

A step behind me makes me lift my eyes from its dark surface, and there, on the other side of the wall, stands Paul Vasher. I had meant to put out a cool, friendly hand to him so easily (if ever we met), looked at him with such careless, friendly eyes, and said "How do you do?" to him so glibly. Why, then, do I stand silent, with uplifted hand, staring at him? I am dumb with pain—not love; I am looking at him in sorrow—not love. Oh! what have the past years held for him that they have altered face, look, and figure, so fearfully? You may be loved for your own sake, Paul Vasher, but never more will a woman love you for your beauty. Gray, haggard, worn—who could believe that you had ever been proud, imperious, passionate? A bitter pain shoots through my heart as I recall the face that I saw in my looking-glass three hours ago—pale it was, and a little fallen; but with such suffering writ on it as on *this?* No! After all it is he who speaks first, and my words used to be so *much* more frequent and ready than his!

"I was going to the Manor-House," he says.

He is standing beside me now. We make each other no greeting.

"Let me look at you," he says, coming a step nearer; "I have not seen you for three years, remember."

He stands looking into my face, line by line, feature by feature, for a full minute; then he turns away.

"You can never have cared as I did," he says, "never—to look as you look to-day."

"Hush!" I cry, starting aside; "we made our last farewells, spoke our last words on that Christmas-morning: in this present we are nothing to each other—*nothing.*"

"And may we not remember?"

"Remember!" I repeat, turning pale. "Do you not see that *there* is the sin, *there* the wickedness? We must not remember—we *will not!*"

"Speak for yourself, child," he says, bitterly. "I am too old now to learn the meaning of the word forget. Have you learned it?" he cries, with the old jealous ring in his voice that I know so well—and it turns me giddy and sick with the memories it brings.

"Why did you come back?" I ask, smiting my two hands together, "*why did you do it?*"

"Why did I? Because if I had not I should have gone mad, or died of longing to hear the sound of your voice, and for a look of your sweet face."

"Then you do not love *her?*" the

erring words leap straight from my heart to my lips without my own volition.

"Love her?" He looks down at the pool at our feet, looks up at God's heavenly azure shining through the exquisite leaves. "*This* is my life with that woman"—he makes a gesture toward the black, foul waters—"*that*"—with a gesture toward the sky—"is my love for you. Tell me," he says, "tell me *how have these years passed with you?*"

"They have not killed me," I say, turning away my white face, "and" (with a little laugh) "they have not made me thin, but—"

Why do I lift my desolate, tearless eyes to those dark, weary ones, heavy with the love that must not, *dare* not be given to me?

He draws a deep breath and turns as pale as death.

Suddenly I step out of the shadow into the sunlight, and he follows me. Half-way across the orchard I turn to him and speak.

"You have come back, Paul, which you should not have done without warning; and we have met, as we should not have done. But this is our last talk together: henceforward we are acquaintances and meet as such. If ever we fall again into such words as we have fallen into to-day, I shall go away and never come back while you are here. You will not drive me away, will you? Paul! Paul! you are stronger than I—help me to be strong too!" By which it will appear that my long night of fierce struggle with my unruly heart has availed me but little.

"Am I stronger?" he says, standing still. "Whether I am or no, you shall not have appealed to me in vain; have no fear—I will not drive you away."

A minute later and he is in the dining-room, and I am sitting in my chamber alone.

———

CHAPTER VIII.

" . . . . No metal can,
No, not the hangman's axe, bear half the keenness of thy sharp envy."

It is a week since mother, sorely
against her will, drove her fat gray ponies
over to The Towers and left cards for Mr.
and Mrs. Vasher. For a week we have
gone out every afternoon immediately
after dinner, lest in the very plenitude
of audacity she should elect to return the
visit. We might have spared ourselves
the trouble, however; for her chariot-
wheels have not turned in at our gates;
and—somewhat to my surprise, I confess
—I come to the conclusion that for once
in her life her haughty spirit is abashed.

I am going to my pretty woodland
this afternoon, alone as usual. Mother
is in the village, Dolly invisible, and I am
hunting for a basket to bring back my
flowers in. Suddenly I bethink me of
the one that contains mother's wools,
and I cross the hall and enter the drawing-room to fetch it. What a noise those
tiresome boys are making! I wish papa
was not so conspicuous by his absence.
It is no use to box their ears, I say to
myself with a sigh: they are altogether
past that. The wools have got entangled
round the handle of the basket, and—
What is that noise in the distance? surely a bell rang? The door opens almost
instantly, and Simpkins announces " Mrs.
Vasher."

The room is a long one, and as she
comes stepping across the space that lies
between us I stand still, with my face
turned toward her. When she is quite
close to me she holds out her hand. I
do not stir, but stand looking from her
false face to her false hand, from her false
hand back again to her face.

"What!" I say, very low. "You
dare offer an honest woman the hand of
a forger? Has not even your varied experience taught you the gulf that lies between the two? You do my father's

house too much honor, madam. But,
since you are here, I will ask your permission to retire."

As I pass her she lays her hand upon
my skirts.

"You shall not go," she says, quietly.
"I came here to speak to you, and I
will."

I cannot struggle with this woman,
so I stand still perforce, scornful and silent, while she scans my face with an intentness that I can *feel*.

"You are very much altered," she
says, slowly. "You are not very pretty
now. What my husband saw in you I
never could imagine."

In spite of my anger I break into a
hearty, joyous laugh.

"It is very strange, is it not? For
you really are a far better-looking woman, and yet he preferred *me*." Some
wicked spirit ever waits on me and informs me how best to irritate Silvia.
Her eyes darken and flame under mine
like those of a furious animal. I never
saw so fair a face so apt at illustrating
ugly passions. "If you have anything to
say to me," I continue, contemptuously,
"release me and say it; it won't trouble
me."

For a moment she draws her breath
hard, looks at me under her drawn brows,
then releases me. "Perhaps you wonder at my coming here?" she asks, sinking into an easy-chair.

"Very much," I answer, laconically.
(What a nerve the woman has!)

"Your father made a great point of
my coming. He does not know the relations that formerly subsisted between
you and my husband, I think?"

"No, or your share in the matter.
You would not have been admitted within his doors if he had. We are honest
folk, we Adairs."

"Indeed!" she says, with a faint
sneer; "then deceit must be rechristened."

"Tell him your worst, madam; and
to hear you talk about deceit is about as

suitable as if the father of lies took to preaching morality. We know nothing here of such womanly accomplishments as spying, forgery, theft; in our part of the world we do not track men for years and marry them when they are mad. Our neighborhood should be the better for containing a lady who is so great a proficient in all these branches of a woman's education."

"Don't call the means I made use of to reach my ends by such hard names," she says, indifferently; "they served me well enough."

"Such ends as they are! " I say, quietly; "and such a reward as they have brought you! "

"Yes," she says, with her old slow smile, the smile of my dream, "they have brought me all I wanted. I was his first love, and now I am his wife, and the mother of his son, and you were never anything but his—*sweetheart*."

"You were his first love," I say, slowly—"true; and he cast you aside like a soiled glove when he found out your real nature, nor could you win him back, though you stooped to the dust to bring him. You are his wife—but did you become a wife in any commonly decent, honorable way? And you are the mother of his child. Yes. Does he love that child? Does he ever look upon him without remembering your immodesty, your perjury, your fraud? Trust me, Silvia, that innocent child will never be any link between you; rather is he a chain to drag you farther and farther away from the man you call husband."

"Yes," she says, deadly pale.

(Have I touched her at last?)

"But, after all, I have conquered, I am Paul Vasher's wife, and you are only Helen Adair."

"Yes," I say, slowly, "only Helen Adair! but she has a pure heart, an unseared conscience, a fair name, and the entire perfect love of Paul Vasher in the past, in the present, and forever."

An infinite content fills my voice as I speak, looking up, with happy eyes, at the blue vault of sky beyond us.

"I am husbandless, childless, lonely; but do you think I would change places with you? "

"Take care," she says, with a low, wicked laughter lying under her sweet voice; "your good name, did you say? You are very proud and sure of yourself now; but take care, take care you don't lose it some day! All things come to him who waits, you know; and I could wait a long while to see your pride brought low."

"You judge others by yourself," I say, with contempt; "but I know that honor is of small account in your eyes. Here we set some small store by the commodity."

"Are you not afraid of meeting my husband again? " she asks. "It must be very hard upon you, poor thing! "

"We do not find it so, madam."

"You have seen him? " she exclaims, thrown off her guard.

"Certainly. Is there anything so extraordinary in that? "

"Sooner or later you will burn your fingers," she says, rising.

"Thank you for your good advice," I say, taking up my basket with alacrity; "but I should say you wanted it all for yourself. You cannot be expected to understand me—or Paul."

"By-the-way," she says, looking in the glass at her own exquisite person, "how did you hear my husband is not proud of my son? Servants' gossip? "

"No; I leave that to you. Have you your spy Jane at The Towers? "

"Yes; she is an excellent wretch. Well, I am going. I intended to see you, and I have done so. I'm glad to find your misfortunes have not broken your spirit. Tell your father I came," she says, from the door; "unless, indeed, you would wish to tell him the whole story."

I ring the bell, and she vanishes.

"Was ever such a woman? " I say to

myself as I sit down; "no shame, no fear, no conscience. No wonder Paul and I were like wax in her hands. Her words cut me like knives, again and again. Did I wince under them, I wonder? I think I touched her once or twice: I am sure I tried hard enough."

I pick up my basket, innocent cause of my being caught, and go out into the garden, my heart beating, my pulses throbbing. How that evil, lovely face brings back to my memory that night at Luttrell when, though I knew it not, such happiness lay before me! Now the warning is fulfilled, and my lot in life is fixed.

My adventures this afternoon are doomed to conclude in a somewhat ludicrous manner, for, in crossing the orchard, I find poor Dolly in a state of siege, standing on a pile of planks against the wall, whither she has been driven by our new and potent tyrant, the ram. He was installed in the orchard last Monday, and a very lively time we have had of it ever since; indeed, it would be hard to say why he is here at all, unless the abundant abrasions inflicted by his horns on the family legs and shins find favor in the governor's eyes. Not but what he comes in for his share, for the ram is no respecter of persons; and only yesterday did we all, from behind corners, indulge in the exquisite diversion of watching him dodge papa round a tree, the governor—to his credit be it spoken—coming off victorious, although with some slight loss of dignity.

To-day it is Dolly's turn. The orchard being the universal high-road to everywhere, we all have to cross it more or less often every day; and she, less spry than the rest of us, has evidently, after long and painful capers, retired to her present perch as a last refuge; while her pursuer, with a perseverance that speaks well for the intelligence of the genus mutton, has stretched himself out on the grass before her, leaving small hope of escape.

"O Nell!" she exclaims, as I ap-

pear, divided between wrath and tears, "I have been up here more than an hour. I was beginning to think that I should be here till *doomsday!*"

"I'm coming," I say, approaching warily from the rear; for I have no notion of attracting Mr. Ram's delicate little attentions to my own defenseless legs.

"Can't you get him away?" cries Dolly, piteously.

Now, with the very best intentions in the world, it is pleasanter to see another person's knees buffeted than one's own; besides, I enjoyed the luxury no later than this morning; and I intend to make no efforts at assistance, save what are compatible with my own safety, so I answer somewhat faintly, "I'll try, Dolly," and hide myself carefully behind a tree.

This sneaking conduct does not at all meet Dolly's views, who, I know, wants to get me into the open, and then, while he is attacking me, make good her own escape. A nice little programme for her, but not quite so pleasant for me; so I think I will stay where I am.

"*Well!*" says Dolly, "I had *no idea* you were so mean! now if *you* were up here—"

"Yes!" I say, with a sisterly wink, "just so. I say, Dolly! have you tried *smiling* at him?"

"Nonsense!" she says.

"Nevertheless," I say—

'There was an old man who said, *how*
Shall I flee from this terrible cow?
I will sit on this stile and continue to smile
Till I soften the heart of that cow;'

his position was *very* similar to yours, Dolly!"

Meanwhile the ram has discovered the new aspirant to honors, and is surveying me with attention; but he does not move, evidently his heart is set on *Dolly.* Emboldened by his apparent supineness, and wishful to do her a good turn, I leave the shelter of my tree, and,

advancing a few steps toward him, make
a frightful face and utter a loud and war-
like "Shoh!" I don't go far, though, for
painful experience has taught me the
painful celerity with which the beast
moves; so when he scrambles to his feet
and rushes at me, I have found time to
interpose the stout body of an apple-tree
between his horns and my petticoats. He
has an excellent notion of dodging, so
have I, and we set to each other as diligently and indefatigably as, now and
again, you may see two people who are
going opposite ways do at a street corner,
first seriously, then angrily, until both
stop to burst out into hearty laughter.
The ram does not laugh though, he is too
much in earnest for that; he has only his
horns and haunches, poor beast; with the
former he defies mankind, with the latter
he feeds it; and life is a very earnest
matter with him indeed.

Meanwhile Dolly, perceiving the foe
to be thus actively engaged, has several
times debated the safety of descending
from her perch, and at this moment elects
to do so; but alas! wicked fate causes
her to lose her footing, and sprawl full
length on the grass, and, in the twinkling
of an eye, the ram has wheeled, rushed
at her, and is rolling her over and over
on the turf in a transport of buffets.

"Help!" cries Dolly.

"Help!" cry I, suffocated with inex-
tinguishable laughter; and, Dorley happily appearing at this juncture, the too-
persevering mutton is beaten off, and
Dolly, very green about the dress, tangled
about the head, and sore generally, is
hustled out of the way.

"I hope that brute will *break* somebody's legs soon!" says Dolly, in tears,
as we go back to the house, by by-ways
and short cuts, fearful of meeting the
governor, "he will never be got rid of—
else—till he has committed *murder!*"

CHAPTER IX.

" Although the print be little, the whole mat-
      ter
  And copy of the father; eye, nose, lips,
  The trick of his frown, his forehead—nay,
      the valley,
  The pretty dimples of his chin and cheek,
      his smiles " . . . .

A MONTH has passed since Silvia came
to see me, and now we are in May—fragrant, blossoming, voluptuous May; and
the world is covered like a bride with the
month's white flower of flowers, that
here and there melts odorously into faintest, palest pink, or burns into vividest
crimson and scarlet. You are very royal
and sweet, you Mayflowers, but I do not
love you so well as my

                  " daffodils
That come before the swallow dares, and take
The winds of March with beauty; violets dim
But sweeter than the lids of Juno's eye
Or Cytherea's breath; pale primroses
That die unmurmured ere they can behold
Bright Phœbus in his strength,"

and all the delicate army that your gorgeous coming has caused to fade away.
They did not wait, like you, till the earth
was warmed and pranked to receive you;
they grew with the grass, and crept up
through the cold, hard ground, braving
the lingering chilly winds and night frosts
to bring us beautiful messages from the
busy, teeming earth-mother. Already in
this fuller spring the indescribably delicate
tints of leaf, and flower, and grass, and
sky, are gone; the fresh, new, impalpable
bloom that lay over all has vanished; the
vague rapture and stir of Nature is over.
It is the fulfillment, not the promise; the
reality, not the dream. Over my head
the apple-blossoms are hanging, rosily
white, pearly pink; they are so exquisite
that I long to take a bough of them in
my arms and bury my face in their cool,
snowy beauty.

As I look up, a thrush, who has been
swaying himself to and fro, hurries away,
and a shower of pink-and-white scented

leaves flutter down upon my head and face—what a feast is this for eye and heart and senses! And so it would have been to me a while ago; now it fills me with admiration, not love. And yet I would not have the days when Nature contented me so thoroughly back again if I could.

> " 'T is better to have loved and lost
>   Than never loved at all,"

sang the poet, with a deeper philosophy than the words at first sight seem to contain. Better is it to have a heart that has only quickened to die, than one that goes beating torpidly on, knowing as little of joy as of pain. I think those who have a great capacity for suffering are not to be pitied, since they have an equal capacity for happiness; to such the great flood of ecstasy that has once swept over their souls, though quickly followed by sharpest misery, more envy may be given than to those whose hearts are watered only by puny rills of pleasure, who can only suffer as they endure—in moderation. And though forgetfulness might bring me a base and sluggish peace, I would not lose Memory—that sad and sweet-faced maiden, in whose face I can look without remorse, and who, though she offers to my lips a full and bitter cup, cannot say, " You mixed it: drink, for the evil is of your own working." I think that, if through fault or sin of mine our misery had been made, I could not have borne it. That is why Paul suffers so terribly, because he knows that his own hand was the means of our undoing. Paul! Paul! and I can give you no word of comfort! no, nor ease your shoulders from one iota of the burden laid upon them.

I have seen him twice, before all the rest. Fortunately, papa is not so far gone in madness and hospitality as to invite Mrs. Vasher to dinner, and as she has been here he is perfectly unsuspicious of the wheels within wheels; and long may he remain so, say I. He, mother, and I, have been invited to a dinner-party at The Towers (ye gods!), but, as papa has fortunately quarreled à l'outrance with every other neighbor invited, and as it might be awkward if he had to take his enemy's wife in to dinner, he has declined for obvious reasons. Mrs. Vasher has returned her visits as she received her visitors, alone, and the county to a man cries fie! upon Paul; and the county to a woman, with a spiteful though true instinct, takes the part of the husband, and calls fie! on the wife.

Sometimes I think I never made a greater mistake than when I made Paul go back to his wife. Upon him I entailed a life of utter wretchedness; what his existence is his face tells plainly enough; and the tongue of scandal even has not been stopped, although my name has not yet appeared in the matter. He might have got over his disappointment in time if he had been away from her, but how can he forget for one moment when Silvia is ever before him, a living witness of the past? God forgive me if I acted arrogantly and unwisely; I did it for the best.

Footsteps come softly over the grass, and Simpkins appears somewhat unexpectedly before me. There are signs of hurry and discomposure on the ancient man's countenance, that nothing short of papa's agency could call up, and I look round hastily to see if that gentleman is harassing his rear.

"You are wanted directly, Miss Nell; Mr. Vasher is here."

"What has that to do with me?" I ask, reddening, as I remember the countless occasions on which Mr. Simpkins has seen us together.

"Mrs. Vasher is dying, Miss Nell; " and may he be forgiven, but a look of positive satisfaction overspreads his face as he makes the announcement.

"And what has that to do with me?" I ask again.

"Oh! nothing, miss, nothing! "

"I don't believe a word of it," I say, promptly. "What is she dying of?"

"Something in her inside, Miss Nell; her 'art, I think."

"Very well; I am coming.—I don't believe one word of it," I say to mysef, as I follow Simpkins toward the house. "It's only another of her tricks. Besides, if she were, why should she want to see *me*, of all people?"

In the drawing-room I find Paul Vasher alone.

"You will come?" he says, meeting me half-way across the room. "Deeply as she has wronged you, you will not refuse her?"

In his voice there is some strange, new feeling. Is it remorse?

"What is the matter with her?"

"Heart-disease. Her mother died in just such an attack as the one I left her in just now. The doctor said she might die at any moment."

"Are you sure?" I ask, skeptically. "People may have heart-disease for a very long while before they die of it. And I can't understand why she should wish to see me."

"Perhaps she wants you to forgive her," he says, in a low voice.

"Do not be angry," I say, after a few seconds' hard thought, "but I cannot go. I could do her no good; and I have a feeling, a conviction even that she is not so ill as you think. Remember her powers of dissimulation. If I go, harm will come of it; and I could not tell her that I forgive her—I do not."

"During the past hour," he says, slowly, "I have begun to feel for her what I never felt before—pity. If you had seen her face when she sent for me—"

"I will go with you," I say, quietly, and leave the room.

Mother and Dolly are to be found nowhere; so I fetch nurse, make her dress herself, and then go down with her to the carriage that is waiting at the door. It is a strange setting out to the house that I have never entered, and to which I was to go as bride, and now I am going there to see Paul's wife, my bitter enemy.

Nurse's amazement distracts my thoughts during the short period that elapses between our leaving the Manor House and reaching Paul's door, where he stands waiting to receive me. He takes us through halls and vestibules, into an octagon-shaped room, looking out on to a gay flower-garden, and leaves us. A queer taste for a man's room; it looks far more like a lady's boudoir. . . .

"Eh?" cries nurse, lifting her finger and pointing toward the mantel-piece; "only look, Miss Nell!"

I start violently as my eyes fall on the picture, which represents a young girl with the first freshness of early youth lying on her lips and cheeks, looking with joyous, happy smile out of her veil of loose brown hair; upon her head is a wreath of poppies and woven flowers and grasses; she wears a white gown, and she is—Helen Adair, as she used to be.

"Nobody 'ud ever know it was intended for you," says nurse, impartially, "you used to look summut like it—but, lord! the difference the paint do make to be sure!"

I look round the room: at the walls hung with pale-yellow silk with a deep rich border of poppies and corn-flowers running round; at the damask curtains, with the same border; at the white carpet, on which the same flowers are scattered in delicate knots. I know now why he uses this room; it was to have been mine. The sex of the occupier is shown by the massive writing appointments, the whips and driving-gloves, the half-smoked cigar on the table, and all the orderly litter of a man's favorite room. And this is my Eden that I have never entered, until I come to it as a visitor to his *wife*. I look up—Paul is standing at the door, and I rise to go to him, leaving nurse behind. At the door of the room where Silvia lies he leaves me, and I go in alone. The room is so darkened that, coming out of the broad daylight, I can barely make out the outline of Silvia's face against the pillows. As I approach her, an elderly woman by her side rises and passes out.

"You sent for me," I say, looking down on her, "and I am here."

Now that my eyes are more accustomed to the light, I see that she is mortally pale, and her breath comes in quick, short pants.

"Do you know that I am dying?" she says, lifting her haggard, lovely eyes to my face. "I dare say you are very glad?"

Desperately ill I see plainly enough that she is; something in her voice tells me that she is not dying, no, nor in immediate danger of death.

"Did you only send for me to ask me that? if so, I am better away."

"Are you so hard-hearted?" she asks between her short pants. "Feel!"

She takes my hand and lays it against her heart, which seems to be leaping out of her body with every beat.

"Do you think that is *shamming?* Sooner or later it will kill me—not to-day, perhaps, or to-morrow, but some time."

She looses my hand and sits up in bed, and her fleece of hair ripples all over her shoulders and the coverlid like a shower of molten gold.

"If I were dead you would forgive me, would you not?"

"I would try to."

"If you knew that I could not live very long, you would forgive me?"

"Perhaps."

"Then say so now," she says feverishly, with her hands clasped over her laboring heart, "that you do forgive me."

"I cannot," I say, slowly; "it is all too sudden. . . . I do not forgive you; would you have me tell a lie? And you seem to have forgotten all that lies between us. . . . how can there be any shadow of friendship between us?"

"I don't ask for friendship," she says, falling back upon the pillows.

How pale and lost and lovely she looks!

No wonder Paul found it in his heart to pity her just now.

"Do you know," she says, opening her eyes, "that it is you who should ask forgiveness of me, not I of you? Paul was mine first, do not forget that, and he might have been mine again, if you had not bewitched him; if I stole him from you last, you stole him from me first. How did you make him love you so well?" she cries with a low wail; "whether with you or away from you, it was always the same—you were the very apple of his eye. Men are not usually so faithful to the absent, or so cold to a beautiful woman who loves them. And all these years that I have been his wife, he has never spoken one word to me, save before servants—never touched my hand in commonest friendly greeting. I came behind him once and put my arms round his neck; he started up—you should have seen his face, there was murder in it; he left me without a word—and for all of this, I have to thank *you*, Helen Adair! Oh! it is pleasant to steal into his room, like a thief, in the dead of night, and hear him cry, '*Nell! Nell!*' over and over again, and toss his outstretched arms into the air; often as I have watched and listened, I never yet heard him whisper, '*Silvia!*'"

A deep pity wells up from my heart as I look down on this passionate, sinful woman, between whose lips the fruits of evil-doing have turned to such bitter dust and ashes. Has not God punished her heavily enough for me to forego my little impotent condemnation?

"If I had known how it would be I never would have tricked him into marrying me—never. I thought that if I was his wife I should regain all my old empire over him; no man ever withstood me yet. My one heart's desire was to make him love me again, then I should have known happiness at last. Happiness! good God! though I have always hated the very name of Death, I shall not be sorry when he calls me; only I dread the cold, narrow bondage, and the thought of the blind-worms creeping over my breast—pah!

"Will you give me some of that medicine? I sent that fussy doctor away; he was no good, and I know the proper remedies. Thank you. I told them just now to send my—"

"Mamma! mamma!" says a gentle little voice outside the door, which opens softly, and on the threshold stands Paul's son, and Silvia's. A breathless calm binds me hand and foot as he stands still for a moment, hesitating, then comes on his little unsteady feet, straight across the room to my side, looking up into my face with Paul's own proud, willful, beautiful brown eyes. And still I do not stir, until, perplexed, he lifts a tiny, dimpled hand and slips it inside mine—and the clinging baby fingers touch some strange, till now unknown chords deep in my heart. . . . I tremble, and a passion of new-born love, fierce regret, and bitter pain, shakes me like a reed, and I bow my head low over the innocent, childish face. Nay, Silvia, it is you who have conquered, not I. To this unsoiled treasure, "fresh from God," you are mother, not I. Through all my years of misery, I have never once felt the loss of my lover as I feel it now, while my arms close around his son.

"You like children?" says Silvia, as the boy slips away from me and clambers over the bed; "I never did."

"Pitty mamma!" says the child, pulling at her loose hair, "pitty mamma!" but he does not kiss her or lay his face against hers, nor does she hold out her arms to him. Silvia spoke the truth, she has no mother-instinct whatever.

"And you do not love him?" I ask.

"No. I might have, perhaps, if he had been any link between me and his father, but he was the one crowning misdemeanor for which my husband never forgave me. I was told he went on like a madman when he heard it. I never loved but one person in my life, and that was Paul."

"Was there ever such a shameless woman?" I say to myself, looking at her. The deathly pallor has left her face, her breathing is quieter, and the bluish tint of her lips is replaced by a tinge of color. I look at the child; they make a beautiful pair. He has his father's eyes, his mother's skin, her golden hair, his father's mouth and chin, with a haughty trick of holding his head, that brings Paul before my very eyes. Father and son, son and father, how my heart aches for you both! —the consolation that the one might afford the other, the love the other might give the one. Somehow the touch of the little hands has smoothed all the resentment and unforgivingness out of my heart. I could not, if I would, speak such words to his mother as I did awhile ago.

"I feel better now," she says, wearily; "I shall not die this time, at any rate. Tell me now, once for all, will you forgive me?"

"Yes, I will forgive you" ("for the child's sake," I add to myself).

"You will?" she cries, sitting up; "you are not pretending?"

"Why should I?" I ask, steadily; "are you?"

"No!" she says, dropping her eyes, "only I did not think any woman living could be so noble. And you will speak to me when I meet you; you will come to see me?"

"We are not likely to meet, and I will not come to see you. Friends we cannot be; no, nor acquaintances."

"Then your forgiveness is an empty form of words," she says, falling back; "I need not have praised you for it. Shall I tell you why you extend to me the form of forgiveness and not the spirit?" she asks, lifting herself upon her elbow. "Shall I tell you why you will not come here? Because you are *afraid of your own heart.*"

There is an instant's silence, in which Satan whispers, "What! Acknowledge your own weakness and his?" and my good angel cries, "Confess it, and be not

led into temptation;" then I answer
coldly: "You are mistaken, Mrs. Vasher;
I am no more likely to forget that he is
your husband than he is to forget what is
due to me. No, I am not afraid to meet
him."

"Then sometimes, not often, perhaps,
but *sometimes* you will come here. You
will not keep up an open enmity?"

"Sometimes!" I say, against my better instincts; then, looking suddenly into
her face, "Silvia, are you quite certain
that whatever of sin and subterfuge there
has been in your past, you now mean
fairly and honestly by me and your husband? Is there any fresh plotting of
wickedness in your heart?"

"Does a dying woman weave plots?"
she asks, bitterly, as she turns away her
eyes from mine. "Is there any further
harm that I can work you, him, or myself? Your heart is not a soft one, Helen
Adair."

For a minute I stand musing, and the
child pulls at my dress; he is tired of the
quiet room, and wants to go away.

"Wattie takes to you," she says, looking at him; "though he never liked
strangers."

The change in her voice brings me
back to commonplaces. "Is that his
name? I am going now. Good-by."

She stretches out her thin hand and
lays it in mine; a queer sensation runs
through me as I look down at it—the
hand that worked my life's misery so
deftly and well.

"You have promised," she says, "do
not forget. You have promised to come
here sometimes and see me and Wattie."

"I shall not forget."

She closes her eyes, and, as we pass out
of the room, I pause to look at her, thinking that she looks far more like a dead
woman than a living one. In the corridor outside several servants are standing.

"That's Miss Adair," says one of them
in a very low voice, as I pass; "her as
master's so sweet on."

Have we any secrets from the detec-

tives who eat our salt, take our wages,
and do our bidding? Wattie trots along
by my side, the nurse follows, at the foot
of the stairs we meet Paul Vasher.

CHAPTER X.

"God protect me from the man I trust, I
will protect myself from him whom I trust
not."

TIME, four o'clock. Scene, a level
sweep of velvet-smooth lawn before The
Towers, upon which are pacing up and
down and sitting about some sixty or
seventy men and women of every size,
make, age, and appearance, and among
them in festive raiment, like unto the
rest, are—oh, wonder of wonders!—
Dolly and I, sitting one on either side of
Mrs. Skipworth. That lady, as a delicate
compliment to the devouring heat of the
day, wears a crimson-colored silk gown,
that makes one glow freshly every time
one looks at her.

"*You* here?" exclaims a young man,
who is walking slowly by, but has now
stopped short to stare at us, "*Nell!
Dolly!*"

"Did you never see us before?" I
ask, rather tartly; "do you take us for
ghosts?"

"Not exactly," he says, recovering
himself, "only I did not expect to see
you here."

He shakes hands with Mrs. Skipworth, and looks about for a chair, but,
as the supply of seats by no means comes
up to the demand, after a little search he
comes back.

"Would you not rather stroll about
than sit still, Nell?"

"I think I would."

"Will you come, Dolly?"

But Dolly, bearing in mind the excellent lines that set forth that "two is
company, three is trumpery," declines
the honor, so we depart without her.

"May I ask why you looked so *astonished* just now when you saw us?" I

ask; "is there anything so very extraordinary in our coming here, pray?"

"Nothing!" he says, coldly; "only you had not told me you were coming, that was all."

"And how could I tell you, when I have not seen you for three whole days? I will tell you the truth," I say, suddenly, my voice falling; "I hate being here; I *hate* it, but I could not get out of it. Mrs. Vasher asked the governor to let us come without my knowing anything about it, of course, and papa said 'Yes,' and told us he had accepted the invitation. Dolly declared she would not come, she is a good hater; mother *got* out of it in some wonderful manner, but all *our* manœuvres were unavailing, and, here we are."

"It was a pity your father never knew the truth," says George; "it seems altogether wrong that you should be the guest of a woman who played you so vile a part."

"Hush!" I whisper, as his voice rises in his excitement, for we are in the crowd now, "and take care"—for with his head lifted skyward, and his thoughts busily engaged, he is taking no heed to his steps, which are encroaching on the train of a lady before us, who looks as though she had seized Fashion forcibly by the nose, and wrested a costume from her, so *bizarre* and outrageous and eye-offending are its properties. If it be true that the test of a perfect toilet is that one does not know of what it is composed, although one is distinctly aware that the person in it looks charming, then are those here present found seriously wanting, for the dress and the manner of it strike the beholder first, the wearer of it after. And yet there are a few beauties, beautifully dressed; a few graceful women with the grace that is almost as great a gift as beauty; a few *grandes dames*, who hold their own against fairness, wit, and youth, by merit of a certain *air du faubourg* and fascination, that it is hard to define, harder still to resist. I wonder why

some women have so much *chic*, individuality, what you will, and others none at all? Hundreds and thousands of women are made on precisely the same pattern, but now and again you come across one who, by right of some sturdy strain of character or independence of thought, marks herself out from the rest, and is not merged in the common ruck, but leads it.

"Do you men never have any bankerings after your lost doublet, hose, velvet cloaks, and other smart trappings, George? I should if I were a man. Now, I have no doubt that blue would be as becoming to some of you as it would be fatal to others; that some particular color sets you off as well as it does particular women, and that the very ugliest of you might be furbished up into something uncommon-looking or picturesque."

"I can't say it ever bothers me," says George, laughing; "but there is one thing I should like to have back, and that is the good old days when a pretty woman was *a pretty woman*, and every one knew it, and a plain woman was a plain one, and every one knew *that;* and the line between Madam Beauty and Madam Ugly was drawn hard and fast. It is all very different now. The plain women make themselves such excellent imitations of their lovely sisters with their dyed hair, painted cheeks, and artificial charms, that it is not always easy to separate the make-believes from the really handsome people—in fact, the only difference between them at a distance is that the former wear veils and the latter do not. Now, our grandfathers were not obliged to look close into a woman's face to find out whether she was beautiful or only pretending to be; they gave hearty, honest admiration to the lass with the ropes of yellow hair, and the skin of cream and roses, and kindly pity to the one who possessed but scanty pepper-and-salt locks and a sallow skin. Nowadays the latter would plump out her head with another woman's hair, and dye her own golden in imitation of the legitimate beauty's fairest adornment, and copy with pigments what the other possesses by Nature's gift. So it often happens that a man, seeing the deceitfulness of the one, doubts the honesty of the other, and his mind gets into a horrible and disgusting jumble."

"Well done!" I say, with much astonishment, as he pauses for lack of breath. "I had *no idea* you were such an acute observer, Mr. George. There is a good deal of truth in what you say, though, and there is a ghastly mixture of false and real beauty about; but for all that there is some contented ugliness wandering about the face of the earth, making no attempt at whitening itself. At any rate, you could not accuse that wreck yonder of being a sham?" and I nod toward a very old woman sitting a little in the background in a wheeled chair. She wears a false, black front, blue-bottle spectacles, and an enormous white bonnet; her mouth is grim as death; she does not move a muscle, or a finger, or an eyelash, No one speaks to her, and she speaks to nobody; she just sits there looking out at the gay scene before her, like a spectre who is silently noting the uselessness, the folly, and the evanescence of it all.

"Why do such people come out at all?" asks George, shuddering. "Pah! —they spoil the look of everything. It can be no pleasure to them to take their aching old bones abroad; they only give the blues to every one who looks at them, and yet they come with the rest until Death taps them on the shoulder and takes them away."

"Poor souls! perhaps they like the excitement—who knows?"

"Mrs. Bareacres is smacking her lips over something," says George. "Another reputation demolished, no doubt. Those old women are perfect emporiums of scandal and venom, out of which a story, redounding to the discredit of every one present, may be fished at a moment's notice!"

"I wonder what mine is," I say, laughing.

"Heaven grant they may never have a chance of making you the subject of their talk!" says the young man soberly —so soberly that I stare at him for a moment in surprise. He used not to be so grave and thoughtful, or think so seriously about people and things. His philosophy is touched with something more of bitter than it was three years ago.

A fat man and a lean woman vacate their chairs, so George and I promptly sit down on them and look about us. Several promising flirtations are in full swing; several lines are being thrown out by dexterous maidens to entice into their nets certain comely fish; there is a buzz of conversation, a flutter of fans, above which rises, sweet and clear, the music of the band hidden in the trees away to the left. In the assemblage the female sex, as usual, preponderates largely, and, beholding the number of petticoats as set against the infrequency of the lavender and gray legs, I feel slightly snubbed and rather small, for is it not an unpleasant reflection that in Great Britain we are supposed to be three females against every male? No wonder men think so much of themselves; no wonder it is considered more honorable in a young woman to possess as betrothed, or lord, ever so pock-marked, broken-winded, weak-kneed, soft-brained a man, than none at all! And Fate, with her unfair fashion of lumping her favors, has a bad knack of giving two or three lovers to one girl who wants none of them, and never a one to another girl who would say thank you for any little mannikin.

"Dolly seems to be amusing herself very well," says George; and I look across to where she sits, soft and round and fresh as the pink roses that lie half on her brown hair, half on her white lace bonnet. Dolly has exquisite blue eyes, and out of them she is looking up, half shyly, half pleasantly, at a very tall, good-looking young man, whom one would, at a moderate guess, suppose to be a trifle shorter than Chang.

"He is a giant," I say, looking at the man, not Dolly. "Why, he must be eight feet."

"Not quite," says George; "in fact he is only six feet four and a half. He is Molyneux of the Fifth."

"I wish they would stand up; I should like to see what they look like together," I say with interest. "Dolly was measured yesterday, and she is exactly four feet eleven!"

"And she will bowl him over like a ninepin," says George; "those little bits of women always bewitch these big men."

"They would look very nice if they went to a fancy-dress ball; he as Tom Thumb, and she as the Kentucky giantess, would they not? But I do hope he will not be *falling in love* with Dolly."

"Why not?"

"Because," I say thoughtfully, "I have a plan in my head about Dolly; I have made up my mind whom I should like her to marry."

"And who may that be? I did not know Dolly had ever seen anybody!"

"George," I say, lowering my voice, "will you promise me not to be angry with me?"

"Don't try me too far."

"Well, then, don't you think Dolly is a little like me, George?"

"Not a bit! No one would ever know you were sisters!"

"Oh!" I say, disappointedly. "Don't you think, though, that on the whole blue eyes are prettier than green ones, and rosy cheeks than pale ones?"

"To some people's taste they may be."

"But not to yours?"

"No."

"Oh!" I say again, dismally.

"You have not told me yet what you are going to make me angry about?"

"I can't tell you," I say, slowly. "Yes, I will, though; I only *thought*, George" (this in a prodigious hurry), "that . . . . for she is very sweet, you know, and a hundred times as pretty as ever I was—that perhaps, *after a bit*, you might get to like her as well as you did me?"

"Did? Was there ever any past tense in my love for you? You remind me, Nell," he goes on, looking at me with half-sad, half-bitter eyes, "of a story I once heard of a man who proposed for a young lady to her father, and, on finding her to be already engaged, the suitor said he was not at all particular, any one of her sisters would do just as well; it didn't matter a pin to him which he married. Do you think I am so accommodating? There never was but one girl in the world that I wanted, and as I can't get her I'll have nobody."

"Dolly would *never forgive me* if she knew what I had done," I say, my cheeks crimson with vexation; "and I have wounded you too. I am very sorry, George—" and, forgetting the people all about us, I put my pale yellow hand into his straw-colored one, and give it a friendly squeeze; he holds mine for a moment, then I draw it away, and looking up see Paul Vasher standing before us.

"I hope you are not feeling dull, Miss Adair?" he says; and, cold as are our ways and looks to each other always now, his voice strikes upon me like an unexpected douche of ice-cold water.

"Not at all, thank you, Mr Vasher."

He moves away among his guests, and George and I look after him silently: between us Paul's name is never spoken. Dolly goes by with her tall cavalier, giving me a saucy, sidelong look of triumph. She just reaches his elbow. Smiles follow them as they pass, but they are so taken up with each other that they do not see them. As the assemblage ebbs to and fro, scraps of conversation come to our ears. "Pity Adair quarrels so confoundedly with everybody," issues from a knot of men discussing the people present (apparently), "for he has the prettiest family of daughters I ever saw." And a minute later I hear a woman's voice exclaim, " *That* Helen Adair? Impossible! How she has gone off, poor thing!" George's eyes meet mine, and I smile.

"Hags!" cried George, in a fury. "I should like to knock all their spiteful, ugly heads together!"

"Am I so very much altered, George?" I ask, with a sharp pang. "I never was very pretty, you know; and if people say that, I must have grown absolutely ugly."

"You are altered," he says, scanning my face with his honest, tender eyes; "but you have lost none of your good looks; to me you are always sweet and lovely, Nell. You are very pale now, and you do not smile a bit as you used to do, but I don't think you need be afraid of growing ugly, Nell."

"I don't see how I could go off!" I say, laughing, "for that presupposes the possession of more than ordinary good looks at some period or other of my existence, and I never was anything to speak of, except to you, and—" I stop.

"Have you seen my roses?" asks Silvia, coming up to us—beautiful Silvia, in a robe that is all gleaming yellow and blood-red knots of ribbon among her laces.

"No, not yet."

"Then will you come now, and Mr. Tempest?"

"I shall be most happy," he says, stiffly.

Silvia is his neighbor's wife; he cannot refuse to be her guest without folks wondering why, so he comes, but between the pair there is a steady, strong dislike.

"Have you seen Wattie?" she asks, as we are moving away; "I heard him calling out for you just now."

Silvia and I rarely speak to each other on any subject save the child; he is a link between us, and she knows it, but I think she often wonders with a certain pitying scorn at my love for him. Very rarely have I entered her doors, always against my will, but bound by the promise I made her on the day Paul fetched me to her side, and he thought her dying. Well, she looks strong enough to-day, and sometimes I wonder if it was all a trick from the very beginning; and yet the illness could not be a pretense.

"We are going to the rose-garden," she says, tapping her husband lightly on the shoulder with her fan, as we pass where he stands talking to some gentlemen; "will you take care of Miss Adair?"

His face is very dark as he joins me, his wife and George walking on ahead. He does not speak, neither do I; then, for silence is often more dangerous than words, I say, lamely enough, that "the party is a pleasant one."

"Or rather, that you have been very pleasantly engaged!" he says, with a sudden, swift, jealous glance out of his brown eyes, that makes my cheeks paler than ever.

I do not answer, and in another minute we are in Silvia's rose-garden.

It is the month of roses, and this corner is a very feast of roses. From lily white to faintest cream-color and amber and yellow, they melt by every exquisite gradation into richer, fuller tints, fainting away in voluptuous crimson and purple, paling from sea-shell pink to flesh-color. How they mock at our narrow human capacity for enjoyment! How they fill the soul with one drenching, glorious wave of delight, and overflow it, only to be filled again and again!

"I always was so fond of roses," I say, nervously, as I lift my face out of a great golden splendor, with a breath as sweet as its own fairness. "Some people like lilies best, but I do not; they have only one scent, only one face always, and the rose has so many!"

"If you were dying," he says, "and

had to choose the flowers to be laid in your coffin, which would you have?"

"Roses! I should like to be smothered in them! Don't you think dead people know the flowers are there, and smell them? I am sure I should. What made you think of my dying? You forget that I was always a coward about that."

"I had not forgotten . . . . but a strange thought was passing through my mind . . . . of how some people get their flowers in life and some in death, and of how cursed is the man who causes the life's flowers of another to wither."

"Only," I say, gently, "it is God who sends the blight, not man."

I look round, Silvia and George have vanished; there is no one here but Paul and I.

"You will allow me to give you a bunch of your favorites," he says.

"Another time, perhaps. We will follow the others now."

"No, I will pick them this minute," he says; and while I stand a little apart he gathers me a great, glorious bouquet of yellow, crimson, gold, and scarlet. Clearing the thorns from the stalks, he gives it to me and goes away, returning shortly with one snow-white, stainless rose that has no fleck or flaw to dim its absolute purity. "Will you wear this one?" he says; and I take it from his hand and fasten it with my brooch against my throat.

"They are very lovely," I say, looking down on my roses. "We will take them and show them to Dolly."

"Nell," he says, "Nell! are you growing at last to care for that yellow-haired lover of yours?"

"Hush!" I say, holding up my hand and listening. A smile breaks over my face as a certain sound that I know well enough by now is heard in the distance —a scutter of little hurrying feet, a naughty little laugh of mischievous glee . . . . and in another minute Wattie appears before us, his curls tumbled, his cheeks flushed, and the skirt of his frock full of daisies.

"Lallie! Lallie!" he calls out, and down we go on the grass side by side to make our daisy-chain; not the first we have made together by any means. The nurse, seeing that he is with me, goes away. His father does not turn on his heel and go away as he did that first time he saw us together (shall I ever forget his face when he caught sight of us?), he stands looking down on us—on the rapt, intent face of the child, as he hands me daisy after daisy, on my busy hands as I thread them. As I look up from the son to the father, the extraordinary resemblance between the two faces strikes me with fresh surprise.

"You love him?" says Paul.

"Yes, I love him." Does he guess, I wonder, that I love this child above almost all things on earth?

"If you had been his mother," says Paul, jealously, "you would have loved him better than your husband."

"Should I?"

I bow my head over the child that he may not see my face; careless and impatient as I have been with children all my life, does he not know *why* I love his son so passionately, so deeply? The daisy-chain is round Wattie's neck now, and he is nearly throttling me with his kisses and vigorously clinging arms. Gently I set him down and whisper something in his ear, giving him a little push; he hesitates a moment, this little son of not yet three years old, who is worse than fatherless, motherless, then (for he is as brave as he is beautiful) he goes with his little, short, unsteady steps to his father.

"Papa! papa!" he says, in his childish, tender voice; and, no hand being held out to greet him, he clasps his arms round Paul's knees. Paul stoops and unclasps them without a word, setting him aside, not roughly or hastily, but inexorably. A piteous droop comes about the baby lips, and puckers up the baby brow, as Wattie stands alone, in disgrace, as he thinks (a child cannot reason, but it knows when it is slighted and the tender little heart is grieved); then he runs across to me, and hides his head in my breast. Poor, little desolate son! how many repulses have you not had from him before you could understand his ways so well!

"God forgive you!" I whisper to Paul, with burning anger, as I lift Wattie in my arms and press my cheek against his, and so I carry him away through the blooming, fragrant alleys, and leave Paul standing in the midst of his rose-garden alone.

CHAPTER XI.

". . . . Thus do all traitors !
If their purgations did consist in words,
They are as innocent as grace itself—
Let it suffice thee that I trust thee not."

"GEORGE!" I say, in a muffled voice.

"Yes!" he answers in another.

"Supposing somebody comes and *sits down* on us?"

"A little more or less could not make much difference!"

"I wish we had not let them do it. Does not your nose tickle horribly?"

"Rather. That's your fifteenth sneeze, Nell."

"Yes, you ought to condole with me over them, as the ancients did with each other when they were convulsed in like manner."

"I would if it prevented the repetition."

"I wonder when Dolly and Bashan will come back. Supposing they forget us altogether?"

"We should become meat for pitchforks."

George and I have the use of our ears, but of our other faculties not at all; although we are out in a field in broad daylight, we cannot see an inch beyond our noses, and nobody can see us, unless indeed the two mounds that represent us may be supposed to give some grotesque outlines of our shapes. In point of fact, we are snugly buried in the hay, Dolly and Bashan having officiated as sextons, and we are weighed down almost as securely as though solid earth, and not heaps of dried grass, were piled above us. Hay by the handful is one thing, hay in the lump is another; and with our arms and legs laid out straight and flat, and an unlimited quantity of the material heaped upon us, we can move about as easily as though we were in a vice. Not to kill us, however, by too much cherishing, they have put a light covering over our faces, so that, full as our eyes, noses, and mouths are with the pricking, irritating hay-dust, we are still able to draw breath and make ourselves heard.

In the distance are faintly audible the shouts of the hay-makers and the voices of the maid-servants, with which latter this period appears to be one of flirtation and pleasure; shaking grass at the men's heels seeming to please them infinitely better than shaking carpets in each other's face.

"It is not very comfortable," says George, "but I am glad we are buried, because I shall be able to talk to you."

"If you are going to take advantage of my not being able to run away from you, to say things I don't want to hear," I say, with a dignity that is much marred by a tremendous sneeze in its middle, "I consider it *mean* of you."

"I don't think I have bothered you much lately," he says, and through all the hay his voice has a hurt ring in it.

"Indeed you have not," I say, compunctiously; and indeed, since I gave him a certain answer to a certain question, asked doubtfully a year ago, he has not troubled me with one word of love, entreaty, or anything else but friendliness, "only you have looked so sober lately, George, as though you were going to read me a lecture—"

"Would it do you any good if I did?"

"I don't know. One thing I can tell you, though, you will never get a better chance of making me listen to you than you have *now*."

There is a pause and a faint, windy murmur; I think George is sighing.

"Nell," he says, presently, and something in his voice informs me that he is going to disburden himself of the matter that has been oppressing him lately, "I wish you would not have anything to do with Mrs. Vasher."

"I can't help it; I promised, you know."

"It was a great pity."

"I think so too. But supposing you had an enemy whom you believed to be dying, and he asked your forgiveness—wretched, cast down, broken, punished heavily of God—would you refuse your tithe of mercy?"

"If I was quite sure that he meant dying, I might, but I don't think it's very likely. Like Dolly, I am a good hater. If any man had behaved to me as that woman behaved to you, I should hate him as long as I had a kick left in me. Besides, she is well enough."

"She is not; she may die at *any minute*, and that was why I forgave her" (" and for Wattie's sake," I add to myself).

"Creaking doors hang longest," says George, skeptically; "there's nothing like a bad complaint to go upon for a long lease of life. She may outlive us all."

"I wonder if you and I will live to be very old?" I say, thoughtfully. "How droll it would be if you were a dried-up old bachelor at The Chace, I a dried-up old maid at the Manor-House; you would be able to come and see me every evening, and we could play double dummy whist, or *draughts*, if we were weak in our heads. It would be quite proper for you to come when we are both seventy or thereabouts. We shall wear spectacles, of course, but I do hope that never, never shall we stoop to the degrading practice of taking snuff."

"Don't be premature," says George, "you may love it when you come to that age."

"Don't be nasty! And we shall go to church every Sunday in Bath chairs, as grandpapa and grandmamma did side by side, only they went so slowly; we will run races. Perhaps we shall live to an enormous age and be put in the *Lancet* as ' cases.'"

"I hope not," says George, with a vague rustle of hay that sounds like shuddering. "The gradual decay, the loss first of one sense, then another, the tastelessness and weariness of everything, the incessant craving for rest, must be terrible. . . . I would die swiftly, at my best, with my powers in full vigor, be remembered, not dawdle out of existence to the tune of folks' pity, so that when I really went I should be missed. . . . The liveliest sensation one should experience on hearing of the death of a man should be that you are violently shocked—grief should follow in due course."

"I think it would be very selfish of you if you died before me," I say, foolishly enough, "for if there is anything I should hate it would be to leave nobody behind to make a great howl over me. All my brothers and sisters would be married, of course, and have their own selves and families to weep about. It must be unpleasant to live so long that people think it rather indecent of you to be so long about saying good-by, must it not?"

"Very. I don't think you and I will ever sit down to double dummy whist, though, Nell. I don't mean to rust all my life out here; I mean to try to do something, be somebody."

"Be good, my child, and let who will be clever," I quote; "though if you do succeed in doing anything remarkable, which I doubt, you must run back to Silverbridge and tell me all about it, for oh, I shall find it so dull here!"

"Well," says George, "you have more spirit than any girl I ever saw or heard of. Here you are, at the age of twenty-two making up your mind calmly to a long life in this wretched little village, with nothing to break the monotony of it save the deaths and marriages in your family. I tell you it's monstrous, Nell, and you'll never do it."

"I don't know what all the other young women do who have been crossed in love, and aren't lucky enough to catch a fever, or be run over by a postchaise or a railroad-train; they must live some-where, must they not? And one place is as good to live in as another. And I have memory too; if I can't look for-ward I can look back, and Wattie will be growing older every year, you know."

"Good Heavens!" he bursts out, "and that is the life you promise your-self?"

Here he breaks off, and indistinct mutterings follow that the hay does not faithfully transmit.

"If you loved him as I do—" I begin, but a succession of violent sneezes com-pletes the sentence.

A rather loud mutter from George seems to announce the fact that he "*can't understand*" something.

Presently—"Nell!"

"Yes."

"You and I never talk about Paul Vasher."

"No."

"But I want to talk to you about him now—may I?"

I do not answer for a moment; it is like stabbing a fresh wound to speak of him to any one *who knows*, but George was so good to me in that terrible time years ago . . . . so good.

"Yes, you may—only say it as quickly as you can, George."

"Then, Nell, can you tell me why he ever came back?"

"Surely, he had a right to come if he chose!"

"I don't think he ought to have done it."

"If I do not mind it I think you need

not," I say, proudly; "a man may be permitted to manage his own affairs, may he not?"

Having made this speech I instantly repent me of it, as is so often the way with us foolish women. If only we could learn to think first and speak af-ter! . . . .

"I did not mean that, George. I know you only say it for my *good* . . . . but why should he not come back?"

"Because you love each other far too well," says George, sadly; "because you ought never to have met again, never."

"Are you afraid of me?" I ask, so low that surely his ears cannot catch my words, while the blood leaps into my cheeks like a living thing and shames me.

"Not exactly afraid, Nell—but both you and he have had more laid upon your shoulders than mortals could well bear, and—be angry with me if you will, but I must dare to speak the truth—there is danger," he says, slowly and reluctant-ly. If it is bitter to me to listen, it is bitterer still to him to speak.

"Do you think," I say, trembling un-der all the weight that binds me down, "that we are so sinful, so weak, so worth-less? Do you think that I ever for one moment forget that he is another woman's husband?"

"I know you do not," says George; "your behavior has always been perfect; but can you tell me from the bottom of your heart that the mere sound of his voice, the merest chance look at his face, is not the greatest good this world con-tains for you? True, you never forget he is another woman's husband, but do you ever forget that he was once your lover—that he is your lover still?"

He pauses a moment; but I do not answer, and he goes on—

"Can any one help seeing that you are his idol, the very core of his heart; that his eyes follow your every move-ment and step, his ears wait on your every word; that he breaks off in the midst of a conversation if you speak, and loses himself in what you are saying?"

"And do you know," I say, slowly, "that since he came back, three months ago, we have not so much as touched each other's hands?"

"It would be far better if you did," says George, with an impatient sigh— "far better if you *could*, I mean. It is dangerous work, Nell; you are walking on thin ice—some day he will break down, and then—"

"Hush!" I say, pale as death; "do you know what it is that you are saying— do you know that he *loves* me? You do not know Paul, or me. We might meet each other for years and years, just as we do now, content with having a glimpse of each other now and then (I don't deny that it is my greatest happiness on earth to see him, to hear his voice—it is sinful, I dare say, but it is human nature), and never ask, never dream, of being any more to each other—how can we ever be anything to each other all our life long? And if this one consolation were taken from me, if I never saw his face . . . . I could not bear my life. Paul! . . . . Paul! . . . . and that is why I love the child so passionately. . . . I may not give a sign of the love I bear the father; there is no sin in loving the child. When Paul came back, George, I was afraid, just as you are now; I seemed to see all the danger of our meeting . . . . and I tried so hard to make myself cold, indifferent, *uncaring;* but I could not— only after the first meeting was over, I found it so much more easy than I had thought it would be . . . . and I gradually got to feel quite *safe;* and now, do you know that I am not afraid of seeing him? I am almost happy sometimes."

"Happy!" cries George, with a deep, strong urgency in his voice; "ay! as happy as the man who lies down in the snow, and, abandoning himself to exquisite slumber that creeps over him, perishes miserably. . . . Far better and more wholesome for you were your keen, sharp fears, your consciousness of danger, than your present easy sense of security."

"George!" I say, sharply and suddenly, "what is it that you are afraid of —what do you mean?"

There is the silence of a few seconds; brave man, true friend that he is, he pauses before he speaks words that may never be forgiven him.

"I fear," he says, slowly, "that some day this existence will become so intolerable that his love for you will break all bounds . . . . and he will ask you to go away with him."

Dead silence.

"And this is your opinion of my true lover?" I ask; "and do you think I should go with him, pray?"

He does not answer.

"O heavens!" I cry, with a tearless sob, "that I should have fallen so low as for you to think *this* of me!"

"Have I thought it?" he cries, swiftly. "God knows that in my eyes you are the most innocent of his creatures; but, Nell . . . . Nell, are you so strong, is he so strong, that you should fare better than many a woman as fair and pure and proud as you? I don't speak to you in fear, but in warning. I am your brother now; I have taken care of you for a long while past, and if ever any words of mine will keep you from sorrow I will speak them, though you grew to hate me for speaking them to you."

There is a long silence; then I say—

"George, *I thank you.*"

"God bless you, darling!" he says, so impulsively that he seems to be flying straight through the *impedimenta* of hay that divide us; "you are as plucky as you are good; not one woman in a thousand would take it as beautifully as you have done."

"George!"

"Yes, dear."

"I don't think there was ever any fear —not much. But I had never thought of such a thing, never; and, perhaps, if it had really come to that dreadful pass, I should have been so astonished—I might have lost my head and done something wicked . . . . but I don't think I should. However, there is no fear now. . . . Are you always to be doing me good, dear, and am I never to do you any ? "

" You have done me good all my life," he says, heartily; " you have been the one flower to brighten my dull gray garden."

A bitter, bitter pain runs through my heart at his words; is it not hard for him, *hard ?* There he is, free and young, loving me; here am I, free and young, loving somebody else, who is not free to love me. Oh! why cannot I pluck that other love out of my heart, and, putting my hand in his, make his imperfect, spoiled life a completed, happy one ? And I cannot.

" Nell," he says, presently, " do you remember how I have always warned you against Mrs. Vasher—after she tried to make friends with you, I mean ? "

" I remember."

" Well, she has been a worse enemy to you lately than she ever was before; and that is saying a good deal."

" How can she be that ? " I ask, startled; " surely there is no other misfortune left for her to work me ? "

" She has tried, Nell. If ever a woman put another in the way of temptation Mrs. Vasher has tried to put you. Not an opportunity does she ever miss of bringing you and her husband together; over and over again I have watched her manœuvres to have you alone, and smiled at the unconscious way in which you have foiled her—she has been acting a black and wicked part to you both, though neither of you knew it."

" Let me think," I say, slowly; " yes, I remember now. Rarely as I have been to The Towers, she has always contrived some excuse for sending us off together. . . . But what should she do it for—what object could she have had ? "

" God knows! To take your good name, perhaps."

" Yes," I say, recalling her evil threat, three months ago, that "*she would have my good name too.*" " But I can't believe it, George—I did not know any woman living could be as bad as that."

" You remember the day of the garden party at The Towers, when she took us into her rose-garden ? "

" Yes."

" She hurried me away with her, leaving you and Vasher there alone, and when we got back to the lawn she got rid of me cavalierly enough, and I lost sight of her. I should have liked to go back and fetch you, but I was not sure that you would not consider it an interference, so I walked up and down in the outer garden leading to where you were, the two being divided by a thick clump of trees. Any one inside these trees could see what was going on in the rose-garden, but not from where I was, and as I strolled past I saw a bit of pale yellow silk, about the size of a shilling, shining through the thick leaves, and it told me that Madam Silvia was hidden inside, *watching* you."

" And you really believe that she means me evil ? "

" I am sure of it."

" But what harm can she *do* me ? " I ask, persistently. " I don't see how she can do any more."

" Shall I tell you ? " asks George, hesitating.

" Yes."

" She would lead you and her husband into evil, she would shame you to the dust; she could half forgive you for being the girl Paul Vasher has loved so long and faithfully, if she could degrade you in his eyes and your own."

" And this is the woman I *forgave !* " I say, below my breath; " this is the mother of my little angel Wattie! You were right, George, to say I was like a man who has been asleep in the snow. . . . I have been asleep, but I am broad awake now. When do the Vashers go away ? "

" The middle of July."

" When they come back," I say, slowly, " I will go away to Alice or Jack. . . .
I will never meet Paul again of my own
free-will. George! . . . . George! how
shall I ever get through my life without
a sight of him now and then ? "

He does not answer, for what can
he say ? Real comfort he has none to
give me, false he will not offer me, so he
says nothing.

" I am afraid you will be very lonely
in August, Nell," he says, presently;
" everybody seems to be going away but
you."

" I do not mind. It seems so odd
papa's going to Scotland with you; he
has not been anywhere since he came
back from New Zealand."

" No. Dolly and your mother are going to the Lovelaces', are they not ? "

" Yes; and I am to keep house here.
What a muddle it will be! I wish Jack
were coming home for August, not September."

" Ah! you'll not speak to me when
he is here."

" Wait and see."

" They're not dead," says Bashan's
voice, sounding immediately over our
bodies, " for I heard one of them speak."

" We forgot *all about you!*" says
Dolly's fresh voice, with some dismay in
it, as she too leans over our mounds.
" The fact is, we have been eating strawberries, and it does pass the time so
quickly."

And, alas! when we are disinterred
and sit up on end, thirsty, scratched,
blinking, disheveled, with our heads
stuck as full of wisps of hay as a pincushion is full of pins, we find that Dolly
and Bashan have, with a greediness that
has no parallel in these modern times,
very literally confined their attention to
eating them, for they have not brought
one berry with which to cool our parched,
and dry, and dusty throats.

CHAPTER XII.

" Death lies on him like an untimely frost
  Upon the sweetest flower of all the field."

WE are out in the orchard, Wattie
and I, among the unripe apples, that are
day by day taking new shades of glossy
redness on their fat green sides, and an-
nouncing to all whom it may concern
that after their beautiful youth of pearly
blossom, and the long interval of unlovely
brownness and uselessness, they are now
rapidly nearing the respectability and accomplished work of fruition. They need
not be in such a hurry to ripen; they are
better off swinging up there on the bough
than chopped into small pieces by the
cook's knife, or lost to sight through the
agency of my young brothers' vigorous
teeth and appetites. We have been pelting each other with them, Paul's little son
and I, and now he has fallen fast asleep
in my arms, and is far away in the un-
haunted dreamland of childhood. Nothing, surely, can be prettier than a very
handsome child asleep, and Wattie's face
might well linger in the memory of any
one who saw him at this moment—
people, even, who did not see a resemblance, in every lovely curve and haughty
trick of feature, to a stern, proud-faced
man, whom no one would ever call comely
now, who lost his beauty when he lost
all the pleasantnesses of his life, many
years ago.

It is four weeks since he went away,
four weeks since he took my hand in his,
and I left it there because I knew that
henceforward I was going to make it my
care that I should never see his face
again. . . . As our eyes met, how the
passion and misery leaped straight from
his heart to the brown depths; how I
trembled, recognizing clearly enough that
George had not warned me too soon, or
too urgently! . . . He never said a word
beyond good-by, nor did I—people were
all about us—but I saw wild words
trembling on his lips, words that I thank

Heaven he never spoke to me nor I listened to.

Silvia came and wished me good-by; false to the last, she put her hand in mine (he had not touched it then), and wished me well. And I held my peace and said nothing. I let her think I had never suspected all her vile plots, for if I had spoken the words that lay at my heart, how should I have been able to see Wattie, whom, like any other fashionable, heartless mother, she was leaving to the care of servants? She bade her people bring him to me whenever I liked to have him, and he has come nearly every day. Mr. and Mrs. Vasher went away together, but she was going on some visits, to return here in September, while he was to join the Tempests and papa, later, in Argyllshire; he is with them now, I suppose, as the 12th is already past. (When he comes back in September I shall be gone to Alice, and it will be a long, long while before I come back again.)

And while our sportsmen are shooting away so contentedly at the grouse, with no other object than to prove themselves good shots, and make a good meal off the poor birds, other men are shooting, hacking, and hewing at each other like madmen, watering the fair lands of France with blood until they reek, sowing the meadows and valleys with dead bodies thick as the grain of the sower in springtime. . . . For the greed and pride of two men, for the errors in diplomacy of a few more, the land is made one hideous, gaping sepulchre, that opens wide its scarlet mouth and sends its murdered cry of tens of thousands up before God. . . . How the brain reels and the heart sickens as one reads, day by day, of the success of the infernal weapons forged by man to dash out all semblance of humanity in that which God created in his own image! Is not life sweet to those poor fellows who have to lay it down because one crowned head covets his neighbor's vineyard? Oh, a million desolate wives

and mothers, weeping for the husbands and sons who will come back to them never any more, could tell us somewhat of the value to *them* of those mangled, crushed, mutilated bodies that are set down in the returns under the laconic heading of "losses." The day's paper is by my side, but I do not read it, its accounts turn me sick; the "special correspondent" seems to relish his horrors as he writes them down. I used to read his tale of carnage, carnage, carnage! every day, until it rang in my ears like a bell, and my rest was full of blood and slaughter. . . . I never lay me down to rest or enjoy the merest common pleasure, without thinking of these poor Frenchmen fighting this losing game against terrible odds in the burning sun, without discipline, proper food, or able directors. I do not know whether the Emperor of France or the King of Prussia is in the wrong; I never did understand anything about politics, and never shall; but I take the side of the French, for a woman's reason, that they are weakest. Thank Heaven, no brother or friend of mine is in the midst of the fighting! I should make so very sure that he would never come back; for to one mother or sister to whom a man will return, will there not be ninety-nine bereft?

God help you! poor mothers, and grant that your agony of waiting be a short one; better far to know that your son is numbered with the dead than be alternating in the intolerable agony of doubts and fears.

Although every tongue in even this remote Silverbridge wags from morning till night of the news "of the war," an enemy, no less fatal to some than the deadly bullets flying in such abundance yonder in *la belle* France, has crept in upon us and set his mark, first on one, then on another, and drawn them away out of our sight into that straight and narrow bondage that waits for us all, king or peddler, queen or kitchen-maid, sooner or later. His name is Death, and he comes, not peacefully and naturally, but with a fiery burning breath—with a strong clutch at the throat, and a close, hot grasp, under which his victims burn and faint and wither . . . and his other name is Fever. Since mother and Dolly and little Daisy went away a fortnight ago, four little children, two young girls, and one house-mother have died, so quickly, so mysteriously, that lo! they seemed to be here one moment and gone the next. Mother had no idea that fever was in the village when she went, or she would be in fear about the children, and I have not written to tell her—she so seldom has a holiday, and she would come straight back. Nurse says these things are not to be run away from, and that the boys will do better to stay where they are; and Silverbridge village is more than a mile away, so we are not in the midst of the danger. A terrible pang seizes me as I look down on Wattie's unconscious face, and think that even now the phantom hand may be creeping out of the darkness into the light to touch him, my angel of consolation, who is the one pure and perfect thing my life contains. I lay my hand on his head: it is cool; on his cheek, on which lies the exquisite tint that his mother's used to wear (that she has lost so completely lately, whether from pain of mind or body I cannot tell), and that is cool and fresh too.

This child, with his bold, beautiful looks, with his father's eyes, and his own winning, lovable ways, is the delight of my days; he is himself and my lost lover in one. It is Paul who looks at me out of the splendid, willful brown eyes; Paul who lurks in the haughty curves of the little mouth, and smiles at me with all the old resistless magic from these baby lips; and to these he adds his fresh, unsoiled young heart and words, his eager, quick love and childlike trust; and over all is the innocence that only those who have loved very young children can tell of.

I take out my watch—six o'clock, and the nurse ought to have fetched Wattie at five, he should be in bed by now; she is both tiresome and stupid. I am wondering what can have become of her, when Simpkins, that ancient man, appears upon the scene, and his eye betokens trouble.

"What is the matter?" I ask, quickly.

"It's Symonds, Miss Nell; she is down with the fever. She had scarcely got back to The Towers when she fell ill, and—it's a very bad case, the doctor says."

Symonds! Wattie's nurse—the woman in whose charge he has been up to the time she was seized with the fever! O Wattie! Wattie! if my heart could break, I think it would break now, as I listen to Simpkins's words.

"Do you think he looks feverish?" I cry, in a sharp voice that does not sound like my own; "do you know *how people look* when they are going to have the fever?"

"Indeed, Miss Nell, I cannot tell you," he says, sadly. "Their throats just get sore, and their faces flushed, and then God takes them—at least, that was how the other poor souls went in the village."

"Be silent!" I cry, harshly. "Do you want to drive me *mad?*"

I stoop over my darling's face, and my eyes grow to it. Is it here already—does it lurk under this beautiful guise, that deadly, deadly fever?

"You'll not be sending him back to The Towers, Miss Nell?" asks Simpkins, with some hesitation; "it wouldn't be safe—but there are the young gentlemen here to be thought of."

I put my hand to my head in thought.

"He cannot go back there," I say aloud, "so he must stay here. Could he not be put somewhere, a long way from the rest, in case there is any infection?"

(O my darling, my darling, that already it should come to *if!*)

"There's the room adjoining the schoolroom as was fitted up as a bed-room for Master Jack last year, when he sprained his ankle," says Simpkins, thoughtfully. "That's a long way from the nurseries, and down a passage; don't you think that might do, miss?"

"Yes, that will do," I say, feverishly. "Go and have it prepared at once, and ask nurse to have the bed made up instantly; I will come in when all is ready.—"O Wattie, Wattie!" I say, with a shuddering, long-drawn sob, as Simpkins goes away, "could I bear to lose you, my flower, my angel?"

But his face gives me no answer. The black lashes lie heavy and shadowy on the smooth, fair cheeks; he looks as healthy and strong and vigorous as ever he did in his life before, but somehow, *somehow*, I seem to see the outstretched hand waiting to touch him. . . . In my agony I clasp him so tightly that he awakes, and opens sleepy, misty eyes that, when they fall on me, smile in concert with his lips. He stretches himself, and kisses me with a child's spontaneous, unasked-for caress, than which nothing more precious can be found on the whole earth, for it can neither be bought, nor forced, nor stolen.

I was always jealous about the people I loved; I never cared to be liked by people who liked everybody else as well as me—I like to be the *only* one beloved. It is the most exquisite of flattery to be preferred by one who affords his favors to few; and the fact that Wattie has never been known to volunteer an embrace to any living person save me enhances its value a thousand-fold.

His hand is cool enough as I take it in mine, and we go back through the long shadows to the house. He is backward with his talk yet; but he has a language of his own that I understand, and we talk the funniest *shibboleth* as we go along.

The house seems very cool and quiet after the outside world, and Wattie seems somewhat awed, and takes a firmer clutch at my hand as we go down the long stone passage, on whose matting so many vigorous pairs of feet have stamped up and down in their day, and reach the schoolroom.

It is a battered old place enough; walls, books, floor, and chairs are the one as disreputable as the other. A little passage runs out of this room into another of the same size, formerly a place of resort for old books, lumber, and sulky or ill-used people; now it is bare and primitive, with its four-poster, scanty chairs, plain toilet-table, and ill-used washstand. The windows, opening to the ground like those of the schoolroom, and looking out over the court, are open.

The bed is made, and I proceed to undress Wattie, who is evidently much struck with the novelty of everything. He is not afraid, though, and he does not cry; he is too brave a boy for that. I am wondering perplexedly what I can put on him in the shape of a nightgown, when nurse comes in with one of Daisy's old night-garments for him.

"Eh! Miss Nell," she says, after her old fashion, "and are you going to get yourself into more trouble? The bairn ought to be with his mother."

"Only he is not, you see," I say, tying the strings of Wattie's night-gear. "Nurse, have you heard about *Symonds?*"

"I have, Miss Nell, and I fear me the poor wean has run a terrible risk."

"Hush! I cry, sharply, just as I bade Simpkins hold his peace. "It is never possible to tell, nurse; you said so yourself the other day. You know it passes over one person to take another, and it is *impossible to tell*."

"Eh!" she says again, doubtfully; and I could beat her, that she will speak to me no word of comfort.

Wattie is ready for bed, but Wattie will not go. He has escaped from me and is dancing to and fro on the carpet, where the sunbeams are playing at hide-

and-seek; his little pink-and-white toes are like rose-leaves flying hither and thither; the boughs without throw their shadows on his eager, delighted, willful face. O Wattie! through all the years to come shall I ever get you out of my head, as you patter to and fro to-night, a laughing, beautiful little hovering shape in white? Not until the sun in dying has withdrawn his errant sons and daughters does Wattie tire of his play; then I catch him up in my arms, and we roll over and over together on the bed, he shouting with laughter. Then, when he is quieter, to my surprise he scrambles on to my lap, and kneels there; laying his tiny dimpled hands palm to palm, and shutting his hands tight, he makes his evening prayer, something after this fashion: "Peese Dawd—peese Dawd bess pap-a, mem-a, *Lallie;* make 'Otty vay dood boy, T'ist's 'ake. Yaymen." Then, being between the sheets, he pulls my head down on the pillow beside him, clasps his arms round my neck, and in another minute is sound asleep with doubled-up fists. After a while I leave him to go to nurse, for there is much to think of and settle. If any other case of fever happens near us, she is to go away with the boys (who are at school all day at Pimpernel); if Wattie (my lips blanch as they utter the possibility) is already infected, she is to go away all the more. She says she shall take me too, but I laugh in her face; it is so likely that I shall leave him here with hirelings to wait upon him!

"And it will be a pleasant little surprise for your mamma to come home and find you dead and buried, Miss Nell," says nurse, in grim conclusion.

"Only wretched people never catch fevers or die of anything but hard old age," I say. "It is the happy ones, who have so much to leave behind, who go."

I sit by Wattie's side far into the night; but his skin is still cool and fresh, he sleeps calmly, and seems to know no uneasiness; and at last I undress and lie down beside him. I awake suddenly, when the light of the moon is still shining in, broad and clear, tracing silver patterns on the carpet and the wall, and bend my head down to look into my darling's face. What if he have sickened while I lay senselessly, dully asleep? But he looks just as he did when I saw his face last, and I go to sleep again with my arms round him. Wattie went to bed with the sunbeams; he wakes up with the sunlight, and oh! the happiness that fills my heart as he runs about, active and bright, getting into every bit of mischief, bless him! that the place contains. I wash him, dress him, feed him with the bread and milk nurse brings at seven o'clock; then I dress myself, and we go out together into the glorious morning, among the sparkling dew-drops and early radiance that seems to have no knowledge or thought of disease, pain, and death. And all through the day we are so happy together, he and I! No fits of passion or sulkiness ever deform the character of Paul's little son; he is as spirited as he is gentle, led by a word, turned to iron by an injustice, as his father ever was.

"Symonds is very ill," say the accounts gleaned from a distance. Can it be possible, I ask, trembling, that a woman so thoroughly infected with the fever could avoid giving it to the child she was always with? But the day wears on to eventide, and the roses do not burn too brightly in his cheeks, his steps know no flagging, and he goes to bed as he went last night, against his will.

It must be the very early morning, just when the moonlight has gone and the grayness of the dawn has not yet appeared, that I am awakened by a hoarse little voice asking for "water." It is one of the few words that I have been able to teach Wattie's baby-lips to utter. I do not move for a moment; I am like a dead creature who has been slain by one lightning blow from a two-edged sword

—I know what the cry means. . . . I now that Death has called my angel way from me. . . .

Then I rise stiffly, and bring water, which already, *already* it hurts him to swallow. I lay the little head back upon he pillow, I do not kiss him or speak to him; I fall down on my knees by his side! . . . . Wattie! . . . . God has taken all else on earth from me, and now he is beckoning you . . . . my darling! . . . my darling! . . . .

Half an hour later and a man has returned from Pimpernel with the doctor; an hour and he is gone again. He can do no more for the only son of Paul Vasher than the son of a cottager; a few days, or hours even, will determine the issue.

"It is in God's hands," say the servants, as they move to and fro, and the words sound to me in my agony like direst mockery. If it be in his hands, why need he have stricken my flower, my treasure, my ewe-lamb? Somebody takes away the telegrams that I send to the father and mother — though why should they come here? They never spoke to my darling in life, why should they come to look on him now he is going away? He is mine now—*mine;* he wants no one else. And I send the servants and every one away out of the room (I believe they think I am mad), and with the simple remedies they have left for him I take him in my arms and hang over him, hour after hour, watching every change in his face, every throb of his pulses . . . . and his beautiful dumb eyes seek mine piteously in his new, unknown misery. . . . He cannot understand it . . . . he never suffered any pain or oppression before . . . . he seems puzzled and afraid, and if I leave him for a moment he calls after me "Lallie! Lallie!" not with the old merry voice, but in a sharp, altered note, that makes my heart stand still.

The doctor comes and goes; he spends half his time fighting with the grim enemy over this little, resisting frame. A nurse takes up her station in the room, but she never touches him; he takes everything alike from my hand. He has still some hopes of the child, the doctor says, and calls in a greater man than he, and the two consult together; but, oh! I know that Wattie has been called, that he is going—I knew it from the very first. . . . If no one had cared whether he lived or died, he would have lived; as he is more to me than life itself, he is going fast. His sweet, broken babble grows fainter and weaker, then dies altogether. The doctors look down on him in silence. Not all their cunning can breathe life into this beautiful little body—only the Great Physician can do that, and he is drawing hourly nearer; every minute sees a fresh change on the face of my boy.

They go away, these men, saying they will come back presently; they need not come, for they will be wanted by Wattie never any more.

He has always known me right through; he knows me now, and smiles at me with his parched, dried lips, as I give him some cooling drink; he shall be troubled with no more medicine, no more, little Wattie . . . . you had little enough of it in your short three-year-old young life. He has never been fretful, or willful, or complaining, in this illness as other children are; if he had only shown some of his old masterful little ways, I should not feel so *sure* . . . . but he just lies on my knees, fading away before my eyes, and as he grows fainter and weaker a passionate cry rises from my bitter-wrung heart: "If he must go, let me go with him!" But my prayer passes unheeded. I am strong and well, only sick with weeping, worn with watching and fasting, brought to the lowest depths of misery by having the child taken from me; and so it falls that on the third night (he has been very quick about it, my little Wattie, who was always so loath to leave me for an hour even) as he lies on my lap, about six o'clock, he opens his beautiful brown eyes, his hand flutters a little in mine, and as I hang over him in agonized, breathless dread, "Dood-by, Lallie!" he says; a loving smile flickers over his face for a moment, then . . . . he is gone.

CHAPTER XIII.

"Larded all with sweet flowers,
Which bewept to the grave did go
With true-love showers."

My little dead angel is lying alone on the wide white bed, with roses in his folded hands, and tapers burning on either side. You would never know that he had been ill at all to look round the room; it is all so neat, so simple, so fresh. No ugly medicine-bottles or any of the paraphernalia of sickness there; everything looks peaceful, untroubled, *usual*. Through the open windows the moon sends a flood of light that washes the floor, the bed, the waxen features of my darling, who lies there so still and quiet—he who used to run about so indefatigably, whose feet were never tired, whose voice was never still save when he slept; and he is not asleep now . . . . yet that eyeless, voiceless, pulseless shape is my little lad. I am not by his side now; no tears would come to me as I looked down on the little dead face that had smiled on me so lovingly four hours ago, on the lips that had syllabled "Goodby, Lallie!" with the last hovering breath, on the hands that only slackened their hold on mine when death detached them. . . . When I brushed out his beautiful golden curls, and felt them cling round my fingers like living, sentient things, they woke no memory in me of those other times when I had brushed them, finding such trouble in keeping the restless head still . . . . I was as unfeeling, as silent, as placid as he. The nurse has gone away with the rest; she would

have watched with me beside him all night, but she shall not—no one shall do anything for him but me. I am sitting in the schoolroom alone, and the sound of the church-clock striking ten comes with sudden loudness through the silence.

Ten! and at five o'clock Walter was living; I had him in my arms, I was able to kiss him, to call upon him by every foolish name my heart prompted, and he was able to answer me, to put out his weak hand to me, to smile at me . . . . only five hours ago! He cannot be dead; I must have dreamed it . . . . if I open yonder shut door I shall find him there. Ay! but did I ever leave him for a minute while the breath was in his poor tortured little body? O Wattie! . . . Wattie, five hours ago you were *here*, in my arms; but now, *where* are you?

All my life long I have had so keen a pity for dead folk, that it has seemed to me that in some former state I must have loved some one very passionately, who died; but this experience is so new, so strange, so awful, that I cannot grasp it. I pitied them; but did I ever see a human being speaking, smiling one minute, the next a blank, a mockery, a shell, whence is withdrawn the beautiful, loving spirit that I *knew?*

"O God! O God!" I cry, as I rock myself to and fro, "make me *understand*, make me see it; remove this terrible interval that lies between my living Wattie and this dead one."

If only he could come back to me for one brief moment, if only he could tell me about it! . . . I cannot get *hold* of you, Wattie, my angel; you are not dead, so I have no memory of you; you are not living, so I cannot speak to you. . . . To-morrow, perhaps, you will seem farther away; I shall learn to remember.

I go to the window, and look out at the night. May he not be somewhere near me, though I do not know it? Can he have gone so far already? Were you afraid, Wattie, I wonder, when you went forth alone? Did you hold out your hand to me in the awful strangeness of your passing? Is any one taking care of you up there, as I took care of you here below?

" Wattie! Wattie!" I whisper, and my voice sounds hoarse and sinister in the silence, "can you not speak to me?" But no answer comes to me; not a leaf stirs, not a sound is abroad.

Hark! what is that? Hasty footsteps are crushing the gravel, coming nearer and nearer. Who can it be that comes here so late? And farther away I seem to hear lighter steps, that follow after the first. Have the father and mother returned, too late? And my dull heart gives an exultant leap that Silvia should come too late—that Wattie died in my arms, not hers. . . . The steps pass on, retreat, come forward again, and in another minute a man steps into the flood of moonlight that fills the room—Paul Vasher. How wild he looks, how strange! After all, did he love the poor little dead son yonder, only his pride forbade his showing it?

"I thought you would have come sooner," I say slowly; "I have been expecting you for days."

"And I am here," he says, as slowly as I.

His face is pale and set, his dark eyes are flaming under his drawn brows.

"Love," he says quietly, and in his quietness there is a deadly strength that chills me, " I cannot live without you. I have come back to tell you so. . . . Will you end this life of hell and misery, and come away with me?"

But I do not answer; I only fall back before him, and stand with dilated eyes and parted lips, staring at him.

"Are you afraid, sweetheart? Do you believe that the words uttered by a mumbling old priest make things sacred that are not sacred in themselves? Do you believe that you would be any the more my wife if a form of words had been spoken over us? Are the man and woman, forsooth, who are made for each other, and would cleave to each other through time and death and eternity, to be considered less married in God's eyes than the wretches who are bound together by the fetters of expediency, fraud, and the love of gold?"

But I only hold up my hands and wave him back. I am dumb—dumb as my innocent darling lying yonder, dumb as the stones that lie at my feet.

"Sweetheart! wife!" he cries, coming a step nearer, and the old fire has come back to his eye, the old masterful vigor to his voice, "I must have you . . . . I can't live without you. Ever since that Christmas-morning I have been wrestling and fighting with myself as no other devil-tempted, God-forsaken man ever fought, in vain. . . . I knew that the other day when I touched your hand at parting, for the first time for three years and more. . . . When I got to Scotland, a chance remark told me that you were here alone; I set out. . . . You will come with me to-night, Nell, *to-night*. All is prepared, everything is in readiness; no one knows I am in Silverbridge. . . . By the morning we shall be far away . . . . together at last. O heavens!" he cries, with a strong wild leap of exultation in his voice, "at last. . . . I had been very doubtful about you, my beautiful darling. . . . I did not think your love would stand the test . . . . but when you said that you had been expecting me, that you thought I should have been here sooner. . . . I knew then, Nell, that your love was as strong as mine."

A dark shadow crosses the moonlight, a white hand alights like a snow-flake on Paul's arm. He turns, and at his elbow stands Silvia, smiling. She steps through the window, and then we stand in the moonlight, that shows our faces clear as at noonday—my lover, his wife, and I. It is Paul who speaks first.

"So it is you, madam?" he says, slowly. "And, pray, are you following

your old and successful avocation of a
spy?"

"Yes," she says, quietly, "if following one's own husband be spying, for I
have been following *you*. I always knew
you would come back to this girl, sooner
or later, and ask her to go off with you;
and I always knew that, for all her proud
disdainful airs, she would go—*when you
asked her*. Don't suppose that I want to
hinder you from going; on the contrary,
if you do not, I will take good care that
the country rings with the story of how I
found my husband and Miss Helen Adair
alone, at eleven at night, when all her
people were away . . . . arranging an
elopement between them. I wonder
whether it would be you or I who would
be blamed then for not having *got on* together? I don't want to stop you; I
only came after you to shame her.—Ha,
ha! Have I not my revenge on you *at
last*, Helen Adair?"

Paul does not speak, only his hands
clinch and unclinch themselves rapidly,
and his breast rises in short, quick
pants.

"You taunted me once with the possession of a good name, that no living
man or woman could lay finger on," she
says, in her mocking, flute-like tones;
"do you think it is so white and soilless
now?"

"Now," I say, lifting my hand and
beckoning to her, "you will come with
me."

Like a woman who moves without her
own volition Silvia leaves her place and
follows. Again I lift my hand and beck-
on to Paul, who also comes slowly, like a
man in a dream . . . . I open the door,
traverse the short passage, and enter the
bedroom, the husband and wife following. I walk to the bed and look round
at them—they are standing by the door
—and lift my hand once more, and they
come and stand one on either side of the
bed . . . . and they look down on the
dead face of their little fatherless, motherless son Wattie.

"He died at six of the clock this evening," I say, monotonously; then something seems to snap in my brain, and I
fall down like a log, with my arms round
my little dead lad.

.   .   .   .   .

Under God's sky, a man stands holding my hand in his for the last time and
asks me, as though I were his judge, to
forgive him the terrible sin and treachery
into which his mad, sinful love and agony
drove him; and I forgive him, yes, from
the very bottom of my heart, and bid
him God-speed, for I know that just as
surely as that Wattie is laid away out
of my sight under the brown mould at
our feet, so I shall never look on his
father's face again in this life . . . . and
so we say good-by reverently, tenderly,
knowing it is our last farewell, and then
—he goes.

And on the night of the last day but
one of August, in the yet early morning,
he comes to me in my sleep, with the
clear light of the immortals on his brow,
and I awake, knowing full well that he is
dead. Fourteen days afterward a letter
is brought to me, and the superscription
of the envelope is written by a Frenchman. I take it away to my chamber, and
sit down with it in my hand: I am in no
hurry to read it, for I *know;* then I
break the seal.

"Mademoiselle," the letter begins, "I
have a sacred duty to perform to you; I
pray you to forgive me that it is so painful a one. . . . Before Sedan I fought
side by side with M. Vasher, and it was
toward evening that he fell, badly wounded. By good fortune I got him away to a
place of safety, and a good Sister came
and tended him, but he was past human
aid. He gave me your address, and bade
me tell you how he died. . . . Mademoiselle, he was the bravest man, the
truest gentleman, that ever took sword
in hand. . . . He was very restless all
night, but he never complained; and—
forgive me, I had fallen asleep for a moment—toward the very early morning, I

was awakened by his voice ringing out, loud and clear as a trumpet, 'Comin' thro' the rye—*God's rye*, Nell!' then he fell dead. We buried him, mademoiselle, at sunset, and laid on his heart a miniature he had always worn, as he bade us. An hour afterward a lady came; she was very beautiful, and seemed wild with grief. . . . Mademoiselle, she said she was his wife. With humble assurances of my sympathy, I am

"Your faithful servant,

"GABRIEL RISOLIÈRE."

Will they find each other up above, I wonder, my lost lover and my little lost angel? And since I shall go to them, but they will not return to me, I pant, I weary, I burn for the moment when death, "like a friend's voice from a distant field," shall call to me, and, taking my hand in his, lead me to the plains and fields that girdle round the shining city . . . . where shall I not see my darlings stepping to meet me through the unfading, incorruptible splendor of "God's rye?"

THE END.

RHODA BROUGHTON'S NOVELS.

29. RUSKIN ON PAINTING. With a Biographical Sketch. Paper, 30 cents; cloth, 60 cents.
30. AN ACCOMPLISHED GENTLEMAN. By JULIAN STURGIS, author of "John-a-Dreams." Paper, 30 cents; cloth, 60 cents.
31. AN ATTIC PHILOSOPHER IN PARIS; or, A Peep at the World from a Garret. Being the Journal of a Happy Man. From the French of EMILE SOUVESTRE. 30 cents.
32. A ROGUE'S LIFE. From his Birth to his Marriage. By WILKIE COLLINS. 25 cents.
33. GEIER-WALLY. A Tale of the Tyrol. From the German of WILHELMINA VON HILLERN. 30 cents.
34. THE LAST ESSAYS OF ELIA. By CHARLES LAMB. 30 cents.
35. THE YELLOW MASK. By WILKIE COLLINS. 25 cents.
36. A SADDLE IN THE WILD WEST. A Glimpse of Travel. By WILLIAM H. RIDEING. 25 cents.
37. MONEY. A Tale. By JULES TARDIEU. 25 cents.
38. PEG WOFFINGTON. By CHARLES READE. 30 cents.
39. "MY QUEEN." 25 cents.
40. UNCLE CÉSAR. By Madame CHARLES REYBAUD. 25 cents.
41. THE DISTRACTED YOUNG PREACHER, by THOMAS HARDY; and HESTER, by BEATRICE MAY BUTT. In one volume. 25 cents.
42. TABLE-TALK. To which are added Imaginary Conversations of Pope and Swift. By LEIGH HUNT. 30 cents.
43. CHRISTIE JOHNSTONE. By CHARLES READE. 30 cents.
44. THE 'WORLD'S PARADISES. By S. G. W. BENJAMIN. 30 cents.
45. THE ALPENSTOCK. Edited by WILLIAM H. RIDEING. 30 cents.
46. COMEDIES FOR AMATEUR ACTING. . Edited, with a Prefatory Note on Private Theatricals, by J. BRANDER MATTHEWS. 30 cents.
47. VIVIAN THE BEAUTY. By Mrs. ANNIE EDWARDES. 30 cents.
48. GREAT SINGERS: Faustina Bordoni to Henrietta Sontag. By GEORGE T. FERRIS. 30 cents.
49. A STROKE OF DIPLOMACY. From the French of VICTOR CHERBULIEZ, author of "Samuel Brohl and Company," "Jean Teterôl's Idea," etc. 20 cents.
50. LORD MACAULAY. His Life—his Writings. By CHARLES H. JONES. 30 cents.
51. THE RETURN OF THE PRINCESS. By JACQUES VINCENT. 25 cents.
52. A SHORT LIFE OF CHARLES DICKENS. With Selections from his Letters. By CHARLES H. JONES. Paper, 35 cents; cloth, 60 cents.
53. STRAY MOMENTS WITH THACKERAY: His Humor, Satire, and Characters. By WILLIAM H. RIDEING. Paper, 30 cents; cloth, 60 cents.
54. DR. HEIDENHOFF'S PROCESS. By EDWARD BELLAMY. 25 cents.
55. SECOND THOUGHTS. By RHODA BROUGHTON. Vol. I. 25 cents.
56. SECOND THOUGHTS. By RHODA BROUGHTON. Vol. II. 25 cents.
57. TWO RUSSIAN IDYLS: Marcella, Esfira. 30 cents.
58. STRANGE STORIES. By ERCKMANN-CHATRIAN. 30 cents.
59. LITTLE COMEDIES. By JULIAN STURGIS. 30 cents.
60. FRENCH MEN OF LETTERS. By MAURICE MAURIS (Marquis di Calenzano). 35 cents.
61. A SHORT LIFE OF WILLIAM EWART GLADSTONE. By CHARLES H. JONES. 35 cents.
62. THE FORESTERS. By BERTHOLD AUERBACH. 50 cents.

APPLETONS' NEW HANDY-VOLUME SERIES is in handsome 18mo volumes, in large type, of a size convenient for the pocket, or suitable for the library-shelf, bound in paper covers. A selection may be had of the volumes bound in cloth, price, 60 cents each.

⁎ Any volume mailed, post-paid, to any address within the United States or Canada, on receipt of the price.

D. APPLETON & CO., Publishers, New York.

APPLETONS'

Library of American Fiction.

Consisting of Select Novels by American Authors; published in neat 8vo volumes, at popular prices.

D. APPLETON & CO., Publishers, New York.

www.ingramcontent.com/pod-product-compliance
Lightning Source LLC
Chambersburg PA
CBHW031348020726